IMPERATRIX

Also by Russell Whitfield:

GLADIATRIX

ROMA VICTRIX

IMPERATRIX

RUSSELL WHITFIELD

MYRMIDON

Myrmidon
Rotterdam House
116 Quayside
Newcastle upon Tyne
NE1 3DY

www.myrmidonbooks.com
Published by Myrmidon 2015

A catalogue record for this book is available from the British Library.

ISBN 978-1-910183-03-8

Set in 11/14.25 Bembo by Ellipsis Digital Limited, Glasgow

Printed and bound in the UK by
CPI Group (UK) Ltd, Croydon, CR0 4YY

1 3 5 7 9 10 8 6 4 2

*For anyone who has ever sat at a keyboard
with an idea and a dream.
You can do it.*

67 A.D.
Sparta

'It is an honour that she's been chosen!' His voice was muffled by the wall of her bedroom, but Lysandra could hear the anger in it.

'She is my *child*, Arion!' Her mother sounded fraught with tears.

'She is my child too, Kassandra. And it is not the Spartan way to go against the will of the ephors, let alone the gods themselves. Your tears are shameful! This is an honour,' he said again as though trying to convince himself. 'And you have always known this day was coming.'

Lysandra could not understand why they were arguing. Ever since she could remember, her parents had told her that she was more special than the other girls with whom she played. She had been chosen at birth by the Goddess Athene to be her priestess – a fact that the goddess herself had confirmed many times in her dreams. And this, the eve of her seventh birthday, marked the day before she would have to leave home and serve in the great temple on the acropolis.

Her parents continued to argue in the *gynaikon* – the women's room – next to her own. This was her mother's private abode and it was odd that her father was trespassing there. Still, Lysandra supposed, it was an important day for them too and all she wanted was for them to be proud of her. She rolled out of bed, rubbing her eyes and opened her door, padding across the floor to her mother's room. 'I cannot sleep,' she announced as she walked in causing her parents to stop in mid-flow.

'Get back to bed!' they ordered in unison – as was the way of parents.

'I cannot sleep,' she said again. 'You are making a noise – and you told me that I had to go to bed early because tomorrow is a big day and I needed to be strong and not cry. How can I sleep if you are going to keep me awake by shouting next door?' Her gaze challenged them both and she saw the ice-coloured eyes of her father soften and the skin around them crinkle.

He laughed then. 'It has always been the way of Spartan women to upbraid their men! Would you carry on that tradition, Lysandra?' he asked crouching down and opening his arms to her.

She walked to him and put her arms around his neck. 'Rub your beard on my face!' she said. She loved the rough, scratchy feeling of it. Her mother got to her feet and joined them, putting arms around them both. 'Do not cry, mother,' Lysandra said. 'I want to go to the temple.'

Her mother just kissed her over and over again. Eventually she said, 'I know. But we will miss you.'

Lysandra squirmed out of her father's grip and transferred herself to her mother's arms. 'I will miss you too, but when I come home I will be grown up and have lots of stories to tell you. And I will have my grown-up teeth.' This was important: having grown-up teeth was proof that one was indeed an adult.

'You see, Kassandra,' her father said. 'The child has no fear of this and we should have none either. Now it is late . . .'

'Can I not stay up with you?' Lysandra hedged. She was awake anyway and it would now be impossible to sleep. 'Or at least play in my room?'

Her mother placed her down on the floor and kissed her again. 'It is late,' she repeated her father's words. 'You must get to bed.'

'But you said you would miss me!' Lysandra challenged, teasing her mother's long, coal-coloured hair. Parents always said one thing and then told her to do something else, which she felt was entirely unfair.

'And I will.' She put Lysandra down and tickled her under the chin, making her giggle. 'But, still – it is way past your bedtime.'

'But . . .'

'Bed!' they both said at once, pointing at the door.

Lysandra tutted. 'All right,' she sighed and turned, stamping just a little so they would know that she was displeased. She was special, she thought to herself – she should be allowed to stay up late. As she climbed into her cot she determined that she would stay awake anyway and eavesdrop on the rest of the conversation.

She strained to hear what they were saying, but they were now making a point of speaking quietly and then, quite suddenly, she closed her eyes and knew no more.

The dawn was grey and cold and misty rain drifted from the sky, the sort that you could hardly see yet somehow seemed wetter than normal rain. Lysandra and her parents stood by the gate of their home, watching the lone rider approach. All three were soaked through, both Lysandra's and her mother's long black hair plastered to their heads, her father's beard sodden and dripping.

Her mother gripped her hand squeezing tight and Lysandra glanced up at her and gave her a smile. She could see the tears on her cheeks despite the rain and there was a small part of her that was embarrassed by this. She was instantly ashamed of this thought and squeezed her mother's hand back.

Slowly the rider descended into the small valley that surrounded the house like a bowl and now Lysandra could see that she wore the long, red cloak of a Spartan priestess, her head encased in a red-crested helmet that covered her entire face – it had a thick nose-piece and flared cheek guards – Athene herself wore similar and

3

soldiers in the old days used to wear them too. It looked most impressive.

Finally, the rider drew up to them. 'Greetings Kassandra,' she spoke to her mother first as was the Spartan way. 'Arion,' she inclined her head. 'And you,' the helmet tilted towards her, 'must be Lysandra. I am Halkyone.'

'Greetings, Halkyone.' Lysandra stepped forward.

'What is in your satchel?' The priestess gestured at the small bag Lysandra had slung over her shoulder.

Lysandra hesitated, fearing the worst. 'Some toys,' she replied. 'A writing tablet and some fruit.'

'You will have no need of those things,' Halkyone confirmed Lysandra's fears. 'Bid your parents farewell. Be quick about it.' Abruptly she turned her horse's head and walked him away, affording them some privacy.

Feeling somewhat forlorn at the loss of her toys, Lysandra handed the bag to her mother who started to cry anew: she crouched down and embraced her as did her father. Ashamed, Lysandra found herself crying too.

'Come,' her father said, his voice gruff. 'It is not the Spartan way to shed tears.'

They squeezed her tight once more and let her go. Lysandra wiped her eyes on the hem of her tunic and smiled, trying to be brave. 'Farewell mother. Father.' She pressed her lips into a thin line so she would not cry again and turned about, making her way after Halkyone. As she reached her, the priestess did not speak or acknowledge her in any way, simply touching her heels to her mount's flanks. The horse ambled off, Lysandra in tow.

Lysandra turned around and looked down at the house where she had grown up, the small field, the *helots* – her parents' slaves – working on it and her mother and father looking after her. It was all she had known.

'*Lysandra!*'

Lysandra jerked around and looked at the priestess who was riding on heedless of her. It was strange – the voice did not sound like the priestess at all – it sounded more like a man's. A voice that seemed to come from a dream. 'Did you say something, ma'am?' she asked, trotting up to keep pace with the horse.

'I did not,' the helmeted head tilted down to her. 'And do not speak again unless you are spoken to. Do you understand?'

'Yes, ma'am. I understand,' she replied.

'Take your sandals off,' Halkyone ordered. 'Throw them away.'

Lysandra hesitated. 'But the road . . . my feet.'

'They will harden, child,' the priestess chuckled. 'As will you. Obey my order. *Now.*'

Her tone broached no argument, so Lysandra did as she was told, all the while thinking that special children should not receive such treatment. It would, she knew, be better when she got to the temple.

The temple was huge – it seemed to Lysandra that it was more like a miniature Troy than anything else. She started at the thought – it seemed familiar to her somehow as though this was a comparison she had made once before but she could not think of where – or when.

Halkyone dismounted and rapped sharply on the massive wooden doors and, after a moment, they swung slowly open. She turned to Lysandra. 'Go and stand in line with the other girls of your age. Do not speak until you are spoken to. And when you are, make sure you obey your instructions.'

'Yes, ma'am,' Lysandra tried to put on a brave face and not to

5

think about her feet, but inside her stomach was churning with trepidation. She hesitated for a moment, took a deep breath and walked into the temple.

The rain had stopped but the sky was still cold and grey and added to the foreboding nature of the place. The interior was dominated by a large open *palaestra*, which was occupied by a large group of girls arrayed in neat lines. She made her way to join them, refusing to meet the gaze of the red-haired older girl that prowled the ranks, swishing a stick as she did so. She was nearly a grown up – Lysandra guessed she must be at least thirteen years old – a titan's age.

Lysandra stood next to a shorter blonde girl and kept her eyes forward: she had experienced enough of her father's discipline to know that she would get a smack if she did anything other than as she had been told; instead she busied her mind with trying to take in her surroundings.

Opposite the main gates stood a large building – certainly the biggest and most ornate Lysandra had ever seen: the structures in Sparta were simple affairs but this had many columns and pictures carved into the stone and it was flanked by two identical statues of the Goddess Athene, spear in hand. It seemed to Lysandra as though the painted stone eyes were looking directly at her.

There were other buildings that surrounded the *palaestra* – and again this seemed familiar to her, though she knew that could not be possible as she had never been to a place like this. These looked to her like small houses and Lysandra guessed that this would be where the priestesses lived.

They stood in silence for some time and it soon became boring. Her feet hurt, the day was getting colder, the wind whipping through her hair – it was as though the interior of the temple grabbed it from the sky and sent it blasting across their lines.

Someone began to cry and, like a spider scuttling across a web to eat its prey, the red-haired girl pounced. There was a swish, a sharp crack and then a howl of pain. She dragged the transgressor from the line and hurled her to the ground and began to *beat* her with the stick. The girl screamed, cried and begged but the red-haired priestess did not relent. Lysandra had been smacked before but never like this and she had to bite her lip not to cry herself at the sight of it.

Eventually, the girl from the line just curled into a ball and this made the older one stop. 'Anyone else cries or makes a sound, you'll get worse than that!' she announced and gestured to someone Lysandra could not see. Soon two more teenagers came running across, hoisted the smaller girl from the ground and carried her off.

After that, nobody cried, but Lysandra could hear sobs and sniffs coming from all around her. This was not what she had expected at all. If she was special then all these girls must be special too; they had also been chosen to serve the goddess, so it seemed wrong that they should be treated in such a way.

There was movement from the temple. Lysandra watched as a group of priestesses filed out, clad in armour as Halkyone had been, but these women carried spears and great, round shields. They formed up either side of the dark entrance of the building as an elderly woman made her way out to stand between the two lines.

Even from where she was standing, Lysandra could see that the woman was *ancient*: the lines of her face were carved deep, cracks in the granite of her visage. She was small, much shorter than Lysandra's mother, but there was a presence emanating from her, drawing all eyes to her.

'I am the Matriarch of the Temple.' Her voice was strident, much louder than Lysandra had expected it to be. 'Once, long ago, I stood where you now stand. Some of you are afraid. Others homesick, still more confused. Some of you feel all of this and more besides. I tell you now that your childish whims will no longer be indulged. You must cast them aside. You girls are special – chosen by the

7

goddess herself to serve as her handmaidens,' she went on, confirming what Lysandra's parents had always told her. 'You are doubly blessed – chosen by Athene and of pure, Spartan blood. Doubly blessed and so you will be doubly tested.

'We Spartans are superior to all other races and creeds: we are the most sacred race ever to sanctify the earth with the imprint of our feet. Our blood is pre-eminent . . . yes, but we must hone our bodies and our minds. Like swords, they are tools to be forged . . . tempered . . . sharpened. Weakness is not tolerated here. If you are weak, you will be beaten without mercy for, like iron, the harder the body is beaten, the harder it becomes. In time, you will learn that pain – like any other *feeling* – can be suppressed. Controlled. You will learn to serve the goddess, to shun comfort and to excel in any endeavour. You will learn to be Spartans. That is all.' She turned and made her way back inside, followed by her guards.

As soon as the doors had shut, the red-haired girl rounded on the group and began screaming at them to follow her before taking off at a run. Lysandra and the others obeyed at once – as they were supposed to.

There was no comfort to be had, no succour, no relief from the relentless cruelty of the older girls. Everything about the temple seemed designed only to make life miserable. Lysandra cried more in those first days than she had ever done in her life: they had broken her resolve to resist her tears as her hair had been hacked off. The scissors had cut her head in many places, the pain of which caused the dam of her will to break. So she sobbed and screamed for them to stop – and received a beating for it.

Yet, it did not take long to become inured to the constant abuse: Lysandra and the other girls came to expect it as part of their daily regimen; the slightest transgression, real or imagined, would elicit the same response. In time, no one shed tears; they learned to bear the abuse in silence, knowing full well that crying would only bring more punishment.

Their clothes were taken away and they were each given a single red tunic and a thin cloak. These, they were told, would have to last a year and it was their responsibility to look after them.

And what had once been fun now became a constant torment. Lysandra had loved to run – she fancied herself as quick footed, but in the temple, the neophytes were made to run everywhere. Before every sunrise, they were dragged from their beds and sent to run around the compound, sweating and straining, bodies wracked with stitches and sore muscles. The older girls – the acolytes – showed them no mercy. Only when they deemed exhaustion was real and not faked – some had tried that ruse and suffered the consequences – did they relent.

A breakfast of water and blood soup followed and then they were set to marching in step, endless hours of parading up and down, changing formations, breaking into a run and stopping in unison. These things were drilled into them so constantly that Lysandra actually began to dream not of her parents but of the shouted commands from their chief tormentor, the red-haired Melantha.

Melantha.

How Lysandra hated her. She delighted in their every failure even though everyone knew that it was she who was a bad teacher, never explaining anything properly so she had an excuse to hit them. Lysandra swore to Athene that when she was big enough she would take her revenge on Melantha: she would beat her spotty red face in.

The only time they had away from their physical training was in the evening when they were led into a small room to be taught proper religious observance. It was a part of the day they all looked forward to as, coupled with their basic reading and writing, this was a time for stories of the goddess and of Spartan heroes past.

Though she had heard it said often enough, it was in these sessions that Lysandra truly began to understand why the Spartans were superior to all other races on earth. It was clear that they were chosen by the gods and were the pinnacle of what was best in all people, suffering none of the flaws of the lesser races.

Their teacher was Halkyone, the priestess who had brought Lysandra to the temple and whilst she was stern, she never struck anyone unless they really deserved it. Lysandra rarely received a smack: she was by far the best in the class and she – as well as Halkyone – knew it. In her quiet moments, Lysandra thanked her mother for teaching her letters and numbers; though she had hated it at the time, she was now reaping the benefits.

At the end of their lessons, they would make a sacrifice to Athene and stumble, exhausted, to their bunks.

'I don't like it here,' her roommate, Deianara, whispered one night after lamps out. Deianara had stood next to Lysandra on their first day, the blonde girl with whom she had shared a smile.

'I don't think we're supposed to like it,' Lysandra offered. 'One day, we'll be priestesses – it will be better then.'

'But that is *ages* away,' Deianara whined, as loud as she dared.

'It *is* ages away,' Lysandra agreed, Deianara's melancholy rubbing off on her. 'But it also seems that we've been here forever. I wish I were home. But we cannot go home. We cannot ever go home.'

Days turned into weeks and with each dawn the trials the girls endured became ever sterner. From simple exercises and marching in step they were taught the rudiments of combat, armed and unarmed. Weighed down with undersized yet heavy shields, spears and armour, the girls formed the phalanx, wheeling and charging to the high-pitched wailing of the pipes. They learned fast: the beatings for failure here were far worse than anything they had suffered before. When subjected to her own thrashing at the gleeful hands of Melantha, Lysandra was appalled to find that the older girl had made her bleed. She had screamed in protest but received only more punishment for this most terrible of transgressions whilst Melantha had simply told her to 'get used to it!'

There was no time now for homesickness and remorse and Lysandra was coming to realise the truth of her words to Deianara: her parents could not come to her aid in this place. All she had to rely on were her friends, most especially Deianara herself. They shared a bed, stood next to each other in line and soon became all but inseparable.

One morning they formed up on the *palaestra*; instead of the usual array of armour and shields there was a pile of wooden swords. Lysandra nudged Deianara at the sight of them: this, she thought, would make a welcome change.

'Greetings, worms,' Melantha strode out before them. 'Gods on Olympus but you are a pitiful sight! Are you even Spartan at all? More likely you are the brood of bastards foisted on us . . .'

She went on in this mien for quite some time; it was hardly unusual and Lysandra found the whole harangue needless. It was clear to her that she and the group were improving, so it had to be pure mean-spiritedness on the acolyte's part to keep upbraiding them regardless. As Melantha continued, Lysandra stopped listening, her eyes fixed on the cache of wooden swords.

Eventually Melantha barked an order and the line broke up, the girls trotting over to the swords. Lysandra shoved her way to the front: she was taller and stronger than most of the others and she doubted that anyone would take issue with her. Stooping, she selected two weapons that looked sturdy. They were much heavier than they looked.

'Here,' she passed one to Deianara. 'These ones look good.'

'Stop your chatting and get back to your line!' Melantha shouted, 'once you've selected a weapon, back into formation!' She punctuated this by kicking one of the slower girls in the rear, sending her to the ground. 'Now then,' Melantha eyed the group before collecting the final sword from the ground. 'First rank . . . six steps forward! Third Rank . . . six steps back! Give yourselves room, worms! You will need it! What have you noticed about these swords? Any of you?'

After a moment's hesitation, Lysandra raised her hand and Melantha nodded. 'They are very heavy,' Lysandra said.

'Correct. Why?'

'To make our arms strong.'

'Partly. But also, *if* you ever get good enough to use the real thing, it will feel as light as a feather. It's better to sweat now than bleed later! Always remember that, worms! Now, I will show you a basic thrust . . .' Moving slowly, Melantha adjusted her stance, putting her weight forward on her right leg and extending her blade, her left leg shifting back.

She returned to a neutral stance and repeated the manoeuvre. 'See how I am balanced. It is about economy of movement . . . doing more with less,' she stood straight. 'At full speed . . .' she exploded into action, repeating the step so quickly it made Lysandra blink, 'this most basic of attacks is devastating.'

For the first time ever, Lysandra saw a slight smile play about the neophyte's lips: she had probably enjoyed startling them with her sudden, lethal movement. 'Now, worms . . . Thrust!'

The girls reacted to the order but some of them stumbled and lost their balance as they tried to execute the move.

'Slowly, idiots!' Melantha harangued them. 'Technique first, you know that already, how many more times do I have to tell you not to rush? Slowly! Now, do it again!'

Lysandra tried again and found her balance: it somehow felt right as though she instinctively knew how to shape her body. As she settled into the thrust position, her eyes flicked over to Melantha whose nod was barely perceptible. But it was the first sign of approval that she had ever had from the acolyte and she felt a warm glow of pride. As her parents had told her, she was special

– as were all the girls of the temple. But where they struggled, Lysandra excelled. Perhaps, she thought, she was more special than most.

'At ease!' Melantha commanded. 'And . . . thrust! Pathetic! At ease . . . and . . . thrust!'

And so it went on. Each day, they were pushed harder, the swordplay added to the usual regimen of fitness and drill, but Lysandra found herself enjoying the challenge. She was good – better than the others of her age and was soon reaping the benefits of her endeavours with lighter duties. No more cleaning and scrubbing for her, no more doling out food at meal times.

Excellence, after all, ought to be rewarded.

Lysandra awoke in agony.

She sat up, screaming in pain as she looked down at the gaping wound in her side. Blood pumped out all over her thighs. People were surrounding her, two strong men with beards and a woman, her eyes filled with fear and concern.

Another man ran to the cot, a clay pot in his hand. 'Hold her down!' he shouted.

'It's alright, Lysandra,' one of the bearded men said in a weird accent. Athenian?

They pushed her back and though she struggled, the pain was too great. 'Get off me,' she rasped. 'Get off me!' The feeling of two men forcing her onto her back filled her with a terrible fear and she began to scream in terror. At once, her nose was gripped and they were forcing vile liquid down her throat.

'Shhhh . . .' the woman crouched by her, stroking her face. 'Lay still, Lysandra, lay still. All will be well. Try to relax.'

The pain and panic began to recede and the voices in the dark room became distant.

'Will she live?' It was a Spartan voice, full of fear and concern.

'Hard to say. We thought she was dead already.'

'The goddess will protect her.' This from the Athenian. 'She always has.'

'Not today she didn't.'

'The wound is deep,' the Spartan said.

'I've seen this before,' the one who had poured the liquid into her mouth said. Then Lysandra felt a sharp pain in her side, like she had been pricked with a needle. She looked down to see that the man who had poured the drink into her was indeed stitching her side. Somehow, that did not bother her. 'Sometimes, after a really bad wound, the body goes to sleep — almost like it is protecting itself. It can look as though the person is dead . . . but as you can see, that isn't always the case.'

'Yes, but will she live?' the insistent Spartan asked again.

'I told you, I don't know,' the man replied easily. 'As the priest there says — it is really up to the gods now.'

75 A.D.

Sparta

Lysandra opened her eyes to see Deianara leaning over her. 'Gods, Lysandra,' she said. 'Wake up! You are shouting the place down.'

Lysandra blinked a few times, the remnants of the nightmare slipping away from her. 'Sorry . . .' she mumbled, giving her friend a smile.

'It is time to wake up anyway,' Deianara said.

'I feel as though I have not slept at all,' Lysandra complained.

'We have been roommates for eight years — and in those eight years never once have you had enough sleep.'

'That is because you keep me awake with your self-pleasuring every night,' Lysandra shot back.

'You should try it,' Deianara chided. 'It might make you less waspish first thing in the morning. Or I could do it for you. The other girls are all at it, and I'm the only one who lives with *Parthenos* herself. It's very frustrating.'

'We are training to be priestesses of a *virgin* goddess, Deianara. Besides, it is the Spartan way to be disciplined in all things.'

'Really, Lysandra,' Deianara stood and made her way to her own bunk. 'You are incorrigible.'

'I am sure you mean incorruptible.'

Deianara stuck out her tongue.

'Has it really been eight years?' Lysandra said.

'I know, can you believe it? Remember when we first came – they shaved our heads. *That* was awful.' This made Lysandra grin – Deianara was incredibly vain about her long, blonde hair, even though Priestesses of Athene were supposed to be paragons of Spartan modesty. 'And Melantha used to beat us all the time,' Deianara added, her eyes glittering with amusement. After a moment's thought she said, 'She was probably like you – no outlet for her passions. Made her a bully.'

'You know as well as I that she was not a bully.'

'Easy to say *now*. Back then, we really hated her – hindsight, Lysandra.'

There was no arguing that, so Lysandra chose to ignore it. 'We needed discipline and we needed to be taught not to fear pain but accept it as part of life.'

'Spartans fear nothing,' Deianara quoted – without the proper reverence in Lysandra's opinion.

'It is one of the things that make us superior,' she reminded her companion as they began to dress. 'As is proper ritual observance: we need to sacrifice before today's lessons.'

'Well, we had best hurry then. I would not want to interrupt your personal communication with the goddess, Lysandra.'

Lysandra glanced over, wondering if she was being mocked, but Deianara had — for once — managed to keep a straight face and Lysandra deigned not to make an issue of it. She loved her room-mate, but Deianara had a maddening habit of not treating her duties with appropriate solemnity. They had been brought up to embrace their innate superiority over lesser Hellenes and all other peoples and to embrace the hard training of warrior and priest-ess. But much of the time Deianara showed all together too much levity. And she hardly ever got beaten — her back had fewer scars than anyone else who had come to the temple in their group — and, in her more peevish moments. Lysandra felt this to be a little unfair.

After all, it was she, Lysandra, who was pre-eminent in all matters to do with their training. She was the tallest, the strongest, the best with sword, spear and shield and the most intelligent. And of course, the goddess spoke to *her* — even Halkyone had confirmed this was the truth and not something that had grown from a child's imagination.

Lysandra had not shared with anyone that *this* was why she did not indulge in the sexual pleasures that the other girls enjoyed. She was tempted for sure, but feared that if she broke her abstinence, the goddess would cease to commune with her. She glanced at Deianara — indulging a fantasy of being locked in a passionate embrace with her . . .

'What?' Deianara asked, her head cocked to one side.

'Nothing.'

The two made their way to the temple proper to make their morning sacrifices, waving a greeting to Melantha who was on guard.

If the *palaestra* was always full of noise and activity, the temple was an island of serenity. Dominated by the altar of Athene, the temple was austere, its walls decorated only by a frieze that went around all four walls, images of Spartans inspired to feats of greatness by the goddess herself. The statue of Athene behind the altar was far less grand than the exterior one, but Lysandra much preferred it. Far smaller, it looked more real to her, imbued with a sense of life that the grander icon did not have: Lysandra always felt that, no matter where you stood in the temple, the eyes of Athene were always on you and this was a comforting thought.

Lysandra loved this place and knew every inch of it – even those secret areas that were forbidden to neophytes and indeed most full priestesses. Beneath the stone floors was a cavernous library, full of secret knowledge of history and military tactics.

This was part of the reason for the constant tiredness that Deianara had noticed. Lysandra would steal into the temple, avoiding the watchful eyes of the guards, and creep into the library, the entrance to which was situated behind the throne of the Matriarch.

Here, she would pore over the books until the small hours of the morning. It had begun as a challenge to herself – she wanted to see what was forbidden and the truth of it was that most girls who left their quarters at night were out prowling for food or, as they grew older, to meet in illicit trysts and as such, the guards were more often looking outwards than looking inwards. Stealth was a skill that the Spartans had always valued and it pleased Lysandra that she was clearly accomplished at it.

There was already a queue of girls waiting to make offerings and by the time it came to their turn there were only a few doves left in the wooden cages that were placed nearby. Lysandra recalled scrubbing their waste and cleaning the blood away from the altar in her younger days, a task that was thankfully no longer required of her. She selected the best of what looked to be a poor bunch and carried it to the altar.

She whispered her prayers, eyes closed, hoping as always that the goddess would speak to her, but today she was silent. As the Homeric hymn died on her lips, Lysandra slit the bird's throat, allowing its life blood to gush into the altar bowl and enjoying the warm pulse of the liquid on her skin.

'*There will always be blood on your hands, Lysandra.*'

Lysandra started and looked up at the statue: the voice in her mind was unmistakable. *Athene had spoken!* She waited patiently until Deianara tutted and began to fidget. The goddess was clearly not going to elaborate so, with some reluctance, Lysandra placed the dead bird in a receptacle and left Deianara to her prayers, while her own mind whirled with the possibilities contained in the goddess's message to her.

It was bright outside, the *palaestra* now full of girls and women at their training, the air full of the discordant sounds of shouted orders and wooden weapons clacking together. Watching absently, Lysandra plunged her hands into a water-trough to wash away the blood, pondering the meaning of Athene's words.

Blood on her hands. Did it mean that she would spend all her days as a priestess or observing the rituals? Her eyes were drawn to the great statue of the goddess, seeking an answer – and then it came to her.

This temple had been built hundreds of years ago after Pyrrhus of Epirus had invaded Lakedaimonia and tried to conquer the Spartans. Under the leadership of Queen Arachidamia, the Spartan women had taken up arms alongside the men and crushed the invader. The victory was of course inspired by Athene herself and so the temple had been built in case the women of Sparta were ever called upon again to defend their lands.

All their training in arms and military tactics was to honour this ancient promise and with a bolt of divine clarity it occurred to Lysandra that this was why she was so much better than her peers; why she was driven not to seek out illicit liaisons at night but rather break into the temple proper and read the military texts. This was why Athene spoke to her: she had been *chosen*. The blood on her hands would not be that of ritual sacrifice – it would be the blood of her enemies.

'Come,' Deianara emerged from the darkness of the temple and rinsed her arms. 'You are daydreaming again and we have a class to attend.'

Lysandra wondered whether she should share the word of the goddess with her friend but opted against it, feeling that it might be churlish to do so. She smiled. 'Halkyone's classes are always good.'

'I would rather be training,' Deianara said as they moved off. 'It is a fine day and I would test my *pankration* on the sands,' she indicated the girls who were sparring on the *palaestra*.

Lysandra arched an eyebrow. 'Against me, Deianara?'

'Even you cannot win all the time, Lysandra,' she retorted.

'But I *do* win all the time!'

Deianara did not respond for a moment and then suddenly lashed out, clipping Lysandra about the ear and jumped away. 'Got you!' she shouted and sprinted off. Shrieking with laughter and feigned outrage, Lysandra leapt after her, pursuing her all the way to the squat stone building that served at the school house.

Gasping, the two skidded to a halt and composed themselves – it would be unseemly for two senior acolytes to burst into the classroom: exuberance was tolerated on the *palaestra* but nowhere else.

'I am going to kill you one of these days,' Lysandra whispered as they went inside.

'You will have to catch me first,' Deianara nudged her in the ribs. It was true: Deianara was queen of the quick dash and Lysandra, despite her longer stride, could not match her for pace.

The two entered the classroom, Lysandra remembering to adopt an air of controlled nonchalance. The girls in the room were her peers and, in many respects, her competitors and she had to maintain an aura of superiority – especially now as the goddess had revealed her true purpose.

The room was set up much like the mess tent, long benches and trestle tables facing the front, where Halkyone sat at her desk reading. As Deianara and Lysandra strolled to their places, her eyes flicked up and she smiled. Her expression was almost indulgent; if any of them could get away with bending the rules it was Deiannara, and Lysandra was indulged only by association.

'Now that we are all here,' she said, rising to her feet, 'we can begin today's lesson. We shall discuss Thermopylae . . .'

Halkyone began by describing the build-up and training to the battle, focussing on the élan of the Spartan warriors that held off the Persian barbarians at the Hot Gates. The story went on for quite some time, encompassing the entire battle, and Lysandra found herself sighing. This was one battle that they had 'discussed' many times and she felt that there were more relevant campaigns that they could talk about but never did. There was so much more to be learned as she had discovered in the library. Besides which, Thermopylae — whichever way you dressed it up — was a defeat.

'So in many respects,' Halkyone was saying, 'Thermopylae was a Spartan victory.'

It was not, Lysandra thought to herself, but there was little point in bringing it up.

'*What* did you say, Lysandra?' Halkyone's voice rang out.

Lysandra looked around to see all eyes in the room upon her. Had she spoken aloud? She could not have done. 'I said nothing, ma'am,' she replied with a smile. Halkyone liked her after all, but she faltered as she saw a look of iron in the older woman's eyes. 'I said nothing,' she repeated.

'I *heard* you,' Halkyone accused her. 'Everyone heard you say "it was not." Are you so arrogant as to offer an alternative to my lesson?'

Lysandra felt a prick of anger at this: it was not arrogance to speak the truth, even if she had not meant to speak. The thought raced through her mind that perhaps now was the time to show Halkyone and indeed her peers that she knew more than they. That she knew better. That had to be it – the goddess had spoken through her and set this in motion. 'It is not arrogance to speak the truth,' she gave voice to her thought, ignoring the appalled gasps from her fellow acolytes.

'It *is* arrogance to presume that you know more than your instructor, Lysandra,' Halkyone said. 'I can only suppose that you were stating the obvious: in military terms, yes, a defeat. But in moral terms, a victory, showing our superiority over the Persian barbarians . . .'

'We could and should have held them longer,' Lysandra interrupted. Halkyone's eyes narrowed dangerously and Lysandra saw the ire behind them, but she would now not be cowed: the goddess had spoken to her – spoke through her, in fact. 'It was possible to do so.'

'You compare your strategic knowledge to Leonidas's, Lysandra? You believe that *you* know better than the most illustrious Spartan in history?'

'Of course not,' she snapped. 'But after the first day, when the Immortals attacked, Spartiates must have been wounded – unable to carry shield or spear. *I* would have sent these men who could not fight to oversee the Phocian rearguard that guarded the secret pass. You have told us many times that the Phocians were taken by surprise and hence it is my opinion that if there were Spartans commanding them, this would not have occurred.'

'*You would have sent these men!*' The pitch in Halkyone's voice rose with incredulity. 'Be silent, girl. Your arrogance is offensive to me and the memories of our forefathers.'

Lysandra could see that her anger was genuine now and for a moment an apology began to form on her lips but she quashed it – she should not apologise for being correct. 'Are you saying that the Phocian pickets would have been surprised and overwhelmed if under Spartan supervision?' A collective gasp went across the room. Lysandra found that she was rather enjoying the confrontation. All the attention was on her and she was clearly going to win the debate.

'It is enough for you to know that the Spartan way has ensured our freedom. Even now, when the Romans own the world, *we* have never tasted defeat . . .'

'We lost at Leuctra!' The words were out before Lysandra could stop them and she felt suddenly sick with dread.

The rosy tint of anger that had coloured Halkyone's cheeks drained away and her eyes widened in horror. Silence weighed heavy in the room and, despite her outburst, there was a part of Lysandra that revelled in the fact that she was proving to the other class-novices that she knew more than they.

'It is too early in your education for you to know of such things,' Halkyone's voice was tight and controlled. 'But I can guess how you came about this knowledge. You are forbidden to speak that word again – to anyone. You will be punished to remind you of this.' Halkyone's eyes bored into Lysandra's own – harsh, hard and unwavering and for the first time, Lysandra felt a tremor of fear. 'If you are going to spout out the knowledge of a full priestess, *Acolyte* Lysandra, then you will be punished as one. Let us see if your back can support the weight of your tongue,' Halkyone said. 'The rest of you – take her outside. Those of you who have had issue with our *strategos* here are reminded that she is in disgrace and should be treated as such.'

There was a sudden scraping of seats and the girls came at her in a rush. There was nothing Lysandra could do – she was in disgrace and could not fight back. Deianara was closest to her and spun her around, pulling her head to her chest. 'Keep your head down, I will do what I can . . .'

But they were too many and Lysandra was torn away from Deianara's grasp. She saw her go down as one of the girls punched her full in the face as she was dragged out. Blows rained down on Lysandra, now; they pulled her hair, spat on her, kicked and abused her. Through the pain, Lysandra took solace in the fact these were lesser people taking their petty vengeance on their betters but such thoughts soon fled in the disorientating fog of the assault. Some took pleasure in what they were doing, others were simply obeying orders but did not spare their hand. Outside now, they pushed her from one girl to the next, each of whom took her chance to get in a blow and soon Lysandra fell to the ground, curling into a ball as they laid into her.

There was nothing else to do but take it. They had all suffered beatings before and this was no different – Lysandra knew she just had to grit her teeth and get through. There would be worse to follow.

'Enough!' Halkyone's strident voice rang out and at once the constant rain of blows ceased.

Dazed, Lysandra sat up and spat blood from her mouth. Her face felt strange as though it was swollen to twice its normal size. It was numb yet punctuated with sharp pinpricks of pain. She puffed out her cheeks, spots dancing before her eyes.

'Take her to the posts,' Halkyone ordered.

The girls hauled Lysandra to her feet and dragged her across the *palaestra*. All work, she noted, slowly came to a halt as she was pulled along and she heard Halkyone barking orders to form a general assembly. Girls and women began to form their lines as Lysandra was pulled over to the twin posts at the far end of the training area. Here, her tunic was removed and her arms secured to the leather straps attached to the poles.

Lysandra had witnessed this many times before: public flogging was the usual punishment for transgressions. It served two purposes: the first, obviously, to chastise the offender but also it afforded her penance and a chance to show her Spartan virtue. Since their first day at the temple they had been taught to ignore pain, and this was a test of that resolve.

'This acolyte,' Halkyone's voice rang out, 'is guilty of insubordination. She considers her knowledge equal to that of any priestess. Indeed, she believes herself to be the strategic better of Leonidas Agiad himself! The acolyte will learn some humility. Melantha!'

'Ma'am!'

'You were one of the girl's trainers when she was a neophyte. She has shamed you. *You* will carry out the punishment.'

There was silence then as Melantha must have been making her way forward and Lysandra's resolve began to crumble as fear wormed its insidious way inside her. Perhaps if she apologised now she would yet be spared the agonies to come – or at least the worst of it. She opened her mouth but then clamped her jaws shut, picturing the other girls not only in her group but all the rest. She would not falter, she decided, even in the face of her death.

This was a test, she realised. Athene had spoken – now the goddess was putting her on trial, assessing her worthiness.

Rough hands pulled her head up and Lysandra found herself looking at the pockmarked face of Melantha. 'Bite down on this, worm,' she said quietly, pushing a piece of leather between her lips. 'It will help.' Lysandra gripped the band between her teeth, noticing that there was something behind Melantha's eyes – it was not sympathy, Lysandra thought, but understanding. Of course – Melantha had been here before.

'The acolyte is ready!' Melantha announced.

'The punishment will commence!' Halkyone responded.

'How many lashes, ma'am?'

'Until one of you breaks.'

'Ma'am?' Melantha queried, surprise evident in her voice.

'You have your orders, priestess. Carry them out.'

Lysandra tensed, eyes staring straight ahead at the pitted stone of the temple wall. She heard a hiss and sharp crack and for a moment there was no pain. When it came it was sharp, tingling but not as bad as she had feared. Then she was hit again, the tip of the lash scoring into her back. This time it burned, but still – she could bear it. The third blow landed and it made her stiffen in her bonds and she bit down hard on the leather strap to avoid the shame of crying out. Sweat began to ooze from her body as she concentrated on

24

shutting out the physical, compartmentalising the pain, ignoring it.

Again the lash ate into her flesh and she could feel the first rivulets of blood begin to snake down her back as her skin broke under the assault. She breathed in and out sharply through her nose and she heard a strangled cry emit from her throat as Melantha hit her again.

At ten lashes, Melantha paused. 'Acolyte Lysandra, are you broken?' she asked formally. Lysandra was tempted to nod her head, but her pride would not allow it so she shook it, no.

There was a pause and then the familiar hiss and crack followed by the molten bronze fire flooding over her back. Lysandra hung her head low, her black hair now sodden with blood and sweat. Again the lash fell and she bit down hard on the leather strip, the cords on her neck standing out as she tried to bite through the pain. Stars flashed in front of her eyes and, to her shame, she felt tears leak out from beneath tightly shut lids. It came in sickening waves now, peaks and troughs of agony from which there was no respite. She had lost count now, her mind beginning to play tricks on her.

'Acolyte Lysandra, are you broken?'

Lysandra shook her head, no. Athene was testing her worthiness now, testing her true Spartan nature: she would not fail her.

Again, Melantha asked the question and somehow Lysandra realised that she had not moved her head. She shook it with all the vigour she could muster even though the movement nearly made her vomit.

Without warning she was hit again and her body twisted in her bonds, self-preservation disobeying her will, desperate to escape the punishment. This time, Melantha worked faster, the lash cracking onto Lysandra's tortured flesh in rapid succession. Lysandra felt a hot rush as her loincloth became soaked with urine but she was now too far lost in her agony to feel the shame of it.

Three more times the whip exploded onto her back and then

she felt her legs go from under her. Now as the lash fell, she saw bright explosions of light before her eyes and then the glimpse of a darkened room – the room from her dreams.

'Acolyte Lysandra, are you broken?'

Do not give in, a voice from the back of her mind insisted, recalling the lessons drummed into her since the first day in the temple. *You are a Spartan. Spartans do not fear pain. Spartans fear nothing.*

'Acolyte Lysandra, are you broken?'

She made a guttural noise from the back of her throat, an animal sound but it must let them know that she would not be defeated.

'Priestess Halkyone,' Melantha's voice sounded far off. '*I* am broken.'

She heard Halkyone speaking but could not make out the words and suddenly a whiteness filled Lysandra's vision, blotting out everything else.

'She is dying!' A woman's voice pierced the light.

'No, she is not!' This time it was the man with the Athenian accent. 'The goddess will spare her handmaiden. Athene on Olympus, hear our prayer. Save her, we beseech you!'

'I am not dying . . .' Lysandra mumbled. 'I am not dying.'

IV

The shock of the near freezing water startled Lysandra back into consciousness. She gasped, memories of the savage beating coming back to her in a rush and, as they did, her back began to crawl with tendrils of pain.

She was sitting under a small waterfall in the Eurotas and before her was Melantha. The priestess had locked her legs over Lysandra's hips and was holding her head close to her chest so the water did not cascade over it.

'Hold still, worm,' Melantha said. 'You do not want to float away like a lost turd. How is your back?'

Lysandra bit back the automatic and honest response. 'It is much better.'

'Already,' Melantha mocked. 'So as well as being the better of Leonidas in tactics and strategy are you now possessed of Athene's aegis as skin?'

'It is not the Spartan way to admit pain,' Lysandra gasped – all too aware of how pained her voice sounded.

'The water will numb you up soon enough,' the priestess told her. 'If a beating is bad, the pain after is worse. Trust me, I *know*.'

It had been a long time since she had been held by anyone. And despite this being her former instructor and recent punisher, Lysandra found herself taking some comfort from the closeness of the older woman. Naked, their bodies were pressed close together and it felt strange under the cold water. 'What happened,' she asked after some time. 'After you . . .'

'After I had to admit defeat or beat you to death, you mean?' The chuckle in her voice took the sting from the words if not from Lysandra's tortured back. 'I put you in a cart and drove you down here. Immersing the body in cold water after a thrashing is an old trick, Lysandra. Every priestess knows it and passes it on – we all take the lash to harden us against pain. But there is no sense in bearing agony for agony's sake: the trick now is to heal as soon as you can. At the moment you are simply a burden to the temple.'

The cold water was working as Melantha had said it would, the endless drumming on her back seeming to wash away the hurt. 'I will not be a burden for long,' Lysandra said. 'I will heal.' She raised her head to look into Melantha's eyes. 'But why you? Why did you bring me here and not Deianara?'

'Because I asked to,' Melantha replied. 'You impressed me,

Lysandra,' she went on. 'Not many girls of your age would take what you took.'

Lysandra was surprised: this was the first time, save for the formal query during her punishment, that Melantha had referred to her as anything other than 'worm', 'idiot', 'scum' or some other derogation. 'Thank you . . . Melantha,' she said hesitantly.

'Come,' the priestess said. 'My toes are beginning to turn blue and I think yours are too. Slowly now.'

Lysandra bit her lip to keep the pain at bay as Melantha helped her up. The air was cool and she began to shiver as the wind chilled her naked flesh. 'Must be the shock of the lashing,' she said, not wanting to admit to the priestess that she was cold.

'Must be,' Melantha replied, her own skin coming up in goose pimples as the two staggered towards the shore. 'Lie face down on that blanket,' she instructed. As Lysandra did so, Melantha made her way to the cart, patting the mule's flank as she did so. 'I have a pot of myrrh here,' she called, pulling her scarlet tunic over her head and tying it at her waist. 'You will learn to love it if you keep on testing Halkyone as this will be the first of many beatings you are going to get.'

Melantha settled down on the grass beside Lysandra, tipping some of the precious, sweet smelling oil onto her back. 'So, Halkyone told me that you were spouting off about Leuctra. How do you know of it?' she asked as she began to work the unguent into Lysandra's wounds.

Lysandra paused before replying as the feeling of relief spread over her back and the myrrh started to lift away the pain. 'Halkyone forbade me to speak the word,' she said at last.

Melantha chuckled. 'Tell me in generalities.'

'There is not much to tell,' Lysandra said, really just wanting to lie quietly and recover. But Melantha had asked – and could make her entreaty a command if she wanted. 'We are taught that stealth is an admirable quality. I believe that we are subtly encouraged to exploit opportunities to break rules at the temple and as long as we are successful, no one is the wiser. Many of the girls meet to . . .' she trailed off, not quite knowing how to describe these midnight liaisons. 'To . . . well, talk I suppose. Others to steal food. Some for just the thrill of it. I like to read. I want to be the best priestess here. Learning more than my sisters will give me an advantage. So I break into the library to study. I have learned much – and I know that not everything that we are taught is quite the truth.' She stopped short of telling Melantha of her recent communion with the goddess; that was something she had learned, painfully, to keep to herself for the present.

'That should do for now,' Melantha said. 'Sit up – slowly. I will help you with your tunic.'

Lysandra did as she was told.

'So, while the other girls are diddling each other, you are reading apocryphal texts by lamplight. You know, if any other girl were telling me this, I simply would not believe them. Somehow, with you, I find myself hardly surprised.'

Lysandra could not quite work out if that was a compliment or not, but she decided to take it as one, despite Melantha's use of mild vulgarity. 'Thank you,' she said. 'I rather fancy that if we are priest-esses of the virgin then we should not be trying to get around our vows and indulging ourselves with . . . diddling.'

Melantha laughed out loud at this for reasons that Lysandra could not grasp: Lysandra had not been making a joke; she felt very strongly on the matter – though, much as she was loth to admit it to herself, the urges she sometimes felt were almost overpowering.

'Lysandra,' Melantha shook her head. 'You are altogether too staid – even for one of us. Stay here!' she ordered. 'I will return in a moment.'

The lithe redhead made off, leaving Lysandra to stare at the grey, babbling waters of the Eurotas and enjoy the blissful numbness in her back. A short time later, Melantha returned with some dry sticks.

She dug a small pit with her dagger and soon a little fire was burning. Onto this, she placed a pot filled with water from the river. Lysandra watched as she sprinkled some leaves into it.

'What are you doing?' she asked.

'I can see that your studies did not reach as far as Hippocrates,' she replied. 'This is Egyptian opium. It will help with the pain.'

'My back is quite fine now,' Lysandra replied, eager to prove to the priestess that she was as hardy as any Spartan.

'You will know all about it when the myrrh wears off, believe me.'

The two sat in companionable silence as the pot began to boil. The fumes coming from it were the sweetest thing Lysandra had ever smelled and she said as much.

'Opium is a most marvellous thing,' Melantha said. 'It eases pain, brings sweet dreams and sometimes can offer solace when your spirits are down. But it is also very dangerous.'

'Poison?' Lysandra's eyebrows shot up.

'If too much is taken, yes. But it is more complicated than that. If you keep taking it, you will come to depend on it. It will make you its slave and you will not be able to think of anything but the drug. I have read that the same can be said of wine.'

Lysandra answered without thinking. 'I find that quite hard to believe. How can wine make anyone a slave? It is merely something with which you quench your thirst.'

'Who knows.' Melantha grunted and poured the contents of the pot into a cup. 'But I have read about it, so it must be true. Here. Drink it – and mind, it is hot.'

Lysandra took a sip and wrinkled her nose. 'How can something that smells so sweet taste so vile?'

'Just drink it. And make sure you get all the bits down you as well – vile as they are.'

Lysandra took a few more sips, blowing on the water to cool it down. 'I should have shown more control,' she said after a while.

'I should not have spoken out against Halkyone in such a way.' She tipped down the rest of the drink, wincing at the foul taste.

'Perhaps,' Melantha nodded. 'But then, Lysandra, you have always been that way. Always first, always strongest in your group, always the best at everything. Despite today, you will make a fine priestess when the time comes.'

'Thank you,' Lysandra said, feeling a sudden rush of warm affection for Melantha. It was very good of her to take the time to help in this way. She smiled at the priestess, trying to think of a way to express this sudden gratitude. But the words would not come, and after a time Lysandra realised that she was just sitting there, grinning like an idiot. She tried to compose her face into a stoic mask, but was unable to stop smiling.

'How are you feeling?' Melantha asked, but her voice sounded distant and muffled, as though she were speaking through a pillow. Then, to her shame, Lysandra could not remember what the priestess had just said. A spike of embarrassment pierced the sudden balmy veil that had descended over her senses, but it was gone in a moment. Melantha spoke again, asking her how she was feeling.

'I feel . . .' Lysandra languidly shook her head from side to side, enjoying the feeling of her hair playing about her face. 'I feel good. Just right in fact.'

Melantha peered at her for a moment and gave a satisfied nod. 'Yes, I can see that you do. Come on,' she rose to her feet. 'I will take you back to the temple now.'

'The temple . . .' Lysandra agreed and made to stand up. At least she thought she had, but it seemed that her legs had not heard her thought so she remained sitting on the floor. 'Why are you being so kind to me?' she asked. 'This is not the Spartan way.'

Melantha stooped and helped her to her feet. 'You only know what you have been taught so far,' she chided. 'The Spartan way is not only about beating each other with sticks, fighting and reminding ourselves that we are superior to all other people – of course we are,' she added quickly. 'But what makes us so is that we love each other. This is because our blood is pure and untainted. Our Spartan blood is precious and, in times of need, we succour each other.' Melantha was silent for a moment. 'If they choose to punish you as an adult, then I will help you as a sister priestess would.'

Melantha steered Lysandra into the back of the cart and laid her down on her front.

'Sister priestess . . .' Lysandra mumbled. 'One day . . . sister . . . I will fight for Athene.' Despite her earlier reticence to speak of the matter she now found that she needed to speak of it. 'The goddess told me that I will always have blood on my hands. I think I will be remembered as Arachidamia is remembered. As a warrior.'

Melantha's laugh was far away. 'You have a long road to walk before that day, Lysandra. Come on,' she helped her into the back of the cart, laying her down on her front. 'Sleep well little sister.'

Lysandra did not respond and soon the cart was moving, its gentle sway carrying her off to the embrace of Morpheus.

79 A.D.
The Aegean Sea

The pitch and roll of the ship woke her, snatching the dream of her childhood away.

'Ah, it's awake,' her friend Pavo commented as she opened her eyes. 'Did you have sweet dreams, priestess?'

Lysandra frowned, trying to remember. 'I was dreaming of my youth in Sparta,' she said. 'And also – I am not sure that they were sweet. There was a nightmare in there somewhere too – I was lying on a table, covered in blood. I cannot recall it all now.'

'This is a fuc . . . this is a nightmare, too' he said. The soldiers of the Sixth Century always watched their language around her, something that she appreciated; she could not abide vulgarity. 'I *hate* ships,' he added.

'This is my first time on a ship. I too am learning to hate it,' she replied. 'But we have sacrificed to Poseidon . . . *Neptune*,' she corrected herself with a sigh. The Romans could never understand or accept that their religion was an utter plagiarism of the Hellenic pantheon. It was one of the reasons she had sought the position of Mission Priestess at the temple. She was the youngest ever to be granted the honour and the Matriarch had been sure that she, of all the women in the temple, was best suited to give Romans and other barbarians the truth and perhaps make some small part of the world better for her teaching.

She and the legionary were wedged into a corner, surrounded by the men of the Sixth Century. The ship stank as it was and this, coupled with the pungent odour of sweating bodies and belly gas made the air below deck so thick that she felt she could almost chew on it.

'Well, with you on board, everyone knows that if the rest of the legion goes down, we won't. The gods look after their own – eh, priestess?' Pavo was trying to sound lighthearted, but she could see fear in his dark eyes.

Lysandra wanted to reassure him and any of the other men that were listening in; they had faith in her and faith in Athene – or Minerva as they insisted on calling the goddess. 'Though I am a Priestess of Athene, not Poseidon, I am sure that all will be well.' She did not think it prudent to mention that Poseidon and Athene hated each other and it was only the will of Zeus himself that kept his brother and daughter from being at constant odds. Lysandra thought it was all rather childish of Poseidon – clearly, Athene had bettered him in the contest to name the city of Athens and he should have accepted it instead of carrying a grudge over the millennia.

As the thought occurred to her, the ship plunged downwards sharply and she reflexively pushed herself tighter into the corner.

Pavo puffed out his cheeks. 'Scared?' he asked.

'Spartans fear nothing,' she replied at once. Which, most of the time, was true, but in her heart, she was feeling a little uneasy. 'We will be ashore soon enough,' she added.

'And to a new home. I liked Greece, though,' he said.

Lysandra nodded. 'I will admit to some excitement myself,' she replied. 'I have never left Hellas. Indeed, when I came to the legion, it was the first time I had left the temple in Sparta.'

'Your ma and pa must be really proud of you. You know, being a priestess and all – and travelling with the best legion in the empire.'

'I have not seen them in many years,' Lysandra said. 'When I left the temple, I was going to visit them, but then I thought to myself that perhaps I should not see them when I had accomplished . . . well, accomplished nothing in fact. When I return home, then yes – I think they will be proud. After all, I am the youngest priestess to be granted the Mission.'

Pavo chuckled despite his evident nerves at the increasingly violent pitch and yaw of the ship. 'You were the talk of the legion for a bit. A lone girl, dressed up in armour demanding that she should be allowed to travel with us and serve the goddess. No sooner was it out of your mouth than it was all over the camp.'

'That is because you soldiers gossip like old crones.' Lysandra smiled as the memories came back to her.

After the outburst to her old teacher, Halkyone, and the subsequent thrashing, she had kept her own counsel and knuckled down to her work with quiet efficiency. If this had not endeared the other girls to her it had at least gone some way to blunting the outright hatred that the more envious of them felt towards her. She had become the model acolyte and was soon promoted to full priestess – before the others in her group, naturally.

Though Lysandra could have used her newfound status to take revenge on her former peers, she rather enjoyed the fact that she had not. It all went to demonstrate that not only was she physically and mentally superior to them, she also possessed a higher moral code.

When she had asked for the coveted role of Mission Priestess, Lysandra considered that if Athene's message meant that one day she would have to fight, where better to learn about the military than in the all-conquering army of Rome? Also, being with the legion would afford the opportunity to travel to barbarian lands and educate them on correct religious practices. It was all well and good telling stories of Athene to those already familiar with them, but it was the duty of civilised people to educate the savages that lurked in the distant western empire.

So she had donned her armour and ridden directly to the camp of the Fifth Macedonian Legion and spoken to the legate. Clearly he was not a religious man – the Roman upper classes had little respect for the pantheon they so blatantly plagiarised – but the men in the field were a superstitious lot as she would soon discover. Lysandra had won him over with a combination of oratory and competence: she knew how to tend the sick, the goddess was with her and it would be, she had told him, a slight to Athene herself to refuse an offer from her priestess who only wished to serve the goddess.

The ship lurched violently, plunging downwards and causing her stomach to churn. The timbers around them groaned in protest and Lysandra saw the soldiers stirring, sitting up and looking around in shock.

'Stay still, you gutless scum!' snarled Clemens, the Sixth's centurion. 'This is just a squall! It'll pass soon enough!' The bravado was feigned; Lysandra could see the fear in his pallid face. And, as if to contradict him, the ship was suddenly smashed sideways as though struck by the hand of Poseidon himself.

Soldiers were hurled across the underbelly of the ship and all at once chaos erupted, men shouting in fear and anger, Clemens roaring for calm – but to no avail. The famous discipline of the Roman soldier had no place here and the centurion was shoved aside as the terrified troops rushed to escape.

A sick dread welled up inside Lysandra but she scrambled to her feet. 'Come on, Pavo!' she shouted aware of the shrillness in her voice. 'We have to get out of here!' Bare feet slamming on the hard wooden floor, she bolted for the steps that led out of the oppressive tomb of the under-deck, Pavo in tow. There was a crush at the door to the top, men fighting each other to get away.

Even Clemens had given up, he too surging for freedom. Even as she pushed and shoved to escape, Lysandra knew that it was madness: there was nowhere to run, but she was filled with a desperate need to be free of the stygian belly of the ship. She piled out with the others onto the upper deck, ignoring the shouts of the sailors who were frantically trying to keep the ship in order.

Lysandra broke free of the mob for a moment, her eyes widening in shock at the sight of the ocean. Gone was the twinkling, white foamed surface of the sea, replaced by an angry grey churning mass. Above them, the sky was filled with clouds as Zeus added his rage to his brother's, hurling lightning bolts at them from lofty Olympus. She could see other vessels in the fleet bobbing in the tumult, tiny figures of men running here and there on the decks.

'What are we going to do?' Pavo grabbed her and pulled her to face him, his eyes full of fear. 'Priestess, you must pray! Make it stop!'

He was right. Athene had power and she could aid them still. Lysandra opened her mouth to begin the paean, but the words died on her lips, stilled by what she saw.

Taller than a mountain, a huge wave was bearing down on the ship, its white fingers seeming to scrape the sky itself. It moved fast, an unrelenting inexorable mass from which there could be no escape. Movement on the deck ceased as all eyes turned to the wave and for a few moments there was an awed calm amongst them. Then, like the storm itself, it broke and both soldiers and sailors began to scream and shout in terror.

Lysandra turned and bolted towards the stern of the ship. Risking a glance behind her, she saw the wave was almost upon them and made her decision. Legs tensing, she jumped from the ship, hurling her body into the unmerciful ocean.

The water was colder than ice, the shock of it nearly driving the air from her lungs. Lysandra kicked for the surface but suddenly the current took hold of her. Through the murky gloom she saw the ship pounded by the wave's fury, plunging downwards. It was about to take her with it, trying to pull her to the murky depths of Poseidon's realm.

She would not end this way. She was the handmaiden of Athene and the god of the sea would not claim her. Fighting the panic rising within her, Lysandra kicked hard, using all her strength to drag herself from the god's grip. The effort was causing her lungs to burn, but she tried harder. She would not die here, she told herself.

But for all her efforts, she was drawing no nearer the surface and, like the wave itself, she could not hold back the panic as her body begged for air. The strong, assured kicks now became a desperate flurry as Lysandra gave into her fear.

Then, her head broke the surface.

Choking, Lysandra treaded water, looking about her. Debris was strewn over the water and like her, men bobbed about in the furious waves, straining to stay afloat.

'Priestess!' Pavo's voice came to her over the cacophony of waves and shouting men. She turned in the water to see him swimming towards her. 'I'll help you!'

'No, Pavo,' Lysandra coughed in response, but it was clear that he could not hear her. He was just about to head towards her when he cried out in pain and shock and suddenly began to flail about in the water. 'Pavo!' Lysandra shrieked.

'Help! Help me! My legs!' his cries were full of panic.

He had cramp, she guessed. 'Hold on!' she shouted. Exhausted as she was, she could not just let him drown, but the sea was pulling him further and further away.

'Priestess!' Pavo was screaming for her now, then choking as the seawater went into his mouth. 'Help . . .'

With awful suddenness, he disappeared beneath the roiling grey waves. Lysandra held her breath and ducked down, pushing away from the surface she had tried so hard to gain, eyes straining to see him through the dark waters. She swam in the direction he had been, staying under as long as she could, but there was no sign of him. She surfaced and dived again, deeper this time, but Pavo was lost to her and now exhaustion was threatening to overwhelm her. She came up for air and could not summon the strength to dive again.

The waves had carried her far, and she could now only see the occasional flash of a red tunic in the distance as the sea bore her away. A length of mast or spar swept by and she pounced, grasping it and hauling her trunk over its length. It remained afloat and she gripped it tight, knowing that to let go now would mean death for her.

The sea was still churning, but with nothing like the fury that had destroyed the ship. Clearly, Poseidon's anger was now spent, leaving only a cold drizzle in its wake. Lysandra was helpless to do anything but hold on and drift. She kept looking out for soldiers who might also have been pushed out as far as she had, but the only ones she saw were floating dead on the water. It was a sickening sight and she recognised some of them. A short time ago, they had been alive, grouching about their predicament – as had Pavo. His death weighed heavily on her mind: he had been killed trying to help her and – worse – he trusted in her and her ability to summon the protection of the goddess.

For the first time in her life, Lysandra's unshakeable faith in Athene was rocked to the core. The goddess should have come to her aid. Even if this was the domain of the sea god, she had enough power. Perhaps her survival was proof that Athene was still with her. But there was a part of her that wished that she had perished with the rest. The prospect of a slow, lingering death in the middle of the ocean filled her with dread, and it was all she could do not to burst into tears. She bit her lip, refusing to give Poseidon the satisfaction of seeing her cry.

She drifted for hours. The clouds vanished and the sun re-emerged, beating down on her, its heat seemingly magnified by the sea. Everything hurt now, her skin seeming too tight over her flesh, her muscles aching and stiff; fatigue threatened to overwhelm her but Lysandra knew that she could not rest – she might slip off the spar and that would be the end of her.

She kept telling herself this, holding on to the thought with a fierce tenacity, till even thinking itself became hypnotic and she was forced to keep jerking awake; but soon, the battle against both physical and mental exhaustion became too much and she could fight no longer. 'Let Poseidon take me then,' she murmured as sleep dragged her into its own depths.

Lysandra was drowning. Water filled her mouth and the screams of the gulls mocked her as she died.

Panicking she came to full wakefulness, thrashing around to escape certain death. As she did so, she fell away from the spar and her bottom hit the sand.

She sat, waist deep on a shore, coughing and spluttering, spitting out seawater. The tide seethed around her, its hiss incessant, mingling with angry cawing of the gulls that had roused her. Something touched her leg, making her yelp in surprise. She looked down to see the body of a legionary, face down in the surf. She shrieked and scrambled away, half-running, half-crawling onto the beach.

Lysandra took a deep breath, trying to compose herself. The

sands were strewn with detritus from the ships that had gone down in the storm. And there were bodies everywhere, partially obscured by feasting gulls, and with their gear and personal effects scattered around them. It was as though half the soldiers and sailors in the fleet had found their way here.

Wherever it was.

It could be one of the many islands in the Aegean – or perhaps Asia Minor proper. There was just no way of knowing for sure until she found help. As the thought occurred to her, she heard the whinny of a horse. Lysandra turned and there, down the beach, she could see a small knot of men, some mounted, others picking through the flotsam and jetsam that had washed up on shore. She looked skywards and whispered a silent prayer of thanksgiving to Athene. The goddess had not deserted her after all.

'Hey!' she called rising to her feet and waving her arms over her head. 'Over here!' Three riders detached themselves from the main group and cantered towards her. 'Thank the gods!' she said as they drew up to her. The gods, it appeared, offered succour in strange guises. These men all looked hard-bitten and crude – but then, what could one expect – clearly they were not Hellene. One was bald with dark brown skin and bulbous eyes. As he grinned at her, she could see that he had misshapen teeth. The second man had a curled beard and ringlets hung about the side of his face. The third was clean-shaven with his hair cropped close and he had a long aquiline nose that looked as if it had been broken once and had set badly.

'Thank the gods indeed!' the dark skinned one said in accented Latin. 'Our lucky day. How much do you reckon we can make on it?' He turned to the one with ringlets.

'Who can tell?' ringlets replied. 'She looks a mess now, but will scrub up well enough no doubt. And she's tall – shame about the tits, though. Mind you, Stick, we should test the merchandise first.'

The one called Stick rolled his eyes. 'If you must.'

'Tiro?' Ringlets glanced at broken nose. 'Me first?'

'No,' Tiro threw his leg over his mount's head and slid from her. '*Me* first.'

Lysandra drew herself up. 'I am a Priestess of Athene,' she announced, 'recently assigned to the Fifth Macedonian Legion. I am in need of your help.'

'Priestess is it?' Stick eyed her. 'Not any more, I'm afraid. You're a slave now. Gideon and Tiro here are going to fuck you – Jews and Romans – what can I tell you? They're barbarians. Once they've finished, we'll sell you on.'

Lysandra felt almost sick with fear as Gideon also slid from his mount, grinning at her. There was nothing she could do, save for one thing: she turned and bolted, running across the sands as fast as she could. Behind her, she could hear the men laughing at her. Faster and faster her feet pounded on the sand – but she was weak and she could tell they were gaining. Lysandra rushed past a corpse and the gulls, disturbed by her passing, flew up in a fury – behind she heard the two men curse as they were caught in the gaggle, gaining her precious seconds.

She ran on and saw another body; angling her path she headed towards it, hoping to repeat the same trick twice: but this time as the gulls flew, she saw the soldier wore a sword. Lysandra ducked and rolled, coming up by the body and dragging the weapon from the man's scabbard and turning to face her enemies.

She was a Spartan: she would die on her feet with her wounds in front.

Chest heaving with exertion, she raised the weapon as the men drew close to her.

'Oh!' Gideon laughed as he trotted to a halt. 'You should put that down, darling. You could hurt someone. Come on now – Tiro won't take long, but I promise that I'll have you in Heaven in a few strokes.'

Despite her fear, his tone offended her. 'I think not,' she said. 'You will die before I let you touch me.'

41

'Put the sword down, girl,' said Tiro, his tone hardening. 'We don't want to have to kill you,' he drew his own weapon, 'but we will if you try to put up a fight. Got it?'

Lysandra kept her eyes on him, but allowed herself a look over his shoulder. Stick was still someway off on his mount, watching the proceedings. She could not see his expression but she guessed it would be one of amusement. Her grip tightened on the sword and in that moment she realised that fear had fled. The long years of training suddenly kicked in and with omission of thought she leapt into the attack.

Time seemed to slow as she moved across the sand: she saw Tiro's eyes widen as she came towards him, his sword moving to defend – so slow. Even as his guard came up she was through it and her blade speared into his throat. She felt the vibration of it up her arm as the steel parted flesh, bone and gristle; a fountain of crimson erupted from him as he fell back, clutching his neck in agonised astonishment.

Dragging the blade free, she whirled, her salt-begrimed hair whipping across her face as she did so. Her stance was low and she saw Gideon pulling out his sword. It was half way from the leather when she struck, plunging the blade into his groin.

He screamed as he fell to the sand, clutching his ruined genitals, the purplish remains of them crawling down the blade of her sword. 'Oh God!' he shrieked, his voice suddenly high pitched. 'Oh God no! Please God!'

Lysandra advanced on his stricken form.

'Please! Please don't kill me! I'm begging you please . . . I have a wife . . . children . . . please . . .!' Gideon burst into tears, the salty water running down his fleshy face.

Something changed in Lysandra as she stood over him. She knew that she should feel repugnance at what she had done and fear of the consequences. But the truth was she felt a burning, heady rush that filled her to the core. 'I told you,' Lysandra said and rammed her sword into his throat.

She stepped away, the sense of elation that had come over her suddenly fleeing. For a moment, all was still and then she heard the high-pitched blast of a whistle. Stick was blowing for all he was worth and the other riders had heard and now headed their mounts towards her.

Sword in hand, Lysandra turned towards the sun and ran. It was so bright, filling her vision, filling the horizon.

'*Run Lysandra! Run for the light!*'

She knew that voice. She had heard it from the days of her childhood. The goddess spoke to her again!

'*Run Lysandra!*'

Behind her she could hear the pounding of hooves and the shouts of furious men. They were gaining and she gritted her teeth and dug deep.

'*RUN!*'

The light became impossibly bright, searing her eyes and she was forced to close them – but still she forced herself on, running blind now. She heard herself gasping for breath and suddenly was aware of a burning pain in her side.

Then Lysandra opened her eyes. And lived again.

VI

87 A.D.
Dacia

The rain had fallen, making the air smell fresh with the odour of life; now the sky was a cool grey a stark contrast to the lush grass of the plain. It was a rich green that Sorina reckoned had no match in all the world. It sang with life unlike the sand-blasted deserts of Asia Minor where men had to twist and bend nature in order to live.

She watched as the two wings of Sarmatian cavalry thundered across the sodden ground, their hooves an echo like the hammer of the gods beating upon the earth. This, she thought, was as it should be. Women riding to war with their men at their side, united in one noble cause: the destruction of Rome and all it represented.

Six years before, all this had been the stuff of dreams, a waning candle that she had nurtured in the *ludus* of Lucius Balbus. But now, under the guiding hand of the great Decabalus, the tribes of the plains and the warriors of Dacia were united in this undertaking.

'Now,' she murmured. Even as the whisper escaped her lips, the charge wheeled to the left and the horse archers began to loose their volleys at invisible opponents. The light horses did their work and galloped away as moments later the heavy cavalry charged home. In her minds eye Sorina could see the devastated Roman ranks crushed under their hooves and torn by their bloody swords. The disciplined lines would break and the people of the plains would bathe in their blood and make those that survived beg for their deaths. The god Zalmoxis demanded suffering and sacrifice from a conquered enemy.

'They look fine.'

The gruff voice of Decabalus caused her to turn in her saddle; she smiled at him, pleased that he was pleased. 'Aye, lord, they do. Only for you would they train in this way.'

He chuckled at that. 'I think that your constant haranguing and reminders of Rome's military prowess cannot be overlooked, Sorina.'

The wind kicked up and Sorina brushed a greying strand of hair away from her mouth. 'The Romans are great warriors, my lord. No,' she corrected herself, 'they are great *soldiers* as you know.'

Decabalus grunted. 'The world is changing. The old ways, the ways of honour, would not defeat the Romans. We had to change *our* ways − even if it goes against the grain. Drilling, marching, training . . .' he shook his head. 'I can scarcely believe that we are doing these things. Yet, off the back of it, we are making a *civilisation* of our own. Armies . . . mercenaries . . . it all costs money these days and cities are places to make it.'

She eyed him as he spoke. He was every inch the Dacian warlord, tall, bearded and scarred, experienced in battle. His armour was not ostentatious but it was decorated with the scalps and finger-bones of some of those he had killed. 'Whatever it takes to beat Rome, my lord,' she said. 'They cannot be bargained with or appeased: they are insatiable in their desire to rule and conquer. They must be stopped or the whole world will fall under their sway. Our victory at Tapae was only the beginning, though. They will return.'

'I know. They are making their plans as we speak.'

Sorina's eyebrows shot up in surprise. 'You have news?'

'Let us talk in my tent. I will tell you all I know.' Without waiting for a response, he turned about, his mount's hooves flinging up clods of wet earth as she cantered away.

'Yes, my lord.' Sorina nudged her horse and followed him.

Decabalus's tent was huge and its opulence spoke of his great achievements. Above his throne were the five Eagles − the standards of the Roman legions they had destroyed utterly the previous year. No one had ever taken so much from them − and the victory had made Decabalus master of territory far beyond the borders of his own land.

Yet it was not to his throne he went. Shrugging out of his wet armour, which dropped to the floor with a thump, he sat on piled rugs and gestured for Sorina to sit at his side. She removed her cloak and joined him, proud of the honour he was affording her.

'Pour for us.' He gestured to a bottle and cups placed on a low table. 'As you have often said, Rome must launch what they will call a punitive expedition.' Sorina passed him his drink. 'But Rome has problems. In Germania, the tribes are pressuring their legions, in Judaea there is always unrest . . . all across their frontiers the legions are under pressure. They cannot – and will not – draw men from those troubled places to come here. To do so would give a sign of weakness to the conquered peoples and there would be uprisings the length and breadth of their empire.' He downed his drink and winced – *tzuica* was a drink for kings and it tasted of fire, and Decabalus had once presented Sorina with a gift of it. 'No – they must recruit from within and send more men against us. These will not be of the quality that we faced before – but they will still be a *Roman* army.'

Sorina tipped back her cup to cover her surprise. 'You *fear* them?' she asked as she poured another measure for them both.

Decabalus chuckled. 'Only a fool would not. As you said in our council after Tapae – the Romans did not conquer the world by luck alone. We cannot afford to be complacent.' He paused, regarding her from over the brim of his cup. 'I am depending on you, Sorina. You, of all the battle leaders, have a respect for the legions that the others lack.'

Sorina nodded: Decabalus had the rights of it. 'The other chiefs are saying the right things, my lord, but Tapae has changed everything. There is a strong belief in our invincibility now.'

'Which must be fed,' he replied. 'But not overfed. Confidence, not arrogance, yes?'

'Yes. When do you think they will come?'

'Next year. They are not yet ready. That is the only reason they agreed a peace treaty after Tapae. They are paying huge amounts in gold and weapons to ensure that I keep the tribes in check. In return, I have promised them that now that my interests are secured we will go north in search of new lands. Hence our military build-up.'

Sorina shook her head. 'The Romans are not so foolish as to believe such a thing.'

'Of course not. But it is a diplomatic lie that saves face while both sides prepare for the next war. The Romans are buying time with their gold; we are using their gold against them. We have all the advantages – we must ensure these are fully exploited.'

Sorina considered that for a moment. 'Superior manpower . . . short lines of supply . . . the ground is ours and our warriors are confident. Rome will be drawing on the dregs of her army and, in all likelihood, will employ mercenaries to bolster her forces. Men who fight for pay will always lose against those who fight for a cause.'

'It is my hope that they *do* hire mercenaries; it will be easier to infiltrate their ranks. Romans make poor horsemen. Their cavalry is usually German or Gallic. And most Romans can't tell the difference between one "barbarian" and another.'

Sorina laughed at that. 'True, my lord. What will your strategy be?'

'I see no need to deviate from what worked before,' Decabalus replied. 'The situation has not changed – the Romans must bring *us* to battle. They must *punish* us. We'll lead them on another merry dance, stretch their supply lines to breaking point. Your task will be to shadow them from behind. Once the battle is joined, it will be as before. We will hit them from front and rear, envelop them and finish them off.'

'As simple as that?' Sorina raised her eyebrows.

'As simple as that,' he answered.

'You're confident that the Romans will just do as you hope? Last time, they turned on the population in an attempt to draw you out. We cannot allow that. If we mass our forces and hit them hard – we can overcome them by sheer weight of numbers. This would be a sounder strategy than what could become a drawn out conflict.' Sorina eyed him, aware that she had probably over stepped the boundary of rank that separated them but aware too that she must speak up. Caution was not the way to deal with Rome. They had professional soldiers, well used to endless marching with no glory at the end of it. It was their job and they would do it regardless of whether there was a battle in the offing or not. She said as much to Decabalus, but he dismissed this with a wave of his hand.

'As you keep reminding me and everyone else – the Romans can fight. History has proven that they – more often than not – overcome larger forces of lesser-trained troops in open battle. I am proud of our warriors, we have done well in mimicking the Roman ways, but I am not so foolish as to think we can match them, even if we did beat them once before. That was a surprise to them – they will have learned.'

'All the more reason not to repeat the same tactics,' Sorina put in.

'They need a quick victory,' he answered this at once. 'They *need* a battle – to humble us. We can draw them into a hostile environment, stretch their supply lines as I have said. They will turn to 'foraging' – exploiting the locals, which will make them hate Rome even more. *They* will do the work for the main army, attacking those lines. Taking back what was taken from them. This will weaken the Romans. And when they are sufficiently softened-up, I will strike. And you, my battle-maiden, will close the jaws of the wolf.'

Sorina was not convinced, but she could tell there would be no point in forcing the issue: his mind was made up. 'As you say, Decabalus, so it shall be.'

He snorted. 'You are a poor liar, Sorina. You disagree, but your alternative plays into Roman hands. But it is my wish that you remain my conscience.'

'Of course, my lord and I am honoured that you respect my judgement. But I see no reason to cause dissent in council. We must

48

be seen to be united. Conversations like this are best kept to the privacy of your tent.'

Decabalus did not reply for some time and when he spoke his voice was heavy with more than *tzuica*. 'There are other things best kept to the privacy of my tent, Sorina,' he said, placing a hand on her thigh.

She did not flinch at his touch but it was unwelcome and she met his eyes. 'I am to be your whore as well as your conscience?' she asked. It was disappointing: for all his achievements, Decabalus was still a man – a base creature lusting for what he knew he could not have.

'No,' his tone was serious. 'Not my whore. I would take you for a wife,' he added.

Sorina chuckled. Men would say anything before the act and deny it afterwards. 'You have wives,' she said. 'Younger and prettier than me. Wives that can bear you sons, which you know I am too long in the tooth for. Besides,' she removed his hand from her leg, 'you know that I am with Teuta.'

Decabalus looked at her for a while. She could see in his eyes desire, anger, hurt, petulance and then all of a sudden acceptance. 'By the gods,' he laughed suddenly. 'I would have you, Sorina, above all the others, yet you reject me.'

'That,' she rose to her feet, 'is why you wanted me, Decabalus. You must have known I would refuse you – but you still had to try. It is the nature of men,' she added.

Decabalus shrugged and poured himself another measure of *tzuica*. 'Of course,' he said. 'And so I would be less of a man if I did not.' He paused regarding her for a moment. 'You may go.'

Sorina almost laughed her disdain at the dismissal but checked herself before bowing her head and leaving the tent. She took a deep breath of cold Dacian air and wondered suddenly if she had made the right choice. Decabalus could have her removed as a war chief if he so chose. Now, so close to wreaking her full vengeance against the Romans that would be a bitter draught to have to swallow.

VII

87 A.D.
Rome

Valerian could hear raised voices from the atrium – those of his house slave and of Settus. They grew louder and there was a sudden shout of fear mingled with pain followed by a crash. The slave started screaming for help and Valerian sighed and, squinting at the sudden daylight, made his way from the room that had become his prison. He could not remember the last time he had left it. Since his return from Capua after Pyrrha's death, life had lost its meaning. All he desired was to be left alone and perhaps to drink enough to summon the courage to open a vein.

In the atrium, Settus had the slave on the floor and was kicking him, each kick punctuated by an obscenity. 'That's enough, Settus.' He heard his own voice, cracked, harsh and slurred from tiredness and wine.

Settus kicked the slave once again for good measure before turning his attention to Valerian and the shock in his face was evident. 'This cunt wasn't going to let me in. This is the third time I've come round here and been told that you're . . . what is it? *Otherwise engaged*. You look like shit,' he added.

The slave was cowering on the floor, eyes flicking to Settus in fear and to Valerian in desperation. 'Leave us,' Valerian commanded to which the man gratefully scrambled up and fled.

'Where have you been?' Settus wanted to know, walking past Valerian and into the house proper. 'Nobody's heard anything from you in days.'

Valerian followed him inside, the desire to expel him warring with the friendship they had forged. 'What do you want, Settus?' he asked.

'A fucking drink would be a good start.'

'You've just beaten up my slave.'

'And you've lost the use of your fucking legs, have you? Fuck's sake, I'll get it myself then. Cellar?'

Valerian did not answer and, with a shrug, Settus made off. Clearly, he was not going to take kindly to any request to leave. Valerian sat on a couch and put his head in his hands, massaging his temples. The last thing he wanted or needed was Settus and his lies about the amount of wine he had consumed and the number of whores who were so impressed with his prowess they had given him some sort of discount. He decided that if he just sat and ignored Settus when he came back, the former optio would get the message and leave.

Settus returned shortly, bearing cups and a *krater* of wine. He poured for them both, but as he approached Valerian, his nose wrinkled. 'You fucking stink,' he told him. 'When was the last time you had a bath? And why the beard? You fancy turning into a barbarian, is that it?'

'What do you want, Settus?'

'Can't I just come round to see an old friend?' Settus placed himself on the couch opposite. 'Chat about the good times and all that?'

'I'm not feeling well. Perhaps another time?'

'I don't think so. I've already told you, I've been round here three times and been turned away . . .'

'Because I instructed my slave that I was not to be disturbed.'

Settus looked mildly affronted for a moment. 'Yeah, but I'm your mate.'

'And my *mate* should realise when I'm not well and come back when I'm feeling better,' Valerian downed his cup, wincing at the taste. 'You didn't water this?'

'*I'm* not your fucking slave in case you hadn't noticed. Anyway – you're not sick, unless it's up here?' Settus tapped the side of his head. 'Fucking sitting in your house pining after that girl of yours. Look she was a nice bird, no doubt about it, but she's gone. I know it's shit – my wife died in Britannia, but there's fuck all we can do about it when it happens. We can't go with them.'

Like fresh pitch poured on burning embers, anger erupted within Valerian, and he lurched to his feet, spilling wine down his already filth begrimed tunic. 'Get out!' he shouted. 'Get out of my house, *now*!'

Settus remained unmoved. 'I don't think so.'

'Get out!'

'No.'

Valerian leapt at Settus, registering the surprised expression on his face as he slammed his fist into it. The couch up-ended and the two men crashed to the floor, snarling, kicking and punching. They rolled over, Valerian emerging on top as he rained blows down onto Settus in an animal fury. The former optio fought back and heaved Valerian from him sending him crashing into a bust of the goddess Minerva. It fell to the floor and shattered as the two men surged to their feet. Settus opened his mouth to speak, but Valerian gave him no chance and dived in, aiming to use his greater size and strength to overwhelm his opponent.

But this time, Settus was ready and as Valerian came in, the older man moved like a wrestler and used his momentum against him, executing a neat hip throw that sent him crashing onto the low table that sat between the couches. Fury still burning hot, Valerian scrambled from the wreckage of the table and charged in once again, only to be met with a sharp left jab, followed by a thunderous right cross that sent him down on one knee.

Settus kicked him in the chest and followed him to the ground, flipping him on to his front. He wrenched Valerian's arm up behind his back, locking it and effectively pinning him to the floor. The pain pierced Valerian's anger and it fled, to be replaced by shame.

'You fucking cunt!' Settus gasped. 'What do you think you're doing?'

Valerian did not answer, simply going limp and waiting for Settus to release him.

'I wasn't called the hardest man in the Second Augusta for no reason, you twat,' Settus noted and let him go. 'Nice punch though,' he added touching his bloody lip. 'You ready to talk now, or do you want me to carry on using you as a battering ram?'

Despite the melancholy that had been eating away at his soul since Pyrrha had been killed, Valerian managed a grin. 'Ready to talk, I think.'

'Wine's all over the floor, table's all smashed up – that's your fault. We should go out – let your slave clean up this mess. But you need a bath first – I'll even pay, how about that?'

'I don't know, Settus,' Valerian sat up. 'I don't want to go out . . . we'll be fine here.'

'Bollocks,' Settus rose to his feet and offered him a hand up. Clearly, as far as Settus was concerned, the decision was made.

A visit to the public baths was invigorating and, despite himself, Valerian was pleased to have the growth of beard scraped from his face. For his part, Settus always enjoyed the shocked looks his hideously tattooed body garnered in the pool. He called them souvenirs of his time in Britannia, but had once told Valerian in confidence he had got them to better blend in with the locals after marrying a Brigantian girl.

Settus's wife had taken ill and died, leaving Settus with his permanent and indelible reminders of her. And, Valerian assumed, because he had suffered loss, he had now appointed himself as advisor to his friend.

The truth of it was that Valerian had no wish to talk about his grief – after all, there was no point in it. What was done could not be undone and, despite his upbringing in the *equites* class with all its emphasis on Roman *virtus*, he could not help but feel an overwhelming sense of self-pity.

Settus took him to one of his favourite drinking houses where the booze was cheap and the food rancid – but everyone knew the former optio and there would be no trouble from the rough crowd that filled the place from noon till dawn. Valerian found them a booth whilst Settus got the wine. They both drank in silence for a while, Settus clearly trying to work out a strategy to begin his conversation. Evidently, said strategy involved a lot of inane chat, lubricated with a copious amount of wine.

'So,' Settus tipped down another cup. 'Now, I'll fill you in on what's been going on. That Jewish cunt you employed to sort out the finances from our fertilizer business . . . what's his name again . . .?'

'Ezra.'

'Yeah, Ezra. He reckons that things are going better than even he expected. It's funny ain't it? Years of being *in* the shit and now we're making a fortune selling shit. Anyway, leaving the Flavian has eaten into our profits a bit as now we have to bribe the slaves who'll dump it for *us* as opposed to chucking it in the Tiber. A good thing I'm taking care of business while you're sitting on your arse at home. I have to ask why.'

Valerian sighed. 'Look, Settus, I know you mean well,' he began, 'but this is my problem, all right. No offence, but I don't really want to hear that there's more fish in the sea and that we move on. I know that, but right now . . . I just don't want to hear it.'

Settus grunted. 'Well, as I said back at the house – she was a lovely girl, that Pyrrha. I liked her a lot and it was fucking shit what happened to her. But you're right. You do have to move on. And quickly.'

'I'll be all right.'

'You'll have to be,' Settus stated. 'Thing is, I've got a letter here from Sextus Julius Frontinus – he wants to see both of us. Something about "being of service to Rome."'

Valerian laughed harshly. 'Fuck Frontinus and his service to Rome. What has Rome ever done for me, eh Settus?' he drained his cup and refilled it. 'Sent me – well both of us – to Britannia and then after that, I get a tribunate in Dacia. And we all know how that went. You've no idea what they did to me,' he added, squeezing his eyes shut as the memories came flooding back of the night in the forest where they had humiliated him. Raped him. Stripped him of is *virtus* in the most base and effective manner.

'Steady,' Settus raised his palms. 'There's no need to be unpatriotic, no matter what happened.'

Valerian's smile was bitter. 'I'm not a soldier anymore. And neither are you, so you can fuck off with your notions of patriotism.'

'We're still *Romans*,' Settus had the aspect of a man who would not be moved. A part of Valerian held him in contempt for his simple view as Rome being the light of the world. The thought shamed him, but he could not push it away. 'And the Old Man has always done right by us,' Settus added, referring to Frontinus.

'Settus, you are being naïve. The only reason why Frontinus is suddenly extending the benevolent hand of friendship again is because he needs us to do something for him. Last time we were there, he wanted a full report on the battle at Tapae – he wasn't giving you booze and whores for no reason.'

'So . . . so what?' Settus looked confused. 'It's our duty to help him, all right. He's still a general.'

Valerian continued drinking. 'You see him then.'

'Letter says both of us.' Settus stuck out his chin.

'*Valerian says* fuck the letter.' Valerian was aware that keeping up with Settus was making him drunk – and fast. With the loosening of emotions that wine always brought, he was growing more bitter at the unfair lot that fate had dealt him. 'I don't give a shit,' he added.

'That ain't like you,' Settus said. 'You're Gaius Minervinus Valerian, for fuck's sake. *Equites*,' he raised his cup.

'I'm no longer *equites*, Settus. I used to think that regaining my former status would mean something. Now I realise that it wouldn't mean a damn thing,' he drank more wine. 'What's the point, eh?' He asked, glaring at the former optio. 'What's the fucking point? Every time I start to make some headway, it all goes wrong. Rome's taken everything from me. First in Dacia, then in Capua when Achillia killed Pyrrha. I have nothing. I *am* nothing.'

'Listen, mate. You can't carry on like this,' Settus tried what he must have thought was an encouraging smile. 'Maybe Frontinus wants to make clients of us, you ever think about that? We're doing well, I've got loads of contacts in the *subura* and you – well, you're like the acceptable face of our business. Speaking Greek to the upper classes and all that. We're a team, right? You know, just like in the old days, back in the army.'

'We're not in the fucking army anymore,' Valerian spat. 'I'm happy to sell up my side of the business if that's what you're after.' As soon as the words came out, Valerian felt contrite: Settus was not subtle enough to try and manoeuvre money out of him – his concern, however rough, was genuine. And he could tell that he had struck a low blow – reading the hurt in the older man's eyes. That Settus had not got up and given him a kicking for it spoke volumes. 'Look,' he said, his tone less harsh and, he noted, more slurred, 'I know you mean well – and I'm sorry for . . . well . . . you know what I mean.'

Settus grunted in acceptance. 'Yeah, yeah, all right. I think I've made a mistake, though.'

'What mistake?'

Settus jerked his chin in the direction of the entrance to the tavern. 'I invited Frontinus to join us here. I knew I'd get you out of the house but I didn't think I'd be able to get you to go to him.

I'm not as thick as you look,' he grinned. 'But I didn't count on you getting so pissed you can hardly talk.'

'Then I'll leave,' Valerian made to stand, but Settus's hand lashed out and grabbed his wrist as he placed his palms on the table to steady himself.

'Don't,' he said. 'Let's just hear him out – *I* might get something out of it, even if you're not up for it. Don't fuck things up for me as well. Please just hear him out.'

Valerian slumped back down in the booth. *Please* was not a word that Settus used often and the sound of it from his lips gave him pause. It was not fair of him to disavow Settus any chance of raising his position just because he himself felt so wretched.

'He's here anyway,' Settus raised his arm.

Valerian turned and saw the old general weaving his way through the crowd.

He was clad like a pauper, a hood pulled over his rough, green tunic. As he entered, Valerian saw him exchange a few words with a dangerous-looking giant of a man who was evidently his body-guard. Appearances aside, it was clear that the old man was taking no unnecessary risks in the *subura*.

'Sir,' Settus greeted him, and beckoned the serving girl to bring another cup. Valerian just nodded.

'I trust you are both well,' Frontinus began.

'We're fine,' Valerian said.

'As I can see, and I don't blame you for having good drink when the occasion arises. A celebration perhaps?'

Valerian snorted. 'Hardly.'

'Well, that is about to change then,' Frontinus nodded his thanks as the serving girl placed another cup on the table. 'I have news that concerns you both.' He paused, waiting for Valerian to ask what the news was, but Valerian was not going to give him the satisfaction. Frontinus had had a chance to help him in the past, yet he had not been there. And Settus was not going to ask in the presence of his betters. 'Are you not curious?' Frontinus asked.

'Not really,' Valerian responded and tipped back his cup and ignored the sharp pain in his shin as Settus kicked him under the table.

'I see.' Frontinus's face flushed with contained anger. 'I thought this was a bad idea from the start, Settus.' He turned to the younger man. 'I am still a general and – ' he lowered his voice, ' . . . and a fucking senator of Rome. Yet I come to this shithole – at your behest – bearing gifts, yet your friend here is too pissed to hear me out and accord me the proper respect . . .'

'My fault, sir,' Settus held up his hands. 'I thought a few cups would put him in a better frame of mind. He's had a hard time of late . . .'

'I can speak for myself, Settus!' Valerian interrupted. 'What do you want, Frontinus?'

'I don't want anything, boy. I came here to offer you something. But since you don't seem ready to listen . . . '

Valerian snorted. 'Alright. Indulge me.'

Frontinus took a hefty draught of wine, wincing at the taste. And, Valerian could tell that he was struggling to keep his temper. 'My people have told me about your run of bad luck, Valerian. It was a poor show that you were blamed for the Dacian disaster. You were only a tribune after all. But as it turns out, the losses the barbarians inflicted on us there were deemed too serious for the truth to come out. It's been covered up as best we can – and as such, your reputation has been – in some part – restored. By my efforts.'

'You have my thanks,' Valerian responded not sure himself if he was being disingenuous or not.

Frontinus harrumphed, clearly not sure either. 'In any event, the emperor has agreed that you are to be reinstated into the class of *equites* . . .'

'I don't have that kind of money,' Valerian interrupted. 'If *your people* have been keeping an eye on me, then you'll know that Settus and I are purveyors of high quality shit which make the gardens of

Rome bloom. A good living – but not enough to buy my way back in – even if I wanted to.'

'A good thing for you, then, that I have secured you an income from the emperor himself,' Frontinus sat back and let that sink in for a moment.

Despite his melancholy, Valerian was taken aback. The patronage of the emperor was no small thing; even Settus, who always tried to maintain an implacable air looked utterly stunned. 'Why?' Valerian asked. 'Why would you do this? Why would *he* do this? I am . . . nothing.'

'Nonsense,' Frontinus waved that away. 'Valerian, I know you have suffered loss. You were to be married – to the gladiatrix girl. Settus has told me that her death has cut you to the core. If love is ripped away, it leaves a man empty and cold inside: you think I'm too old to remember? I am not.'

'You have my thanks,' Valerian murmured. Perhaps he *had* been too quick to jump to conclusions.

'Think nothing of it,' Frontinus said. 'I have been remiss. We served together and you were a damn fine officer. I could – and should – have helped you before. But Rome is a demanding mistress. I serve her still. And so should you.'

'I could be of no further use to Rome.'

'I disagree. As does the emperor. Domitian now sees you as a man with unique experience, the only man of quality to survive the Battle of Tapae. A man with good cause to hate Dacia. A man whose hand would not be stayed by mercy. The emperor has decreed that a new war must be proscribed against these savages who have inflicted so cruel a wound upon Rome. Dacia must be punished – *summa exstinctio.*'

'*Summa exstinctio,*' Valerian repeated. Total war – the utter destruction of an enemy – women and children included, was an unprecedented order.

'Just so,' Frontinus said. 'They will pay in blood for what they have done to us. To you,' he added, his eyes telling Valerian that the old general had a fair idea of what treatment he had received at Dacian hands.

'And you wish me to serve as your tribune?'

'Gods no!' Frontinus exclaimed. 'That would be a waste of your experience. Your orders are to take command of a legion, my boy.'

Valerian was stunned. 'A legion,' he repeated, wondering if he was now so drunk that he was hearing things.

'Indeed,' Frontinus nodded. 'You will serve under Tettius Iulianus in the coming campaign – should you accept the emperor's generosity of course.' He left this hanging for a moment. It was obvious that an imperial command of this nature could not be refused – you did not spit on the emperor's hand when he extended it.

'Fuck me!' Settus put in, the matter already decided in his mind. 'We need more wine here. A lot more wine.'

Frontinus reached across the table and gripped Valerian's wrist. 'Your emperor offers you a chance for vengeance,' he whispered. 'Take it. Take it and punish the barbarians for what they did to you. And to Rome.'

'Revenge!' Settus raised his cup.

'Revenge.' Frontinus did the same.

Valerian hesitated. Could he wash away the pain he now felt with the blood of the Dacians? Perhaps, he thought, and perhaps not. But it couldn't make him feel any worse. 'Revenge,' he said and drunk deep of his wine.

A part of him hated himself for being so easily swayed. He knew that Frontinus was playing him like a lyre and he guessed that the Old Man knew that he knew it. But he was in an impossible situation – no man could refuse an Imperial edict and expect to survive. And, even if life had no meaning anymore, Valerian had no wish to end his existence under the torturers' knife or as food for the beasts of the arena. Better to die fighting and take as many Dacians as he could with him.

He became aware of a looming presence outside the booth: Frontinus's bodyguard had approached and leant in to whisper in the old man's ear.

On receiving the message, Frontinus broke into a broad grin. 'Well, gentlemen,' he said. 'I will leave you to your entertainment.'

'Good news, sir?' Settus enquired, evidently curious as to what the bodyguard had said.

'Yes, I think so,' Frontinus replied. 'It appears that Achillia has survived her bout with *Aesalon Nocturna* after all. She lives again – and I am pleased, I rather liked the girl.'

It was all that Valerian could do not to snort with derision. The fates were playing with him again. They give him a legion with one hand but insured that the woman who killed his love was delivered from death with the other. It was almost funny.

Settus jerked his chin at him, indicating that he should rise, and he did – albeit unsteadily.

'*Salute*,' Settus acknowledged Frontinus formally – as a soldier should.

Valerian did not hesitate – he had made his pact. '*Salute*,' he repeated.

Frontinus eyed him for a moment before nodding. 'I will be in touch,' he said before turning abruptly and taking his leave.

VIII

Lysandra was bored.

Bored of being cooped up in Rome's Temple of Minerva Medica, bored of being told she must rest and, most of all, bored with being told of how lucky she was to have survived the bout with *Aesalon Nocturna*. If anyone had been lucky, it was *Aesalon* herself – one fluke blow had settled the issue. Lysandra's own survival had nothing to do with luck: the goddess had intervened – not only because she had seen that the Roman woman's 'killing' blow had been a stroke of luck but also because she now had a new purpose for her. And Lysandra burned with the desire to find out what it was. She knew she had received visions while in the grip of the fever after her injury but she could only recall fragments, snatches of her childhood and past. But the goddess had spoken to her again, of that she was certain.

Her friends – Telemachus, Thebe, Titus and Kleandrias, along with the bodyguards Cappa and Murco, had been constant companions during her rehabilitation, but even their company was beginning to irritate her. Of course, they meant well but there was only so much they could talk about during their daily visits – and now these visits had turned into a general debate about what was best for her and where she should go next: Kleandrias was all for a visit to Sparta; Telemachus and Thebe urged that she should get back to the Deiopolis as soon as possible; Titus said that she should stay in Rome whilst he and others took care of work at the temple; the bodyguards – rightly – that she should do as she wished.

She knew that Telemachus was correct as always. The Athenian priest had a way of seeing to the heart of the matter and truth of it was, she had forged the Deiopolis in the fire of her will. The women there needed her, and the crushing loss of Varia proved that should her attention wane, disaster awaited. But Titus was also correct: there was something that she needed to attend to in Rome first.

'You have made the right choice,' Telemachus agreed when she told them as they gathered around her bed. He glanced at the others with an I-told-you-so look on his face, which was a typical Athenian trait.

'Yes,' she said. 'But the healers will not let me. I fear that these

Romans have no concept of the Spartan constitution – we heal faster than lesser peoples. I am ready to leave this place now.'

'It is not their fault,' Kleandrias put in. 'They are only treating you as they would anyone else . . .'

'I am *not* anyone else,' Lysandra shouted, frustration at being cooped up bubbling to the surface. 'I am Lysandra of *Sparta*!' She was about to say more, but the effort of shouting pulled on her wound and, to her shame, she winced. 'But my own wishes aside . . .' She calmed herself with effort. 'You are my friends, not my nursemaids. As you say, the Deiopolis needs attention. Titus . . .' she addressed her old trainer. 'You, Thebe and Telemachus must return to attend to matters whilst I am away.'

'I'm sure all is well there,' Thebe assured her.

'I would feel better if you did, however.'

Thebe opened her mouth to protest, but Telemachus cut her off. 'If you insist,' he said.

'I do insist,' Lysandra replied. 'My friends, I love you all dearly and I am grateful to you for watching over me. But, as I have said – I am nearly whole again.'

'I don't know, Lysandra,' Thebe began. 'We should stay – or at least I should.'

Thebe was a caregiver, steadfast and loyal, and an example for the women of the Deiopolis to look up to – she needed to be back there. 'Cappa and Murco will be close by,' Lysandra assured her. 'They will continue to see that I am well cared for. Is that not so?'

'Aye, lady,' Cappa affirmed. 'We'll let nothing happen to you.'

'Nor I,' Kleandrias rumbled.

Lysandra smiled at her countryman. Of course, Kleandrias felt accountable for her so-called defeat as he had largely been responsible for training her. That was probably a correct assumption, but it would be churlish of her to point this out – so if the man wished to stay to assuage his guilt then she should allow it. Besides which, she enjoyed his company and it was clear to her that he adored her and she was big enough to admit to herself that she rather enjoyed the attention. When they had first met, she had been in awe of him – now the situation was reversed.

'Very well, then,' Telemachus nodded. 'Lysandra – Athene, as always, walks by your side. We shall make ready to return – dare I say – home.'

'You have given up on your Athenian roots, Telemachus?' Lysandra arched an eyebrow.

'I've lived longer in Asia Minor than I've spent in Athens,' he scratched his beard ruefully. 'I think that it is my home, now, yes. But there is a part of me that wants to see the city of my birth once more.'

'I will always be Spartan, no matter where I live,' Kleandrias put in.

'Naturally,' Telemachus responded smoothly.

Thebe looked to be on the verge of tears. 'You will do as the healers say, Lysandra?' she asked. 'You two won't let her leave here till they say she is fit,' she turned to Cappa and Murco.

'We promise,' Murco's response was as bland as the man himself.

Thebe did not look convinced but sighed. 'Just make sure,' she said. She moved to the bed and embraced Lysandra, kissing her on both cheeks. 'Be well, sister,' she said and pulled her as close as she could without hurting her. One by one, her friends said their good-byes and departed, and as soon as the sound of their footsteps had passed from earshot, Lysandra turned to Cappa. 'Pass me the stylus and wax pad, please.'

'I thought you were in a bit of a hurry to get rid of your mates,' he grinned. 'What have you got in mind?'

Lysandra grinned back. 'Rematch,' she said, her heart beating fast with the anticipation of it.

'A *woman*?' Tettius Iulianus was aghast. 'No, Frontinus – that is at best madness and at worse an affront to the gods. I will not have it.'

Frontinus had expected this reaction and was prepared for it. The two men were reclining in his *triclinium*, well fed and watered as they discussed the forthcoming Dacian campaign. 'She is no ordinary woman,' he replied.

'She's still a woman – a Greek and a *gladiatrix*,' disgust was evident in his dark eyes. 'Rome will not associate herself with such an abomination. *I* will not associate myself with it. There are plenty of mercenary commanders out there, men still loyal to the empire – and their own purses. We will use them.'

'I think you're rather missing the point,' Frontinus responded. 'Decabalus has spies everywhere – as do we. He *knows* we are planning a punitive expedition as we know he is well prepared for it. When he hears that Valerian has been given command of a legion, he will believe that we are desperate for quality leadership – the boy's shame is well known, so why would he be chosen for a command?'

'I wonder that myself.' Iulianus was sour. 'I have better men for the job.'

'No, you do not. Despite what he's been through, I know that the boy has the gift of command. I served with him in Britannia and Cambria.'

'Cambria.' Iulianus shook his head. 'A gods-forsaken shithole if ever there was one.'

'True,' Frontinus said. 'Nevertheless, the decision has been made – by the emperor,' he added – a little needlessly, but if Iulianus was going to be obstructive then he ought to be reminded that Frontinus had Domitan's ear. 'It makes sense. All Valerian has to do is give you time to complete your work. You will not fail. But . . .' he paused, choosing his words, 'war is a dangerous business my friend. If things go awry then all the blame can be laid at his feet. Of course, we don't anticipate things going badly. And, naturally, in victory, you will take all the plaudits and he will remain anonymous. History will remember Tettius Iulianus – Gaius Minervinus

Valerian will not even be a footnote – unless he fails, in which case he will become the Varus of the modern era.'

Iulianus grunted, mollified by the flattery but obviously remained unconvinced. However, Domitian had agreed with Frontinus – so he had to accept it. 'And how does this fit in with your insane scheme for the gladiatrix?'

'Ah,' Frontinus motioned for a slave to pour more wine for them. 'I spent time in Asia Minor as you know. To the Greeks there, she is a heroine of almost divine status. She is the *Gladiatrix Prima* still – they worship her. You know of young Trajanus?'

'A man to watch, I'm told.'

'He had a frieze of her commissioned for her battle with the former champion.'

'But your gladiatrix is not *Gladiatrix Prima* in Rome. She was defeated. By a Roman, I might add. I imagine your purse is still stinging from your ill-placed faith in her.'

'Indeed,' Frontinus felt a glow of inner satisfaction as Iulianus began to walk into his trap. 'She should have died – but she did not. Did you know that, before she became a gladiatrix, she was a Priestess of Athene? It could be said, her goddess has spared her for another purpose.'

'Nonsense. She was spared by good Roman surgery and medicines.'

'As any educated man knows. But the vast majority of mercenary soldiers are not educated. We can use this to our advantage. It is my intention to spread the word of the "divine intervention" among the Greeks in my former province of Asia Minor and indeed on the Greek mainland. I will then dispatch Lysandra – Achillia as you know her – to recruit mercenaries from the Greek peninsula and bring them to Dacia. All this will be conducted away from the prying eyes of Decabalus. In this manner, we reinforce Valerian's legion with another, cover your actions against the Dacians and give any relief or flanking force a nasty shock. They will think they are facing a rearguard, after all – they will learn a costly lesson.' He leaned forward on his couch. 'Iulianus, I know this woman. She is extraordinary. Her training in her Spartan temple coupled with her unique celebrity makes her an ideal choice. Nobody will suspect her – and through her we will ensure your victory in Dacia.'

'I don't need a woman to cover my back,' Iulianus snapped.

'She won't be – as far as everyone is concerned, that task falls to Valerian. Lysandra will be . . . edited out of dispatches, so to speak. Unless everything goes wrong, in which case her involvement will be blamed on Valerian. That way, even if you lose . . . you don't lose at all.'

'We cannot afford to lose,' Iulianus sat back, deep in thought. 'We have to win. Rome cannot suffer another defeat in Dacia. It would portend the end of the empire.'

'Which is precisely why we should seize every advantage we can,' Frontinus concluded like a lawyer. 'Iulianus, I know it is distasteful. But nobody will expect it. And there is something else. Valerian reported that the men hesitated to kill the Dacian warrior women – it is a perverse and un-natural thing to send a woman into battle, but the barbarians have no such compunctions. Lysandra has women of her own that can combat this . . . fear. She owns a school of trained killers: years ago, she led them in a mock battle for the emperor. I might add she handled them well.'

'A *mock* battle,' Iulianus shook his head. 'Marvellous.' He sighed. 'I suppose you've already got Domitian's approval for this?'

'The emperor is a great admirer of Lysandra.' Frontinus smiled.

'All this assumes that this woman of yours will do what you ask. She may refuse.'

Frontinus chuckled. 'I think I can persuade her. In fact I know that I can.'

'How can you know?'

'Because,' Frontinus replied, 'it will flatter her ego. Which is, I might add, prodigious.'

67

'This is madness.' Iulianus's hawk-like face crumpled in defeat. 'I won't be associated with it.'

'You won't be,' Frontinus assured him. 'Unless you lose. So it's best for all of us that you do your job and allow me to do mine. Do we understand each other?'

'Yes, I think that we do,' Iulianus got to his feet. 'I will take my leave of you, Frontinus. I have a war to prepare for.' He stalked out, fury hanging about him like a mourning pall.

There had been plaudits, of course. Many and varied, humble and extravagant; these coupled with the boons from an elated Domitian had almost doubled her already vast fortune.

But now, weeks after her victory over the Spartan, Aemilia Illeana found that all the wealth in the world was no substitute for the thrill of facing down an opponent in the arena. She had indulged herself in any and all number of diversions, but after the sexual thrills had passed and the hangovers from too much wine had faded, she found that she was left with nothing.

Well, not quite nothing, she amended. She was still the most beautiful woman in the empire – despite the scars that had been delivered by the impossibly tough Spartan. Illeana picked up a hand-mirror and looked at the one down her cheek – it had not been a deep cut and, now that the swelling had gone, managed in some strange way to almost enhance her looks, drawing attention to her cheekbones and her otherwise flawless skin. But if the cut to her face had not been deep, the one to her shoulder had; it pained her still, having cut deep into the muscle. She knew in her heart that though she would return to fitness in time, she would not be able to rely on it in the arena. Other fighters might bear to fight at a level less than perfection, but not *Aesalon Nocturna*. She had to be at her peak – all the time. She knew that, even with a suspect shoulder, she would still be a dangerous opponent. Perhaps *the* most dangerous. But she could no longer be sure.

Illeana rose from her empty bed and walked to her balcony, wondering what to do for the day. As always, the first thing that occurred was to begin training again: even if the life of a fighter was denied her, there was no reason that she should not keep her skills honed. But as she raised her arm to the ceiling to test her wound, it ached and she knew that today was not the day. She could run and do light callisthenics to keep in trim – but anything else would just damage her shoulder further. It was frustrating in the extreme.

She recalled the conversation she had had with Pyrrha before she had been killed and she had told the youngster the truth. It was the sheer *thrill* of combat that attracted her to the arena. There was nothing like the high it gave her, not drink, not drugs, not sex. And it was ultimately depressing that it was lost to her forever.

Illeana called her slaves to her and demanded that they prepare her bath. Perhaps she would visit the *Ludus Magnus* – if only to watch the fighters at their work. She needed to feel some sort of connection with the place again – perhaps as a trainer. She had, after all, trained Pyrrha. That the girl had been killed was not her fault. No one on earth could have defeated Achillia – no one except her, of course.

Illeana had heard that, in defiance of the gods themselves, Achillia still lived. It was incredible to her that the Spartan survived; she knew she had struck a killing blow, seen her fall all but dead to the sands. Yet, somehow, she had clung to life. Illeana found her lips twisting in a half-smile: despite her arrogance and overweening piety, the Spartan was a woman to be admired. Almost her equal in many ways. She herself was not so conceited as to think that, on another day in another battle, she would have been guaranteed a victory. It had been a close fight; the closest she had ever fought. It could easily have been the Spartan who struck the decisive blow.

But she had not, and *Aesalon Nocturna* emerged as *victrix*. Again.

The thought lifted her mood as she slipped into the warm, petal-strewn waters of her bath. Perhaps becoming a trainer was the way to go: it would not replace the ultimate thrill of *knowing* that each moment in the arena could be your last, but she recalled the peaks and troughs of emotion she had felt when she watched Pyrrha fight and die. Different of course, not as intense as personal combat, but perhaps in time it would satisfy her.

'*Domina*?' the unobtrusive voice of her body slave, the ancient and wiry Naso interrupted her reverie.

'What is it,' she asked.

'There is a message here for you. From one Lysandra of Sparta.'

'*Lysandra*?' Illeana sat up in the water. 'Well?' she snapped, 'read it!'

Naso cleared his throat with air of a man who was going to deliver an unpopular message to the *plebs*. 'To Aemilia Illeana From Lysandra of Sparta, Hail,' he began. '*I trust that the grievous wounds I inflicted upon you are healing well and you will soon be able to fight again. The victory had the touch of Fortuna as I think we both know and I am sure that your Roman public, accustomed to gladiatorial displays, know this as well. I shall, therefore, offer you a chance to redeem your honour and permit you to fight me again. If you have the courage. I expect your response forthwith.*'

Illeana was stunned for a moment. All fighters had to have confidence, but this bordered on the delusional. *She* had won the fight, not Achillia – *Lysandra*, she corrected herself. Yet this challenge read as though the opposite were true. It was ludicrous and Illeana found herself chuckling at the audacity of the woman.

She glanced down at the scar on her shoulder. It was a livid reminder of their fight. Illeana knew that if she had not managed an instinctive lunge at Lysandra – more by luck than judgement – this blow would have seen her defeated. She closed her eyes, thrilling at the fear in her belly. She was afraid of Lysandra – to come so close to defeat yet still have achieved victory had taken almost everything she had to give – an experience she had neither need nor desire to repeat. She had won; Lysandra had lost – and Illeana had nothing to gain or prove by fighting her again. Only a fool tempted the fates.

'Do you have a response, *Domina*?' Naso, ever the professional, queried.

'Yes,' Illeana thought for a moment. 'Yes, I do. Tell her that I have retired from the games as *Gladiatrix Prima* and *Victrix*.' She paused thinking for a moment. Lysandra was an intriguing woman – there was a part of Illeana that wanted – needed, in fact, to get to know her better. No one had ever pushed her so close, no one had ever dragged the reserves from her that the Spartan had – and no one had ever made her afraid. 'Naso. Add that it would be my pleasure and honour to meet Lysandra of Sparta. My respect for her prowess is considerable and I would like to raise a cup to her bravery – we are both champions and there should not be enmity between us.'

They were, she realised, similar creatures. As she was already feeling the abyss of emptiness left by her retirement, so must Lysandra. The challenge was most likely bluster, but in it Illeana wondered if perhaps she had found a kindred spirit.

Moesia

Valerian tried very hard not to grin at Settus stalking up and down the ranks of recruits like a lion choosing which prisoner he would devour in the arena. His first act as legate of the IV Flavia Felix legion had been to order Settus's instatement as centurion. For Valerian, it was the least he could do – Settus had been a friend to him when he was down; and, if he was honest with himself, the legion would need men like Settus to mould the recruits into soldiers.

Recruits was almost too fine a word; as the newest centurion, he had to give Settus the lowest ranking century – the Tenth of the Tenth cohort. But for Settus he knew it was the fulfilment of a dream; and, if he knew Settus, the beginning of a nightmare for the unfortunates who had been assigned to his century.

Valerian glanced up at the iron-grey sky. It always rained in the east, he thought to himself: just like Dacia. The legion had marched from Italia to Moesia to train in earnest and, as any veteran of the last campaign knew, the weather could get on top of you. As he thought it, a light drizzle began which would have been an omen anywhere else in the world.

He nudged his horse forward as Settus and his optio finally had the men arrayed to his satisfaction. 'These are your recruits, Centurion Settus?' he said, his voice carrying to the rear ranks.

'I'm afraid so, legate,' Settus said with a sigh and a slight shake of his head. Both of them had heard the 'welcome speech' enough times and knew exactly what to say in front of new men. Such was the army, Valerian thought: it never really changed. He regarded the men and could not keep the disappointment from his eyes. Ex-slaves, old men and boys had been pulled in to bolster the numbers and Valerian knew well that the Commander in Chief, Tettius Iulianus, was none too pleased to have him on his staff. As such, the Felix Legion received the worst of the worst. 'They don't look as though they'll be any good to Rome, centurion.'

'That's very true, sir, very true. Not at the moment. But I'll knock 'em into shape. Or Optio Slanius here will make sure they'll die trying to get there.' Settus's optio flexed his shoulders on cue. He was huge and had the aspect of a boxer – flat-nosed, chip-toothed and scarred. The grin he gave Valerian was evil and he looked again at the recruits, now feeling some pity for them.

'Carry on!' Valerian nodded and retreated, deciding to watch for a few moments before returning to his command tent.

'I am Sallustius Secundus Settus,' Settus began to pace again. 'Or, to you useless fucks, Centurion Settus or *sir*. Forget what your old man might have told you about "real soldiers" and "doing all the work": I'm a fucking officer and you will address me as such. Forget that and . . .' He raised his vine staff. 'I will ram this so far up your arse you will be able to pick your teeth with it.'

Someone in the middle ranks sniggered at that and Settus drew to halt and smiled. But there was no warmth in it. 'Yes, I know. I'm a funny man. I crack myself up. Like now, for instance. The comedian there has just earned you lot extra fatigues. If you don't know what fatigues are yet, come the end of the day – you will. And I'll still be laughing. Something tells me you won't. Now,' he began to pace again, 'it's obvious to me that you are all less than the shit on my boots. But I will make soldiers of you or you will die in the attempt. Work hard, do as you're told, perform well and you will find me benevolent, kindly and like a second father to you. Fail me and you will curse the day your whore mother spat you out of her poxy cunt. Any questions?'

He halted and glared at everyone and no one in particular. Every man in the century had the good sense to keep their eyes front and their mouths shut. Settus picked on a tall, rangy old-timer who was front and centre. 'You!' he screamed into the man's face. 'What's your fucking name?'

'Caballo, sir!'

'Caballo? Are you taking the piss?'

'No, Centurion Settus!'

'I like you, Caballo,' Settus leered. 'Ex-slave are you? Or have you seen time in the legions before? Come back for one last crack at the big payday?'

'Ex-Slave, sir. Manumitted because I'm here to fight the barbarians, sir.'

'So, slave,' Settus got in close, invading the taller man's personal space. 'Any questions?'

'Not at the moment, sir.'

'Well, well. That's good, Caballo, very good.' Settus resumed pacing. 'You lot should learn from this man. He may have been a slave but he seems to have some sense. "Not at the moment" he said. And he's right. Asking a question is not a bad thing. Asking it twice *is*. Don't make me waste my autumnal years telling you the same thing over and over again.

'Now,' Settus moved on, 'whatever Caballo was before, he is now a recruit in my century. That goes for the rest of you. You are all equally worthless in my eyes and here's your first lesson for free. You will work as a team: the only worth you have in this life from this moment forward is the worth you prove to me and my commanders. But mostly to me. What happened in the past is in the past – and there it will stay. In other words, any ganging up on someone because he was a slave or a prisoner or anything else, you will answer for it. My century; my rules. Am I clear?'

Settus got a mixture of 'yes sir' and 'yes Centurion Settus' but he seemed satisfied.

'Let's begin shall we? Turn to your left. The other left!' he screamed as someone – inevitably got it wrong and was duly pounded on the back by the eager Optio Slanius's vine staff. 'Right foot first . . . and right . . . left . . . right . . .'

Valerian had seen enough. He dismounted and hailed an idle legionary to take his horse to the paddock as he wandered through the vast camp back to the *praetorium* – his command tent situated at the very heart of the legion and surrounded by its guardsmen and standards. The men on duty saluted him as he approached but Valerian could read the disdain in their eyes. No one respected him and he knew it: his inexperience of field rank was a heavy enough cross to bear for the few veterans in the legion but – worse – he was unlucky. The irony of being given command of the Felix – 'the fortunate' legion – was not lost on him, nor, he suspected on anyone else. Word had got around that their new commander was the highest ranker to survive Tapae: to have such a man leading them on a return to the site of his former defeat was a bad omen.

Valerian entered the command tent and threw his wet cloak onto a couch. He should, he thought, be a man revitalised. Frontinus had been true to his word and had delivered everything he had promised – the patronage of the emperor, the command itself, exoneration and a chance for revenge on the Dacians. But the drunken feeling of resolve that had filled him in Rome had long since fled, and now Valerian could barely shake the feeling that he was being set up to fail even though there was no good reason for the suspicion.

He sat at his desk, trying to push the depressing thoughts away, but the truth of it was that being so near to Tapae had brought close the horror he had experienced at barbarian hands. His sleep was restless, the nightmares had returned and with them the fear – and he put his rising paranoia down to this. But paranoia aside, nobody in the legion had faced the Dacian hordes before – nobody except him. And with the men he had at his disposal, Valerian doubted if they would make much of an impression. But it was his task to ready them – to prepare them. And if he could, perhaps his family name would be saved from the ignominy he had brought upon it. Perhaps *virtus* could be his again.

Valerian turned his attention to the endless pile of paperwork that he had to attend to. Bureaucracy was the key to the success of Rome's legions as surely as the tip of the *gladius* and the shield wall. Checks and balances, supplies and requisitions, sick and active duty lists, all had their part to play in the smooth running of the machine. Valerian could have turned much of this over to his subordinates but he felt that the responsibility should be his and his alone. If the

Felix succeeded in the task set for her then all would know that it was the hand of Gaius Minervinus Valerian that had guided her. And if she failed . . . he smiled grimly as the thought occurred to him. If she failed, it really would not matter to him as he would be dead. He had made his peace and would never allow himself to fall into Dacian hands again.

Valerian worked for some hours, agonising especially on the punishment details. There was a part of him that wanted to be Crassus-like in his judgements but another that wanted – maybe needed – his men to like and respect him. But in his heart he knew that respect could only be won on the battlefield, so Valerian was happy to go along with the penalties noted by the duty officers: they knew best after all.

It was, Valerian realised, as he signed a flogging order, time for the daily meeting with the centurions and tribunes that made up his staff. He set his paperwork aside and composed himself, calling out to have scribes sent to him at once. Everything said had to be recorded and analysed later – he could not afford to miss anything vital, but the sad fact of the matter was that the daily reports all tended to be the same.

Slaves filed into the tent bearing the benches that would seat the staff, followed closely by disgruntled looking scribes – Greeks mostly, and Greeks were only suited to soft climes and softer lifestyles. Here, at the cold, damp edge of the world, they were out of sorts. Soon after, the officers entered, filling the *praetorium* with the harsh gutturals that all centurions had to master as part of their job.

'Gentlemen,' Valerian raised his voice in greeting and was pleased as the conversation died down at once. They might not respect his person, but at least his rank still carried some weight. 'I will hear your reports by century,' he turned his gaze to the grizzled form of Mucius; grey haired, grey eyed and almost pale grey in colour, Mucius looked as though he had been cast from sword iron. As *Primus Pilus* – the first spear – Mucius commanded the legion's elite first cohort when in battle. When not in action, the First of the First – the leading century was his dominion.

'Sir,' he got to his feet and snapped a salute. 'I have seven men down with minor ailments,' he said, his gravelled voice filling the tent, 'caused by this fucking climate, but nothing that will keep them out of the next war I'll hazard.' The men in the room chuckled. Everything about Mucius screamed *military*, making Valerian feel inadequate and grateful in equal measure. Like Settus and the rest, the man was a born soldier. 'Training is progressing well,' Mucius continued, 'but that is to be expected – we don't have conscripts, slaves, freedmen and associated scum in the First.'

His glare and tone bordered on insubordination, challenging Valerian, testing him. He swallowed, trying to think of some suitable put down but nothing came to mind and Mucius's flicked to one of his fellow officers, his face fixed in an I-told-you-so expression. Valerian rose to his feet. 'Conscripts, slaves, freedmen and associated scum,' he repeated. 'You forgot old men and boys, *Primus*,' he addressed Mucius by the soldiers colloquial for his rank. 'Yet, these conscripts, slaves, freedmen, associated scum, old men and boys make up the greater part of this legion. They, like us, are committed to win or die in the defence of Rome . . . or am I to take it that your view differs from that of our Lord and God, the Emperor Domitian? After all, it was his genius that allowed the replenishment of this great legion from this . . . associated scum. Perhaps . . .' He swallowed. 'Perhaps you think that you know better than he? After all, you're a man of your experience, all scars and medals and proven valour? Or am I mistaken? Perhaps you criticise the quality of your brother soldiers out of too much love for your own men. This I can understand, but it is bad form for a senior officer to cast aspersions on the troops of his peers. Do it again and I will break you, Mucius.'

'Break me?' Mucius had been turning more and more purple

with each syllable of Valerian's public dressing down. 'Break *me*? The legion wouldn't stand for it.'

'They'll stand for it because they're Roman soldiers, you arrogant bastard. They obey orders – *my* orders. Let me be clear . . .' Valerian raked his gaze over the assembled men. 'I know that my appointment here is not a popular one. And you need to know that I don't care what you think. Not one of you has faced the Dacians – I have . . .'

'Yes,' Mucius interrupted. 'And you lost.'

Valerian opened his mouth to speak – but Settus had shot to his feet.

'The legate was serving as a tribune not as commander, you arsehole!' Settus glared at Mucius – who glowered back. 'You don't fucking scare me,' Settus informed him, 'so stop giving me the eye like I'm one of your bum-boys in the First. Your lot are all soft bodied and gaping arsed – '

'One more word and I'll kill you, Settus!' Mucius's hand strayed to his sword.

'Keep dreaming, shitcunt.'

'ENOUGH!' Valerian was a little surprised at the power in his voice: anger had got the better of him and it had worked. 'The pair of you will sit down, *now*, or I swear by Minerva I'll have you both crucified!' The two men hesitated, their blood up, but Settus gave way first and sat. Thinking he had achieved his moral victory, Mucius finally lowered himself to the bench. Valerian composed himself. 'As I was saying . . . none of you have faced the Dacians. And the *Primus* is right: we were hammered by them. We cannot afford to let that happen again. The responsibility . . . the fate of the empire rests with all of us. So get over yourselves and think of Rome . . . your woman . . . your kids or your dear old mother – I don't care what. But for the sake of the gods, we need unity, not a pissing contest. Clear?'

There was a moment's hesitation before the centurions responded as one. Valerian shook his head and puffed out cheeks before turning to the scribes. 'Is shitcunt one word or two?' he asked, and, to his relief, most of the men laughed – more from the release than the quality of the joke he reckoned. 'I think we can scrub the last few bits from the record. Now,' he turned back to the centurions. 'Where were we?'

Rome

The house was adequate, located in the heart of the Roman capitol – and it was priced accordingly. Still, despite the exorbitant rent she had agreed to, Lysandra was satisfied. If she was honest with herself, she would have paid double to be free of the Temple of Minerva Medicus. And, while she was being honest with herself, she was confident that the priestesses were glad to be free of her as well. Since news of her recovery had reached Rome's Hellene expatriates, they had flocked to the temple to catch a glimpse of her, hailing her as some sort of demigoddess.

Perhaps they were right. She had always walked close to Athene and had survived where no one else could or should have. Of course, she could not state this publically and had accepted the praise and goodwill with her customary humility knowing that, to these simple folk, a few words from her or a touch of the hand would mean a great deal.

But it was not only amongst the poor that her fame had spread. Rich Hellene merchants and equestrians also paid court to her, sending her gifts and endless correspondence. They loved her – one of her own had made good and shown the Romans that Hellenic valour was still strong.

Further proof of that was in the letter before her. It both angered and pleased her at the same time.

'*Aesalon Nocturna* refuses to fight,' Lysandra tossed the note on the huge pile of papyrus and wax tablets that littered her desk.

Ever near, Kleandrias grunted. 'What did you expect? Only a fool would face you twice, Lysandra.'

'You seem to be forgetting that she defeated me.' The words were poison on her tongue.

'She was lucky,' Cappa said. He and Murco were lounging on couches, playing dice half-heartedly.

'Yes,' Lysandra agreed. 'She was. And clearly she knows it to. I smell fear beneath her platitudes.'

'Platitudes?' Kleandrias raised his eyebrows and Lysandra gestured that he should read the missive.

'It reads like respect,' he said after a moment.

'She fears me.'

'Yes, of course.'

Lysandra could tell that he was soothing her and it irked her. However, she chose not to make an issue of it.

'But still,' he went on, 'there is nothing here that reads false. You are a champion and so is she – like Hector and Achilles,' he added with a smile. 'Both great warriors – Hector fell but that . . .' he trailed off as Lysandra glared at him. 'You are still a champion, Lysandra.'

Petulance was not an admirable trait and Lysandra tried to force her pique away. If *Aesalon* would not fight, there was one of two things she could do about it: accept it or try to shame the woman out of retirement. Sting her pride – anger her back into the arena. For a moment she imagined herself giving an oration to the Hellenes of Rome, calling the so-called *Gladiatrix Prima* a coward and urging them to march on the Flavian Amphitheatre demanding that a rematch be held.

She pushed the idea aside – it was beneath her to act in such a way.

Despite the fact that it was *Aesalon's* training that had led to Varia's death, she could not find hatred in her heart for the beautiful Roman. Varia had chosen her path – and her death was Lysandra's to bear – her punishment for sins committed.

The truth of it was that *Aesalon* had fought with honour and grace and, on the day, the better woman had won, as hard as that was to accept. *Aesalon* had been lucky – Lysandra knew that she was by far the better fighter than the Roman – and she guessed that *Aesalon* knew it too. The Roman version of Tyce – Fortuna – was capricious, even her own beloved Athene was sometimes at her whim. So it must have been on the sands that day.

She picked up another letter.

'What is that one?' Kleandrias queried.

'Another marriage proposal,' Lysandra tossed it to the ground. 'Have a slave take them to the scribes – I will draft a general response that can be copied.'

'Will you ever marry?'

Lysandra looked up at Kleandrias, grinning. 'Gods, no. I prefer women. Much less complicated than men, generally more intelligent and certainly less demanding.'

'I just thought that . . .' Kleandrias trailed off. 'You know . . . children and so on.'

'I hate children, Kleandrias. They are noisy, smelly, petulant and irritating. Much like men, in fact.'

Cappa and Murco chuckled, but it was evident that Kleandrias failed to see the funny side at all and looked rather hurt. She had probably offended his machismo.

'Let us say that when we are both old and grey I will marry you,' she offered an olive branch as she turned her attention back to the letters. 'We shall live out our dotage together, educating the younger generations on Spartan virtue.' She paused, an ornate scroll catching her eye. 'Interesting. Domitian's seal.'

'The emperor!' Cappa exclaimed. He and Murco sat up, their game forgotten. 'You have a letter from the emperor?'

'You seem surprised,' Lysandra was nonchalant. 'I have met him before.'

'So have we,' Murco commented. 'You know – me and Cappa were Praetorians. For his father.'

Lysandra ignored him. 'Ah. I am invited to a *symposium* at the palace. In honour of my battle with *Aesalon Nocturna*. It seems that we two are the toast of Rome at the moment.'

'Can we come?'

Lysandra glanced up at the two bodyguards, amused. 'It seems my children and men analogy carries some weight. I believe in Roman society it is unseemly for a woman to travel unescorted. You two are my bodyguards. It is your job to accompany me. And you, Kleandrias, if you wish it. I shall need someone with whom I can disdain Imperial high-living after all. These Romans are well known for their decadence.'

Appearances had to be maintained. Despite her hatred of makeup and hairdressing, Lysandra knew that she would have to adhere to protocol. It would be unseemly to arrive at the Imperial palace wearing a simple *chiton*. At least she had enough in the way of jewellery: gifts from her admirers had seen to that, though most of it was gold and Lysandra preferred silver. But that would send out the wrong message – according to the outrageously camp freedman she had hired to advise her on Roman high fashion.

Despite his irritating lisp and Rhodian accent, he seemed to know his work well, as he should given the huge amount of money his consultancy was costing her. In Rome, it seemed that everything was about turning a profit, but judging by the reactions of her bodyguards for the evening, it was money well spent.

He had dressed her in her customary red, an exquisitely cut *stola* that served to soften the hard, angular lines of her physique. The

Rhodian had wanted her to wear a long-sleeved garment but Lysandra had refused: her forearms were criss-crossed with scars, the marks of her trade and she wore them with pride. If the *symposium* was in honour of gladiatrices then to Lysandra's mind it would be absurd to pretend that they were anything other than what they were.

'You look like Athene herself,' Kleandrias breathed as she emerged from her room.

'Aye,' Cappa agreed. 'The goddess come to earth.'

He nudged Murco who added a self-conscious 'Very nice' which, from the taciturn Roman, was high praise indeed.

Outside, Lysandra could hear the raised voices – as though there was a crowd close to the house. Intrigued, she made her way to the balcony to see what the commotion was all about.

No sooner had she emerged she heard an excited shout of 'there she is!' Looking out into the street she saw a throng of people – old, young, rich and poor. On sight of her, they cheered and began to chant her name. Through the mob, a group of Praetorians were trying to forge a path, their bodies forming a cordon around a huge litter, borne by harassed looking slaves.

Lysandra raised her arm in acknowledgement to the crowd – clearly, some of Rome's Hellene population had come to send her off to the palace in style and the gesture touched.

'They love you,' Kleandrias noted as he came to stand next to her. 'It is strange, do you not think, that as a Spartan, it should be you that can unite the Hellene's in this way?'

'Not really. Five hundred years ago, our pre-eminence was etched into the *psyche* of the lesser peoples of Hellas. Even after Leuctra . . .' she trailed off, recalling her childhood in the temple and how the very mention of the word had earned her a beating. ' . . . And those dark times that followed, all men knew – and still do – that Sparta is the epitome of all virtue. In the modern arena, I bring those virtues into stark relief, Kleandrias. I am beautiful, I am honourable and I am deadly – all the things people expect a Spartan to be.'

'As is right and proper,' he agreed. They both watched for a few moments longer as the Praetorians pushed their way to her door. 'We should go.'

Lysandra raised her fist to the sky, which sent the crowd into a frenzy and the chanting of her name began anew. 'It is a good way to begin the evening,' she murmured as she followed Kleandrias.

The litter was large and spacious and the slaves were excellently trained: Lysandra's journey through the city was smooth, swift and altogether pleasurable. Whilst she appreciated the admiration of the mob, it was still pleasant to be closeted away from their unwashed attentions.

The journey through the Capitoline district was surprisingly fast; no one was going to argue with the pack of Praetorians that escorted her and it seemed to Lysandra that she had hardly had time to settle in the litter before it was placed gently on the ground and the door slid open by a grinning Cappa.

'It's been a few years,' he offered her a hand out.

It was all Lysandra could do not to gawp at the beauty and sheer scale of the *Domus Flavia* – Domitian's royal place. She recalled thinking that Sextus Julius Frontinus's governmental residence in Halicarnassus had been opulent, but compared to this place it was a pauper's hovel. In the Roman fashion, everything was on a huge scale – like the Flavian Amphitheatre. She recognised it not only as a work of art but also as a political statement. Everything had to be bigger and more grandiose than anywhere else in the empire. Huge statues adorned the avenue that led to the inner sanctum of the Flavians, fountains pumped clear water from the Tiber in intricate displays, each cunningly arrayed to catch the light of what seemed like thousands of torches. Marble – so much marble: it must have cost tens of millions of sesterces to construct this place.

'What do you think?' asked Murco as she looked around.

She recovered herself. 'It is overstated,' she sniffed.

The bodyguard chuckled as the Praetorians directed them to the palace proper. Lysandra kept her eyes front, refusing to be overawed by the opulence around her. That was the expected reaction and it had always been her way to defy expectation. And the truth of it was that, despite the scope and lavish expense, it was all a little crude and smelt of new money. Unlike the great – and superior – classical constructs of the Hellenes, which were in the main to honour the gods, this place was clearly a monument to the power of humankind and as a result was somewhat crass.

The Praetorians led them to a lush and beautifully decorated anteroom. 'You'll need to wait here,' the centurion in charge told her. 'Your men will come with us.'

Lysandra regarded him for a moment before responding. 'These men are my bodyguards,' she advised him. 'I should not be separated from them.'

He was an older man, perhaps in his fifties; despite his military demeanour, he had kind eyes and a friendly visage. 'This is the *Domus Flavia*, lady,' he said. 'The home of the Emperor of Rome: probably the safest place in the world. And, even if it wasn't – I've seen you fight. I'm confident that if any assassins are abroad you can handle them. Your men will be safe enough too – they will be treated as honoured guests. You have my word.'

'I am not sure,' Kleandrias drew himself to his full impressive height. 'I will stay with Lysandra.'

'Us too,' Cappa added with far less enthusiasm.

'My orders are to leave the lady here till she is summoned by a steward. 'Look,' he raised his hands placatingly, 'what they'll do – because this is what they always do – is announce her so she can make a big entrance. She can't do that with you three in tow. It's all part of the show, lads.'

'Sounds fair enough,' Cappa was obviously looking forward to the 'honoured guests' part of the evening.

'My duty is to be with Lysandra,' Kleandrias folded his arms, making her smile.

'I can see that Spartan virtue triumphs over Roman decadence yet again. Go, Kleandrias – keep Cappa and Murco safe and do not allow them to swim too deeply into their cups.'

'Orders are orders, Kleandrias,' Murco said, edging towards the door.

Kleandrias ignored him and gazed at Lysandra for a long moment, his eyes going soft as he did so. 'If that is your command,' he said at length.

'It is.' She sat on one of the couches, eyeing the low table that was full of sweet meats and wine.

'Well, that's that then,' Cappa said. 'Lead on, centurion.'

Lysandra felt like an indulgent mother as the men trooped out. She poured herself a cup of well-watered wine and glanced around the room, wondering when she would be called in. Despite herself, she was a little excited. Of course, she had met Domitian before, but to be invited to the palace was an honour indeed.

The door to the anteroom opened once again and Lysandra made to rise. But it was no steward who entered.

In the doorway stood the unmistakeable form of Illeana – the *Aesalon Nocturna*.

Lysandra remained composed, but her heart thumped hard in her chest. She saw the start in *Aesalon's* eyes as she entered: the *Gladiatrix Prima* had not been prepared for this meeting either. However, she too hid her feelings well, her full lips lifting in a smile as she entered. Lysandra was struck by her beauty – she was more than beautiful, she was magnificent. Her *stola* was as white as new snow, perfectly accentuating the dark auburn of her hair and piercing green of her eyes. Lysandra had once thought that Eirianwen was perfection, but looking at *Aesalon Nocturna* she knew otherwise.

'Achillia,' she greeted her as Lysandra rose. 'I am pleased to see you.' She paused as they kissed each other on each cheek. 'You have recovered well.'

Lysandra sought a barb in the remark but could see none, the Roman's comment appearing genuine. 'I heal quickly,' she replied as she returned to her couch. 'As do you – that blow would have finished anyone else.' She raised her cup in a toast – 'to your fortitude, *Aesalon Nocturna*.'

Aesalon sipped from her cup. 'Illeana, please . . . Lysandra? And yes – the blow would have finished anyone – it finished me, but I was lucky enough to have struck first. If I had missed . . .' she trailed off. 'But it is past.'

Lysandra regarded Illeana over the rim of her cup. 'But we will fight again.'

'I don't think so,' Illeana responded. 'There is no need – I have no desire to fight you again. Nor do I have to.'

Lysandra felt her face pinken with annoyance. 'You are afraid to face me again. You were lucky, by your own admission. I deserve a chance to set things right.'

Illeana laughed softly, the sound almost musical to Lysandra's ears: it was, she thought, difficult to remain hostile to someone who rivalled Helen of Sparta herself. 'Afraid? Yes, of course. Our fight was close – too close. We could have died – you *should* have died. Yet here you sit. If we fight again, I may kill you – or you may kill me. That is hardly a desirable outcome for either of us. You are a warrior, Lysandra and I have never met your like.' She gazed at her for a long time before continuing. 'And I know you think the same of me. We are sisters of a sort, don't you think?'

Lysandra considered that for a moment. There was no hatred between them, no real enmity, even over Varia's death. The truth of it was that the blame for that could not be laid at Illeana's feet: if she had not trained her, Varia would have found someone else to do the job. 'In a manner of speaking,' she said at length. 'But I would even the score with you, Illeana.'

'I have retired,' there was finality in her voice, despite the smile that came to her lips. 'Actually, *you* have retired me. My shoulder,' she touched it, 'will never be the same again. I would always be at less than my best. And that is something I cannot tolerate.'

Lysandra pressed her lips into a thin line, a mark of her irritation. Yet for all that, she understood Illeana's feelings on the matter. Knowledge of a debilitating injury would make her a lesser fighter. It was hardly her fault that she was not possessed of superior Spartan breeding and suffered from the weaker constitution that so plagued the lesser races of the world.

The door to the anteroom opened before Lysandra could respond and a steward entered. 'My goodness,' he said as he breezed in. 'I've seen you both in the arena, but I must say that seeing you both up close is indeed breathtaking.' He lowered his voice. 'A good thing the emperor's wife is not attending the celebration – I rather think you two would have upstaged her.'

'Clearly there is nothing wrong with your eyesight,' Lysandra said as she rose to her feet, realising she was a full head taller than him: there was a part of her that always enjoyed looking down on others.

'Quite so, quite so,' he agreed. 'Now, if Rome's own Venus and Minerva are ready, the emperor has summoned you both.'

'Athene,' Lysandra corrected as he led them out.

The steward took them down a beautifully decorated corridor at the end of which was a set of large double doors. The corridor itself was flanked by statuary; busts of great Romans from the distant and recent past. Lysandra felt the eyes of history on her and was, despite herself, impressed. Of course, it was the Roman way to err towards self-ostentation. Hellenes preferred to honour the gods as was right and proper.

'Here we are then,' the steward said as they reached the doors. 'I shall announce you. *Aesalon Nocturna*, you will make your way to the couch at the emperor's right hand, Achillia to his left.' Lysandra bristled at that – the position on the right was the position of honour, but there was nothing to be done about it. However fortunate Illeana had been, it was she who had emerged as *victrix*.

The steward opened the door and stepped in front of them both. 'Titus Flavius Domitianus, Lord and God, Emperor of Rome!' he began. Lysandra was stunned at the noise the little man was able to generate from his compact frame. 'I present to you the two finest gladiatrices in the empire, they who recently graced the sands of the Flavian Amphitheatre. I present first the worthy defeated, champion of Asia Minor, the Spartan Achillia!'

Lysandra squared her shoulders and breathed out sharply through her nose; she was, she realised, nervous. She stepped past the steward into the imperial *triclinium*. It was vast. Lysandra had seen lavish before, but this was beyond anything she had encountered. There must have been a hundred guests, reclining on couches or standing and mingling with others. Flute girls and lyre boys dressed in next to nothing played and danced amongst the revellers and the scent of incense hung heavy in the air. In the centre of the room, on a low plinth two wrestlers struggled with each other, watched half-heartedly by some aficionados of the sport.

As she entered, all eyes turned towards her and there was a round of polite applause, which she acknowledged with her customary dignity before making her way towards the emperor's dais. He had not changed much in the years since she had seen him, save for gaining a few extra pounds in weight. But he still had that brooding, handsome face and the piercing black eyes that she remembered so well. He smiled as she approached and bowed. 'Hail, Caesar,' she said.

Domitian gazed at her. 'Apparently, it is now the custom for my guests to prostrate themselves at my feet – that is what the liberal writers would have you believe anyway.'

Lysandra met his gaze. 'I do not believe everything I read, Caesar. Especially the words of liberals who I rather think would serve the empire better as food for the lions.'

Lysandra had managed to draw a chuckle from her host. 'Of course,' Domitian said. 'I imagine that liberals are not fashionable in Sparta – even today.'

'Though I have not been home for many years, I am sure that is the case,' she replied. 'Their pomposity disgusts me – whining about the strength of the very empire that affords them the luxury of their complaints.'

'Very perceptive,' he said, gesturing that she should sit at the couch on his left. 'You serve the empire, then, Lysandra of Sparta?'

'I serve the goddess Athene, Caesar. It would seem that her will and the empire's are in concert.'

Domitian was about to reply when the steward announced Illeana, his deep baritone seeming to fill the room. As the *Gladiatrix Prima* entered, the Romans in attendance went into rapturous applause – more than she herself had received, but that was to be expected. The acclaim washed over Illeana and she lifted her chin, her eyes hooded as she drank it in. With effortless poise, she made her way to the dais and bowed.

'Hail, Caesar,' she said softly, appraising him as he clearly appraised her.

'Illeana,' Domitian purred. 'You look magnificent. A goddess.'

'Caesar flatters me,' she responded.

'You are deserving of flattery. You are *victrix*,' he added, forcing Lysandra to resist the urge to sigh. 'Your battle with Lysandra was magnificent. As a Roman, I had hoped you would win, but I have seen her fight before and I feared for you.'

'Lysandra is the most dangerous opponent I have ever faced,' she acknowledged her with a glance and a nod of respect. 'The truth, Caesar, is that on another day it would be she and not I that won the battle. Fortune was with me.'

'Beauty, skill at arms and modesty,' Domitian indicated that she should sit. 'You are a woman of many virtues.'

'And vices,' she added as she sat and Lysandra was sure that she winked at her emperor as she did so. The realisation hit her that they must be lovers or at least had shared the same bed at one time or another.

Domitian continued to flirt with Illeana, leaving Lysandra to take in the surroundings. Far across the room, she could see Cappa, Murco and Kleandrias. The two Romans were enjoying the hospitality, drinking laughing and grabbing at the wine slaves as they went past. Kleandrias was doing his best to look unimpressed.

'Thinking deep thoughts, Lysandra?'

The voice startled her and Lysandra looked up to see Sextus Julius Frontinus approach the couch. 'Frontinus,' she rose, genuinely pleased to see him. He held out his hands and she took them in hers, kissing him on both cheeks.

'May I?' he indicated the couch.

'Of course.'

He groaned as he sat. 'Gods, that's better. The trouble with making deals is that they're normally done standing and I'm at an age where I'm more comfortable reclining.'

'What kind of deals are you making these days?'

Frontinus took some wine before responding. 'We're going to war, Lysandra. You must have heard about the catastrophe in Dacia.'

'I was in training then,' she responded. 'Of course, I know that there was a defeat, but I am sure that it is only a temporary setback.'

'Quite,' he said. It seemed to Lysandra that he was going to say something else, but stopped himself. 'Well, you have come a long

91

way, haven't you? From shipwrecked priestess to *Gladiatrix Prima* and now you sit at the hand of your emperor.'

'He is not my emperor,' Lysandra corrected. 'Sparta is a client state, not a conquered territory, Frontinus.'

'Of course. Slip of the tongue. I'm getting on a bit, you know.'

Lysandra grinned. 'I rather think, Frontinus, that you are not as decrepit as you would have everyone believe. This must work for you in your . . . deal making.'

He chuckled. 'Perceptive as ever. Politics is like being in the arena in a way. Show them you are weak when you are strong . . .'

'. . . And show them you are strong when you are weak. An old adage and a true one.'

Frontinus glanced at Domitian and Illeana. 'You were unlucky,' he commented. 'As was I. I lost a fortune betting on you, Lysandra.'

She shrugged. 'I would have more sympathy if you were a poorer man. But everyone knows that Croesus would envy your fortune. But you are quite right. I *was* unlucky.' As she spoke, the injustice of it all welled to the fore. 'I should have another chance, but Illeana states that she has retired, thus denying me. It is most frustrating. On another day . . .' she trailed off, wishing with all her heart that she could go back in time and change the fight. Do something that would have altered the outcome.

Frontinus nodded. 'Who can know the will of the gods? There is a method in everything they do.'

'Of course. But even I struggle to see reason in this.'

'Perhaps because if you had won, the *Roman* emperor would not have been so magnanimous as to invite the Hellene *victrix* to a celebration – which would mean that you and I would not be sitting here now.'

Lysandra chuckled. 'Frontinus, I count you as a friend, but really – I would rather have won the fight.'

'I would speak to you – privately.'

Lysandra narrowed her eyes at this. Frontinus was shrewd and, friends or not, she knew well that the old man only ever used people to his own advantage. But, despite herself, her interest was piqued. 'Why?'

'I will tell you. In private.' He looked around again. 'This will soon degenerate, Lysandra – and I know you well enough to realise that orgiastic behaviour is not one of your vices.'

'I thought that that was all a scurrilous rumour.'

'It is for the most part, but the emperor finds you gladiatrices irresistible. He is enamoured of Illeana. He will wait till the . . . er . . . well, when everything starts, and then take her to his private rooms.'

'He is a man' Lysandra looked over at them to see Domitian gazing at Illeana like a lovesick youth. 'She is the most beautiful woman I have ever seen: it is no wonder he is under her spell.'

'Quite. Will you walk with me? Unless of course I have misread your appetites?'

Lysandra stood abruptly. 'No, you have not.' She offered him her arm, which he took and hauled himself up.

'Of course . . . now everyone will think I am taking *you* to a private room.'

'My virtue is well known – even in Rome,' she replied. 'But if people come to the wrong conclusion, it may serve only to enhance your reputation. I do not care either way.'

The two made their way through the *triclinium*, Lysandra giving Kleandrias a reassuring nod as they did so. Cappa and Murco were clearly drunk already, hooting with laughter at some joke that was probably childish and lewd. Kleandrias made to walk towards her but she shook her head – and noted the anger in his eyes as she did so. Sometimes he took his duties far too seriously.

Frontinus led her into an anteroom, the centrepiece of which was a huge, tabletop map. Lysandra arched as she made her way to it. 'You wish to give me a geography lesson, Frontinus?'

He laughed at that. 'Not quite, but it will serve to illustrate a point.'

'What point?'

Frontinus turned serious then. 'This is Dacia,' he pointed to an area of the map.'

'I know.'

He ignored her. 'This is where the Roman army crossed into Dacian territory and this,' he indicated an area near a mountain pass, 'is where they were defeated.'

Lysandra considered the scenario for a moment. 'Were they caught strung out on the march?'

'No. This was a pitched battle. Full deployment.'

Lysandra folded her arms and tapped her chin with her forefinger. 'Full deployment. Then they were outnumbered. Hugely.' It was the only logical conclusion: the modern Roman army could not be defeated any other way save by overwhelming numbers. They were too disciplined, too well equipped. And too well led.

'Yes they were outnumbered. But not overwhelmingly,' Frontinus said. 'Cornelius Fuscus was in command. The Dacians, under their new king, Decabalus, would not be drawn out, so he was forced to march into the interior.' Lysandra opened her mouth to speak, but he pressed on. 'He left good lines of supply and communication, ensuring that marching camps were constructed along the route. What happened was this. He engaged the main force here at Tapae, but was caught in a pincer movement – and annihilated. Five legions, Lysandra. All gone.'

'A disaster,' she agreed. 'Rome will not make the same mistake twice, I am sure.'

'Rome does not have enough legions left to mount a similar campaign.'

'That is absurd. You can recruit new men and recall some from overseas.'

'It is not as simple as that. Yes, we have recruited new men, but there are only so many regular troops. To recall other legions would weaken our frontiers – and news of this defeat is spreading fast.

Like in the arena – we have to make our enemies think we are strong when we are weak.'

Lysandra looked at him over the map. 'Why are you telling me all this?'

'The secondary attack was led by women. Specifically, Sorina of Dacia. I am sure you remember her.'

At the mention of her name, Lysandra felt the familiar stab of hatred as the barbarian's face was brought to mind. 'Yes. I remember her.'

'My reports tell me that our soldiers struggled in the face of this unexpected assault. The truth of it is, Lysandra, that many men hesitate to kill women – some out of honour; some from pity; some from disdain or incredulity that they could be a threat. This allowed the attack to open our lines and . . . well. You can guess the rest.'

'Then your men will have to learn to be more disciplined – and perhaps more ruthless.'

'And again, here is the problem. Many of our recruits are older than usual or ex-slaves.'

'I find it hard to believe that Rome struggles for manpower.'

'Yet it is the truth. The empire is vast – it needs policing and no empire, no matter how strong, can wear such a loss so easily. So Rome needs your help. *I* need your help.'

Lysandra frowned, unsure as to the old man's point. 'How can I help you? I am rich, yes. Is it money you need – taxes?'

'No. I need you to fight. To lead.'

'I?' Lysandra was more than taken aback. 'Frontinus – I know how backward Roman views are when it comes to women.' It was true. Only in enlightened Sparta were women afforded their true worth. 'I cannot lead a legion – no one would accept it. And I cannot believe that even with a dearth of manpower there are no Roman generals left.'

'You led an army for the emperor,' he reminded her.

'But that was a show – a spectacle.'

'You are right.' His shoulders sagged, defeated. 'I was desperate.

I *am* desperate, but I should have realised that such a task would be beyond even you.'

Lysandra felt the recrimination like a slap in the face. 'It is not beyond me,' she snapped. 'I know tactics and strategy better than most of the aristocrats you put in the field. As I proved to you those years ago. It is simply a matter of acceptance: I am fully aware of my own abilities, but others are not. Rome would not countenance it. Nor would the soldiers. No – it is not possible.'

'I am not asking you to lead a *Roman* legion,' he said, his eyes meeting hers. 'Rather a mercenary one. And I would need your veterans. Gladiatrices who would not balk at the prospect of killing women the way men might. Decabalus . . . and Sorina hold all the advantages now. I need to turn the wheel on them. Surprise them. And there is something else to consider.'

'What?'

'Look at the map. Let us say you are the Dacians. If you defeated Rome again, which way would you go? Where is the richest territory?'

Lysandra's eyes were drawn to the beautiful cartography. She swallowed. 'Moesia.'

Frontinus raised his eyebrows. 'And then?'

'Hellas.'

'Yes,' his voice was quiet. 'Hellas. So you see, Lysandra. The only thing that stands between Decabalus, Sorina and your homeland is a few legions of old men and raw recruits.'

You will lift your shield in defence of your homeland.

The words of the goddess echoed through her mind as she stared at the map. The hairs on the back of her neck stood up and her skin raised in goose bumps as the enormity of the prophesy welled up within her. A sense of destiny hung over her and in that moment she realised her purpose.

'I will help you,' she said.

★

It was empowering to make the master of the world all but weep with joy. The rush of it was far greater than the physical pleasure of sex. He was lost in her, worshipping her, loving her.

She gazed at his face as he thrust into her, urging him to greater efforts, her sweat mingling with his till finally, with a sob of the purest ecstasy, Domitian came into her. He continued his strokes, eking every last moment of pleasure he could before finally rolling off and onto his back, chest heaving.

'I can have any woman in the world,' he gasped. 'But it is you I desire above all others.'

'Caesar flatters me,' Illeana repeated the words from earlier in the evening. It had become a private joke between them. She laid her head on his chest, pressing her body close to his as he expected a lover would.

'Say the word and I will divorce my wife.' He always said this and she knew that in the aftermath of his passion he meant it. 'I will make you my empress and we shall forge a dynasty such as the world has never seen.'

'But Caesar would tire of me after a while,' she teased. 'I am so fine a prize because you cannot possess me.'

'I am emperor. I can possess whatever I desire. And I desire you, *Aesalon Nocturna*.'

'For now,' she rolled away from him and rose from the bed, seeking a jug of wine. She felt his eyes on her, knowing the effect her body had on him.

'You are Venus,' he said.

'Perhaps,' she glanced over her shoulder and then poured wine for them both. The goblets were huge and adorned with jewels. 'Parthian workmanship?' she asked.

'I don't know. Maybe.'

Illeana returned to the bed. 'You are master of all you survey, Caesar,' she toasted him.

'For now.' His countenance changed, becoming more pensive — almost angry.

'What troubles you?'

'Dacia,' he answered. 'It teeters on the brink of disaster since Tapae. We must respond in force. But we don't have much force to respond with. Hence Frontinus's scheme with Lysandra.'

'What scheme?'

'He means to use her as a "surprise weapon" against the Dacians. As leader of a mercenary army. She has a vast fortune as you know — his plan is to sideline Dacian spies having her recruit troops and materials. That way, we can raise another legion and no one will know.'

'Lysandra is going to war?' Illeana arched an eyebrow, her interest — and excitement — piqued.

'Yes. With her women too. The Dacians have a large band of horsewomen that have caused us much trouble. Women warriors are an affront to Mars for a very good reason. There is no real way to defeat them in the truest sense: there's no honour in victory, and if they should defeat you the disgrace is all the greater. No wonder Frontinus affirms that our soldiers have trouble fighting those of the fairer sex — if Dacian women can be described as such. Lysandra's gladiatrices will have no such compunctions. But I fear we risk a lot on this . . . hunch of his. He places much faith in her.'

'She is unique,' Illeana said after a moment. 'If I believed in them, I'd say there is a touch of the gods about her. She should be dead, Caesar — I cut her down. Yet — she lives. She is clearly one of Fortuna's favourites, and what better trait is there for leadership? I think, perhaps, Frontinus's faith is well placed.'

'Would you gamble an empire on it?'

'No — but then there's no real choice is there? If Lysandra can raise her force in secret, it cannot hurt your cause.' Domitian kissed her then, but her mind was elsewhere.

'Enough talk,' he murmured, placing his wine cup aside.

Illeana found that she was no longer in the mood for sensual gratification, filled with a fire of a different kind. Yet one did not deny an emperor – even if one were *Gladiatrix Prima*.

Frontinus had spoken long into the night, Lysandra furiously taking notes as he did so. As dawn broke over the city, she asked to take her leave and sent a slave to find Cappa, Murco and Kleandrias. Kleandrias had fallen asleep; the others long since passed out from over indulgence: they had to be carried to a *lectica*, much to the disgust of Kleandrias.

'They are supposed to be protecting you,' he told Lysandra as he stalked down the road away from the palace. 'And they are in your *lectica*. You are not supposed to be walking – you're supposed to be in the litter. All they did was drink and fornicate. It was disgusting.'

'Quite so. I take it you did not indulge,' Lysandra glanced at him.

'I did not. And I did not think your tastes ran to much older men like Frontinus. You said you preferred women.'

Despite herself and everything that had transpired the previous evening, Lysandra felt gratified by Kleandrias's jealousy for reasons she could not quite fathom. 'I rather think,' she said after a few moments, 'that you are mistaken in your assessment, Kleandrias. I thought you knew me better.' He looked chagrined, which she enjoyed. 'I have much to think on after my conversation with Frontinus – which I will share with you once I have analysed the situation.'

Kleandrias made to respond but thought better of it. They walked in silence back to the house where Lysandra retired at once to her rooms and began to go over her notes.

If his battle strategy was simple, the logistics were not. Frontinus's plan was all about secrecy – his fear of this Decabalus discerning his intentions bordered on paranoia. He was even convinced that the Dacians had spies in the imperial treasury, monitoring what military equipment was being bought and sold – an indication of the strength of forces ranged against them.

Thus Lysandra's command was to be independent: she would raise the money to hire the mercenaries herself by selling her assets to Rome. Once victory had been achieved, her funds would be returned – with interest. But of course, the most valuable asset she possessed was the Deiopolis itself. It was worth millions – and she would need millions to raise her army.

It was galling – but she realised that the temple had now served its purpose. Athene had called upon her once again – and the Deiopolis had provided her women with all the training they needed to support the cause of the Olympians. Fighters, healers, logistics – all were there in microcosm. It was clear to her that the goddess had this in mind from the beginning.

Lysandra sat back in her chair and rubbed her eyes: there was so much to do, to organise. She had little time. But, for now, she was exhausted. As she sat in the chair, the gravity of what she had agreed to suddenly welled up inside her.

It was one thing to lead in a mock battle – an entertainment – but quite another to go to war for real. Yet this is what she had been trained for in the Temple of Athene so long ago. The purpose of her sisterhood was to defend Sparta against invaders as they had done when Pyrrhus had attacked. Now that training would be put to the test.

It seemed to Lysandra that her entire life had been heading towards this moment. Every trial she had faced, every victory she had won was a preparation for this – her greatest challenge. Fitting then that Sorina was among the enemy.

She brought the older woman's face to mind – she could recall

100

every line and contour, the chestnut coloured eyes and the brown hair just beginning to streak with grey at the temples.

No barbarian army can stand against civilised troops.

It was the argument that had first brought them to blows in Lucius Balbus's *ludus*: Sorina had gone on to disprove that statement, crushing the flower of Rome's army at Tapae. Now Lysandra would even the score.

She was Spartan — war was in her blood. More, she was steeped in martial lore and far more tactically astute than the career generals who used the military as a stepping stone to political power. They were amateurs and, despite her lack of experience, she was the professional in this matter. She had proven this at Domitian's birthday and more on the corpses of those she had slain in the arena. What Roman general had actually felt the slick warmth of blood on his sword hand before leading his troops to battle?

There were no war-tricks that Sorina and her band of savages could pull off this time — Frontinus's strategy would not allow it. No, this would be a battle that would play into Lysandra's hands and negate the great advantage of barbarian horse tribes.

The orders from Frontinus were clear — *summa exstinctio*. She was to take no prisoners for slaves: she must kill every Dacian. Lysandra smiled slightly, imagining the agony this would make Sorina feel before she herself fell. She deserved it for what she had done to Eirianwen. Sorina should have stayed her hand, let her win. Eirianwen was in the flower of her youth, Sorina in the autumn of her life. Sorina, who claimed to love Eirianwen as a daughter, but not enough to sacrifice herself for that love.

Lysandra would make her pay. 'Athene,' she whispered. 'Let me have my vengeance.'

Her head nodded on her chest and she felt sleep begin to claw away at the edge of her consciousness.

'Lysandra?'

Her eyes snapped open as Kleandrias entered her rooms. The

101

spark of anger at his intrusion was doused as she saw he was carrying a tray with food and drink on it. 'I thought that you might need some refreshment.' His eyes fell on her notes. 'Battle plans? For another mock battle?' he asked as he placed the tray down.

Lysandra smiled. 'Not exactly.'

'Well – what exactly?'

'Sit,' she ordered, gesturing to the chair opposite hers. She told him then, enjoying the look of surprise and, she fancied, amazement on his face as the news was imparted.

'*You* are to do this?' he asked.

She did not like his intonation. 'You think I am incapable of such a task, Kleandrias?'

'No,' he grinned. 'But you will need my help. As you know I was a soldier – a mercenary. I am well-suited to helping you.'

His smile melted her pique and she met it with one of her own. As he spoke she was reminded of the first time she had met him, all full of bluster and pride. 'Of course. I was counting on it.'

'What are your plans?'

Lysandra slid her notes over to him. She was pleased to see him nodding as he read, proof if she needed it, that her thinking on the matter was right.

'Your Deiopolis?' he looked up from her script. 'I do not understand.'

'Frontinus believes that the Dacians have spies in the Roman treasury. He wishes me to sell my assets to Rome – this will pass the notice of any spies as the purchase will not be for weapons. It will be for land – they can hardly be looking out for such things.'

'He is sure there are spies, then?'

'He seemed so. It does not matter either way. We need money to raise troops and this is the most expedient way of turning stone to gold.'

'It is a sad thing though, Lysandra.'

She frowned, tiredness now making it hard to think. 'How so?'

'You have told me everything about that place. It was once your *ludus* – now it is your temple. You have shed blood for it. Sometimes, things are worth more than money.'

'There is no other way. Besides – after my fight with *Aesalon Nocturna,* I walked the banks of the Styx . . . Athene appeared to me in a vision. She said that I would lift my shield in defence of my homeland. I see now that the vision was true. The Deiopolis was made for this purpose. *I* was made for this purpose as was Arachidamia so long ago. I am her . . . offspring.'

Kleandrias nodded. Like any Spartan he knew the story of the princess who led the women of the *polis* in battle against the Epiran warlord, Pyrrhus. 'You will call on your Sisters of the Temple then. They have been there for centuries, training for a war that never came. Now it would seem that war is upon them.'

Lysandra's breast swelled with pride at the thought. 'I will lead them out,' she replied. 'A Spartan to lead Spartans in battle. You will be by my side.'

'A good beginning,' he said.

She nodded. 'Leave me. I must rest. Then I will draft orders for the Deiopolis. They must prepare.'

'One question.'

Lysandra regarded him for a moment, fighting the urge to yawn. 'What is it?'

'You are assuming that all the women of the Deiopolis will want to follow you. Want to go to a war. Lysandra, they are not all like you, surely. Some will be unwilling. Afraid.'

'Then they will answer to the gods!' Lysandra snapped. 'I will have no one with me who is not . . . with me.' She squeezed her eyes closed, calming herself. 'I am not going to conscript my women, Kleandrias. All will have a choice. Any who refuse will have a pension and my goodwill.'

'And for those who join you?'

'I will have Frontinus ensure that they are granted Roman

citizenship and a lump sum of cash in addition to their regular pay – on completion of the mission. And exemption from tax if I can.'

'A sweet deal if every I heard one.'

'Rome is desperate. Frontinus will agree to my demands – he has no choice. If he did, do you really think that he would approach me?'

Kleandrias thought about that for a moment. 'Perhaps he would. Is there a better strategos in the empire?'

She smiled. 'We shall find out soon enough.'

XIV

Dacia

There was a change in the air, the cold fastness of winter fading into brighter mornings and longer nights. Sorina could taste blood in the wind too: the summer would bring days of slaughter.

The warriors' training was going well enough, but it went against the grain. The Dacians were unused to order, preferring instead to embrace the chaos of battle and fight as champions should with skill, courage and honour.

But the Romans had no honour. To them, war was not a sacred thing, it was merely a process by which they achieved their aims and, as had been proven with the blood of countless thousands, they could not be defeated using the old ways of war.

Decabalus knew this and had mimicked their methods, dealing them a crushing blow that served well to keep the host in check.

Even so, there were divisions in the tribes – those utterly loyal to Decabalus and those becoming unsure by the interminable lingering before the war began.

'They are a problem.' Decabalus said to her as they sat on the rich rugs that decorated the floor of his tent. 'A problem you can help me deal with.'

Sorina smiled. 'I think you overestimate my sway with them, my lord.' It was true: she had a reputation as warrior and war-leader, but she was old. The young always disagreed with the old; it was the way of things.

'The Romans are beginning to move,' Decabalus scratched at his beard. 'My spies provide me with information on their legions,' he added both with a sense of pride and as if he sought her approval.

'You have spies in Rome?'

'Slaves. The Romans trust them to do everything and don't notice them doing it. It would seem they can only muster three legions to send against us. *Three!*' He laughed and slapped his thigh. 'Three to do the job that five could not do before. And I know that one of these legions, the Felix, is of low quality. Old men, slaves . . . the dregs of their empire.'

Sorina grunted, eyeing the jug of *tzuica* placed on the low table between them. 'So you meet them on the field and crush them. We have the warriors to overwhelm them.'

Decabalus picked up on the hint and gestured for her to pour for them. 'The legate in charge of the mission is Tettius Iulianus. This one is no Cornelius Fuscus, that's what I'm told. A hard man and a wily general. I anticipate more than a handful of trouble if I allow him to call on all his resources.'

Sorina nodded her agreement. 'It is wisdom not to underestimate the Romans, my king. This has been my counsel to you and the war chiefs.'

'It intend to make them divide their forces. Which is where I need your help.'

'How?' She leaned forward.

'You will lead a strong force – comprising those that are less than enthusiastic about my ways of making war – to the north. The story is that you are looking to recruit more warriors from those tribes that have not already provided them. It may look like intimidation. It may look like a show of just how powerful we've become if we can afford to send a war host to sweep up extra warriors. But I don't care how it looks. What I want is for the Romans to know about it. This will force them to divide their army – they must guard their supply lines and their backs. A legion, I think, will be assigned to this – in all likelihood the Felix.'

'But this strategy plays into their hands!' Sorina exclaimed. 'They will pick a strong position and fortify it. Poor quality troops or not, we would lose thousands to them before we overwhelmed their defences!'

'Yes,' Decabalus nodded. To Sorina, it seemed that in the low lamplight his eyes took on a feral gleam. 'Thousands of those that question my authority and those that were slow to answer my call.'

Sorina drained her *tzuica*, wincing at the liquor's acrid bite. She had thrown it back to hide her shock and disgust: disgust at Decabalus for planning to waste tribal lives so casually; disgust at herself for realising that it was necessary if the king was to retain an iron grip on power. She poured some more *tzuica* for herself and met his gaze. 'You think like a Roman,' she said at length.

'To win, I must.'

'I know,' her reply was quiet.

'Then you know I am right.'

She did not reply, staring at the floor, hating the truth in his words.

He must have taken her silence for reticence. 'Sorina, you are the only one I can trust to do this. That is my plan, laid bare to you. No one else knows the truth of it. I don't have to say that I will remember those that aid me.'

And those that don't. Sorina knew the threat was implicit. It irked her – he need not have bothered. 'I will always aid you, Decabalus,' she said. 'I hate Rome and all it stands for. This . . . sacrifice is worth it.'

XV

Moesia

'What happened, Settus?'

The fact was that Valerian knew all too well: Settus was sporting a black eye and three men from Mucius's First of the First had ended up mysteriously in the infirmary with broken bones and head injuries. The centurion was drawn up to attention in the *praetorium*, doing his best impression of stoicism.

'I fell, sir. Banged me head.'

'At ease, Settus.' The older man relaxed slightly, but was still on his guard – which irked Valerian a little. 'Cup of wine? I'm a legate – it'll be better than the piss they're giving you, these days.' Without waiting for a response, Valerian poured two cups for them. 'Sit down,' he gestured to the chair opposite his desk.

'Thank you, sir.'

'You want to tell me what's going on?'

'I fell, sir.'

'For fuck's sake, Settus! I need to know – I can't have my centurions at odds with each other. So can we drop the pretence that we've just met. Permission to speak freely granted, alright?'

'I can't be seen to have special treatment,' Settus thrust out his chin, which from hard experience Valerian knew meant that he was as set as concrete on the matter.

'I'm not giving you special treatment, you idiot. I'm asking you for a favour. None of those bastards trust me and nobody will tell me anything. So, what's the story?'

'Not much to tell,' Settus tipped back some wine. 'That cunt Mucius has given his lot free reign to take the piss out of my men. It got out of hand at our *tabernae*,' he referred to one of the encampment's drinking houses.

'*Your tabernae?*'

'That's right. First of the First have no reason to be at our end of the camp unless it's on business or they're looking for trouble. It was the latter.'

'So you took it upon yourself to deal with the situation?'

'No, I . . .'

'Right,' Valerian sighed. 'You fell.' It saddened him a little that a distance was growing between himself and Settus. It hadn't occurred to him that it would happen, but of course, from Settus's point of view, if he was seen to be the legate's pet, then his life would be intolerable with his peers. But warring factions within the legion were intolerable to him as legate – it all needed to be stamped out. 'How are your men progressing?' he changed the subject.

'That Slainius – my optio – is a vicious bastard. Even *I'm* scared of him. But the men are terrified. So we're getting the best out of them, I reckon.'

'Don't exaggerate to me, Settus. I'm serious – I understand the whole my-century-is-the-best speech – but I need to know.' He didn't add it, but the *as your mate* suffix was implicit.

'They won't let you – or me – down, sir. One of the lads – Caballo – is showing signs of leadership. Which, by the way, is a fucking contradiction, because he's an ex-slave, but who knows the way of the gods? What I mean to say is – I know what I'm doing. Slanius is enough of a sadist to keep 'em on the straight and narrow and Caballo gives them a shoulder to cry on. And he does a really good impersonation of me which cracks the men up.'

Valerian held back a smirk at that, imagining someone lampooning Settus. 'So you reckon they'd hold their own in some field work? Bit of friendly competition with the other centuries?'

Settus gave Valerian his crack-toothed grin. 'They'd fucking relish it, sir.'

Publius Mucius Cinna was the son of a soldier, who in turn was the son of a soldier. He knew with certainty that he – like his fathers before him – would die in the service of Rome. Not for Mucius the drooling, piss-stenched years of senility, his memories of the glory days lost to the confusion of the aged. He would end his days under the eagle.

He counted himself an honest man, a trait, his father had warned him all those years ago, that would land him in trouble one day. And it had.

He could pretend that his position of the Felix Legion's *Primus Pilus* was an honour gifted to him for years of loyal service. But the truth of it was, it was demotion to the shittiest legion in the empire.

Legion? From his hilltop vantage point, Mucius looked on as the men marched out on exercises. Out of the five thousand that made up the Felix, his century had the only men worthy of calling themselves soldiers. The rest . . . it was all he could do to refrain from spitting as the thought came to him.

The legion – like some giant, iron-plated snake, undulated over the gently hilled Moesian countryside. These barbarian lands were all the same, Mucius thought bitterly – green, wet and stinking – muggy in summer, freezing in winter. It was as though the gods had become bored with the north and just decided that Germanian topography was all that the savages deserved.

The rhythmic thump of a horse's hooves on damp grass dragged his attention away from the legion.

The legate.

Mucius bit down on his own teeth to stop himself from sneering. If the Felix legion was barely worthy of the name, its commander was a disgrace to the banners. A boy, foisted upon better men by the idiot politicians in Rome. And worse, a *cursed* boy, the taint of defeat hanging around him like a pall.

'Morning, *Primus*,' Valerian nodded at him.

'Sir.'

The legate turned his attention to the marching men below. 'Not bad,' he murmured. 'Not bad at all.' Mucius kept his counsel, but his distaste must have been written all over his face. 'You disagree, *Primus*? You may speak freely.'

'I've served with better, sir.'

'As have I. But, we have what we have. We must . . . do what Romans do. Find a way to win.'

'With that lot? They'll shit themselves at the first sign of the enemy and run away. They're not proper soldiers — they're . . .'

'Yes, I know — geriatrics, children and slaves. But it's your job — you and the other centurions — to make them soldiers.'

'My men *are* soldiers.'

'That's not enough, *Primus*. You are a fine officer — your First of the First is the cream of our somewhat clotted legion — but it cannot win a battle alone. I need you to show some leadership here.'

Mucius bristled. 'Am I still speaking freely?' He waited until Valerian made a gesture of acquiescence. 'All right, then. I don't need a lecture from you, legate. Maybe you should look to your other officers.'

'Like Settus?'

Mucius didn't answer. He didn't have to.

The legate sighed and turned his attention back to the marching troops below. 'This little feud between you and him needs to end,' he said after a moment.

'He lacks respect.'

'For what? Your position as First Spear in the empire's shittiest legion? Like it or not, Mucius, Settus – and I for that matter – served with Sextus Frontinus. We won with him.'

'That was then,' Mucius was pleased to point out. 'This is now.'

'True enough,' the younger man acknowledged. 'Very well, Mucius. Very well. It might please you to know that, as part of this exercise, I've given orders for one of my centuries to secure an area. From which they could, say, harass a legion on the march, interrupt supply lines – that sort of thing.' He looked pointedly to the north – in the distance, Mucius could make out a thickly wooded forest.

'Go on.'

'I'm sure that by now they're dug in deep, like ticks. As you know, we don't have any auxiliaries at this time, so if these manoeuvres were the real thing, I'd need to dispatch an elite force to get rid of this potential threat to the security of the legion . . .'

'You're setting my men against Settus's?' Mucius didn't know whether to be pleased or affronted.

'Well . . . yes.' The legate shrugged. 'I reckoned that it was probably for the best that this contest had a conclusion, don't you?'

'It's not going to be a contest!' Mucius looked again towards the forest, suddenly eager to be back with his men, eager to be getting to grips with the tattooed little upstart.

'Don't be so sure, *Primus*,' the legate said. 'He's no fool. But whatever the outcome, you two will shake on it and that will be an end to it. Do I have your word on that?'

'You do, sir,' Mucius agreed – hastily, he recognised. Too hastily.

'I'm not setting you up,' the legate said as though reading his thoughts. 'Settus knows that your unit will be out looking for him – his men are armed with practice weapons, so he also knows there'll be a fight. But that's all he knows. Your job is to locate his force and take him out. I'll have judges put in with your men – as I have

111

with his. So . . .' Valerian gestured to the distant forest. 'Over to you, *Primus*.'

'What do you think?' Mucius eyed the foreboding trees with a degree of suspicion.

His optio, Livius, twisted his lips. 'Shit, I don't know. What was it the legate called us – an elite force? Elite force, my arse.' He lowered his voice. 'This is auxiliary work, *Primus*. We've no business slogging our way through that,' he indicated the black barked trees. 'We all know what happened to . . .'

'For fuck's sake,' Mucius cut him off. Livius was steady and level-headed – but he could also nag like an old wife. 'If I hear the name *Varus* one more time today, I'll break you to the ranks.'

'I'm just saying, is all,' Livius held up his hands defensively.

'Varus was ambushed and outnumbered,' Mucius gritted. 'All we've got to do is find Settus and his slaves and give them a kicking.'

'Then why ask me what I think?'

'Professional courtesy.'

'My arse.'

Mucius glanced back at his century, idling on the grass. The men were – like himself – pretending that entering the forest wasn't scaring them. But it was – everyone knew that these barbarian woods were cursed and ghosts lurked in the mists. But they had a mission.

'All right,' Mucius tapped his chin. 'Let's see. Livius, get a *contubernia* ready. No shields – I need them moving fast and light. Skirmish line – fifty feet apart. Get 'em out scouting and reporting back at regular intervals. I'll get the rest ready to move. We'll follow them up. Clear?'

'Yes, sir.'

Livius saluted and made off to carry out his orders, leaving Mucius once again to turn his attention to the forest. 'All right, Settus,' he murmured. 'Let's see what you have.'

XVI

The Deiopolis, Asia Minor

Life was good, Telemachus decided. The goddess was good. After years of loyal service, she had finally rewarded him. Life in Lysandra's Deiopolis was everything he had imagined it to be and more. Lysandra had made beautiful what was once hard and cruel, building upon the grounds of her old *ludus*, converting the houses and cell blocks to places of work and worship. As such, each of the twelve Olympians had their own sphere of influence within the compound.

Yes, most of it was rudely designed – aside from the complex's centrepiece, a magnificent statue of Athene crafted by the famous Apollodorus of Damascus – but, for all that, it was a grand place. Tourists flocked to it and paid handsomely to pray at the feet of Hellenic pantheon – especially the Temple of Aphrodite that, despite the obscene fees charged by the priestesses for their services, was by far the most profitable enterprise in the entire place.

Telemachus had just visited there himself – a perk of the job for which he did not have to pay – and he supposed that this was the reason for his bonhomie. That and the fact that he was becoming a very rich man for doing what he had always done – administering a temple.

Hands behind his back, whistling a jaunty tune of his own devising, he made his way to his quarters, smiling and nodding in greeting along the way to the priestesses and temple staff that knew him.

The sun was sinking, casting an orange light onto the white stone of the Deiopolis – it was his favourite time of the day. As the sun set, the sounds of the temple became somewhat muted, save for the clack of wooden swords coming from the Temples of Ares and Athene. It served to remind him that, as grand as the place was now, it had been bought and paid for in blood and gold earned on the sands of the arena.

It was time for a cup or two of wine, he decided. A reward for the efforts of the day – and he needed one after the exertions at Aphrodite's Temple.

His quarters were of adequate size, kept neat and tidy by his own hand. Telemachus could not abide mess and disorder and it had shocked him to see how the usually disciplined Lysandra conducted her business affairs. Then again, Lysandra was hardly gifted with acumen of that kind.

Unusually, his secretary, the big-haired Nikos, was waiting for him as he entered.

'Sir . . .' Nikos began.

'Telemachus,' the priest corrected – for the umpteenth time. 'I'm not Spartan, I'm not a trainer and I'm most certainly not a soldier. Come on,' he threw his arm around the younger man's shoulder. 'I need a cup of wine. And so do you, by the look of you,' he added, noting Nikos's tense expression.

'Old habits,' Nikos acknowledged.

The two entered Telemachus's office – a homely affair, less severe and more tastefully decorated than the bleak cell from which Lysandra liked to work. Perhaps that explained the mess of her accounts – chaos out of all that order. 'Sit down,' he bade Nikos, pouring wine for them both before he sat at his desk. Everything was cleared – aside from two, sealed leather message tubes: one of them bore Lysandra's name, the other, the seal of Sextus Julius Frontinus.

'The messenger said they were urgent and were to be opened

only by your hand,' Nikos took a hefty hit of wine. 'His horse was half dead.'

'I hope you – '

' . . . Offered him lodging and had his horse tended to at the Temple of Artemis. Of course.'

'I'm surprised the priestesses didn't pepper you with arrows.'

'They may be mean-spirited towards men, Telemachus. But they love animals. And shooting.'

Telemachus let his mouth twist in a half-grin to mask his concern. The one thing Lysandra was not prone to was panic. Arrogance, obstinacy, parochialism and ruthlessness, yes. But never panic; the fact that she had seen fit to ensure the messenger underscored the urgency of her communication worried him. 'Let's see what they want, then.'

'Shall I leave, sir . . . Telemachus?'

'Why?'

'Well, because the messages were for your hand only and the Lady always insisted that private messages were to be read in private.'

'The Lady isn't here. You're my secretary for now, so my rules apply – alright? And besides,' he broke the seal on Lysandra's tube, 'you'll be writing the response anyway. Better handwriting than mine.' He pulled out the scroll and began to read. After a few moments, he put it down and laughed.

'I feared it was bad news.' Nikos looked relieved.

'It is.'

'Then why are you laughing?'

'Hubris.' Telemachus said, recalling his cheeriness of a few minutes ago. 'Nikos – please would you go and find Thebe and Titus and have them come here. At once.'

Nikos set his cup down and made off, leaving Telemachus to open Frontinus's messages, hoping it was all some terrible misunderstanding.

It was not.

115

'She can't be serious,' Titus said. He, Telemachus and Thebe were on some hastily gathered couches in the office. Wine and food had been brought, but it was largely untouched.

Telemachus regarded him from under his eyebrows. 'How long have you known Lysandra?'

'A bit longer than you.'

'And in all that time, have you known her indulge in comedy?' There was no answer to that. 'She's serious all right. The goddess has spoken to her,' he added. Titus was about to talk again, but Telemachus overrode him. 'You Romans view the gods differently to us, Titus. I am a priest – I know that Athene speaks to – and sometimes through – Lysandra. For all of her . . . foibles . . . Athene loves her. As she loved Odysseus – *Ulysses* – I suppose.'

'But this is madness!' Titus leaned forward on his couch.

'It is not!' This from Thebe. 'You know her. You know what she can do. That sort of thing can only be inspired by the Gods of Olympus. Lysandra died – and lives again. If Athene calls . . . don't roll your eyes at me, Titus . . . Lysandra must answer. As must we. All we have,' she gestured at the surrounds, 'all we do, we owe to her.'

'To be fair, you did your share of bleeding in the arena, Thebe,' Titus raised his cup in a peace gesture.

'That's as maybe. But no Roman senator commissioned a frieze of Thebe. They do not still speak of Thebe in Halicarnassus and beyond. There is no statue of Thebe in Corinth – '

'So, she's serious,' Telemachus interjected. 'And it falls to us to help her.'

'Let's hear it again – the short version, though,' Titus amended hastily.

Telemachus sighed. 'I laid out a map on my desk,' he said, swinging his legs off his couch and moving towards it.

'We are to sell the Deiopolis to the Governor of Asia Minor,' he said. 'The price over the odds – but not excessively so. With the money, we are to fund Lysandra's recruitment of a mercenary army to support the Romans in defence of the Empire against Decabalus – his Dacians . . . and Sorina's Amazons. Frontinus has engaged propagandists amongst the gathering places of Hellene mercenaries. Their task is to rally them to the Roman – or rather Lysandra's – cause. Her fame as the woman Athene saved will assist in this.

'The priestesses of this temple also play a part in this plan,' he went on. 'We *must* convince as many as we can to march with us.'

'What about the ones that don't fight?' Thebe asked. 'They're not just Priestesses of Ares, Athene and Artems – '

'Logistics,' Titus interrupted. 'You can't have men and women marching together. But the Deiopolis has everything a campaign needs in terms of skills. Cooks, woodcraft, leather workers, armourers, healers . . . everything. Lysandra,' he smiled, despite himself, 'thinks of everything, doesn't she?'

'There are women that have left here that fought in Lysandra's spectacle,' Thebe said. 'Many are still local. They would fight for her, I know it.'

'Then it'll be down to you to convince them,' Telemachus said. 'Now look,' he pointed at the map. 'We're here. We need to get *here* – just outside the village of Ceramos – one week before Saturnalia. It's a natural harbour as you can see.'

'Turn of the year is only four months away,' Titus said. 'It takes six months to train a legionary. We – '

'That's taking a civilian and making him a soldier,' Thebe interrupted. 'Our people can already fight. Most have already seen a battle.'

'A *mock* battle,' Titus pointed out.

'Lysandra trained us well. Marching. Drilling. Many hundreds moving as one. I remember it well – the others will too. I led my women with honour.'

117

Titus rubbed his beard. 'Rome must be desperate to countenance this. I know our girls fought for Domitian's spectacle, but would they stand in a real fight? With men?'

'Doesn't that come down to training?' Thebe's eyebrow was arched, her response barbed.

'Yes and no,' Titus adopted his 'voice of experience' and it was all Telemachus could do to refrain from rolling his eyes. 'Morale is key. If they're fighting *for* something – that's the thing. I can tell you, the many times I've faced battle . . .'

'They will be fighting for something,' Telemachus said quickly, cutting off the inevitable lengthy yarn. 'There is Lysandra, yes. They know the goddess favours her. And, let's be honest, they owe her. They've lived a life here like no other.'

'Even so,' Titus said. 'Gratitude only goes so far. You'd be asking them to leave all this behind and go to a war.'

'Athene speaks through Lysandra,' Thebe folded her arms. 'All the women in the Deiopolis know this. They will answer her call – the call of the goddess.'

'It's never a good idea to bring religion into a war,' Titus muttered.

'Nevertheless – it will be the glue we need to hold this . . .' he almost said 'madness' but stopped himself in time. 'This . . . army together. And besides . . .'

'Besides?' Titus raised both eyebrows in question.

'If the women go, they will be granted Roman citizenship, land in Asia Minor and a life-long pension. Frontinus's word on it.'

'I will do my part of it,' Thebe announced. They both looked at Titus.

'And I,' he agreed. 'Lysandra has never asked for anything from me in all these years. She asks now, and I will not refuse her.'

'She asked plenty of me in the past,' Telemachus smiled. 'But she's my friend. More like my younger sister, in fact.'

'I admire your loyalty, priest. But what can you bring to a war plan? It is a dangerous business.' Titus had no malice in his voice and Telemachus was not offended by the question – though a part of him felt that he should be.

'An army cannot function without finance, Titus. I will ensure that all goes according to plan. Make sure that everyone gets paid. And that Rome keeps her end of the bargain.'

'I'll drink to that,' Titus grinned, scooping up his wine cup. 'Who knows with Lysandra,' he added. 'With her in front, we might even survive.'

'Spoken like a true believer,' Thebe nudged him.

They raised their cups and drank, each of them knowing in their hearts that soon after the Kalends they would probably all be dead.

XVII

Rome

'I think I will just leave most of it.' Lysandra eyed the clothes and ornaments strewn all over her bed with weary eyes. Her rented apartments were a scene of unorganised chaos as slaves, supervised by a short-tempered Kleandrias, filed her correspondence and packed her belongings in a frenzy.

'I dunno . . .' Cappa was lounging against a wall, picking his nails with a dagger. 'There's some nice stuff in there. Gifts and all that.'

'I have "nice stuff" back at the Deiopolis, Cappa.'

'You're going to sell the Deiopolis, though,' Murco said. 'And Cappa's right – there is some nice stuff from your admirers. It'd be wrong to just toss it.'

Lysandra glared at them, knowing they were right and allowing herself to be piqued by it. 'You pack it then!' she snapped, and strode off, knowing that they were exchanging a what's-wrong-with-her look between them.

She went to her balcony, on edge, nervous and testy – unlike her usual self. She didn't know why.

'*Yes, you do,*' the voice at the back of her mind whispered.

Lysandra looked out over the Capitol. It was a beautiful city, a testament to what Roman money could do with Hellenic artistry – in places at least. A lot of Roman architecture bordered on the vulgar. Like the Flavian Amphitheatre. She could see it from the balustrade; she could see it everywhere she went in the city, its towering walls seeming to mock her.

'Let it go,' Kleandrias had counselled her many times. 'Some you win, some you lose.' It was true. No one, not even she, was invincible. And that, she realised, was why she was so anxious. Frontinus was asking a lot of her – maybe he was asking the impossible. She realised in her quieter moments that he had played her like a lyre, appealed to her pride and got the result that he wanted.

Lysandra smiled, despite herself. As a younger woman, she would never have realised this, assuming that his assertions of Spartan superiority – and perhaps more importantly – *her* superiority were correct. In the former he was of course right. In the latter – he was probably right.

'Lysandra.' Kleandrias's deep voice interrupted her self-depreciation. She turned to face him, forcing herself to smile. He returned it, his hard visage softening somewhat. 'I have messages for you,' he said, handing her two wax tablets.

'From Bedros,' she eyed the first. 'A merchant captain,' she explained, noting Kleandrias's blank expression. 'A good man and a good friend. Useful in a fight too,' she added. 'He will transport us as requested. For a fee, naturally.'

'Naturally,' Kleandrias agreed. 'I'll have your acceptance of his terms sent off straight away. And the other?'

Lysandra opened the tablet. What she read hit her like a physical blow.

'What is it?' Kleandrias took a step forward, concerned.

'It is from *Aesalon Nocturna*,' Lysandra said. 'She wants to meet. Tonight.'

This was no formal invitation, Lysandra knew. No need to dress in Roman finery, no need to adopt airs and graces that the Romans so valued. It was clear from her missive that Illeana wanted to talk – about what she had not said, but it could only be their rematch.

Cappa and Murco escorted her through the streets, weaving their way through the heavy press of people and traffic. Wagons were not permitted into Rome before sundown, but at night the streets became a stinking free-for-all. At least Illeana's *domus* was far enough from the *subura* for them to arrive relatively free of grime.

The *Gladiatrix Prima's* abode was situated on the Quirinal Hill – its opulence unobtrusive in that it was surrounded by places equally lavish. Cappa whistled appreciatively. 'See, this is the life,' he said.

'You think my apartments are unworthy of you, Cappa?' Lysandra queried. She was making light, she realised, to hide her nerves.

'I think your apartments are wonderful,' Murco soothed – unconvincingly. He rapped on the gates to Illeana's *domus* and waited. It took some time for an old slave to arrive. He wrestled with the locks, begging their pardons.

'This is the *Gladiatrix Prima*, Lysandra,' Cappa announced as though daring the old man to contradict him.

'You are expected, lady,' the slave looked past Cappa and directly at Lysandra. 'I am called Naso. Aemilia Illeana awaits within. I will escort you to her and ensure your slaves are tended to.'

'They're not slaves,' Lysandra put in, mollifying the outburst she knew would come from Cappa. 'These men are my bodyguards.'

Naso peered at her as he opened the gate. '*You* need bodyguards?'

'No. But someone needs to keep them employed.' Smirking, she moved into the courtyard with Cappa and Murco in tow.

'Follow him,' Naso said to the two, gesturing to another of Illeana's slaves who lurked discreetly in the darkness. 'He will see to it that you are refreshed.' Ever the professionals, both men waited till Lysandra gave them a slight nod.

'You're sure?' Murco queried.

'Enjoy the wine.' Lysandra clapped the taciturn bodyguard on the shoulder; Murco fancied himself an authority on wine and always drank it like a barbarian – unwatered – prophesying that one day everyone would drink it like that. Both Lysandra and Cappa knew well that this was a bald excuse.

'This way, lady.'

Naso led her through the *atrium* and into Illeana's home. It was exquisite, its mosaic floors depicting scenes of gladiatorial combats. There were busts of Roman gods – and the Emperor himself.

'The *tricilinium,* lady.' Naso opened the door to the dining area. It was low-lit and another slave, a vaguely handsome German-looking creature, stood in the shadows, armed with a bowl and towel. 'He will see to your needs,' Naso advised her before walking out backwards, bowing his head.

The German flexed his shoulders as he regarded Lysandra with what looked like open lasciviousness – which she found mildly insulting. 'Just wash my feet and legs,' she commanded, sitting on one of the lush couches. 'My *lower* legs,' she added as the slave undid her sandals.

As he washed her with the warm, perfumed water, Lysandra noted that the mosaic and décor in the *tricilinium* were overtly sexual – the usual god-ravishing-mortal scenes. The Corinthians, Lysandra decided, had a lot to answer for.

'Will there be anything else?' the German asked as he dried her legs.

'My hands and arms,' she instructed. He did as he was bid and she dismissed him, reclining on the couch. The room was silent but

Lysandra fancied that the beating of her heart could be heard. She was nervous and chided herself for it.

The door opened once again. It made Lysandra jump but it was merely yet more slaves this time bearing food and wine. But behind them came the *Aesalon Nocturna* and again, as every time she saw her, Lysandra was struck by her magnificence – the woman truly was blessed by the gods. She was strange, those green eyes and full lips would look odd on anyone else – but Illeana was pure perfection. Lysandra realised she was staring and rose to her feet to greet her host.

'Illeana,' she said as the Roman approached.

'Lysandra.' Lysandra felt herself flush as Illeana's plump lips brushed both her cheeks before moving to her couch. 'It is good to see you again without the pomp and ceremony of an imperial audience.'

'Quite so,' Lysandra moved to her own couch. A slave handed her a wine cup, which she raised in toast to the *Gladiatrix Prima*. Illeana watched her, her green eyes seeming to look into Lysandra's heart. 'I am honoured to be invited to your home.' She left the unasked question hanging – why?

Illeana chose to leave it unanswered. 'I have the ear of the emperor,' she said. *That and more*, Lysandra thought to herself. 'He tells me that you have been selected for a unique mission on his behalf.'

Lysandra frowned. 'This is so, but it is not something I am at liberty to discuss, Illeana. I thought that you had invited me here to discuss a rematch. Is that not so?'

'If I were to offer that, you could not accept, am I right?'

Good sense warred with the injustice of her defeat – and injustice won out. 'No,' Lysandra answered, trying hard to keep any tautness from her voice. 'I would fight you again tomorrow.'

'And if you lost?'

'I would not.'

Illeana's smile was disarming. 'Even so, it would be a hard fight. The risk of injury would be great. I imagine that Domitian would be displeased if the architect of his scheme were to be put out of action – in victory or defeat.'

It was hard to maintain any sort of aggression against Illeana. Lysandra realised that she herself would not – and had never been – so gracious in victory. It made losing to her somehow more bearable. Even if it was still excruciating. 'That is true,' she acknowledged. 'But I would avenge my . . . defeat. If you agreed to fight me, I would risk the wrath of the emperor.'

'I'm sure you would,' Illeana agreed. 'As would I, if I were in your place.'

'But you are not in my place,' Lysandra failed this time to keep the bitterness from her voice.

'I was about that much away from it,' she held up her forefinger and thumb.

'That much may as well be a mile.'

Illeana took a sip of wine, regarding Lysandra over the rim of her cup. She remained silent for some time. Then at length, she spoke. 'Lysandra, we're similar creatures, aren't we? When it all comes down to it, fighting in the arena is not really about fighting at all. It's about living on the edge – doing things that no one else can do. You know, as well as I, that you're never so alive as when you're facing death.'

'I fight for the glory of Athene and the honour of Sparta.'

Illeana chuckled. 'Yes, of course. And you don't enjoy the roar of the crowd in the least and never relish the defeat of an enemy.'

Lysandra recalled her first victory in Halicarnassus that seemed so long ago. 'In my first fight I felt guilty afterwards, but the more I fought, the more I came to enjoy it.'

'How old are you now?' Illeana asked. 'Twenty-seven?'

'This is so. You are twenty-six.'

'If I had not retired, how many years do you think I would have left in the arena? Five? Ten maybe?'

'Perhaps longer,' Lysandra thought of Sorina's lined and hateful visage.

'But sooner or later, someone younger will rise. Someone quicker. Stronger. Or perhaps just someone luckier.'

Lysandra raised her cup in agreement. 'No one can defeat Chronos. Or Tyche. Fortuna, for that matter.'

'Lysandra, like you I've done more in my twenty-six years than most women – most men – could even dream of. I have riches. Fame. I am beautiful. But my curse, such as it is, is to always want more. I need . . .' she gestured, seeking the right word and could not find it. 'More. And because of that I will fight you again.'

Lysandra's eyes widened with shock at the proclamation. She had hoped, *prayed*, for this, and now her faith had been rewarded.

'But there is one condition,' Illeana said.

'Name it.'

'I've never fought in a *war* before.'

Moesia

The century drew to a weary halt at Mucius's command, the men sinking down onto the damp earth of the forest. The fear of ghosts had worn off some time before. Truth be told, the deep varying shades of greenery and soft earth made the place quite pleasant – or it would have been if Mucius had not been trying to slog through it in armour and helmet. He sympathised with the men; lugging a *scutum* through the woods would be no fun at all. They had been searching for some hours and it was slow going.

'*Primus.*' Livius jogged up. Like everyone else, he looked tired and drawn. This was a different kind of fitness to what they were used to.

'What is it?' Mucius took a hefty swig from his water skin. It was warm but delectable.

'Enemy sighted,' the optio reported. 'Looks like a scouting party. First *contuburium* is tracking them.'

'Let's take a look.' Mucius was well pleased. He motioned for the century to stay put while he followed Livius to the advance party position.

Centurion and optio crouched in the deep foliage, looking at Settus's 'scouts'. The two men were unarmoured, their red tunics a bright splash of colour in the perpetual twilight of the forest. They had no spears either, just their swords strapped tight to their right hips. They were ambling along, chatting – clearly not expecting any trouble. Mucius nudged one of his own scouts, motioning for him and the others to keep track of the two as they disappeared into the foliage.

'Take them out?' Livius queried when they were safely out of earshot, back with the main body of the century. 'Give them a kicking, threaten to cut their balls off if they don't tell us where Settus is?' He threw a look at four black-clad men that Valerian had seconded to the century to judge proceedings.

Mucius grinned. 'Tempting. But if they're due back, it'll tip Settus off that we're on to him. If we leave them be, they'll lead us right to him.'

Livius twisted his lips. 'Could be a trap, though? Hang out some bait for us to snap up. I mean, those two twats were pretty shoddy – even for Settus's mob.'

'Even so – we've been slogging around here for fucking hours. I don't fancy spending the night here, do you? After all, you were the one shitting yourself about the fate of Quintilius Varus.'

The optio ignored that. 'I'm just saying that we don't want to walk onto a right hook if we can avoid it.'

Mucius weighed it up. Settus and his tenth century needed to be taken down a few notches, that much was certain. But Livius made a good point – losing to the tattooed little runt would be unthinkable. And unbearable. 'You think Settus has it in him?'

'*You* said Valerian reckons he's no mug.'

'Yeah, but Valerian is a dickhead.'

Livius rolled his eyes. 'He's doing all right.' He paused. 'What are we going to do then?'

Mucius was cursing himself for not throwing caution to the wind and springing a surprise on the Tenth. They'd tracked Settus's scouts and the men were plainly not bait – they were just useless. Still, for all that, they'd led the First right to Settus's encampment and they were, as Valerian had predicted, 'dug in like ticks'.

Settus's men had set up a ditch and rampart – and not a great one by the looks of it – in a large forest clearing. Hunkered down in the undergrowth with Livius, Mucius could see the little bantam cock striding around his defences as though he were Caesar at Alesia. There was a patch of clear ground that would afford the First a good run at the barricade, which is what Settus wanted of course.

'*Primus.*'

Mucius turned to see one of his scouts crawling through the vegetation. 'What is it?'

'As you thought, sir . . . no way around the flanks and Settus has cleared a path to the rear – which'll make that another front anyway. It looks like we'll have to do it the hard way.'

'And no pickets?'

'No, sir. He might as well be sat up there shouting "try it if you think you're hard enough". The prick.'

'All right, good work,' Mucius gave him a nudge. 'Get on back to your mates and get your gear on.'

'I can't believe that he was just sitting here waiting the whole time while we were creeping around expecting an ambush,' Livius noted.

Mucius glared at him. 'You made me think that,' he shot back. 'I should never have listened to you.'

'It's my job to point out angles you've not thought of.' Livius was defensive. 'Your job is to act on the information. It's not my fault if you make the wrong call. From time to time,' he amended.

'Fuck off.'

'Orders?'

'Nothing fancy here,' Mucius jerked his chin at the encampment. 'If we give them time to prepare, it'll go harder for us.'

'Ah. The usual subtle approach then. I'll tell 'em to charge on enemy sighted. Sir.' He slid off through the undergrowth to deliver the orders. Mucius liked Livius – but, gods, the man could be sarcastic.

He turned his attention back to Settus's camp. A frontal assault was always going to be costly in terms of men, but sometimes it just had to be done. Besides which, Settus's amateur geriatrics would not be able to hold up a sustained assault from his men. If Settus thought a ditch and rampart would be enough to tip the odds in his favour, he was sorely mistaken.

After some time, Mucius heard the tramping of booted feet and the cursing of his men as they laboured through the brush. The sight of them breaking cover would scare the shit out of Settus's ragged little band.

Mucius stood as the first line of legionaries shoved their way through the bushes. 'That's it, lads!' he shouted. 'Those bastards have been yanking our chain most of the fucking day. Time to make them pay!' He dragged the thick wooden training sword from the loop at his hip. 'Let's get 'em . . . First of the First . . . CHARGE!'

The men let out a war cry and ran at the defences, hurdling the ditch as they went. Settus was on the rampart above, screaming at his men to loose javelins. Blunted spears arced out, clattering the First as they stalled at the ditch. Mucius cursed as he saw men dropping to the ground left and right. Settus had dug pits that in a real conflict would have been layered with caltrops – each a stout wooden base with a metal barb. They were called 'daisies' by the men and could be as effective at bringing down infantry as horses.

Mucius gritted his teeth as the black-clad judges went around informing the 'planted' that they were out of the game – he was both impressed and annoyed at Settus's forethought. 'Come on!' he shouted, as the First scrambled out of the ditch. Cursing, he picked his way across the ground, trying to avoid the caltrops.

Mucius sensed rather than saw the spear hurtling towards him – sometimes in battle, the luck of the gods prevailed. He hurled himself to the ground and felt it part the transverse horsehair crest of his helmet. Looking up, he saw Settus making a 'wanker' gesture at him, a chip-toothed grin all over his face.

But Settus had problems of his own. The First of the First were hard, experienced men and they were making short work of the Tenth's defences. Mucius hauled himself up. 'That's it, lads!' he exhorted, moving across the ditch. 'Let's get 'em!' The First roared in response and, with a suddenness typical of battle, they were through – and the real fighting started.

It was a game, true enough. But there was pride at stake for the First – they were not going to be bested by the Tenth; even if this task was beneath them, they took to it with gusto, shields smashing forwards, wooden blades pulping noses and bruising flesh.

Mucius scrambled over the barricade. 'First of the First! Form a fucking line, you dozy twats!' he shouted. 'Form line! Let's roll them over. Livius!' He called out to the optio – just in time to see Settus's own Number Two, Slanius, kick Livius in the balls and shove him back over the rampart. Livius rolled down the short hill, clutching himself and flopped into the ditch, out of the fight.

'They're forming up!' he heard Settus scream at the top of his voice. 'Tenth century, form line! Form line!'

To their credit, and Mucius's surprise, the Tenth did a fair job of getting themselves together and locking shields. Just as his own men hit them like a battering ram. The sound of shield crunching on shield was loud – just like a real battle, he thought with a grin. But there was no clash of steel here, just the staccato thudding of wooden weapons and the occasional 'clang' as a man took a blow to the head.

The judges moved up and down the lines, calling out as they decreed men were wounded or killed – and it was clear that the First were going to overwhelm Settus's bastards in the short order. 'Come on,' Mucius urged them on. 'They're going to break . . . BREAK THEM!'

Settus's line was wavering – even if the little upstart himself was fighting like a man possessed, trying to win the battle all on his own. But the class and cohesion of the First was – as Mucius knew it would be – too much for the men of the Tenth. One by one, they were beginning to fall as the First pushed them back.

Settus forced his way across the melee of struggling men, heading straight for him. Mucius grinned and beckoned him on, ready to settle their score.

The high-pitched sound of whistles cut through the fighting, stopping both Mucius and Settus in their tracks. It was over.

Mucius looked behind Settus to see that the Tenth had been completely rolled over – it was senseless to continue the fight as more men could get injured needlessly. Despite wooden swords, there was minor carnage on the battleground and Mucius was surprised to see that the Tenth had done some damage to the First. His men knew they had been in a fight, of that there was no doubt.

He turned his gaze towards Settus and felt the eyes of his men on him. Both the Tenth and First knew what this was really about. The First had beaten Settus's men, but that outcome had never really been in doubt. The real question was who had the toughest commander. 'All right, Settus,' he said, loosening the leather chin-straps of his helmet. 'Get out of your armour and let's settle this.'

Settus's grin was eager. 'Let's get on with it.'

They both began to remove their kit, and as they did so, the injured and unhurt alike began to shout encouragement to their respective champions. It was for the better, and he realised the wisdom of the legate's move. Whatever the outcome of his personal battle with Settus, the men would wear it. There was now even some lighthearted banter going on between the two groups of bloodied and battered soldiers.

Neither Mucius nor Settus waited for the judges to get involved. Once stripped down to their tunics and boots, Mucius looked over at his smaller opponent. 'Ready?' he asked. Settus didn't answer – he just ran at him.

The two men collided, Settus taking Mucius around the waist in a shoulder charge. They crashed to the ground, rolling over and over, each trying to gain purchase on the other. Snarling, Mucius emerged on top and rained down punches on Settus's face. Settus was not done, however – he grabbed Mucius's arm confusing him for a moment. Then, agonising pain lanced through his wrist as Settus bit down hard.

Cursing, Mucius rolled away, as did Settus. The little man was up fast, blood oozing from a cut above his eye. The sound of the men shouting encouragement was loud in Mucius's ears as he closed on the still-eager Settus. Mucius swung a vicious right, aiming to knock Settus out of the fight, but the Tenth's centurion was fast, blocking the blow with his left and countering with a hook of his own that slammed into Mucius's cheekbone and following up with a straight right that crunched the cartilage in his nose. Then Settus was on him, raining in punches.

Mucius covered up like a boxer, taking most of the blows on his forearms. His head cleared and this time it was his turn to barge forward. He stooped and grasped Settus around the waist. Fury roared through him and Mucius straightened his legs, lifting the shouting and cursing Settus up and heaving him back. The Tenth's man crashed to the ground in a heap. Mucius turned fast to see Settus on his hands and knees, about to rise. He lashed out with a kick to the other man's jaw, sending him down before he could get up.

Settus was stunned – Mucius could see it. He waded in with his boots, kicking Settus in the back, the ribs – anywhere he could land leather. The First of the First screamed encouragement and then took up the chant '*Primus, Primus, Primus!*' and beneath it, a collective groan from the Tenth.

He swung a huge kick, but Settus rolled away, his own boot lashing out, kicking the knee of Mucius's standing leg. He crashed to the damp earth on his back, winded, willing himself to get up. But the expected onslaught from Settus did not come. Mucius rose to see him standing off, gasping for breath, his fists raised.

It looked as though he was there for the taking, but Mucius had been in enough bar brawls to see that Settus had something left and was probably trying to lure him in. He too put his fists up and they circled to the screams of advice from their men.

He lashed out a kick, trying to smash Settus's bollocks to sauce, but the little man was too canny, side stepping and then wading in with his fists. Mucius responded in kind – he was the fresher man now – and he was bigger, stronger and tougher than the Tenth's centurion. Once the burst of Hercules's rage had left him, Settus could be picked apart. Mucius softened him up with a right cross that staggered him, but Settus came straight back with a thunderous body punch that almost made Mucius vomit. Not that he had time as Settus's fist crashed into his cheekbone, staggering him. White light flashed in front of his eyes and he swung a punch in desperation, hoping to fend Settus off. He felt his fist hit flesh – and it was enough to halt the other man.

Mucius spat out blood, spirals floating in front of his eyes. Settus was still standing, blood sheeting down his face, staining his chipped teeth. His eyes were gone, but he was still on his feet. Mucius was all but done and he knew it – he had to finish it now. He moved in, opening up with a barrage of punches. Settus took some on the arms and to the face, but still he didn't fall, responding with hooks and straight punches that smashed through Mucius's guard, snapping his head back.

He hit back, a vicious, lancing right that connected with the point of Settus's jaw. The Tenth's centurion staggered, his legs dipping and his guard dropping low. Mucius swung a huge blow with his left, knowing that when it connected, Settus would be put to sleep.

'Wake up! Come on . . . are you all right? He's out of it.'

Mucius opened his eyes to see the faces of Lucius and Settus's optio, Slainius, hovering over him. He felt ill. 'What happened?' he asked, his voice sounding as though someone else was using it.

Lucius rolled his eyes. 'You walked onto a right hook.'

'They didn't call him the hardest man in the Second Augusta for no reason,' Slainius added. 'That's what he keeps telling us, anyway. Can you get up?'

Mucius felt utterly drained and all he wanted to do was lie there and let the pain sink into the damp earth. He looked to one side to see the Tenth celebrating, shouting and cheering, some of them lifting Settus aloft – which looked painful. To the other side, the First of the First, looking, by and large, taken aback. That wouldn't last long, he knew – they'd be eager for payback soon enough. Mucius had lost the fight and had to take it on the chin – literally and figuratively. He sighed. 'Yeah.'

Slainius hauled him to his feet. 'Good fight, *Primus*,' he nodded and walked off to his own century.

'Unlucky,' Livius shrugged.

The men of both centuries had gone quiet now, seeing he was back on his feet. He steadied himself, drawing in a lungful of air. 'Centurion Sallustius Secundus Settus!' he shouted. 'On parade!'

Settus, now set down by his men, looked left and right, unsure what to make of it. But he was a soldier. He marched out, stood before his superior, snapped to attention and saluted. 'Yes, *Primus*,' he responded, dark eyes glittering with supressed anger. He suspected, Mucius guessed, that he was about to be punished for his victory.

'At ease,' Mucius gave him leave to stand loose. 'Your men fought well!' He invoked his parade ground lungs, ensuring that his voice would carry. 'Stood against the finest in this legion, holding their ground against better men. There's something to be said for men that fight when they know they can't win. What do you reckon, First?' His men pounded on their shields in appreciation; it was an art that Mucius had down pat, able to praise the winners and the losers in the same breath.

'Thank you, *Primus*.'

Mucius regarded him. 'And *you* fought well. A little too well for my liking!' This raised some guffaws amongst both sets of men. 'We've had our differences, you and me, your men and mine. We've met in the field and sorted it out. As men should. I would put it behind us, if you would.'

Settus nodded. 'Yes, *Primus*.' Mucius didn't think he meant it, but Settus – like Mucius himself – realised that Valerian was right. The legion came first. 'Good!' he shouted. 'Good. Then your lads and mine will have a few drinks tonight. At *our* end of the camp. First round on First!' The Tenth cheered at that and, given that they had won the day, the First looked magnanimous enough.

Settus met his eye, nodded once and saluted before making his way back to his men.

Brundisium, Southern Italia

Brundisium was just as chaotic as Lysandra remembered. The incessant buzz of a thousand conversations assaulted her ears, punctuated frequently by shouting, laughter and cursing. The thump of bare feet on wooded gangplanks, the crash of broken freight (followed by the roars of enraged captains and shrieks of punished sailors) coupled with the overriding stench of seaweed was a strange balm after weeks and months in the city.

Or perhaps it was that after a period of inertia, she was once again moving forward – albeit in a direction she could not have foreseen. She glanced at Illeana who was taking in the chaos around her whilst Kleandrias pushed would-be purchasers away.

Having received Lysandra's promise that she could join her on the 'Dacian adventure' as she had taken to calling it, the Roman had attached herself to Lysandra's coterie like a barnacle to a ship. To be fair to her, Illeana was no passenger – she added funds to their cause and, truth be told, Lysandra was coming to like her.

But there was a price – both Illeana's fame and her beauty. If someone could possess too much of a good thing, it was her. She could strike down man and woman, beggar and emperor with her eyes. Lysandra thought that if she herself walked with Athene, then the Roman gladiatrix must be touched by Aphrodite. But this could only be more evidence that she had indeed been chosen by the gods

135

to fulfil this mission. If Athene and Aphrodite were at odds in Ilium, they would not be so in Dacia.

She allowed herself a moment of fancy, imagining that she was a female Jason with Illeana as her Heracles, accruing a group of heroes to travel with her on an epic adventure to save her homeland. She looked across at Murco who was picking his nose as they walked; feeling her eyes on him, he tried to pretend that he was in fact only scratching. In any event, it brought Lysandra crashing back to reality.

It was slow going as the group were buffeted this way and that by the crowd, but finally Lysandra spied their destination. The *Galene* was moored, one of a thousand other ships in the dock but Lysandra's heart lifted at the sight of it. *Her*, she corrected mentally. Her captain, Bedros, was leaning over the side of the ship, forearms resting on her stout wooden beam. He laughed aloud as he saw her approach and then disappeared from view.

'Friend of yours?' Illeana arched an eyebrow as, moments later, Bedros was charging down the gangplank towards them.

Lysandra had no time to respond as Bedros was upon her, lifting her up in his altogether too hairy embrace, kissing both her cheeks. 'Lysandra the Spartan,' he said.

Lysandra was prepared to indulge his unseemly display – truth be told, she had a place in her heart for the merchant captain. 'Bedros,' she grinned. 'It is good to see you again. These are my companions – Kleandrias, Cappa, Murco and . . .'

'The *Aesalon Nocturna*,' Bedros identified. Illeana inclined her head as though being recognised was her due and Lysandra tried not to grind her teeth in annoyance.

'Aemilia Illeana,' the *Gladiatrix Prima* favoured Bedros with a smile.

'Come aboard, come aboard,' the captain beckoned them. 'All has been made ready,' he added. 'We can sail anytime.'

'Sooner than later, then,' Lysandra said. 'There is much to be done and I have little time to do it.'

'Then we'll set sail!' Bedros laughed and rubbed his hands together. He turned away and began bawling at his men, many of whom Lysandra recognised from her first voyage on the *Galene*.

'We don't really like boats,' Cappa whispered to Lysandra as the captain made off.

'The *Galene* is a ship,' Lysandra corrected, remembering that Bedros took umbrage at this kind of elementary mistake.

'Huh. Who cares?' Murco put in. 'You can't trust the sea,' he added.

'Most sailors call it "The Great Green", Lysandra informed him, pleased that she could impress her nautical knowledge on them all.

'I don't care what they call it,' Murco looked around as though he could be heard by all and lowered his voice. 'It's dangerous.'

'If you know a better way to Sparta, I would like to hear it,' Kleandrias said. 'Are you scared of a little water?'

'No,' Murco lied. 'We're just saying it's a big risk is all. Right, Cappa?'

'Right.'

'Enough,' Lysandra said. 'Bedros will have made all the offerings to the gods that are necessary to protect us from the wrath of Poseidon. *Neptune*,' she added before her bodyguards pretended they didn't know who she was talking about.

The two looked at each other. 'But *you* used to be a *priestess*,' Cappa said. 'Still are, really. You could – you know, add some extra prayers. Athene favours you.'

Lysandra could not help herself. 'Yes, but she and her uncle Poseidon are not friends. Invoking Athene in Poseidon's realm could be seen as a slight – I have made that mistake before.'

'What happened?' Murco's eyes were wide.

'The first time I set sail the ship sank. The second time we were attacked by pirates.'

'And the third time?'

'This is the third time,' she grinned and clapped him on the shoulder. 'Let us hope that Poseidon has had his fill of me.' She moved off, leaving both men staring after her. There was silence for a moment before Kleandrias and Illeana erupted into gales of laughter.

Despite the fears of her two bodyguards, the clouds did not darken nor the seas turn to mountains when the *Galene* was on open water. The ship dipped and rose on the waves, causing both Cappa and Murco to vomit over the side, their superstitious apprehension lost in the misery of seasickness. Even the ever-redoubtable Kleandrias's skin was slick with sweat and he had a grey pallor; he was bearing illness with stoicism and determination – better than Lysandra herself had. She recalled being in the same position as Cappa and Murco, hurling her guts into the Great Green and looking just as undignified.

Lysandra made her way aft – it was one of the few places on board where any kind of solitude was available to her. She looked out over the water, her mind churning like the white water in the ship's wake. It was happening.

You will raise your shield in defence of your homeland. The words of the goddess echoed through her mind. She recalled an earlier vision: that of blood on her hands. She had considered her achievements as a gladiatrix the fulfilment of that message, but the truth of it was that there was more blood to spill. And not only her own.

'Thinking deep thoughts?' Kleandrias came and stood next to her; it was uninvited and rude of him, but Lysandra guessed that he wanted to talk to take his mind of his seasickness.

'Yes,' she answered. 'It is heavy responsibility that I bear, Kleandrias. All my life I have served the goddess. I cannot remember a time when I have not,' as she spoke she realised the truth in her words. 'And now . . .'

'And now you sail to your destiny.'

'Yes. The Temple . . . Balbus's *ludus* . . . the battle for Domitian . . . it has all been to prepare me for this.'

'The goddess has marked a path for you, Lysandra. She has chosen wisely.'

138

Lysandra smiled at him, grateful for his support. 'She offered me a choice, you know. She said that I had earned my place in Elysium. Or I could get back my life and defend my homeland. Our homeland.'

'Lysandra,' Kleandrias turned her to face him. It was, she felt, over-familiar of him, but she allowed it. 'Duty, honour, service to the Athene and Sparta herself are what defines you. That is why you were chosen. And that is why we will win. You are . . . the best of women.' He looked at her with a strange intensity that she had not seen before, his hard hands tightening on her biceps as he did so. The fervour of the goddess, she surmised.

'Thank you, Kleandrias.'

'We will be home soon, Lysandra,' he said – and for a moment, he had the look of a man who was about to kiss her, but he blinked and his lips went tight as though he was embarrassed by his words. Kleandrias looked into her eyes for a moment longer before turning away and making his way back to Cappa and Murco who had – for now – ceased their puking.

Lysandra turned her eyes back to the Great Green. Despite Kleandrias's words, her heart was heavy with trepidation. And not a little fear of what was to come.

Sarmatia

'It still does not sit well with me, Teuta.' Sorina whispered in the dark quiet of their tent. Outside, the sound of music and laughter was loud – as it always was when the tribes gathered in peace.

Teuta sighed. 'It must be this way. You said it yourself – many, many times on the way here.'

Sorina took the barb. 'I did, didn't I? Perhaps to convince myself. But Decabalus plays a dangerous game here. Or, I should say, he has me playing a dangerous game.'

Teuta did not answer, leaving Sorina to her thoughts. It was the way of things lately. Teuta was not as she had been in Balbus's *ludus*; things were simpler there, but since their return to Dacia, Sorina had reclaimed her mantle leaving Teuta with little honour, little to do and little reputation other than that of Sorina's lover.

They had ridden long and hard, leaving Dacia as Decabalus had bade them, travelling north, taking his messages to the wilder tribes of Sarmatia. They had come at Sorina's word – her voice was second only to the King of the Dacians. Her life had many strange tributaries, she thought. From Clan Chief to the basest of the base – slave and gladiatrix. But then, to rise to the top, she became queen among them: *Gladiatrix Prima*. And now, free, she was more than Clan Chief. She was the proxy of the King of Kings. And because of that, the Sarmatians had answered the call – as they had done before.

'Sorina!' A man's voice sounded from outside their tent. 'The Chiefs will see you now.'

'You must do what you think is right, Sorina,' Teuta said.

Sorina smiled. 'That's what I'm afraid of,' she said and rose to her feet. 'I shall be back soon.'

'And I shall wait – as always.'

Sorina was about to offer her a sweet word, but Teuta turned away. She sighed and left the tent to see a bodyguard of three waiting for her. Big men, tough, long-haired and raw-boned – they were still what the Dacians had once been, she thought to herself: people of the plains, they rode the endless grass seas, fighting, living, loving and dying with only an earthen *kurgan* to mark their passing.

140

The life of the encampment swam through Sorina's senses – the smell of meat on open fires, voices raised in passionate song. Here and there, a shout of anger and the crack of a fist into flesh; she looked around to see the campfires stretching far into the night; from a hilltop, it must look as though the stars themselves had fallen.

She was led to the main hall at the heart of the encampment – a semi-permanent structure of wood and earth. Guards were posted, but like everyone else they were enjoying a cup of ale and a talk. The men assigned to her stopped and motioned her in. Sorina thanked them and made her way inside.

It was like a scaled-down version of the camp inside; the addition of a roof doing nothing to dampen the celebratory atmosphere. Herein were the lords, the mightiest warriors and shield-women, clan chiefs and their partners. It was the very antithesis of Rome with its rules on separation: here, men and women sat together as equals, their status earned by the sharpness of their blades or their minds. Prowess and wisdom were not assumed to be purely male qualities and this was manifestly clear in the woman on the high throne at the far end of the hall.

She was tall, big-boned and strong limbed, her dark hair razored short at the sides and spiked with lime; her keen grey eyes found Sorina's own the moment she came into the room and her acknowledgement was a slight smile. Around her were men and women of the Sarmatians, the Getae and even a few Scythians.

The Clan Chief let her stand in the hall for long moments and Sorina tolerated it, knowing that this was all part of the game. She was in another wolf's lair now and, if she wanted to run with this pack, she would have to prove herself. Sorina returned the woman's smile with a half-grin of her own. Even with the lost years in the *ludus*, she'd been at the game longer than this puppy.

At length, the woman raised her hand and, after some time, the music, talk and laughter stopped. All eyes turned to Sorina.

'You are Sorina,' the woman spoke. 'Clan Chief and Right Hand of the Lord Diurpaneus – now called Decabalus.'

'Now called,' Sorina's voice rang true in the still, 'for his victory over five Roman legions. Even now their Eagles decorate his halls, the scalps of their generals hang from his warhorse.'

'I am Amagê – I speak for the Sarmatians gathered here. Other tribes too have lent me their voice for this meeting.' She let that hang for a moment. 'I speak for all of them.'

Sorina was impressed. 'Your prowess must be great indeed,' she acknowledged.

Amagê laughed. 'Oh, it is. *But that is not why they chose me,*' she added in Latin. Then she said something else in a language that Sorina recognised but could not understand. Amagê stopped. 'You have no Greek, then?'

Sorina gritted. 'I have no Greek. I hate Greeks.'

'And Romans, I've heard tell.'

'There's truth in that,' Sorina agreed.

Amagê's grey gaze was piercing and Sorina knew that her mettle was being tested here. 'Why? Because they made you a slave and whored you to fight naked for their pleasure.'

Sorina was surprised at how Amagê's words affected her. For the briefest of moments, her years in Balbus's *ludus* burned bright as the sun in her mind's eye. The good times with Eirianwen, Stick and Catuvolcos. And then Lysandra. Always Lysandra, raven haired, long-limbed and strange-eyed. And evil-hearted. Sorina blinked to see Amagê's eyes still on her.

She had the magic, Sorina realised. Eirianwen had the sight, like her Druid father and this woman too had been touched by the gods. Sorina cleared her throat, aware that the silence lengthened about her. 'What you say is true,' she replied. 'I was made to fight for their pleasure. Do you know why?' her pale brown eyes swept the room; she was given no answer. 'You?' she pointed at Getae clan lord. 'You?' this to a Scythian. 'No? I was captured. Fighting them.

Fighting, it would appear, for you. I'll hazard that very few among you have wet their sword in Roman blood.' Many dark looks were thrown her way.

Amagê, however, merely smiled. 'Your prowess is well known,' she acknowledged. 'But what need have we to fight Romans? We have no quarrel with them.'

'Other Sarmatians and Getae think otherwise,' Sorina replied. 'They ride at the side of Decabalus.'

'Other Sarmatians and Getae are fools, then. Let Decabalus lord it over them if he wishes. He does not rule here.'

'Yet you still gather at his behest to hear my words?'

Amagê's lips lifted in a half-smile – she was enjoying herself, Sorina realised. 'His deeds give his words weight,' she admitted. 'But as I say: we have no quarrel with Rome, nor does Decabalus rule in the north. And we're hearing your words at his *request*. He would not send Sorina of the Dacians unless he wanted something. What does he want? As if we didn't already know.'

'Your swords,' Sorina said. 'Your bows. Your horses. Your courage. You say you have no quarrel with Rome? I once thought as you did. I remember – when I was young . . .' She looked meaning-fully at Amagê who could not have seen more than twenty-five summers, ' . . . that our elders counselled thus. And they were wrong. Rome is a ravenous wolf that will eat the world. Her hunger will never be sated – because for Rome to endure, the beast must be fed! Rome needs armies – armies need to be paid for. To pay requires booty, booty requires conquest, conquest requires land. You have no quarrel with Rome?' She threw up her hands. 'Rome will have one with you if Decabalus is not successful.'

'And yet, the great Decabalus has already defeated five of their best legions,' Amagê responded. '*Their Eagles decorate his halls and the scalps of their generals hang from his saddle.* What need of the great man have we . . . barbarians of the north?'

Sorina hesitated. She approached a crucial point in the game. A wrong word here could end her cause. Perhaps her cause *should* end. Decabalus did not need these warriors – he wanted them to fight and die so that they might bend the knee to him more easily. Thin their numbers – and give them a share of his glory in return for their vassalage. But with these tribes . . . victory was assured. Honour warred with hatred of Rome in Sorina's heart – and hatred won as she knew it would.

'He doesn't need you,' she said – and it caused a ripple of shock amongst them. Talk began to babble, cut short when Amagê raised her hand. 'He *wants* you. As do I.'

'You?' Amagê raised an eyebrow. 'Why?'

'My hatred of Rome is well known,' she met Amagê's grey gaze with the pale brown of her own. 'Some can see that clearer than others. I would have you ride with us because your strength will ensure our victory. Rome cannot endure two defeats – not any more. If we win, fire will ignite across her borders – burn down her gates and leave the way open for *us*. Rome has vast lands and her innards are soft. You could make kings of all of your people on her wealth.' That got a response from most – the thought of hard gold always did.

'But more than that,' she pushed on, 'there is the future to think of. Your sons and daughters – their sons and daughters and so on through the ages . . . would you have them know only the name of Decabalus, conqueror of Rome? Sorina, the woman who hated Rome and brought it to its knees? Or would you have the bards sing of your names too? So that your descendants will visit your *kurgan* and tell *your* story – not a Dacian one?'

She was going to say more, but her voice was drowned out by shouts and cheers. Beer-fuelled aggression and lust for gold coupled with the promise of fame were a winning combination. Amagê was looking at her from under a hooded gaze, a smile playing about her lips. Then, the Clan Chief raised her cup and in that moment, the promise was made.

It was a black victory; the deceit in which she was complicit sickened her to the core.

Sparta

It had been many years, Lysandra realised.

Too many.

She could have returned many times, but had baulked at it. There were reasons, of course. She twisted her lips in self-reproach: reasons or excuses? It no longer mattered. She was *home*.

Home. She had once denied it, saying that she could not return here. But now, as she overlooked the city, her heart was full when she had not realised it was empty. It would be unseemly to shed a tear and this was not the Spartan way – but Lysandra had to bite her lip to stem the gamut of emotions running through her. By her side, Kleandrias also had set his jaw tight and she knew that he felt the same.

Cappa, Murco and Illeana were with them, hanging back. For once, the two bodyguards refrained from comment, allowing she and Kleandrias a moment to take in the city below.

It had not changed at all, Lysandra realised, recalling her last sight of it – looking over her shoulder as she rode away – a Mission Priestess riding to a Roman Legion. The Fates, she thought, have had their fun with her since then.

She looked east and fancied she could see the outline of her parents' smallholding, and in her mind's eye she could see the gate, the *helots* at work in the field. She heard the sound of her mother's voice, singing the *Hymn to Athene*. Her father's laughter. She had been a child when she had left for the temple and perhaps she was only imagining what she thought she remembered.

'So this is Sparta,' Illeana had nudged her horse forward to stand by Lysandra. 'I had not expected it to look so modern.'

'I suppose not,' Lysandra agreed. 'I imagine that everyone still thinks of it as it was in Leonidas's day. But that was more than five hundred years ago now.'

'But the people are still as they were then,' Kleandrias put in. 'Most of them anyway.'

Illeana favoured him with a smile. 'This is true. I have spoken to people who have visited here. It is a popular place with Romans to take a vacation – there are many cities in Greece that have ancient things in them, but none that live in the ancient way. I have heard it said it is like living history.' This last she directed at Lysandra who was clad in her armour and scarlet war-cloak, her full-faced Corinthian helm tucked under her arm.

'Let us be about it then,' Lysandra said, placing the helmet over her head, enjoying the languid weight of its red horsehair crest.

'Impressive,' Murco commented.

'Shut up and get in line,' Cappa cut him off. 'We ride in her wake.'

There was no need to be nervous. Yet, as she rode through the city, her stomach churned and sweat beaded and crawled down her back. Even if Sparta was home, she had never really known it. Her childhood had been spent cloistered in the temple, her youth with the Fifth Macedonian Legion and then on the sands at Halicarnassus. She knew everything about her city – but had never lived as part of it.

People stared at her as she rode past, mouths agape at her spear and her war finery. The Priestesses of Athene could still inspire awe, then; even the Roman soldiers on guard duty did not stop her or request she hand over her weapons as was common law. This religious tolerance was one of the reasons for their success as an empire, she knew. All Rome wanted was land, taxes and a nominal acknowledgement of the Emperor's supposed divinity; everything in a conquered territory was left much as it was. Not that Sparta had been conquered, of course. She was unique. But, looking around, it was clear that the city through an adult's eyes was not as anachronistic as she had thought.

It was very much a small Roman town, replete with forum and theatre. If Sparta had never been conquered, she had certainly been subjugated. Much like herself, Lysandra thought. She lived away from here, fought in Roman tournaments and was in the service of a Roman governor – even if Athene *had* willed it. Then again, the goddess was pragmatic.

'Look there!' Kleandrias pointed, steering his horse to the left – annoying pedestrians as he did so. He dismounted and turned, grinning all over his face. 'Lysandra, look!'

And there it was. Lysandra slid out of the saddle and approached the plinth. It read: This statue of Lysandra the Spartan, Gladiatrix Prima of Asia Minor was raised by the Spartans and paid for by L. Balbus.

'I told you,' Kleandrias said.

Lysandra could not help but smile, recalling her old *lanista*, Balbus; typical of him to mention that he had paid for it. The statue was tall, depicting her holding a sword aloft, her face serene. It looked nothing like her, of course – she wondered briefly who had modelled it. The woman could be here, now, she realised, walking by and wondering why a priestess was admiring the work.

'You will live forever now.'

Lysandra turned to look at Illeana, hearing a note of wistfulness in her voice. 'It is not the first work on me,' she said. 'There is another, commissioned by Trajanus. It is a frieze, smaller than this, though.'

147

'There are none of me,' Illeana replied. She didn't add 'even though I defeated you', but it was implicit.

Lysandra was surprised she felt no irritation at this. 'That is probably because no artisan could do you justice,' she said.

Illeana smiled her smile, and Lysandra felt the warmth of it. 'We should go?'

They paused at the foot of the hill that led to Sparta's acropolis. 'I must go on alone from here,' Lysandra said, her voice sounding disembodied from within her helmet.

'I will take the others and find us lodgings,' Kleandrias offered. 'The Last Stand is an inn of good repute.'

Lysandra nodded and turned her horse's head away. She swallowed; this was somehow more nerve-wracking than waiting at the Gate of Life in the arena. She rode up towards the temple. It was no longer such an imposing place to her eyes – the Deiopolis was many times its size – but still, as the shadow of the walls fell upon her and the helmeted heads of the guards tilted in her direction, she could not suppress the shudder that crawled down her spine.

'Halt!' one of the girls on the wall shouted down to her. Lysandra recalled that duty well – and in her time, no one unannounced had come to the gates. 'State your business!'

'I am Lysandra of Sparta,' she called back. 'A Mission Priestess. I return . . . home for a time. I would speak with the Matriarch.'

'Wait there!' The girl disappeared from view and the other priestesses on the ramparts fingered their spears as they looked down at her. She heard shouts from within. She had known her arrival would cause a stir; the temple had few unannounced visitors and she knew she must now be the most famous priestess of all: she who had gone out into the world and gained honour fighting in the name of the goddess. She hoped Deianara would be there, Halkyone and Melantha too, and wondered if and how they had changed.

The girl returned to the walls. 'You will wait!' she shouted down. 'The Matriarch comes at no one's beckoning.'

And that, Lysandra supposed, was to be expected.

Afternoon wore into evening as she stood vigil. She would not give them the satisfaction of removing her helmet or war gear. She had dismounted knowing full well that a dignified display of Spartan stoicism could be ruined by the horse farting or becoming agitated.

At length, the great doors of the temple began to open and, in the shadows of her helmet, Lysandra smiled. Her heart beat fast in her chest and her mouth was dry – again, she was reminded of the Gate of Life.

An honour guard stood, holding torches to keep the dark at bay. They marched out towards her; like herself, they were armed and armoured, faces and identities obfuscated by shadows and bronze. There were no words; they flanked her and waited for her to step forwards.

Lysandra took a deep breath and walked into the home of her childhood; it was unseemly, but she was all but overcome by the emotion of it. Her eyes flicked here and there as she entered the temple, the great statue of the goddess dominating the courtyard, the *palaestra,* and of course the whipping post. She could not stop her head from titling towards her old barracks – and memoires of it flooded over her like the tide.

To her left and right, the priestesses had assembled and before her, on the steps of the temple, the Matriarch awaited, Halkyone by her side, her expression taut and stern. Lysandra stopped at the steps and knelt.

'Rise and show your face.' The Matriarch's voice was weaker than she remembered – but then she was ancient now. Lysandra stood, removing her helmet, her eyes lifting to meet those of the old woman. 'Speak then, Lysandra.'

Lysandra gathered herself. Everything that had happened to her since the ship had been wrecked, all her trails, her achievements – all of it had led her here. The hand of the goddess had guided her home, and Athene did nothing without purpose.

'Nine years ago,' she began, 'you chose me to be the Mission Priestess – the youngest ever,' she added. 'I have travelled far – to Asia Minor and to Rome herself. I was made a slave . . . a *slave*, but I honoured the goddess still. Through the strength of my arms and my faith in her, I triumphed. I gained my freedom and I have raised a temple to her and all the gods.

'But my Mission is not complete. I thought to live out my days in a temple of my own building. Grow old there. But this is not the Will of Athene. No,' she paused. 'She speaks to me still and when I hung on a thread between life and death, she offered me a choice! Elysium . . . or that I would "lift my shield in defence of my homeland". I now know the truth of her words.

'War is coming, sisters. From the north. You know that the Romans were defeated there by Decabalus. They plan to strike back against him – but it is a gambit. If they are defeated, the road to Hellas is open to the barbarians and they will fall upon this land with fire and fury.

'The Romans came to me and asked me to lead men – and women – in battle against the foe. And this is why I am here – my Mission . . . my journey . . . all of it was to bring me home. I call on you now, sisters. As we did so long ago against Pyrrhus, so we must do again against this Decabalus and his . . . allies. It is time for us to march out against the enemies of the goddess and raise our spears in her honour. In doing so, we glorify her and we defend not only Sparta but all Hellas.'

Lysandra fell silent – and the silence endured. The Matriarch regarded her, expressionless – but she saw Halkyone's mouth twitch in approval and she was proud.

'You dare to come here, Lysandra?' The Matriarch said. 'You, who have been gone for nearly a decade? You, who have whored yourself for your Roman masters? You, who has built monuments not for the glory of the goddess but for her own self-adulation? They tell me that there is a statue of you – *gladiatrix* – in the city below; that the fools in the council allowed it because some rich Roman demanded it. Your former *owner*.' She laughed, a harsh, wheezing sound from the cracked bellows of her lungs. 'Owner. Yes. Last I remember, no Spartan called herself slave. No Spartan would permit it. I would rather die than submit – unlike you, whore, who would cavort naked for the pleasure of a Roman mob.

'You always were a vainglorious child,' she went on, each syllable she uttered burning into Lysandra's mind. 'I indulged it – this was *my* hubris, my hope that a child in my charge did indeed hear the voice of the goddess. And here, standing before me, is the result of it. You are an abomination, Lysandra. Your overweening vanity insults me, this sisterhood, the city of Sparta and the goddess herself.' She looked Lysandra in the eye. 'I cast you out! From this Sisterhood and from our *polis*. You are *xenos* – a foreigner – now, Lysandra. Halkyone – take her cloak and her weapons! She is not Spartan, she is not of this temple and she has no rights to any of it.' Halkyone hesitated, her expression aghast. 'Do it!' the Matriarch shouted; years of ingrained obedience to command kicked in. Halkyone walked down the steps to Lysandra.

The words of the Matriarch swirled through her like a bitter gale. How could she have been so wrong?

Halkyone approached her, her lips pressed into a thin line, eyes narrowed. Lysandra could read the shock in them, the disbelief. She did not resist as her old teacher tugged the scarlet war-cloak from her back. She herself cast the helmet to one side, the impact of iron on stone too loud in the stillness of the temple. She gave up her spear but when Halkyone reached out to pull her sword from its scabbard, Lysandra's own hand went to it. Her eyes met those of the older woman and she shook her head slightly.

'No one will have my sword,' she said, over Halkyone's shoulder to the face of the Matriarch. 'Unless they can take it from me.'

'Does your arrogance know no bounds?' The Matriarch screeched from the steps.

Something inside Lysandra snapped then. She walked past Halkyone and placed her foot on the bottom step. '*My* arrogance,' she said. 'The arrogance is yours, old woman. You, who has not set foot in the real world since before you bled as a young girl. You, who hide the truth of what was from those that should know it. I understand why.' She heard her voice echo around the *palaestra*. 'I understand that we must preserve the history and the myth of Sparta. I know that we are pre-eminent, our blood makes us better than all others. But I had expected you – of all people – to recognise when the goddess called. In this temple, we train for war. War is coming. And Sparta, for all her courage, will be laid low if we do not meet this threat. I fight in the name of Athene herself . . .'

'Silence!' the old woman all but screamed it. 'You are cursed, Lysandra. I curse you – in the name of Athene – I curse you. May her hand guide the furies to rend your soul.'

Lysandra looked up at the great statue of the goddess and then to the lined, ancient face of her Matriarch of the Temple. 'Curse me?' she hissed. 'Curse *me*! You do not have the right or the authority to do so.' She heard the women of the temple gasp at her words. Lysandra advanced up the steps towards the Matriarch. 'Athene!' she shouted. 'Hear me, Oh goddess. Hear me who has served you in blood. Hear me, Lysandra *of Sparta* who has honoured you and raised a temple by her own hand. I beg of you . . . strike me down now if I am not your Handmaiden. Strike me down!' She stopped half way up the steps, her ice-coloured eyes burning with anger. 'You, Matriarch, are cursed,' she spat. 'I curse *you*. In her name,' she gestured at the statue. 'You cannot unmake who I am, old woman.'

She thought for a moment that the Matriarch would take a step back, but she did not; she had more steel in her than that. 'You place much stock by your sword arm, Lysandra,' she said. 'And you bandy curses before the goddess in her own temple. We shall see who is cursed.'

Lysandra baulked then, seeing with clarity into the old woman's thoughts. 'Still your tongue, Matriarch! Do not say it! Do not. You accuse me of arrogance and vainglory? Do not let your own spill the blood of my sisters.'

'They are not your sisters, *xenos*. You have offended me and the goddess in her own house. The goddess demands to see you punished . . .'

'I will not fight here.'

'Then you are doubly cursed as a coward too.'

That stung. 'Do not speak of matters of which you have no understanding, Matriarch. I will go — with sadness in my heart. I believed that we, the sisters of this temple, would lead others in defence of Hellas — as warriors of Athene. I have learned now that you preside over nothing but a shallow reminder of how great we once were.'

She turned her back on the old woman and made her way down the steps, fury flowing through her like strong wine.

'You will not leave!' the Matriarch shouted. 'Bar her way! And strike her down if she resists.'

The assembled priestesses flowed like water into a phalanx, an impenetrable wall of bronze and iron. It was beautiful to see — the precision that she so admired now turning its spears on her. Lysandra turned back to the Matriarch. 'You old fool! *Please*. Do not do this!'

'Deianara!' the Matriarch's voice rang out. 'Step forward.' She held Lysandra's gaze for long moments.

And smiled in triumph.

Moesia

The night – as nights invariably were in Moesia – was cold. Valerian hated the cold and he could well sympathise with the legionaries that had pulled guard duty on such a wretched night. As he empathised, he felt the first drops of rain hit his head and cursed under breath, now regretting his decision to not wear his helmet.

He made it his habit to walk the camp at night – he had done it when he was a tribune and saw no reason to stop now that he was a legate.

Legate.

His lips twisted at the thought. He was hardly that, but at least – thanks be to the gods – the legion had stopped sliding into anarchy and had begun to perform well. Better than well.

He climbed the steps that led to the rampart and strolled along, coming to the first sentry, who snapped to attention. 'Sorry, sir,' the man said. He looked tired and well over forty. 'I know who you are, but centurion's orders – password please.'

'What's your unit, soldier?'

'Tenth of the Tenth, sir.'

'One of Settus's . . . men.' He was going to say 'lads' but that would have been disingenuous.

'I have that honour, legate,' the man said and Valerian couldn't tell if he was being sarcastic.

'Your name?'

'Caballo, legate.'

Valerian recalled that Settus held this man in high regard – or at least, considered him a force for good in the century. 'Good to see you on alert, Caballo. Carry on.' He made to move off.

'I'll still be needing that password, sir,' Caballo said.

Valerian raised his eyebrows. This was all about procedure and he was impressed that – despite their genial conversation – Caballo was sticking to the letter of the law. He thought for a moment, recalling the centurion's meeting of earlier where such things were set. Of course, Settus had chosen it. 'Ah yes,' he said. 'Ugly cocksucker.'

Caballo nodded, his smile a white slash on his face in the darkness. 'Can't say as I've ever noticed an ugly cocksucker myself, sir.'

'How so?'

'I've always got me eyes shut.'

Valerian chuckled and slapped the man on the shoulder before moving on. He made his way along the ramparts – it took almost an hour a night to complete the circuit – a singularly unpleasant duty in the rain. On the other hand, he didn't have to stand out all night in it like the sentries did. What was two hours of his time to listen to their jokes, their complaints, their ambitions? It was good generalship, he had read. And, at least if he didn't feel like a proper legate, he could at least give an impression of one to his men. It seemed to be working: he didn't often read utter contempt for him in their eyes, even if that could have been attributed to their centurions beating the respect into them.

It was colder still when he made it back to the *praetorium*; gods, he was looking forward to getting out of his wet clothes! 'Not long to go before your changeover, lads,' he said to the two sentries on guard outside his command tent. They had the good grace to smile, though Valerian was sure they hated him for going into the warm.

And it *was* warm in the tent. Valerian desperately wanted to just

155

lie on his bunk and rest, but the slightly painful ritual of armour-removal needed to be performed. Whoever designed the *lorica segmentata* was a genius, he decided, but still – one could never get the stuff off or on without losing a few layers of skin. Rather than a leather cuirass, Valerian had opted to wear the standard issue kit because he felt that the men would warm to him more if he did. Still, legionaries had their mates to help them out of the stuff. Having untied the leather thongs that held the front of the strips closed, he shrugged the armour back as far as it would go before it wedged – defiant – at his triceps. Next was the humiliating jumping up and down routine to get it to slide down his arms; a quick turn and he snagged it by the neck piece before it hit the floor with a crash.

Neatly done.

He hung it on its stand, relieved to be out of it for a few hours at least. He disrobed as fast as he could, ruing the state of his wet boots. He stuffed them with wool, hoping they would soak out by morning. Of course, as legate he could have someone do all this for him – but Valerian considered that it probably wouldn't send the right message to the men.

Finally out of wet clothes, he dropped a dry tunic over his head and went to his desk to review orders and correspondence.

'Sir!' A sentry's voice.

'What is it?'

'Visitor, sir – requests audience.'

'At this hour?' Valerian was at once irked and intrigued. Of course, his rhetorical question got the standard military response: silence. 'Send him in.' *Fucking couriers*, he thought.

The man – clearly *not* a courier – entered, rain plastered and doing his best to look unfazed by the filth of the northern weather. Valerian rose as the man saluted, eyes narrowing. It took a moment, but he recognised him.

'Hail, legate,' the man said. 'I am . . .'

'Quinctilius Spurius Nolus,' Valerian rose and greeted him,

extending his arm – and noting the confusion in Nolus's eyes. Of course, Nolus would not remember him.

'Forgive me, sir,' Nolus stuttered, now thinking he had made a blunder.

'You did me a kindness a few years ago,' Valerian smiled. Nolus looked mortally embarrassed that he did not recall the incident and Valerian pushed on. 'Your slave . . . Tancredus . . . He was once mine. I came to your house . . .'

'Which was once yours – yes!' realisation dawned on Nolus's face. 'You were . . .'

' . . . Different then,' Valerian brushed over Nolus's discomfiture. 'Fortuna has smiled on me once again,' he added. 'At least – I hope she has. Please, allow me to get you some wine.' He moved to his desk and poured. 'It's not the best, but . . .'

'When on campaign, sir,' Nolus finished, scooping up the cup and draining it in a single swallow. He winced. 'Not bad.'

Valerian chuckled. 'Very politic, Tribune Nolus. I'll have dry clothes and some food brought.'

Valerian allowed himself to indulge in some small talk as they ate but he was burning with curiosity. As soon as their dishes were cleared, he cut to it. 'You're not here to sample the delights of the table,' he said.

'No, sir,' Nolus agreed. 'I've been 'here' for a few days now.' He cleared his throat, clearly uncomfortable. 'My orders – direct from Iulianus – were to observe and assess your men.'

Valerian did not show his pique at this; he had almost expected it. Even if Frontinus had raised him from nothing, it did not necessarily follow that his peers would consider him anything but. He forced a smile. 'And what is your assessment?'

Nolus shrugged. 'You command a legion. From afar, it looks no different to any other. Only up close can you see the calibre of men in your charge. They're hardly the pick of any crop . . .' he held up a hand, ' . . . but that is no fault of yours. I see that, despite their disadvantages, they are more than capable. It is my opinion that – with the material to hand – you have excelled.'

Despite himself, Valerian was pleased. No, he realised. More than that – he was *relived*; indeed he felt a sense of vindication. Even if his peers looked down on him, it was gratifying to know that his men – and by proxy, he himself – had made the grade.

'I will make my report,' Nolus said.

'Not tonight, unless you have orders to get right back,' Valerian was feeling like the soul of magnanimity. 'It's a filthy night. Speak to the guards – have them get you a billet on my orders.' He rose to his feet and extended his arm, which Nolus took.

'It is good to see Fortuna smile on you, sir.'

'Let's hope she smiles on us all in Dacia, tribune.' Nolus did not respond; he broke the grip, saluted smartly and made his way out into the night.

Valerian stared at the tent-flap for a few moments, trying and failing to be irritated by the fact that the man had been spying on him. It would have stung if he had been found wanting. But as it was, he felt the warm fire of confidence burn in his belly.

Sparta

They had taken her – at spear point – to an anteroom off the main temple. It was small with a single couch and a bench; a place for messengers to be refreshed. Food and water was brought. Lysandra did not feel like eating, but knew she must. As she forced the flatbread into her mouth, the question kept resounding in her mind – *why?* Why was the Matriarch doing this?

She finished the last of the bread and, still chewing, she removed her cuirass and let it fall to the stone floor – too loud in the small room. Her red tunic was soaked with sweat and she downed more water, knowing that if she had to fight, too little water would exhaust her quickly

Fight.

Again the question. Why?

The door to the room opened and Lysandra's heart beat faster, the feelings unfelt since her bout with Illeana beginning to stir in her gut.

'You have grown, worm.' It was Melantha. She was out of her armour, she too wearing the simple red tunic of the temple. She looked good, Lysandra thought; strong, assured and confident. Nine years had passed and they suited Melantha well.

'Is it time?' Lysandra asked.

'No,' Melantha sat on the bench. 'But soon.'

'Why?' Lysandra asked.

Melantha arched an eyebrow. 'Big question. Why are you here? Why did you come back? Why . . .'

'Do not play with me, Melantha,' Lysandra snapped. 'I'm no longer a child.'

'Were you ever?'

Lysandra did not respond, meeting Melantha's gaze with her own.

'You ask why?' her old instructor said. 'Why you were not feted as the returning heroine? Why are we now at this moment not sharpening our spears in preparation to join you in a war we know nothing of or care little about – '

'No,' Lysandra cut her off. 'None of that. Why is the Matriarch trying to make me fight? Hate me all you want, cast me out. You can even say I am no longer Spartan if it pleases you.'

'It does not please me. Nor any of the others, I suspect. The Matriarch is old, Lysandra. Older than anyone has a right to be. Her whole life, she kept her body fit and strong – now, it sustains her whist her mind . . . does not.'

'She is mad?' Lysandra arched an eyebrow.

'No . . .' Melantha frowned. 'It is hard to explain. Sometimes, she seems quite fine. At others she seems not to know who we are or where she is. We think it is at these times that she speaks to Athene. But clearly, these communions have taken a toll on her. She is not as she once was.'

'She remembered me well enough,' Lysandra muttered, hearing the petulance in her own voice.

'You went too far,' Melantha shrugged. 'Hera's tits, Lysandra. You cannot curse the Matriarch of Athene's Temple on her own steps in *Athene's* name! You have always had some front, but by the gods – '

'By the gods, Melantha, I do not care what anyone thinks – my mission is at the behest of Athene herself. I have the right of it, not the Matriarch.'

'I am a Priestess of Athene,' Melantha replied. 'You, however, are not. I take my orders from the Matriarch.'

Lysandra looked straight at her. 'But you do not agree with them.'

'It is not the Spartan way to speak ill of one's leader.'

Lysandra almost laughed at that – because she had heard herself saying such things so many times in the past. 'Very well,' she said. 'I believe that you do not agree with her. You keep your own counsel.'

'Wisdom from worms,' Melantha's mouth twisted in a half-smile. She turned serious then. 'Halkyone now pleads with the Matriarch,' she said. 'She asks for no blood to be spilt. But it is a hard ask – to entreat such is an admission that she fears that you will win.'

'Fears?'

'You have been gone a long time, worm,' Melantha rose to her feet. 'The Matriarch may have cast you out just now, but the truth is, you left this place years ago. It is my guess you had chances to return, but you did not. Deianara is one of ours – who do you expect us to want to win?'

'She cannot defeat me. And I have no wish to defeat her.'

'I know,' Melantha's face was grim. 'I know.'

Shadows danced on the *palaestra*, the wind catching the flames of the lit braziers that lifted black smoke to the sky – a hecatomb to the gods. The Priestesses of Athene had assembled, surrounding the training area, their spears planted. They looked to Lysandra like so many statues, unmoving and unyielding. Despite the nervousness she felt as she moved to the sands, she found she was still proud of them – this is where she had been made. No matter what the Matriarch said, she was still one of them in her heart.

They had sent an acolyte to oil her body in the anteroom. They were to fight *gymnos* – naked – as was the Spartan way. Lysandra remembered that her first bouts in the arena were fought such, but for a different reason. Romans were titillated by the sight of naked flesh. In Sparta, to exercise unclad was the norm. It was, she thought, so like yet unlike preparing for the arena. Lysandra still felt the familiar tingle on her flesh, her nerves coming alive as the girl applied the unguent to her. But there was no sense of purpose. She had once told the gladiatrices of Balbus's *ludus* to think of another fighter as the enemy, to show her no mercy.

Those words mocked her now, as they had before when she faced Varia. Varia who had died on Lysandra's blade, punishment for her hubris.

She stepped on the cold sands of the *palaestra* and glanced up at the temple steps. The Matriarch sat in a chair, flanked by Halkyone and Melantha. Then, the ranks before her parted and Deianara walked towards her. Lysandra's heart quickened at the sight of her child-hood friend.

She had flowered into true womanhood – beautiful in a way that Lysandra herself could never hope to be. Her body was muscular but lacked the hard, angular shape of her own and her front was free of the scarring she had accumulated over her career as a gladiatrix.

With her blonde hair slicked back with oil, Lysandra realised with a start that Deianara looked much like Eirianwen. She pressed her lips into a thin line at thought of the woman she had loved more than life itself.

A priestess broke ranks and walked over to her and pressed a *xiphos* – the Spartan short sword – into her hand. She looked across to see another do the same with Deianara. Wordlessly, the women walked away, leaving them alone on the sands. Lysandra advanced – and, after a moment's hesitation, so did Deianara.

They halted perhaps five feet apart, swords held loosely by their sides. Lysandra looked into the eyes of her friend. She saw no fear – but Deianara was Spartan; she would not show her foe any emotion.

'The combat will begin,' the Matriarch's voice rang out. 'To the death.'

Deianara dropped into her fighting stance – her weight was too far forward for one-on-one battle, Lysandra noted. Too used to the shield wall, too used to training for close quarters fighting, too used to fighting other priestesses where these weaknesses would not be exposed.

She skipped forward, her blade thrusting straight for Lysandra's chest. Even as she skipped aside, she could hear Nastasen's voice echoing in her mind: '*First rule: You get an instant kill on the red,*' as he daubed paint on her pale body. '*Always remember, go for the red first, because if you don't, your opponent will . . .*' She had a chance to slice Deianara's side open but, as she sidestepped, she managed to still her hand – her instinct to kill screamed at her in frustration.

Deianara turned. She knew how close she had come. 'Please, Lysandra,' she said. 'My orders are to kill you. I must obey them. I will not stay my hand as you just did.' She did not wait for a response but launched into an attack – thrust, step in, thrust, high-cut, side-cut . . . Lysandra could read each move before Deianara had begun it. She had learned the same steps, the same attacks. Good enough to defeat most, she knew. She had used them to great effect as a novice in the arena. But she was not a novice any more.

Iron struck iron as Deianara pressed in; predictable or not, she was good and Lysandra knew all too well that she could not continue to parry and evade forever. One mistake was all it took and Deianara would have her. Her friend struck out again – this time Lysandra stepped forward as she warded the blow away, moving to inside Deianara's guard. Her left fist swung up in an uppercut, cracking into Deianara's jaw, snapping her head back. She staggered back, but Lysandra gave her no chance to recover, her foot lashing out and kicking Deianara straight between the legs.

The blonde gasped in pain, doubling over – and Lysandra was on her. She cast away her sword and grabbed Deianara's wrist, twisting it, making her lose her grip on her own weapon. The hold still in place, Lysandra forced the arm up behind her friend's back to between her shoulder blades; at the same time she clamped the blade of her forearm into Deianara's throat.

Deianara gagged, her fingers scrabbling at Lysandra's arm, trying to tear it away from her neck; at the same time, her feet stamped down, trying to catch Lysandra's instep or shin – anything to make her let go. Lysandra pressed her foot into the back of Deianara's knee, taking her – face down – to her knees. Lysandra made sure that she faced the dais and looked directly at the Matriarch as she applied the chokehold.

Deianara became frantic at the lack of oxygen, her struggles increasingly desperate. The eyes of the Matriarch did not waver, but even from the distance that separated them, Lysandra could see the gleam of irrational hate in them. She squeezed harder as Deianara's strength began to ebb away. The struggles became more sporadic till finally her hand fell away from Lysandra's arm.

She dropped her to the ground. 'I rather think,' her voice rang out, 'that if I was cursed by Athene it would be me lying there. As such . . .' she shrugged, 'I would take my leave of you and this place.' The Matriarch clenched her firsts in fury — and Lysandra smiled at her as a young acolyte ran up clutching her tunic. She threw it over her head and turned her back on the temple.

XXIV

Sparta

'. . . Utterly surrounded and outnumbered, it was a desperate fight,' Kleandrias said as slaves removed their eating bowls and refreshed their cups. *The Last Stand* was, as the Spartan had promised, of good standing. Illeana insisted that they have their own section set aside from the other patrons, but even she had winced at the price of it.

Their repast done, Kleandrias was regaling them with a story that was either made up or heavily exaggerated. But she liked the aging warrior, his love for Lysandra so blatant and obvious that only the narcissistic gladiatrix could fail to see it.

'But I know the cut of tribal warriors,' Kleandrias went on, 'and I stepped from the ranks and challenged their leader to single combat.'

'What happened?' Illeana indulged him, a slight smile playing about her lips.

'His centurion tore off his balls for breaking ranks in the middle

164

of a contact and assigned him to latrine duty,' Cappa said, nudging the chortling Murco.

'Our centurion was already dead at this stage,' Kleandrias was clearly annoyed that the two were not taking his tale at all seriously.

'You weren't there,' Illeana said to the two bodyguards. 'Kleandrias is clearly a mighty warrior.'

'If you say so, my lady,' Cappa said, doing a bad job of looking chagrined.

Illeana's eyes told him to behave and she turned back to the Spartan. 'What happened?'

'It was much like an arena battle,' Kleandrias began, a faraway look in his eyes. 'My blade was already red with the blood of my enemies . . .' He stooped as the door to their anterooms opened and Lysandra walked in.

She was not wearing her armour and helm – only her sword, slung over her shoulder from a baldric. Her hair was slicked back, wet with oil and her skin was black with sand. She had clearly been fighting. The question was with whom. And why?

'Lysandra,' she rose to her feet as the Spartan walked towards their dining area.

'Leave me!' Lysandra snapped. At once, Cappa, Murco and Kleandrias got up and made way, Kleandrias's eyes full of concern. Yet he did not speak as he made his way towards the rooms that had been set aside for them.

Lysandra threw herself onto a couch and poured a hefty measure of unwatered wine. She looked over at Illeana, as though questioning why she was still here.

'I'm not your servant,' she said. 'Nor your employee.'

'Stay if you want,' Lysandra shrugged. 'I will be poor company.'

'You're always poor company, Lysandra. What happened?'

'Matters did not go as I expected them to.' The Spartan tipped back her wine and refilled her cup.

Illeana waited but Lysandra was clearly doing her best to 'go native' and act as though she was the paragon of laconic speech – despite the fact that, although she would never admit it herself, she usually was as garrulous as a senator. 'Kill anyone?' Illeana asked at length.

'No,' Lysandra replied. 'Though they wanted me to. The Matriarch is quite mad,' she murmured. 'Quite mad. She made me fight Deianara – a childhood friend. I was skilled enough to overcome her without killing her.'

'Not the homecoming you expected,' Illeana poured more wine for herself, noting that Lysandra threw hers back at pace.

'No,' the Spartan admitted. 'I thought . . .' she hesitated. 'I thought that the Matriarch would be proud of what I have done. What I have achieved. I have honoured Athene,' she stated.

'I know,' Illeana agreed. It was the truth – if Lysandra was anything it was religious. Illeana had little truck with the gods, but she knew that such Romans who acknowledged their existence realised that they were fickle and untrustworthy. They could be bargained with – do something for them, they were supposed to do something for you. That was the modern way of looking at things. But then Lysandra was a walking anachronism and her attitude towards her goddess whilst unusual was hardly surprising once you got to know her. 'You honour her all the time – even when life deals you harsh blows.'

'Varia,' Lysandra raised her cup, her lips pressed into a thin line. She drank and poured more. 'I expected the priestesses to rally to our cause. But they did not – the Matriarch refused. She sought to punish and humiliate me – as though making me fight as a gladiatrix in front of my former sisters would shame me.'

'And it did not.'

'Certainly not,' Lysandra's inherent haughtiness shone through. 'She even cursed me in Athene's name!'

'That must have been hard to take.'

166

'Hardly. I cursed her back – in Athene's name.'

Illeana laughed. 'Why am I not surprised?'

'Why are you here, Illeana?'

The question caught Illeana by surprise. But that was Lysandra for you. She had given Lysandra one reason and it was the truth. The hidden truth was that she found the strange Lysandra intriguing. Attractive even. She was a creature like Illeana herself – the only one she had met who could match her. The only one, she guessed, that would truly understand her. However – these were thoughts she could not share. 'As I told you,' she said at length. 'I've never fought in a war before.'

'Nor have many people. Some would say that most would not want to. You have everything a mortal could desire. Fame, wealth and beauty, the love of the people and your emperor and clearly the gods. You could die,' she added, her voice now a little heavy with wine. 'Why risk it?'

'Because life without risk is not life,' Illeana replied. 'Why did you let me come, then? If we fight again, I could kill you. You risk the same as me.'

'That is different,' Lysandra responded.

'No it isn't. Not really. You know as well as I that only when Hades is on your shoulder do you truly feel alive. This is an opportunity never afforded to a Roman woman – at least not that I know of. I want to know what it's like.'

'And then?'

'I'll think of something else,' Illeana smiled and was pleased that Lysandra did too. 'If we live, you and I have to fight again – as per our agreement. That in itself will be challenging enough.'

'There is truth in that,' the Spartan agreed. 'Do you know anything of leadership? Of tactics. Of battle?'

'Gods, no!' Illeana waved that away. 'Just give me a sword and let me at them.'

Lysandra looked vaguely affronted. 'I am afraid that is not how it works. You will have to learn a different way. A new way. To fight as a soldier is not to fight as a gladiatrix.'

'How so?'

'On the battlefield, you are not *Gladiatrix Prima*. You are part of a team – each person supports the other. It is the barbarian way to indulge in personal glory and single combats and other such nonsense. But I will write notes so that you are prepared as well as you can be.'

'So that I'll survive in order that you're not robbed of your revenge?' Illeana could not resist teasing.

'So that you will not let the side down.'

Illeana frowned – and then realised it was she who was being teased. She sobered then for a moment. 'How do matters with these priestesses affect your plans?' she asked.

'It is not ideal,' Lysandra admitted. 'They are all highly trained. They have been taught the arts of war since an early age. In terms of morale for the other women I have sought, they would have been invaluable. As it is . . .' she shrugged. ' . . . It will have to be you and I that inspires them now, Illeana.'

'I'll drink to that.' And she did.

It was a decision she regretted in the morning.

Illeana consoled herself that no one who knew Lysandra could have an inkling that the Spartan's capacity for alcohol matched her fortitude in battle. In the arena, it was as though Lysandra did not feel pain; at the altar of Bacchus, she seemingly knew no limits.

They left Sparta that morning, heading back to their ship. Illeana spoke little and her companions let her be, aware of her plight. She took some satisfaction that Lysandra too looked a little pasty. She glanced over at the Spartan who was looking down at a small farm holding.

Her home, she surmised. She remembered fragments of their

conversation the previous evening: Lysandra deigned not to visit her parents as the Matriarch had gone further than simply casting her out of their sisterhood. She had cast Lysandra out of Spartan society and whilst Lysandra herself seemed to think that the Matriarch had no right to do this, she feared that it would shame her family and no amount of cajoling would move her.

Illeana's horse grunted beneath her, tossing its head and nearly throwing her from the saddle. The other mounts too were suddenly skittish, all rolled eyes and gritted teeth.

The ground beneath them began to tremble – it was slight, but still frightening and disorienting. Illeana gripped her horse's reigns, afraid and unsure.

'We should dismount,' Kleandrias advised, swinging his leg over his horse's head and dropping to the ground. 'Poseidon is angry,' he added as they followed suit. 'The Earthshaker is abroad in Sparta.'

'An earthquake?' Murco asked, fearful.

'Aye,' Kleandrias said. 'We have them often – small tremors only, Murco.'

'Sometimes not,' Lysandra put in. 'In times past, Poseidon has struck hard.'

'But we should be away anyway,' Cappa urged, not willing to show that he too was as spooked as the horses – and Murco, of course.

They walked away from the city of Lysandra's birth. No one said it, but Illeana could not help but think that first Lysandra's expulsion from her temple and now an earth tremor were bad omens for their forthcoming expedition. She frowned and pushed the thoughts aside – it was best to leave the religion and augury to Lysandra who believed in such things.

The Deiopolis, *Asia Minor*

Telemachus was tired. But that was nothing new these days. Preparations for Lysandra's campaign continued to gather pace; it was as though they had pushed a massive boulder from a cliff top, momentum built on momentum. It was all he could do to keep up with everything and, as such, he rose early and slept late.

The Deiopolis was a hive of activity, alive with the sound of construction, saw on wood, the hiss of the forge and the music of the blacksmith's hammer. It was no secret that Lysandra was beloved of Athene – but Telemachus could not help but think that the lame god, Hephaestus, would be looking down from Olympus and smiling on them.

As Titus had pointed out months before, the Deiopolis had everything that was required for a military campaign in terms of skills. The cottage industries that had once turned a profit for the running of the place were now applied to the logistics of war.

He strolled past a team of women straining to package up yet another *ballista* – an artillery piece that could fire iron tipped bolts as thick as a man's thumb over huge distances. He had seen them tested on the plains outside the temple and the sight had sent shivers down his spine as he imagined the reality of hundreds of bolts streaking towards their enemies. The effect would be devastating.

Not that that was something Telemachus wanted to dwell upon.

Unlike Titus or even Thebe, he had never held a sword, never thrust iron into another's body and felt their lifeblood gush out over him. He looked over again at the women – girls really – hoisting their prefabricated kit onto a waiting cart and realised that soon they could lie dead or dying in some cold field in Dacia.

He turned his head away – it was easier to think of the numbers, to bury his head in the logistics of it and not dwell on what he was a part of. Besides, the alternative was worse: if the Romans and Lysandra failed, the horrors that would be unleashed on the civilised world would be the stuff of nightmares – Tartarus made real on earth. The barbarians would show no mercy and revel in destruction for destruction's sake. Everything that the Hellenes and Romans had built over hundreds of years would be torn down, to be replaced by a bloody anarchy where the only law was that of the sword.

The women were looking at him, bemused, and Telemachus realised he was staring. 'Good work,' he said, offering a smile and a wave. They responded in kind, their expressions still somewhat mystified. He made off quickly, ears reddening in embarrassment and made his way to the walls, climbing the steps that led to the ramparts.

Below on the plains, Thebe was working with her troops, their booted feet kicking up dust in great plumes. Even from here, he could hear shrieks of laughter and curses in equal measure as they marched up and down to the shrill sound of pipes. There were over two thousand of them out there; as he had predicted, the lure of money, land and citizenship was enticement enough for these women. What else, he wondered, had life offered them. Life in the Deiopolis was good – those that chose to leave and not found happiness beyond the walls must have welcomed the chance to serve again – despite the risks. Besides – most, if not all of them, had seen battle before, even if it had only been the spectacle laid on for Domitian's birthday. Thebe and Titus had argued about that but Telemachus had agreed with the former gladiatrix – it was all real enough when the dying started.

Thebe rode up and down the line of the 'legion', a close eye on the dust-coated women who cursed the heat and her relentless drill and equal measures. But drill, she knew, would save lives. She was not Lysandra – she could not inspire them, tell them tales of the goddess to make them believe they were invincible. But she knew how to train women for battle.

Thebe glanced up at the ramparts of the Deiopolis and spied Telemachus. She lifted her hand in greeting and the priest responded in kind; Thebe liked the Athenian – he had been a rock for Lysandra in a way she could not be, their shared devotion to the goddess giving them a common ground.

A crash and shrill cursing dragged her attention back to the drill. Helena, a *lochagos* – a line commander – was berating one of her troop who had fallen over her own feet and thereby thrown the whole section into disarray. In battle, it would be different: the formation would just keep moving forward and the girl would either have to get up or be trampled on; that was the harsh reality of battle.

Lysandra's instructions had been typically detailed. She wanted her veterans to fight as they had been trained for years, armed with short sword and *secutrix* shield – smaller than the legionary's *scutum*, which was designed for a man's strength. Otherwise, her infantry was similar enough to legionaries in kit and formation, but they would be supported by elite *hypaspistai* – heavier armoured troops modelled after Lysandra's beloved Spartan phalanx. Backing up the heavy infantry were large numbers of lightly armed troops – archers and slingers mostly, trained by the taciturn and demanding Priestesses of Artemis – who, it seemed to Thebe, hated everybody.

Arms and armour had been procured from the Romans – and it was hit and miss surplus that was of inferior quality and had to be repaired before it was fit for battle. It was fortunate, she thought, that they had the resources at the Deiopolis to deal with this issue or the girls would be sent to fight without the right kit – tempting disaster.

What had surprised both Thebe and Titus was the massive amount of artillery Lysandra had ordered constructed. Onagers, the huge, heavy catapults; the bolt-throwing ballistas; their lighter, more mobile cousins, the scorpions, together with the archers and slingers gave Lysandra an impressive missile force.

Her eyes flicked across the field to where Titus was directing yet another barrage from the artillery. The women under his charge were becoming extremely proficient – she remembered from her days as a gladiatrix that 'the centurion' had no end to his patience for drill. She had learned this from him – the key to survival was endless repetition.

Thebe turned her attention back to the marching gladiatrices, holding a whistle to her lips. Three short blasts – the order to charge – was taken up by the pipers and the line lurched forward, the shouts of the *lochagoi* mingling with the laboured breathing of the troops. She gave them a hard run before ordering the light infantry to rush in and cover their flanks.

This was an innovation of Lysandra's. Conventional wisdom dictated that though heavy infantry were effective when grinding forward, they could become easy prey if their formation was broken up by enemy troops. But few soldiers had fought in the arena. The women of the Deiopolis had drilled as a team – but each of them was lethal at close quarters when fighting as an individual. All had the small shield of *Thraex* slung about their shoulders and were armed with the *gladius*. It would be a nasty surprise for the Dacians if they thought the fight was over if they got in amongst them.

The light troops sprinted into position and assumed good order in reasonable time. Thebe smiled. They would all be ready to fight in Ares's arena soon.

XXVI

Taenarum, Laconia

Lysandra leant on the bow of the *Galene* and stared out at the coast of Laconia. She had tried to put the disappointment of the temple behind her, but the incident stayed with her, troubling her waking hours and haunting her sleep.

She still seethed with the injustice of it. How *dare* the Matriarch cast her out! And mark her a *xenos* – a foreigner – to boot. The old woman's word may carry weight in Sparta, but she could not take that away from Lysandra. She recalled her darkest days in Balbus's *ludus* when she felt unworthy of her sisterhood and her *polis*. It was not, she realised, for the Matriarch to take that away from her – only Lysandra could decide if Lysandra was worthy of calling herself Spartan. In the ease with which she had defeated Deianara, Athene had shown them that Lysandra had the right of it.

And, she thought bitterly, to make her fight her childhood friend was vindictive cruelty on the part of the Matriarch. It could have been any of them – even Halkyone, but no – Deianara had been chosen to spite her.

Bedros approached her – a little fearfully, she noted. She forced herself to smile, banishing her grim expression for a moment. 'Are we close?' she asked.

'Aye, I came to tell you that,' he said. 'I think we'll beach tonight and get to Taenarum tomorrow. Early.'

'Good. Saturnalia fast approaches and I must have everything in

174

order. Speaking of which . . . have you furthered my additional request?'

Bedros tapped his nose. 'Your instructions were to keep it as quiet as possible. Which is not easy when you're talking to sailors. But never fear – I have arranged everything – as discreetly as I could.'

This was a matter she had written to him about in the utmost secrecy. She had not even confided in Kleandrias so desperate was she to keep this part of her mission concealed. 'I hope so, Bedros,' she said. 'Everything depends on this.'

The usually bluff sailor sobered. 'I understand,' he said. 'I've spoken only to men that I trust. You will have what you need.'

'What do you need?' Illeana – obviously bored – had drifted in and caught part of their conversation.

'Just things for our mission,' Lysandra tried to sound blasé.

Illeana's arched eyebrow told her how effective her attempt had been. 'What things?'

'Just things.'

Bedros just shook his head and made off, leaving them to it.

'I thought you said that it was important for me to know about tactics.' Illeana actually pouted her over-plump lips, her forehead creasing in a petulant frown.

'It is,' Lysandra soothed. 'This is strategy. Totally different. You do not need to worry about the details,' she went on. 'There is enough for you to learn as it is.'

'Yes, about that . . .' Illeana said. 'I've read your notes. I'm sure that everything you say in them is right. But I will be honest with you, Lysandra – I don't really understand any of it.'

Lysandra frowned. 'How could you not? It is perfectly clear.'

Illeana chuckled. 'To you, maybe. Some people are leaders – you are. I have to say I don't know why, but people follow you.'

'What do you mean?' Lysandra was almost affronted.

Illeana stepped closer and Lysandra felt the magic of Aphrodite

175

about her, distracting her, filling her senses. 'You're rude. Arrogant. Terse. And intolerant. Yet those men,' she flicked her eyes to Cappa, Murco and Kleandrias who were arguing about something or another, 'would die for you.'

'It is because I live the Spartan way,' Lysandra huffed.

'Maybe,' Illeana said. 'But it seems to me that not even the Spartans live the Spartan way anymore.'

Lysandra opened her mouth, but the words died on her lips. Illeana was right in some respects. Sparta itself was no longer the warrior state with its *agoge* and invincible warriors. Despite the fact that it had never been conquered by the Romans, it was – to all intents and purposes – a small Roman town with Roman laws. 'They do in the Temple of Athene,' she said after a time.

'And yet they say you are no longer one of them, no longer a Spartan?'

'That is the right of the Matriarch,' Lysandra gritted. 'I feel it is unjust, of course. And I will say to you now, Illeana, that she cannot take away my birthright. She can cast me out of the temple, but being Spartan . . . no, that is mine. Not hers. I serve Athene – the goddess herself.'

She felt the goddess on her, cutting through Aphrodite's veil. 'The Matriarch is wrong. I am right. I cursed her – and she will die knowing that Lysandra of Sparta went to war and did not shame herself, that she fought in the defence of Hellas. I offered her a chance for glory and greatness and she spat in my face!' Lysandra waved a dismissive hand. 'Then so be it – Sparta will be on the battlefield. In me and Kleandrias. I will win because my way is the *true* Spartan way, the way that trusts in the gods.

'You say that I'm vain . . . arrogant, was it? You are not the first to say so, Illeana, nor will you be the last. But my conviction comes from my trust in Athene and I will walk her path – no matter how steep. I will win without the Spartans and prove to the Matriarch that I did it with lesser peoples.'

176

Illeana smiled at her then. 'So now I know why they follow you.' She leant forward and her lips brushed Lysandra's in a kiss that was not altogether sisterly but nor was it one of passion. She turned and walked away as Lysandra gaped after her. The Roman looked back over her shoulder and smiled. 'I'm teasing you, Lysandra,' she said.

Lysandra blushed and turned her eyes to the sea, finding that after the exchange, her mood was lighter and her thoughts calm. Illeana had that effect on her, she realised. Perhaps it was the spell of Aphrodite, she thought, protecting her favourite. Lysandra reminded herself that she and Illeana had a bargain concerning a rematch – and she could not forget that. But with Illeana's kiss still tingling on her lips, the prospect of facing her with a sword in her hand was somehow less appealing.

The noon sky was grim, Helios well withdrawn behind a veil of grey clouds as the *Galene* docked at Taenarum's harbour, named for the hero Achilles, which Lysandra counted a good omen, given her arena name. The *Galene* one of only a few vessels on the water-front and the wharf hosted none of the chaos Lysandra had seen at Brundisium.

'Fighting season is well under way,' Kleandrias commented, indi-cating the other vessels. The best men will be hired already. But there are always mercenaries looking for work.'

'I am sure we can make good with what we will find here,' she replied. 'I will be counting on you, Kleandrias. You know this place.'

The warrior gazed at her, his eyes softening. 'It gladdens my heart to be of service.'

Lysandra smiled, pleased that he clearly understood the impor-tance of the task and the pivotal role she would play. Of course, Kleandrias knew that the Matriarch had named her as *xenos* and, as a Spartan, he had the right to look down on her now. But it was a testament to the man that he saw through the old woman's false-hoods. 'We should find lodgings, then,' she said. 'It is early still and we can make a start.'

'That would be best, yes,' Kleandrias agreed. 'The nights here tend to be bawdy and not a place for ladies of quality.'

'You mean that whores will be abroad.'

Kleandrias coloured. 'Well . . . yes.'

'Some would say that a gladiatrix is the lowest whore of all,' Lysandra shrugged. It was true – she had heard so many obscene suggestions thrown at her from the stands that she rather felt she was an expert on the subject of all things carnal. Even if it had been a while.

'Then I would strike that person down for his insult,' Kleandrias was vehement. 'No man – no *one* – will insult you while I live.'

'Then it would be best if you did not attend my next match, Kleandrias. Or else you might have to kill the entire Flavian Amphitheatre.'

He knew she was teasing him. 'Spartans do not ask how many,' he quoted King Agis, 'but where they are.'

This made Lysandra laugh – she was now the one being chided as this was precisely the kind of answer she often gave.

'You should laugh more often.' Kleandrias looked as though he was going to add something else but stilled his tongue. 'We should be about it, then,' he finished.

Lysandra nodded. There was work to be done.

Taenarum was unlike anything Lysandra had seen before. It was a small town with squat buildings, narrow streets and stench that outranked even Rome's epic foulness. Bedros and his crew had departed already – headed straight for a dive they knew well, leaving Lysandra and her companions to find lodgings in what Kleandrias optimistically referred to as 'the better side of town'.

Despite the fact that the streets were all but deserted, he, Cappa and Murco formed a protective cordon around her and Illeana and Lysandra could tell by the look on the beautiful Roman's face that she was less than impressed by their machismo – especially as they were all armed. This garnered some looks from what few passers-by there were – a woman with a sword was something rare.

Kleandrias stopped outside an inn. 'This is the most expensive place in Taenarum.'

'This?' Illeana affronted. 'This is a hovel.'

'This ain't Rome,' Murco said.

Lysandra refrained from commenting – she, after all, had lived in a cell for a number of months – which hardship she guessed none of them had endured. Instead, she eased past Kleandrias and led the way into 'Taenarum's finest' – the heroically named *Helen's Palace*.

It was dark inside, incense hanging heavily in the air to cover the smell of wine. There was a drinking area with tables and a small stage for bards; set back from this were a large number of booths, which offered privacy for conversation and other matters. Whores lounged about, and looked surprised at the early arrivals. A long bar separated customer from patron; a bored-looking ancient with a bald pate and long, iron grey hair about the sides and back. 'Greetings, friends,' he said, creaking into life as they approached him. He squinted. 'Is that . . . Kleandrias?'

The big man smiled. 'Yes, Philemon, it is.'

'By the gods!' Philemon reached for a krater of wine and banged it on the wooden counter. 'It's been a while, boy. I thought I'd never see you again.' He poured them all a cup – himself included. '*Hades or Croesus!*' he toasted.

'*Hades or Croesus!*' Kleandrias responded and drank his wine.

Lysandra and the others did likewise, mumbling the toast as well, strangers at a familiar meeting.

'You'll be needing rooms, then?' Philemon eyed Lysandra and then Illeana. 'Zeus, Hera and Athene,' he said. 'This one's a looker. Your wife?'

'No . . .' Kleandrias began, but that was all Philemon needed to hear.

'I could make you a fortune, girl,' the innkeeper informed Illeana – who Lysandra knew to be one of the richest women in Rome. Despite herself, she felt a little affronted that Philemon had given her no more than a passing glance. 'Men would pay gold to be with you,' the innkeeper added.

Illeana laughed, instantly disarming him. 'They already have,' she said.

'Ahhh,' Philemon nodded sagely. 'This your servant,' he jerked his chin at Lysandra. To either side, she saw Cappa and Murco wince.

'Certainly not!' she snapped. 'We need rooms. Food. And less observation from you, old man.'

Philemon shook his head. 'Spartan women, eh?' he winked at Kleandrias. 'You're in luck,' he added. 'Season's almost over as you can see, so we're pretty empty. Rooms a-plenty. Are you sharing?'

'No,' Murco said.

Cappa looked surprised. 'You're paying for your own room?'

'If it's a choice between that and chewing on your farts, I'll pay.'

'We're not sharing,' Lysandra interjected. 'Rooms for all of us. See to it, Kleandrias. And . . .' she rounded on Philemon. 'Food, as I said. Wine.' She stalked off, annoyed, looking for a booth that would accommodate them, Cappa and Murco in tow.

As was their wont, they made her sit first so they would be on the outside to protect her – and she noted Illeana's amusement as the gladiatrix joined them with Kleandrias. 'So,' Lysandra said. 'This place seems deserted. There are no men here.'

'The men will come into town at night,' Kleandrias said. 'For now, they will be on the Field of Ares – drilling, idling and hoping.'

'Hoping?' Illeana asked.

'Aye, hoping that they will get a contract.'

'Even now? You said that the fighting season is well underway?'

'Yes, but you can always rely on the Parthians – killing each other isn't seasonal for them, so there's always a chance a prince or lordling will want to hire on men for a spot of dynastic murder.'

'How do *we* hire men?' Lysandra asked.

'Just go to the Field.' Kleandrias nodded his thanks as Philemon and a slave brought their food. 'It is like buying slaves,' he expanded. 'You view the merchandise, decide what you like and then you haggle. And at this time of year, we will get a good deal.'

'It seems all too easy,' Lysandra said.

'That is because it is easy. The Romans need mercenaries too – specialists for jobs they do not excel at.'

'Name one,' Cappa snorted.

'Cavalry,' Kleandrias stuffed a piece of flatbread into his mouth and chewed, evidently enjoying Cappa's expression of outrage. 'Light infantry, archers . . .'

'They're all auxiliary jobs,' Murco said. 'It's not really proper soldiering is it?'

'If you say so.' Lysandra decided to end the bickering before it started. 'Finish up. We will go to the Field of Ares and be about our business, then.'

'As you say,' Kleandrias acquiesced.

XXVII

Sarmatia

They moved. Slowly, inexorably, a vast sea of humanity creeping over the endless sea of grass that was the plains. The sun was not too hot – bright enough to warm the skin and make the day pleasant. Behind them were the old, the too young, the hunters and gatherers, all those who were needed for this fight, yet would not be part of it.

Sorina felt more at peace than she had done in many years. This was the life she had left behind so long ago, the life that the Romans stole from her. Even after she had returned home after her years as their slave, things had changed in Dacia. Decabalus had united many of the tribes under his banner, villages were becoming towns, towns had grown into cities and only those on the fringes of his rule still lived the old ways. Even his soldiers now drilled and practised the Roman way of war.

It was, Sorina knew, the only way to beat them. But here, as she rode free, she wondered if in destroying Rome they would recast themselves in its image? She looked to her left and Amagê caught her eye; the Clan Chief smiled and winked at her as though she somehow had instigated all this and Sorina was a piece in her game of *latrunculi* and not the other way around.

Sorina forced herself to smile back, but her deceit – no, her betrayal – eroded her heart. Her conscience told her that to cull the tribes that had proven resistant to Decabalus's rule was wrong. These people – Sarmatians, Getae, Scythians and the few Northern Dacians – were all that were left of her way of life. Yet, Rome could not be defeated without them and nor could they win without the guiding hand of Decabalus. The tribes had tried before – many times – and failed.

Only Decabalus had met them in open battle – five legions – and destroyed them. Sorina recalled the day in stark relief, its images bright in her memory. For all their vaunted discipline and training, their superior arms and armour, the Romans were bested, defeated by their own arrogance and their own weakness. She had seen them – men who were killers and rapists – stall when faced suddenly by a woman with a sword. She had cut them down herself, payment for their vacillation. She had seen too, that they could not comprehend how they – the barbarians – had adapted and did not fight in the way they were expected to. They did not simply rush onto their spears and die, as Lysandra had once goaded her.

Lysandra.

Sorina wondered what had become of the Spartan. Dead, she hoped or living in squalid misery, suffering as she had made Sorina suffer. No punishment was too harsh for the arrogant sow. But in her heart, Sorina knew that her wishes were simply those – wishes. Lysandra was a civilised woman – she had impressed this enough times at Balbus's *ludus*. She knew their ways, how to make her lowly status work for her. Lysandra of Sparta was doubly a whore – a whore in the arena and a whore for the civilised ways. The truth of it was that Lysandra probably lived in the lap of luxury and laughed herself to sleep each night at the fate of Sorina.

Sorina prayed to the Great Mother that some day there might be a reckoning. She swept her gaze over the great host of plains-people. Countless thousands here; more with Decabalus. They would crush the Romans and the gates of Lysandra's beloved Greece would be flung open. They would descend on her homeland and ravage it, burn the temples of her Goddess Athene and make her people suffer. Men would die. Women would be raped and children would be made slaves – a consummate revenge on both Sparta and Rome's empire. But it would not stop there, she knew.

Rome – that was the ultimate prize. And Decabalus was right: when they had destroyed the punitive force sent against them, other peoples on the fringes of Rome's imperium would begin to rise – the myth of invincibility, once shattered, could never be pieced back together. She had met people from all over the Roman dominion: Britons, Gauls, Germans, Iberians, Egyptians, Ethiopians, Numidian's and more. Disparate, distant and unalike, they were united by one thing – their hatred of Rome and her ways. She had seen it in the *ludus*, how the freer peoples had stuck together whilst Greeks and

Romans wore their gladiatorial servitude as though it were some mark of honour.

Their world, she realised, was coming to an end. The empire would fall, as all empires must. She wondered if Rome would be the last empire the world would ever know. That would be the greatest gift she and these people could give to the Great Mother: to eradicate the stain of 'civilisation' from the earth and return it to its free and natural state.

Or would Decabalus think to make himself emperor? Would he replace Domitian as king of the world and turn Dacia into Rome? No, she told herself at once. That would not happen. She would not allow it to happen. She served Decabalus because he was the bringer of doom to the Romans. He had the vision and the power to make her dream real. But she would kill him if he took on the Roman purple.

'Thinking black thoughts?'

Amagê's voice snapped Sorina from her reverie.

'You read me easily, Amagê. When we first met, I thought you had the magic.'

'I do,' Amagê laughed. How else do you think I manage to keep these people from each other's throats?'

'Can you read minds?' Sorina kept her voice neutral, but her heart hammered in her chest. If what she said was true, Amagê would know that her mission was half-truth-half-lie. And the tribespeople of the north were not famed for ending the lives of traitors quickly.

'In a way,' Amagê admitted. Sorina tried to look away, but something compelled her to meet the eye of the younger woman. 'More like I can see what is in someone's heart written on their face.' She held Sorina's gaze for a long time and the Dacian could find no words worth saying. Amagê reached out and put her hand on Sorina's shoulder. 'The cares of the world seem to rest here, Sorina. There are some things that you cannot control and for which you are not responsible. People make decisions for all kinds of reasons – some-times they are obvious, other times they are not so. It is the way of things.'

'As you say,' Sorina agreed. She looked away to see Teuta watching them. Her lover's face was taut with jealousy. And a resigned bitter-ness.

Amagê noticed it too and her hand slipped away from her shoulder. 'You see,' she said to Sorina, her eyes flicking to Teuta. 'The magic isn't so hard, is it? Can you read *her* thoughts now?'

'She's young, like you. I think she is tiring of me.'

'She is young, yes. But not like me. There's no one like me.'

The Clan Chief steered her horse away without further comment, leaving Sorina behind her. Sorina turned her eyes to Teuta and shrugged; doubtless there would be words tonight.

Taenarum, Laconia

Kleandrias led the way and, Lysandra thought, he was rather enjoying his role as expert on all things Taenarum. He was, in some ways, very similar to Titus with his love of storytelling with an inference on his own military prowess; even now, as they travelled towards the mercenary encampment, he was regaling all of them with another tale of his adventures.

As he talked, she wrapped her war-cloak closer about herself and her mind drifted back to the temple again. Her recent experience there dominated her thoughts, blackening her mood and giving her a craving for drink, which she had long believed to be under control.

She pushed it aside: it *was* under control. She need only be aware of it.

She did not need the Priestesses of the Temple, but she could not deny that they would have been a worthy addition to her forces. But the Matriarch's betrayal had stung her. Even if the old woman was at the end of her sanity, Lysandra was surprised that Athene had not provided her the wisdom and foresight to welcome her back. Perhaps some people were beyond even the help of the gods.

They left the town and rode for some time along a well-maintained road; to either side of them the land was bare but not barren. Winter was approaching fast, but Taenarum seemed to be none the worse for it.

'This is a rich town,' Kleandrias told her when she brought it up.

'I've never met a bunch of soldiers that kept their surroundings in such good nick,' Cappa said. 'Usually, it's a free-for-all.'

'Usually,' Kleandrias agreed. 'But this is not an army on the march or on campaign. Indeed, it is not an army at all, but more a collection of specialist companies – and they rely on the port and supplies it brings. Tearing up the countryside would bring down the wrath of not only the Romans but also their fellow swords-for-hire.'

'Don't shit on your own doorstep?' Murco offered.

'A singularly disgusting if accurate appraisal,' Lysandra muttered, causing Murco to flush with embarrassment.

Further comment was cut short as the ground beneath them trembled. The horses bucked and skittered, eyes rolling as Lysandra and the others wrestled for control of their mounts. For a moment it was still – and then again came another tremor – this time, greatly diminished.

'This Earthshaker of yours seems active,' Illeana said. 'Sea gods should stick to the sea.'

'And mortals should not speak ill of the gods,' Lysandra snapped.

Illeana irritated her further by mouthing her words back at her and pulling a sour expression.

'Let us move on,' Kleandrias interjected.

The encampment was huge.

It sat in a valley through which ran a fast flowing river – ideally placed for sanitation and fresh water. It was set out like a Roman marching camp, yet had no ditch and rampart. Blocks of semi-permanent quarters were arrayed in the correct order and from her vantage point Lysandra could see men making their way about the camp. Beyond was a wide, open field – here, she assumed, the men practised their drill, though none were abroad at this time.

'Impressive,' Illeana said. 'I like the way it's all in blocks.'

'It's standard,' Cappa informed her. 'All camps look the same.'

They steered their mounts down into the valley. There were no guards, but they were met as they approached by a stocky Hellene who wore a satchel around his shoulder.

'All right, lads,' he addressed Kleandrias, Cappa and Murco, not deigning even to give Lysandra and Illeana more than an appreciative glance. 'You here for work or to hire?' Lysandra recognised the Corinthian accent at once, bringing Thebe to her mind.

'To hire,' Kleandrias said.

'You've left it late in the day.'

'We are aware of that,' Lysandra broke in. 'Where can we stable our horses?' The Corinthian looked at her as though it was her horse that had spoken. 'Speak, man!' she barked, irritated at his hesitation. She expected it of course, but it still exasperated beyond reason that outside of Sparta, men could accept women as equals.

'Wind in your mouth, bitch,' the Corinthian said. 'You ought to give her a beating, lads. The fit one knows her place at least.' He gave Illeana a black-toothed grin.

'The horses?' Kleandrias asked.

'Leave 'em with me,' the Corinthian said, reaching into his satchel.

'You don't think I'm hanging around here for the good of my health, do you? Here,' he handed Kleandrias a token from the bag. 'Collect them from me, back here . . . I'll bill you – it's five sesterces a day, mind. Each.'

'Twenty-five?' Kleandrias raised an eyebrow. 'I am not sure that is right, friend.'

'I'm not your friend, I'm the stable master,' the Corinthian thrust his chest out. 'Come back in the summer if you want cheaper rates. How do you think I pay for fresh hay and feed, eh? You think the farmers around here give a shit? Give us lot lower rates because there's no custom at this time of year? No, they bloody don't . . .'

'All right,' Kleandrias cut him off. 'Twenty-five.'

'You want to keep those women close,' the Corinthian advised. 'The men are well behaved for the most part, but there's always someone who can cause you trouble.'

Lysandra lifted her war-cloak to show him her sword. 'We can take care of ourselves.'

The Corinthian's eyes widened. 'Sword dancers, eh? I saw that in Persia. Are you doing a show later?'

'If you're lucky,' Illeana purred, at once mesmerising the irritating lout. There was a part of Lysandra that was becoming a little jealous of the Roman woman's apparent power over all and sundry. Probably, she reasoned, because Illeana had a similar effect on her.

'He could be right, though,' Cappa said to Lysandra as they moved into the encampment proper. 'Maybe we ought to rethink this – let me, Murco and Kleandrias handle the signing on bit. You two are already attracting attention,' he indicated a group of men who watched them go by, their expressions amused.

'We shall have to get used to it, Cappa,' Lysandra said. 'All of us. The men we take on will be facing women in battle. They will be fighting alongside women in battle.'

'It sounds pretty liberal to me,' Murco observed.

'That's because it is,' Illeana said. 'Besides – I'll lay you any money that there's not one man here who could match me – or Lysandra – with a sword.'

'Well, there is that,' Murco conceded.

'So how does this work?' Lysandra wanted to know. 'Do we just put up a sign saying "swords wanted" and wait?'

'No, no,' Kleandrias replied, the irony clearly lost on him. 'There is an office at the centre of the camp – the *praetorium* of this encampment. We go there, speak to the officer-on-duty, tell him the details of the job . . . then we wait.'

They continued on, Kleandrias leading, Cappa and Murco flanking herself and Illeana – and they were attracting attention from the men billeted in the encampment – most stared and some shouted out predictably crude comments, but there was no untoward behaviour and their journey to the *praetorium* was otherwise uneventful.

As they arrived, they were confronted by two guardsmen who looked sharp and alert – even if they were a little long in the tooth. Thus far, she was more than impressed by this place – it was well organised, clean, tidy and seemingly upheld good standards of discipline.

'Is the officer on duty?' Kleandrias asked. 'We are hiring.'

'Good to know,' one of the men grinned. 'I'll take you in.' He turned and banged on the door and, without waiting for response, opened it and led them into the *praetorium*.

The room was large and pleasantly warm, dominated by a large desk behind which sat the officer-in-charge. He rose, a smile creasing his handsome face. 'By the gods,' he said. 'I knew we would meet again, Lysandra.'

She could not help herself from grinning. 'Greetings, Euaristos.'

The Deiopolis, Asia Minor

'They look very grand,' Telemachus observed. 'You should be proud, Thebe.'

The former gladiatrix waved his praise away, though she enjoyed hearing it. 'I only told them what to do. It is they who have made the accomplishment.'

On the fields outside the Deiopolis, the women of the temple rushed to form up, their booted feet pounding on the damp earth. The days of dust were past now; Saturnalia approached and the weather was turning, rain and cold wind the constant companions of the women as they drilled.

Titus had taken command for the parade. 'A commander,' he had said to her, 'should watch from afar as her people do the work.' The acknowledgement of her role was praise indeed from the centurion.

The *hypaspistai* and other regular infantry took time to get in line – there was no getting away from this, she knew. Heavy infantry was not so called for nothing, even if they were carrying less kit than their male counterparts would have been.

'Nervous?' the priest asked her.

'A little,' she admitted. She looked to her left where the small band of Romans, Sextus Julius Frontinus amongst them, were assembled. Ostensibly, they were here to formally complete the purchase of the Deiopolis, but Thebe and all the women on the field knew that they were essentially here to assess them. As though he felt his eyes on her, Frontinus turned his head towards her. She looked away quickly, back to the troops on the field.

The formation was simple: a solid block of *hypaspistai* in the centre, with the swordswomen protecting their flanks. In turn, lightly armed slingers stood to the left and right of the infantry blocks, an offensive buffer for their slower moving counterparts. Arrayed behind them were archers; these women, trained hard by the merciless Priestesses of Artemis, considered themselves the elite. Even those that had not been women of the temple had taken on the religious practices of their trainers and all had taken to oiling their hair and tying it into a queue to mark themselves as different from the rest.

At their backs, raised up on a long rampart, was the artillery. Thebe had been a slave, a gladiatrix and then a woman of the temple – she had never seen these war machines until their construction at the Deiopolis – and they terrified her. They were like mechanical beasts, groaning and taut before they spat death across the field.

A woman's voice rang out and she could hear – even from this distance – the clank-clank-clank of the ballista ratchets, the creaking of the onager ropes being pulled tight. After the awful creaking and groaning of the war machines was finished, the woman barked another command and everything on the field lurched from stillness to motion.

The sound of the artillery being released was terrifying, sounding to Thebe like a hydra – the hiss and thump of the onagers, the sharp retort of the ballistas and scorpions spitting their missiles into the distance.

The awful noise was accompanied by the wailing of pipes as the foot soldiers advanced under a canopy of arrows launched from their rear.

'I cannot imagine facing that,' Telemachus said to her.

It was true. In the arena, Thebe had known fear, but there was a way to overcome it – to fight *back*, to get to grips with your opponent and hurt her. The thought of walking in closely packed ranks as death fell from above was a horrifying thought.

The infantry plodded forward until they were at the apex of the artillery's range, then the music of the pipes changed and, as one, the women raised shields and drew swords. It was smooth, the countless hours of practice now paying dividends. A few more steps and another change in the cadence; her soldiers broke into a slow, loping trot. To charge in formation was impossible for the *hypaspistai*, despite Lysandra's claims her Spartan Sisterhood had perfected it. Thebe had found that only the last few steps could be managed at full sprint. But a slow, relentless jog had been worked on and perfected.

All the while, the archers kept pace, shooting, running forward and shooting again, their 'spindles' spiking the earth in front of the infantry.

'It's a waste of material,' Telemachus noted. 'How many broken arrows will there be at the end of this?'

'It's necessary,' Thebe told him. 'These Romans have to see that we will not shame Lysandra.'

The infantry slowed and changed formation, refusing a flank and forming up on an echelon to counter the threat from an imaginary enemy; again, it was smoothly done and then came the climax.

A shrill, wailing tune floated to them across the breeze and the women began to reorder. Behind them, archers began to trot forwards and on the flanks, the light infantry ran towards their slower moving counterparts, who began to form into circles. This was a difficult manoeuvre but an essential one – it was the only defence they had against cavalry. Inside the ring of flesh and iron, the light infantry and archers could pepper enemy horse with shafts and stone.

If it came to this, Thebe was in no doubt it would be a war of attrition – either the enemy would break the circle and her troopers would be killed. Or the spears and swords of the Deiopolis would stand firm and win the day.

As the women drew to a halt, she looked across at the Romans and hoped they were impressed.

Credit to the secretary, Nikos – he had done wonders with the dinner hosted within the walls of Athene's sanctuary in the Deiopolis. It was by far the grandest of the buildings therein – an extravagance to which even Lysandra herself had admitted.

Frontinus had dismissed his aides and he, Titus and Thebe reclined on couches. Telemachus had absented himself. He was, Thebe thought, probably on the field at this very moment, collecting spent arrows and ballista bolts.

They were served by the Priestesses of Aphrodite, each one chosen for their exquisite beauty, and entertained with lyre and voice by the women of Apollo's temple. The food was excellent and Thebe was well pleased – the ex-governor could not fault their hospitality.

'I enjoyed your display,' the old man said once their main repast was done. He nodded his thanks as a girl filled his wine cup. 'It was ragged in places – but that's to be expected given the time you've had to train your women.'

'Thank you, sir.' Thebe bristled inwardly, but held her tongue. It would not do to argue with the man – she had done her level best with the troops and that was all she could do. She was not, after all, Lysandra.

'But for all that, they seemed adequately prepared. Field battles are not a parade ground after all.'

'They're well prepared,' Thebe said. 'Most – myself included – fought in your spectacle for Domitian. Those that didn't, still have experience of the arena. All of us have put iron into their foes at one stage or another. This, I think, is the main thing, sir?'

Frontinus regarded her and she knew she was being assessed – he seemed affable enough, but Thebe knew his mind was as sharp as a razor. 'Quite right, young lady,' he agreed. 'Quite right. All the training in the world can go to Hades when confronted by the enemy. That's why we have centurions.'

'We have them too, sir,' Titus said. 'Sir, if I may be blunt – '

'I would expect nothing else,' Frontinus's interruption was softened by a grin.

'We have done as we have been instructed. We are aware as to why these women are needed – your notes to Lysandra made this quite clear. *I* am aware that your colleagues must think this absurd, that Roman soldiers will not baulk from the dirty task of killing women. And they are right – some Roman soldiers won't mind at all. But most will. It is an unnatural experience for a soldier, and every instinct tells him that to put his blade into a woman's belly is wrong.'

'There's truth in that,' Frontinus agreed. 'Young Valerian – you remember him – told me as much. As have others – serving in Germania for instance. That Chattian bitch Auriane gave the legions out there more trouble than they could deal with. But you're right,' he added. 'They do think it's absurd.'

Titus gestured for more wine, ensuring that their guest's cup was full. 'Your colleagues do not know these women.' Thebe was surprised at the earnestness in his voice. 'You do – it was under your patronage that our former *ludus* flourished. You elevated our women from a sideshow to something that men of quality could appreciate. Thebe has done good work. Those girls you saw today will not disgrace her. Or you. I have seen battle many times. Many times. I was a centurion once, sir. And I was a trainer of gladiatrices. I know the look in the eye of a killer. And our *soldiers* have it.'

Thebe felt her cheeks colouring at Titus's words. The centurion was so sparing as to be frugal with his praise. To hear it lavished in such a way filled her with a sense of pride that she had not felt in years. She served Lysandra – as Lysandra had delivered them all from slavery and given them a life they could not have imagined – it was

194

her duty. She did not begrudge the Spartan's legendary prowess – or her prodigious ego. But the Deiopolis, the winning of freedom, the battle for Domitian's spectacle – all this had been Lysandra. For once, Thebe herself was centre stage – and it was good to know that she had not been found wanting.

'I hope so,' Frontinus said. 'They'll need it.' He was silent for a moment. 'Are they ready?' he asked, earnestly. 'Are you sure?'

'Yes,' she heard herself answering. 'I am certain they are. All is in order. Lysandra's instructions were to have the troops ready and march them to Ceramos by the Saturnalia. The troops are ready, the supplies and transportation prepared and built. All that remains is to march.'

'Ceramos is a natural harbour,' Titus said. 'Where are we going after we get there?'

Frontinus smiled. 'Taenarum.'

'For mercenaries?'

'Yes. And to meet with Lysandra. Gods willing, she will have recruited the soldiers that you need.'

'And after Taenarum?'

Frontinus reached into his toga and produced a scroll. 'Here are the orders. Take them to Lysandra at Taenarum.' Titus was about to speak, but Frontinus stilled him with a wave of his hand. 'Secrecy is all,' he said. 'I trust you, of course, but the wrong word in the wrong place at the wrong time could jeopardise everything. You will find out soon enough, Titus.' It was clear that that was an end to it. 'Have you given them a name?' Frontinus asked suddenly.

Thebe exchanged a confused glance with Titus. 'I'm not sure what you mean, sir,' she said.

'A name – all legions have a name,' Frontinus explained. 'Normally chosen from the place they are founded, though some are more fanciful – Gemina, Minerva and so forth. Is that not so, Titus?'

'Yes, sir,' the centurion agreed, colouring a little as though he should have thought of this. 'It's good for morale,' he said to Thebe.

'It makes you feel part of something – something you would be ashamed to let down.'

'We can name them 'Carian,' Thebe said. 'We are in Caria – here is where they were formed.'

Frontinus laughed. 'Yes we could, but surely there's something more apt.' Thebe was acutely embarrassed as both she and Titus floundered under the old general's gaze. 'I have it,' Frontinus said. 'They are Greeks, mostly – I know what the Greeks are like, we can't use a good Roman name. Let us call them the Heronai.'

Thebe raised her cup in toast. 'The Women of the Temple it shall be.'

Moesia

The *praetorium* was warmed by the comforting glow of the brazier, warding off the winter chill of Moesia.

Valerian re-read the message from Tettius Iulianus for the umpteenth time. Clearly, Nolus's report had not done the Felix Legion a disservice – because Iulianus's inferences were those of surprise at the Fourth's apparent fitness for battle. He had ordered them to move out and prepare for 'a holding action if necessary'.

'What do you think?' he asked Mucius. He had invited the *Primus* – and Settus – to the *praetorium* as his most senior and most trusted officers respectively.

'He's a cunt,' Settus offered. This garnered a look from Mucius. 'Don't leap to his defence,' Settus admonished. 'He assigned *you* to *this* legion,' the little man reminded his superior. 'You may be First of the First, but you're First of the First of the Last.'

'That's because the rest of you are fucking useless!' Mucius retorted. 'I'm here to inspire you lot.'

'You couldn't inspire a stiffy in a brothel, Mucius.'

'That's not what your mother keeps telling me.'

'All right,' Valerian interjected, gratified by the apparent improvement in their relationship. 'I meant of our orders, not what you think of Tettius Iulianus.'

'Vague,' said Mucius after a moment. 'And I don't like vague.'

'I don't see it that way,' Settus said. 'Look. Orders are to march into barbarian country, prepare a defence and wait for re-enforcements. And kick the shit out of any cunt that comes near us. How is that vague?'

'Because it doesn't give us any intelligence on the strength of the enemy, what kind of re-enforcements we'll be getting and – crucially – how long we're supposed to hold the ground for.'

'Well at least it tells us where the ground is.' Valerian muttered.

'And that doesn't sit well either,' Mucius added. 'It's almost as though we're being sent in . . .' he stopped as realisation hit him.

'Yes, quite,' Valerian agreed.

'What?' Settus looked from Legate to *Primus* and back. 'What?'

'As bait, you twat,' Mucius informed him. '*Summa exstinctio* is a rare order, Settus. We're to go in and clear this city . . .'

'Town,' Valerian corrected.

' . . . Town. Kill everything and wait for back up. If that's not sending a signal to the barbarians to come and carve our balls off, I don't know what is.'

Settus failed to look moved by this. 'So,' he asked. 'So what? It's a fuck load easier defending a position than it is marching around Dacia looking for hairy arsed bastards to kill. Let 'em come to us, that's what I reckon.'

Mucius rolled his eyes. 'This probably won't be a town as we know it, Settus. It'll be some barbarian shithole with a two-foot high fence for a wall . . .'

'Then we'll build a fucking wall, you idiot. You should sack him and make me *Primus*,' he told Valerian.

'Assuming we have the time,' Valerian noted, 'you're right, Settus.' The Tenth's centurion gave Mucius a 'told you so' look, which Valerian was prepared to indulge. 'All this would explain the lack of cavalry at least,' he went on. 'Anyone who can ride has been requisitioned by Iulianus. I've requested a few *turmae* for reconnaissance purposes, though.'

'How many is a few?' the Mucius asked.

'Two or three,' Valerian admitted. 'Four if we're lucky.'

'So sixty to a hundred and twenty men,' the *Primus* pulled a face. 'Better than nothing,' he conceded.

'So you say,' Settus complained. 'Three horses each, those cunts. They get through supplies like nobody's business.'

'Speaking of which,' Valerian said, 'our target is on the river. We won't die of thirst and hopefully we can get resupplied if needs be.'

'What's the name of this pisshole, anyway?' Settus wanted to know.

'Durostorum,' Valerian replied. 'We're going to attack Durostorum.'

'Never heard of it,' Settus admitted.

'No one has, probably.'

Mucius laughed. 'Legate,' he chided. 'Aren't you supposed to say something like "we will punish the enemies of Rome and the name of Durostorum and the IV Felix Legion will echo down the ages"?'

'It will if we fuck this up,' Valerian said.

'*Summa exstinctio* won't sit well with some of the lads,' Mucius said after a moment. 'I've never carried out that order.'

Valerian sat back in his seat. 'As you say, it's a rare order.'

'Fuck 'em!' Settus waved it away. 'They all deserve to die. First, because they've defied the Empire, second . . .' he trailed off, meeting Valerian's gaze, ' . . . second because they more than gave you a rough time, didn't they? You should want to wipe the bastards off the face of the earth.'

Valerian pushed the memories of the aftermath of Tapae aside, the images still vivid and painful in his mind. 'I hate them,' he admitted. 'Even the women. But the children . . .'

'You're both going soft,' Settus snorted. 'Look . . . *summa exstinctio* is the order, all right? I shouldn't be telling you this.' He stabbed a finger at Valerian. 'You're the boss. And you fucking think too much – I blame reading for that,' he added. 'We've all been in a sacking,' he expanded. 'You know what it gets like when you take a town. Women raped, kids spitted, old people killed for sport and the men – well, they *have* to get killed. And all that is good for our lads, gets it all out of their system.'

'That's true enough,' Mucius said. 'But you know as well as I do that it wears off after a night or two. The lads can only get so pissed and fuck so many locals. If you've been there, you know what it's like. Once it's all over, the old ones are left alone, the women and kids taken as slaves or left alone as well.'

'Yeah, well not this time.' Settus folded his arms. 'Besides which . . . If we've got to hold a position, we can't be guarding prisoners and all that crap – they'll turn on us first chance they get. Better we kill everyone and nick their supplies. The lads'll crack on once they've had the orders. Better we do it when they're pissed up, though,' he admitted. 'For once, Mucius is right – some of them have kids of their own and that can make a man hesitate.'

Valerian found himself envying Settus at that moment. The world was simple for him – get an order, obey it. And the little man was correct – he should have no qualms about ordering the *summa exstinctio*; the Dacians had all but ruined him.

But not all Dacians. Toasting revenge with Frontinus in a Roman bar was one thing. Ordering innocents to their deaths was quite another. But he was in command now – a legate. And with that came responsibility; after all, it was his *virtus* that the Dacians had taken from him – and part of Roman *virtus* was doing one's duty, whatever the cost. 'The orders are explicit,' he said. 'We will carry them out.'

Taenarum, Laconia

'Lysandra!' The handsome Athenian leapt to his feet and rushed across the austere *praetorium*. She braced herself as Euaristos embraced her, kissing her cheeks and holding her close. Cappa and Murco had met the aging enthusiast before and knew his ways but, she noted, Kleandrias bristled at the Athenian's familiarity.

She blushed, remembering that the mercenary captain had almost bedded her when they were both out of their minds on cheap wine. Almost, but Dionysus had blunted Euaristos's spear that night.

'It is good to see you!' he said. 'And Cappa!' he broke away from Lysandra and took the bodyguard's arm in the warriors grip. 'Murco. Still dreaming of fine wines, my friend.'

'Good to see you too, mate,' said Murco, his usually mournful expression lifting.

It didn't take Euaristos long to be drawn to Illeana. 'Ahh,' he said. '*Aesalon Nocturna*. I am honoured to meet the greatest gladiatrix in Rome.'

Illeana appraised him for a moment, clearly pleased that he knew who she was. 'A pleasure,' she said. 'But I am *Aesalon* no longer. I am just Illeana now.'

Euaristos waved that away. 'You will always be *Aesalon Nocturna,* my lady, just as Lysandra's legend as Achillia will live forever. I am humbled in the presence of greatness.'

Illeana's eyes flicked towards Lysandra and she gave a half-grin in response. He may well have been somewhat over effusive, but Euaristos knew how to complement a woman.

'I have heard of your battle in the Flavian,' Euaristos went on. 'Everyone has, in fact. You have become something of a legend, Lysandra – the gladiatrix of Athene whom the goddess saved. Even in defeat to the mighty *Aesalon Nocturna*, you triumphed. A fine tale.'

'And a true one.' Lysandra felt a glow spread across her face. 'This is Kleandrias,' Lysandra introduced the big man. 'A fellow Spartan, my former trainer and dear friend.'

Euaristos offered Kleandrias his arm and it was taken; the tell-tale bulge in Kleandrias's biceps told her that he was squeezing way too hard as men were wont to do. However, as effete as he looked and acted, she knew well that the Athenian was a hard man and would not baulk. They matched each other for a time until it became embarrassing.

'We are here on business,' Lysandra announced, ending the contest.

Euaristos broke away and made a show of shaking his arm. 'Strong grip, friend,' he chided.

'It is the Spartan way,' Kleandrias replied. 'We measure a man by the strength of his arms.'

'I see you and Lysandra have the same book of stock responses,' he mocked, which made both Cappa and Murco snicker.

'Please,' Euaristos gestured to a bench at the other side of the room. Lysandra glared at her bodyguards who, suitably chagrined, went and got the seat and placed it in front of Euaristos's desk. 'So,' Euaristos clasped his hands in front of him, eyes never leaving Lysandra's. 'Business.'

'We are here to hire men,' Kleandrias began.

'You are?' Euaristos interrupted. 'Or Lysandra is.'

That threw Kleandrias somewhat. 'Of course, Lysandra,' he sputtered. 'But I am a former mercenary. I know your ways.'

'And I know Lysandra. I think she's quite capable of putting out her terms, don't you, friend Kleandrias?'

Kleandrias bristled but there really was no comeback to that. Lysandra was grateful for the fact that Euaristos was treating her with the deference she deserved. She was a little tired of Kleandrias leading the way and Illeana being the centre of attention. 'The goddess is indeed with us,' she said. 'Euaristos, I could not have hoped to have found you here.'

'Likewise,' he grinned.

Lysandra let his easy and predictable charm wash over her. 'We have been tasked with a matter of great importance. You have heard by now of the battle at Tapae?'

'Of course. Not good news,' he shook his head. Lysandra's eyes were drawn to his temples – he still dyed his hair. 'But Rome will endure. She always does. I expect that this Decabalus will soon be decorating a cross.'

'Would that were so,' Lysandra replied. 'But the ramifications of the battle are far reaching, Euaristos. The fact of the matter is that Rome does not have the manpower to crush the Dacians. Not without weakening her frontiers elsewhere.'

'How do you know this?'

'Because Sextus Julius Frontinus told me. I am here at his – and Domitian's behest.'

'You're not serious,' Euaristos leaned back in his chair. 'Of course, Rome hires mercenaries, but for specialist work – cavalry mainly. We've had no contracts from them. This season is almost over – everyone's gone to Parthia. Again.'

'That is unfortunate,' Lysandra said. 'But I assume that the Romans did not anticipate such a drastic defeat. Five legions were lost, Euaristos. *Five.*'

'By the gods,' the mercenary commander paled. '*Five*. The news was that Rome had suffered a set-back and nothing more.'

'Of course,' Lysandra said. 'What else would you expect them to say? The truth is somewhat different. Tapae is the greatest disaster since Varus marched into the Teutoberg Forest – and he only lost three legions.'

'Very well,' Euaristos said. 'I accept that. But why are you here, Lysandra? With respect, Rome has generals aplenty. And you are . . .' he hesitated . . . 'well . . . you're . . .'

'Yes, I am a woman. Who would suspect that Rome would assign a Greek woman to this task? It is an obfuscation,' she explained. 'Frontinus will send troops what troops he can muster. Decabalus will know of this – Frontinus assures me that he has spies and I have no reason to doubt it. It is my task to recruit a legion if I can. A surprise for the Dacians. They will expect three legions ranged against them. *My* legion will be the fourth. And Decabalus will have no idea that we are coming.'

'I need a drink.' Euaristos was earnest.

'I'll go,' Murco offered. He got to his feet. 'Come on, Cappa.'

'You don't need me to hold your hand,' Cappa retorted.

'No, I need you to pay.'

'Fuck's sake . . .' Cappa grumbled.

Lysandra was grateful for the interlude – it allowed Euaristos at least a few moments to digest what she had told him.

The Athenian rubbed his temples. 'We don't have that many men here,' he said. 'Half a legion at most. And they're not the highest quality. The best men . . .'

'Have gone to Parthia and it's late in the year,' Lysandra said. 'I have other troops – I hope to raise at least three thousand. Veterans of my battle for Domitian's birthday.'

'Your battle for Domitian's birthday was comprised solely of women. You're not seriously proposing that you march female soldiers into a war.'

'The Dacians do,' Lysandra said. 'As do the Gauls, the Britons and the Germans.'

'But they're all savages.'

'That is true. But civilised men baulk at killing such creatures. This was the undoing of the Romans at Tapae. They baulked at killing women. And were killed by them. That is why I *will* march female soldiers into a war.'

Euaristos shook his head. 'I am not sure that even you can do this, Lysandra. The men will not take you seriously.'

'They will take my gold seriously, though. I will pay them a third more than their standard wage. I have the money and I have the backing of Rome and her Emperor.'

Euaristos shrugged. 'We can but try. I am with you, of course. The others . . . I will arrange an assembly. You will speak . . . and we shall see.'

'Yes,' Lysandra said. 'We shall.'

Dacia

There was no change in the landscape, but Sorina could feel in her bones that they had crossed into her homeland. The taste of the air, the feel of the wind on her face, the music of the Mother's breath on the grass – these were of Dacia now.

The night was cold but not wet and the host celebrated the crossing into a new land. Thousands of men and women drank and made merry, singing the old songs and praising the god Zalmoxis.

Sorina had drunk herself into melancholy. She was in no mood to celebrate – guilt lay heavy on her shoulders, dragging her down. She berated herself for being a coward too; in her heart, she knew she should tell Amagê the truth. That they were all Decabalus's cat's paws, that he wanted to whittle down the numbers of tribes that had – as he saw it – defied him. Living amongst the Clans once again, Sorina had realised that defiance was far from their minds. They simply didn't care.

But she was afraid. To assuage her guilt would probably cost her life and wreck Decabalus's strategy. He was right: the truth was they needed the plainspeople to trap the legions and destroy them or the cost to Dacia would be very high. She knew from bitter experience the effectiveness of Rome's war-machine. Even in defeat, they would extract a heavy toll and, despite Decabalus's assurances, she did not believe that the legions sent this time would be such easy prey as Fuscus's men had been.

Fuscus had had five legions at his disposal and all the arrogance that an unbeaten army facing a 'barbarian' enemy could muster. He had paid for his overconfidence with many thousands of Roman lives – his own included. The next general they sent would not be so vain, she knew. Rome had not become master of the west by being stupid. Rome was a wolf, a tenacious, cunning creature that never gave in. Rome would win or Rome would die. This was their credo.

Sorina weaved her unsteady way through the camp, forcing herself to smile as those that recognised her embraced her. Each touch, each kiss on the cheek that she returned felt like a betrayal and she was eager to return to her tent and drink more so that sleep would claim her.

She found her tent – no easy task with her head fogged from beer and her path diverted by a milling sea of humanity. Sorina felt a weariness press down on her as she sighted her destination, a heaviness that permeated her very bones.

She lifted the flap to find that the tent was occupied.

Teuta lay on her back, legs splayed as one of Amagê's warriors fucked her. Teuta's eyes were squeezed shut as he penetrated her, teeth gritted, her skin slick with sweat. Her gasps and moans of pleasure were punctuated by the warrior's guttural enjoyment. Empty jugs were in evidence, left haphazardly on the floor.

The man stopped, feeling the cold draught of night air on his buttocks and Teuta's eyes flew open. 'Sorina!'

'Join us, woman,' the warrior said, his voice thick with intoxication. 'I am man enough for you both.' Teuta squirmed away from him, trying to cover her nakedness.

Sorina looked at them both. The smell of their lust hung heavy in the air. Teuta's nipples tight and pinched, the warrior's cock engorged and slick with her juices, his public hair damp.

'I just came for a drink,' Sorina said, her surprise numbed by the alcohol in her blood. She was not hurt – Teuta was young and her body was hers to do with as she pleased. Besides, Teuta was jealous of Amagê and Sorina knew her well enough to realise this was probably her way of getting even.

'I'll give you something to drink,' the warrior suggested.

'I am not for men,' Sorina said shortly, lifting a skin from the floor of the tent. 'Teuta – throw him out when you're done with him. And clean up,' she added.

She exited fast, back into the chill of the night, leaving them be. This had been coming; Teuta was not the Teuta of old, the gladiatrix of Lucius Balbus.

As soon as the thought came to her, she knew it to be unfair. Teuta was still Teuta – it was *she* who had changed. She was no longer *Gladiatrix Prima*. She was Clan Chief and the Right Hand of Decabalus. And Teuta was nothing but her lover. What could Sorina give her now? A home, wealth and a shoulder to lean on.

But she could not fill her belly with seed – and though she seemed young to Sorina, Teuta would soon be too old to bear a child.

It hurt that things between them could be reaching their winter. Perhaps she could mend it, Sorina thought. She would talk to Teuta on the morrow – she owed her that and much more.

Irritation hit her now as she sucked in a breath of cold air. Not because Teuta has chosen to fill herself with cock, but that she had chosen Sorina's tent to do it in – consigning her to a night of sleeping by someone else's fire.

She looked around to see the strong shape of Amagê walking towards her. She could tell by the Clan Chief's gait that she too had been over-indulging. The younger woman had a sack of beer swinging from her left hand.

'I thought this was your tent?' Amagê said – too loudly – as she approached.

'It is,' Sorina shrugged. 'It was. Teuta is within. She is . . . not alone.'

'Ahh,' Amagê threw her fleshy arm around Sorina's shoulder. 'You are not . . . interested?'

'No – they're young. I'm old, drunk and tired. And I'm not for men.'

'I'm drunk and tired too. Lay your head with me?'

Sorina's heart lurched with shock. She did not want to spend any more time with Amagê than necessary but she knew that to refuse would be to offer insult. She forced a smile. 'You honour me.'

They walked through the encampment, sharing the sack of beer; the liquor was doing its work on Sorina and, she could tell, Amagê too. The Clan Chief spoke of the coming battle and how she would carve up their enemy – it was the heartfelt boast of the drunkard – and the Earth Mother would hear the truth in her words. To drink before battle was to honour the goddess.

Thunder rolled across the sky and cold spits of rain began to fall.

The two women began to hurry, but as soon as they increased their gate, the sky split and let fall a heavy downpour, soaking them.

Sorina was sorely unimpressed by the freezing deluge – especially as Amagê was so drunk she couldn't find her way. They took several missteps and had to double back through crowds of people, all of them eager to be inside – which slowed their progress.

Amagê's tent – when they eventually found it was capacious, befitting a woman of power. Sorina was grateful as she parted the flap and stepped into the warmth. The interior was well stacked with hides that kept out the draught and ensured the floor was dry and a brazier gave out a dim orange light that swathed the tent in shadows. Amagê's belongings were stacked to one side, packs, bags and an assortment of weapons – won in battle and given as tribute, Sorina guessed.

'Agh!' Amagê cursed as she stumbled in. 'Fucking rain! Put more wood in the brazier, Sorina.' Sorina did as she was bidden as Amagê began to strip off her clothes, kicking them here and there. Her body thick and strong, her breasts heavy and her belly round – like the Earth Mother, Amagê was a vision of the fertile woman in her prime.

The Clan Chief wrapped a cloak around herself as Sorina too began to disrobe. Amagê's grey eyes never left her as she did so; her gaze embarrassed Sorina for reasons she could not tell. She had been naked in front of thousands of Romans, heard their screams and insults. Perhaps, she thought, it was just because she was long in the tooth. She remembered a time from years ago, she had seen Eirianwen swimming back at Balbus's *ludus* in the flush of her youth and felt the same way.

She was older now.

And Eirianwen was dead.

'By the Mother!' Amagê said. 'You're hard. Lean. Like a Roman statue.'

Sorina grimaced. 'I need a cloak.'

'Here,' Amagê rummaged around and tossed one to her. 'Sit by me.'

'Not more beer,' Sorina said, forcing a laugh. She had had enough.

'No,' Amagê said. 'Not beer.' She rose to her feet and went to her packs, the cloak wrapped around her and returned a few moments later with a small vial.

'I thought you were tired,' Sorina said. She could only guess what narcotics Amagê was planning on ingesting on top of a lake of beer and knew from bitter experience that the after-effects were seldom worth the experience.

'I was, but no longer. Put your tongue out.'

'Amagê . . .' Sorina drew back a little. 'I must rest.'

'You are a guest in my tent,' Amagê reminded her. 'Enjoy the hospitality I offer.' Sorina struggled to think of an answer that would not be rude, but none came to mind. 'Put your tongue out,' Amagê said again. She did so and the Clan Chief reached out and shook the vial, depositing two drops. Sorina swallowed. 'Disgusting,' she said.

'Yes,' Amagê agreed. She tipped a few drops into her mouth, swallowed and winced. 'But it will make your head and your skin sing.'

'And ache tomorrow?' Sorina forced a grin.

'No,' Amagê said. 'It will give you sweet dreams, a light head in the morning – and calm guts.'

Sorina found that hard to believe. And she was tired of the game. 'Why am I here, Amagê?'

'I rescued a sword-sister from a wayward lover and a cold night in the rain. You should be thanking me.'

'And I do. I am in your debt. But you are wise beyond your years. You have the magic and you are Clan Chief of your tribe and others. Those that rule do not think and act as others do, nor do they do much without reason.' Sorina swallowed and felt her eyebrows rise slowly as the narcotics began to swim through her system.

'I do have the magic,' Amagê admitted. 'And the brew we have drunk helps me see things. Now we will see them together. And we will stop the game and share some truths.'

Sorina wanted to back away – to flee even. But she could not. 'What game?' She blinked and puffed out her cheeks. 'By the Mother, this is strong stuff.' She gazed at Amagê, noting her slate grey eyes, her hair, shaved at the sides, the stubble and razor cuts on her scalp coming into sharp relief. She forced herself to concentrate. 'What truths?'

'Didn't you just say that a Clan Chief does not think as others do? You come to us with talk of Decabalus. That our swords are needed to beat the Romans . . . and yet, we don't rush to battle. There's no urgency in our march. Why?'

'You rule here, not I,' Sorina hedged. 'The tribes march at a pace you set.'

'And you have not come to me and asked me to hasten. Do you want the Romans to arrive and be ready for us?'

Sorina narrowed her eyes, hoping this would somehow disguise her thoughts. But Amagê was looking straight at her, peering into her heart. It was hard to think clearly – the narcotic was fast working and strong – and worse, she was not hardened to it. She could not tell Amagê everything. Nor could she lie outright. 'Yes,' she said at length. 'We do want that. We want them all in one place where we can annihilate them. To do that, we must make them feel secure. Decabalus plans to draw them inland from the River Olt; force them to stretch their supply lines.

'Decabalus knows they will have a rearguard – a single legion to hold us. Not because they underestimate us but because – after Tapae – it is all they can spare. If we give them time to dig in and feel secure, the Romans will believe they have the better of us. They are in for a shock,' she smiled. 'We are to destroy the rearguard and march to the rear of the main Roman army – as we did before. We will trap them between our forces . . .' Sorina clapped her hands together sharply, making Amagê jump in shock. 'And finish them.'

Amagê started to laugh, obviously amused and embarrassed at her reaction to Sorina's clap – a fact for which Sorina was grateful. She could feel the heaviness in the mood of the room lift. 'You scared me like a child,' Amagê admitted.

'It seemed like the thing to do,' Sorina grinned, hoping she had done enough to assuage Amagê's line of questioning.

'And what now is the thing to do?'

'I want to see what dreams your potion gives me.'

When Amagê leaned forward and kissed her it was a surprise. But with the drug now coursing through her system, Sorina felt her body betray her will and respond, a warmth flooding into her belly. Her mouth parted and Amagê's tongue caressed hers; the Clan Chief leaned in, the cloak falling away from her body, revealing her heavy breasts, nipples already taut with lust. She bore down on Sorina, kissing her with a hot, eager intent, laying her back and pressing her to the ground.

Sorina tried to rise and roll Amagê onto her back, but she resisted, continuing to kiss Sorina's lips and neck, her tongue gliding lower till it found her breast. Amagê's teeth played about her nipple, nipping and teasing it with agonising slowness. Sorina gasped in pleasure, unused to and thrilled by another woman taking the lead.

Amagê was strong and urgent in her hunger; she sucked hard on Sorina's nipple, drawing it into her mouth – and then bit hard on the sensitive teat. It hurt, the spike of pain a sharp contrast to the pleasure. Again, Sorina tried to regain control and again, Amagê denied her. She moved down Sorina's body, her body hot and slick with sweat and Sorina opened her legs, eager and expectant.

With Teuta it was different – she was soft, gentle and giving. But even in giving, Amagê took. Her lips and tongue explored Sorina's lust soaked sex with madding intensity, drinking her in, enjoying her excitement even as Sorina cried and begged for more. Amagê put her hands at the back of Sorina's knees and lifted her up, pushing her tongue into her anus. The drugs in her system coupled with this unknown and forbidden pleasure pushed Sorina close to the edge and Amagê must have felt her victory close at hand.

Her palms slid down the back of Sorina's legs to her waist and then she pushed her onto her knees; Sorina did not have time to draw breath as Amagê once again licked her, this time her fingers pushing in and out of her, exploring the most intimate parts of her – something she had not allowed Teuta to ever do.

Amagê's fingers pressed and teased her nub and Sorina heard herself moan, a low animal sound from the depths of her being and, like fire, the final ecstasy ripped through her with a shuddering, fierce intensity that she had never known. Her fists clenched the carpets beneath her, every tendon in her body taut with lust.

With the fire still burning in her, Amagê gave her no respite. Her strong fingers gripped Sorina's hair and pulled her towards her, forcing her head down to between her legs. Amagê was soaked with lust and Sorina was eager to taste her, desperate to satisfy her needs.

And soon it was Amagê who cried out and begged for more.

XXXIII

Ceramos, Asia Minor

Despite all the training, the endless hours of weapons drill and callisthenics, nothing quite prepared the body for simply walking mile after mile weighed down by armour and kit.

As the Heronai trudged across the sparse Carian landscape, Thebe recalled her first view of the place through the bars of the cage that had carried her to Balbus's *ludus*. The brief recollection took her mind off the pain in her feet, the weight of the helmet on her head and the annoying pain under her arm as every so often her mail shirt pinched her skin.

She should have listened to Titus; for once, the world-weary voice of experience was right and a horse would have been the better option. But the truth of it was that none of the women had horses aside from the pack animals that drew the supplies and thus, neither she – nor any of the commanders – would have them either. The *good for morale* and *we must endure what they endure* sounded fine back at the Deiopolis, but now, nearing the end of the first day of the march, she was sorely regretting her decision.

On her right, at the front of the marching train, Titus forged on, pretending he wasn't suffering. On her left, at least bereft of armour and weapons, Telemachus huffed and puffed, deigning not to curse, but instead keeping up a steady liturgy of complaining that at once amused and annoyed.

'I'm thinking I need to check on the supplies,' he said, waiting for Thebe to give him permission to take a break.

'If you think it's necessary,' she replied. 'Might take a while to get back up here, though.' It was petty and pointless, but Titus got a laugh out of it and Telemachus did his best not to look like he was sulking.

'We'll need to call a halt soon enough,' Titus offered the drowning man a spar. 'It's getting late in the day.'

'This is nowhere near twenty miles,' Thebe said.

'Nearer twelve or thirteen,' Titus agreed. 'But that's the way of it. These girls aren't legionaries and they're not used to this. Call an early halt and we'll go for an extra mile or three tomorrow. Besides,' he glanced at her, his grin laden with mischievous spite, 'they still have to make the ditch and rampart.'

★

213

That particular exercise had not endeared anyone to Titus. It took far longer to build the famed 'marching camp' in the field as they discovered and the ditch and ramparts had been completed by torch-light. Thebe felt for the women tasked with the backbreaking work of digging and piling the soil and felt that it was – while they were in Caria at least – pointless. She said as much the following morning.

'It's not pointless,' Titus informed her, his manner curt and profes-sional when she challenged him on it. 'They'll thank me for it if we have to do it for real in hostile territory. Besides,' he added. 'It helps with cohesion – though they carp and complain, it builds morale. Nobody likes building a marching camp but, by the gods, it unites everyone in hatred of the bastards that made them do it. At least at first. After a time, it's just another part of the day.'

They were on a rise, watching as the Heronai got themselves together for the march; like everything else, it was taking much longer than anyone – Titus included, – had anticipated. 'How are your feet?' she asked Telemachus.

'Amazingly, the swelling went down as soon as I took my boots off,' he admitted.

'That'll change on the march,' Titus advised him. 'But at least the blisters will numb up when you keep walking on them.'

'Marvellous,' the priest muttered.

'This is taking too long,' Titus observed as a pack mule bolted; chaos ensued on the plain below as the animal careened through the mass of women and material, knocking both aside with impunity.

Thebe recognised Helena's voice from her vantage point, the file commander screeching at her charges to catch the mule – much to the hilarity of those that were watching on and, no doubt, offering less than helpful commentary. 'What can we do to speed things up?' Thebe asked Titus.

'Not a lot,' the centurion admitted. 'The *lochagoi* will have to handle their own women,' he went on. 'The time for putting an arm around the shoulder or putting a boot up an arse is something you have to learn. There's a lot more to this than just being able to fight.'

'Maybe,' Thebe said. 'But that's the most important part of it.'

'Give them time,' Telemachus put in. He was walking around in circles attempting to numb his feet. 'We have a few days yet before we reach the coast.'

The trio watched for some time as the Heronai got themselves in order; Titus was right, Thebe thought. There *was* a lot more to it, but when the women eventually got themselves into the line of march, the main body of the army was an impressive sight. Their iron helms and armour glinted and the dust rose as their booted feet pounded the earth – the sound of the march added its own musical cadence to the scene. Behind the soldiery, the dust-covered artillery and baggage train forged their own less glorious path towards the coast.

'We should go,' she said, eliciting a muted groan from the priest.

Titus laughed. 'It will only be a few more days.' He rose and clapped the Athenian on the shoulder.

Telemachus looked singularly unimpressed.

The second and third days of the march were a slog; Thebe herself was footsore and suffering, but she dared not complain. At the front of the army, she marched beside Titus and she knew he was waiting for her to admit to her discomfort, but the part of her that was the fighter – the gladiatrix – refused to submit. Telemachus, however, had developed a 'sprain' and had to travel with the baggage train to rest.

Titus pushed them hard. 'You and all this lot are years younger than me,' he said as they pounded over the arid scrubland. 'This should be easy for you. I remember when I was a young man in the legions, we once had to embark on a forced march . . .'

'You think we will be there today?' Thebe cut him off. She had heard the 'forced march' story before.

Titus looked a little hurt. 'Yes. By mid-afternoon, if we keep up this pace. That's where we went wrong on this forced march . . .'

'Good. The women need a little rest,' Thebe said.

'There will still be a marching camp,' Titus stuck his jaw out, sulking.

'Of course,' Thebe agreed. She put her head down and kept going, forcing her protesting muscles to keep at a steady, mile-eating stride. Behind her, she could hear the women swearing and complaining – a thousand small things. Blisters, weapons unbalanced, needing to piss but not wanting to fall out of the marching line, stomach cramps at their bleeding time – all, she reckoned, to help them keep their minds off the march. Complaining was cathartic.

They pushed on, Thebe noting that the ground began to rise as the sun began to turn orange in hue. They were getting close and the thought of it gave her a renewed vigour.

'I can smell the sea!' someone in the ranks shouted. 'We're close, girls!'

Thebe glanced at Titus who looked well pleased. 'What?' she said.

'Morale is good,' he replied sagely. 'You've picked up speed. As have they.'

The rise grew steeper, punishing Thebe's calves as she pushed onwards. Finally, she reached the top and raised her hand to halt the line, but the words died in her throat. Below her to the east was the tiny village of Ceramos; to the north and filing to the west, the beach was black with beached ships.

'Halt!' Titus bellowed, making her jump. 'The Heronai will split by thirds. Construct the camp!' His command was greeted by a chorus of swearing and complaining, cut short by sharp words and some kicks from the *lochagoi*. He turned to Thebe. 'Those aren't military transports.'

'I'll take your word for it,' Thebe said. He must be correct – she knew well that the Romans loved uniformity and there was a huge variety of crafts hauled on the beach – none of which looked particularly military even to her unschooled eye. 'We should go and see what's what.'

Titus grunted in the affirmative. 'You and you!' he pointed at two women from the ranks. 'Fall out and come with us. The rest of you . . . get on with it!'

They made their way down the slope, grateful bodyguard in tow. As they drew closer, they could see the first campfires being lit and the sounds of raucous laughter floating to them, cutting through the gentle hiss of the waves.

There were no guards posted anywhere, just groups of men drinking, dicing and playing music. There were women too – from Ceramos, Thebe surmised, some bringing the sailors food and drink, others offering more earthy services.

'The villagers must be making a fortune off this lot,' Titus observed.

'Hey, hey!'

Thebe started as one of the sailors spied them and got to his feet; as he did so, she noticed her bodyguards' hands straying to their sword hilts. 'You Thebe?' the man asked. He had a lyre in his hand and, despite his hawk nose, had a friendly and open face; Thebe guessed he was in his forties.

'Yes,' she said.

'I'm Hermaloas,' the sailor informed her. 'Bedros asked me to keep an eye out for you lot. You weren't hard to spot,' he added, gesturing to the two Heronai who relaxed visibly.

'Bedros, of course,' Thebe said, recalling the apish sea captain who had once served Lysandra.

'Come with me,' Hermaloas bade them.

They walked with him, through the throng of men, both Thebe and her Heronai doing their best to ignore the offers that were thrown their way and the urges to be shown what a 'real sword' could do. 'Get used to it,' Titus advised her. 'I'm well used to the

217

sight of women at arms,' he went on. 'But outside of the arena, nobody's seen anything like it. You're still novelties.'

Thebe glanced at him. 'Novelties that are putting their lives on the line to protect them,' she snapped. Titus opened his mouth to respond but clearly thought better of it.

'Hey, hey!' Hermaloas shouted at a group of men. 'Bedros!'

'Hermaloas!' Bedros jumped to his feet and rushed over. 'Titus!' he took the centurion's arm in his own before turning to Thebe kissing both her cheeks. He reeked of wine and she realised he was more than a little drunk. 'What do you think?' he gestured expansively at the beached ships.

Thebe was momentarily at a loss. 'Impressive,' she said after a moment. 'There are many and they look . . . really big.'

'Too many!' Bedros tapped his nose. 'All these men can be trusted. Well, most of them anyway. We'll get you and your girls to Taenarum, don't worry. And I've warned the men that there's to be no funny business going on with you lot. I'll cut the balls off of any man that defies me.'

'I'm sure that won't be necessary,' Thebe glanced at her bodyguards whom she now realised were rather enjoying the dubious attention they were getting. She leaned closer to Titus. 'Get back to the camp. Post a double guard tonight, Titus. Anyone caught . . . you know . . .' Titus refused to help her as she floundered. 'I won't tolerate fraternisation,' she said. 'Anyone caught is out – no pay, no land, no nothing. I mean it.'

Titus regarded her for a moment, something like genuine respect in his eyes. He saluted and made off. The simple gesture made Thebe's heart swell.

'You want a drink?' Bedros almost shouted. 'Come! You too, girls!' He grinned at the bodyguards.

Thebe forced herself to smile. Bedros was Lysandra's man. Her choice. It would be a snub not to entertain him.

XXXIV

Dacia

Sorina regained consciousness, her head and stomach reeling from the previous night's indulgences – despite Amagê's assurances to the contrary, the Clan Chief was still fast asleep, oblivious to the noise of the encampment outside.

She rose and stumbled, still feeling the effects of the drugs. Gathering herself, she dressed with haste, thinking back to the night before. The indulgences had been good – desperately needed in fact – but in the cold light of day, she wondered why Amagê would pick her of all women to share her tent.

'I like you, Sorina,' Amagê mumbled, making Sorina jump.

'I'm not sure I like you anymore,' Sorina forced a smile. 'I feel terrible.'

Amagê propped herself up on her elbow. 'That's not what you said last night.'

'That was last night.'

Amagê smirked. 'I enjoyed it. Enjoyed *you*. It has been a long time since I've met anyone like you.'

'There are plenty like me,' Sorina was brusque.

'No there aren't. There are wives of clan chiefs or their daughters, but these days, it is mostly the men who rule. But you, Sorina, are not like most women. You are like me – and that is rare, is it not?'

'Perhaps today,' Sorina admitted. 'I don't know how things

changed; I was a slave of the Romans for many years. When I returned home, things were different.'

'More different in Dacia than with us,' Amagê said. 'But even in Sarmatia, things change.'

'Eventually,' Sorina grinned. 'You northerners are a rough sort.'

Amagê laughed at that. 'Lucky for you that we are,' she said after a moment. 'Otherwise you'd be running back to Decabalus swordless. You got your wish because you know that we love a fight.'

'You could have said no,' Sorina reminded her. 'And you still could send me back swordless if that is your wish.' This, she knew, was hedging. But she was a little tired of Amagê holding all the advantages.

'I could not, and well you know it,' the Clan Chief replied. 'Not without losing face and facing a challenge to my status. The Clans are sold on the fight – so a fight they will get.'

'Good.' Sorina moved towards the flap of the tent, eager to be away. The air was cloying and her head was still thick.

'Why not stay with me today?' Amagê suggested. 'I'm sure Teuta will not mind. My man will keep her entertained.'

'*Your* man?' Sorina arched an eyebrow.

'Of course.' Amagê sat up, the covers falling away from her body; Sorina was aroused at the sight of her nakedness – and annoyed that she was so. 'I wanted some time with you so I arranged for a handsome warrior to amuse your lover. I think she was enthusiastic enough anyway.'

The admission sent a mild spark of anger through Sorina. 'I am pleased that it worked out so well,' she said. 'We all enjoyed the night. But I am with Teuta – and have been for years.'

'Things change,' Amagê was blasé. 'People change.'

'Some people,' Sorina replied, careful with her tone. She did not want to anger the younger woman, but she was riding along a path that she was unsure of. 'We have been through a lot together.'

'That is past,' Amagê said. 'This is now. You are different now, are you not? No longer the slave, but the queen. The Right Hand of Decabalus, Warrior of Tapae and now, Bringer of the Northern Clans.'

Sorina puffed out a breath she did not know she had been holding. She sat on the floor, realising that there was no getting away from this conversation. 'What are you saying, Amagê?'

'You and I are alike. We are strong. We are *equals*. That is a rare thing for women in this world.'

Sorina smiled. 'You sound like I did when I was younger.'

'That is because it is true.'

'I am with Teuta,' Sorina said again, the words sounding frail even in her own ears.

'She is not your equal. In life. In bed. Tell me the truth – was last night better than with Teuta?'

'Nothing can beat the thrill of new flesh, Amagê,' Sorina said. 'But life is not all about that. There is friendship. Trust. Companionship. These things take time and must be earned by both partners.'

Amagê's grin was crooked. 'Are you rejecting me, Sorina?'

'You make it sound as though we were to be wed. We got drunk, we lay together. It was good. More than good. But I could not cast Teuta aside because . . .' She hesitated, unsure what to say next – and Amage's hooded gaze was smug because of it. 'Because I am loyal.'

'But you do not love her.'

'I don't love you either.'

'Not yet,' Amagê turned and lay on her front. 'Go then,' she said, surprising Sorina that there was no anger or malice in her voice. 'Run to Teuta. But remember last night, Sorina. And if you change your mind, you have a way out. After all, it was not Teuta who came to her tent and found a man riding you, was it?'

'If things were another way, Amagê, I would be with you. As you say, we are the same. And, I will admit – it thrills me that you would want me in your bed. And at your side.'

Sorina made her way to the tent flap. As she placed her hand on it, Amagê spoke again. 'One thing . . . I have decided that today will be a day of rest. After which, we will march in haste.'

Sorina dropped her hand. 'I told you Decabalus's plans,' she said. 'We must let the Romans think they are safe – it is a ruse.'

'I don't care.' Amagê rolled over to look directly at Sorina. 'A ruse that works well for Decabalus, perhaps, but not so well for the Northern Tribes. I've never fought Romans before, but I know that a well-fortified position takes many lives to overrun. Better for *my* people if we catch them before they are ready.'

Sorina met her gaze evenly, refusing to let her anger rise. 'As you wish,' she said. 'I am sure the end result will be the same.'

'I'm sure it will for the Romans,' Amagê rolled onto her front once again. 'But I think your Decabalus will not be best pleased. Many of the northern tribes defied him, did they not? I can't help but think that he would have been pleased if our numbers were thinned. As it is – he will be disappointed. But we all deal with disappointment.'

Sorina bit down a retort. 'I will see you soon, I hope,' she said and left the tent quickly, leaving Amagê alone.

The air outside was cold and sharp; Sorina took a deep lungful, letting the breath of the Mother clear her head. She walked away from the Clan Chief's tent at haste, hoping that distance would lessen the spell Amagê had cast. The truth of it was that she desperately *wanted* her again; Amagê was right, the passion they had shared had taken Sorina to heights that she had not felt in years. They *were* equals – in life, in bed and, she reckoned, with sword in hand.

And Amagê was perceptive – more perceptive than Decabalus had foreseen. The fact that the Clan Chief had worked it out on her own was a weight lifted from Sorina's shoulders – shoulders with her head still attached. Amagê could have taken umbrage at

Sorina's deliberate obfuscation of the truth and her rejection of her advances.

But she had not. Which made Sorina want her all the more.

XXXV

Taenarum, Laconia

Lysandra eyed the *latrunculi* board as Euaristos made yet another error, allowing her to take the game. She looked up at him and raised an eyebrow. 'You let me win,' she noted.

Euaristos spread his hands. 'Of course not,' he lied. 'It is merely that you are the superior *strategos*.'

'I am,' she replied. 'So there was no need to let me win.' Cappa and Murco got a laugh out of that, but not Kleandrias, who made a show of reading a scroll. Illeana was combing her hair, something of which she never seemed to tire.

At Euaristos's orders, a barracks had been laid aside for Lysandra's party and Euaristos, it seemed, had decided to join them. The Athenian had gone to great lengths to show hospitality, ensuring that they were well stocked with food and the best wine he could find. The surroundings were 'spartan' as Cappa and Murco kept saying as though it were a huge joke. Walled and floored with undecorated wood with low sleeping bunks and a rough-hewn table, it was, like the rest of the encampment, of Roman design. Several braziers were set about the room, giving a warm hue to the lamplight.

'Tonight's the night, then,' he said, placing the *latrunculi* pieces back into their box. 'I am sure that all the men will be yours to command, Lysandra. Your arrival here is all the gossip to be had. It seems that your famous prowess and beauty pre-empts you.'

'Are you trying to charm me, Euaristos?' Lysandra smiled, enjoying the attention. She could feel Illeana pout into her mirror; the Roman was unused to not being flattered first.

'Of course,' Euaristos was airy. 'You have held my heart captive since the first day I saw you.'

'Then you will find that fancy words aren't the way to a Spartan woman's heart,' Kleandrias snapped, looking up from his book. 'It is deeds of arms that inspires the heart of the Lakedaimonians,' he added. 'Not . . . poetry. Or whatever you call it.'

'I call it manners,' Euaristos replied. 'And it looks to me as though the lady finds my manners pleasing.'

'I am here!' Lysandra snapped. 'Do not talk about me as though I were not.'

Kleandrias looked chagrined. 'I do not like his platitudes.'

'And I don't like your attitude.' Euaristos rose to his feet – as did Kleandrias. 'You are my guests here. Have I not provided for you? Have I not ordered the men gathered so that Lysandra may speak to all at once – on the Saturnalia, I might add. What have you managed to achieve, Kleandrias? Save for training her to a defeat . . .'

Kleandrias balled his fists and Euaristos turned side on – ready to fight, a move not lost on Lysandra. She was about to speak when Illeana turned from her mirror.

'Now, now,' she said. There was something in her tone that made everyone – Cappa and Murco included – look over at her. 'Gentlemen, it is obvious to me that you are two fine warriors. Handsome. Strong. Brave. You both – as do we all – believe in Lysandra's cause. Yet, it is the way of warriors to compete – I understand this better than either of you.' She got up and walked towards them and Lysandra knew that the touch of Aphrodite was on her. She could feel it. 'But for all that, I ask you for her sake that this rivalry be put aside. Such petty things are for lesser men. Like Cappa and Murco,' she finished.

Lysandra saw Kleandrias visibly relax, charmed by the beauty of the Roman and Euaristos sat back down, the beginnings of a smile forming.

'Thanks very much,' Murco muttered – not offended but playing up to the joke. Cappa began to chuckle; it was infectious and soon, he, Murco and Euaristos were laughing like schoolboys, the heavy cloud of tension that had shrouded the room lifted. Kleandrias forced a smile and offered Euaristos his arm. The Athenian took it and as he did so, Illeana looked over to Lysandra and winked.

'I am going to walk among the men,' Kleandrias said. 'To see how the mood is.' Cappa and Murco rose too.

'Good idea,' Cappa agreed. 'Maybe we'll have to change a few minds . . .' he trailed off, catching Lysandra's eye. 'But I doubt it. Come on, Murco.'

Illeana looked over at Euaristos. He managed to hold her gaze for a moment before he spoke, realising that he had been dismissed as well. 'I will return when it's time,' he said. 'Do not worry, Lysandra. The men here know of you. They know you walk with the goddess.' He nodded to them both and then left them alone.

Lysandra watched him go. 'Well?' she said to Illeana.

Illeana poured herself a cup of wine and offered some to Lysandra, who shook her head and raised a hand. The Roman took Euaristos's place opposite her. 'He's in love with you, you know,' she stated, a grin touching her lips.

Lysandra was taken aback both that Illeana would mention something like that – and that her thoughts were occupied with such things. Besides, she was wrong and Lysandra knew it. 'Euaristos is a ladies' man,' she replied. 'He's charming and flattering – '

'Not *him*! Kleandrias!'

Lysandra's eyebrows shot up. 'Do not be absurd,' she said. 'He is my dear friend and sometimes trainer . . .'

'Who looks at you with adoration and is sorely jealous of your Athenian peacock.'

'Ah,' Lysandra waved that away. 'We are Spartans — as a people we find the Athenian ways . . . distasteful.'

Illeana did not respond, giving her words time to sink in. It could not be, Lysandra told herself. She entertained no such thoughts and it was impossible that Kleandrias did. Certainly, he was honest, brave and loyal to her, but then — as Illeana herself had said — she inspired others, did she not? She met the Roman woman's gaze and, as she had the irritating knack of doing, Illeana seemed to be staring into her heart and holding up a mirror to her soul. 'That,' Lysandra said at length, 'is a complication I could do without.'

'I just thought I would point it out,' Illeana replied. 'He is a good man. Maybe you should consider him?'

'I do not have time for such diversions,' Lysandra snapped. 'I have only ever loved one person. She is dead. And that is that.'

'A waste.' Illeana shrugged, giving Lysandra a spike of anger. Losing Eirianwen had been too much to bear and she had sworn she would not allow herself to endure such hurt again. She had sworn — but that had been long ago, and looking at Illeana made her regret her vow — and then feel guilt that she did so.

'I appreciate your concern,' Lysandra sounded taut in her own ears, but if Illeana noticed her irritation she did not show it. 'But there is nothing to be done about it.' She was about to change the subject, but Illeana, being Illeana, was relentless.

'You prefer women, then?'

'Of course. As do you, if I am not mistaken. You kissed me, after all.'

'That was because you are so adorable, Lysandra.'

Lysandra laughed despite herself. 'You are mocking me.'

'Of course I am.' The beautiful Roman reached out and took Lysandra's hand in her own. 'Just remember that he has feelings for you. Treat him kindly.'

'I will keep that in mind.' She wondered for a moment if Illeana's words and deeds were prompted by self-interest. Lysandra recalled before their first fight, the Roman had tried – and failed – to put the seed of doubt in her mind. Perhaps she was trying to play with her emotions now. She was about to question her but the words died on her lips. Illeana had nothing to gain. And, though the realisation was bitter, nothing to prove. She was *victrix*.

Lysandra withdrew her hand. 'I must prepare to address the men and convince them to join me.'

'Athene is with you.' Whatever gravitas that statement should have had, Illeana spoilt it with a mocking wink.

'You really should take the gods more seriously,' Lysandra muttered.

'I there are gods, they seem to indulge my blasphemy.' Illeana shrugged. 'Why should I change?'

Illeana left soon after – purportedly to find Euaristos, but Lysandra guessed that the Roman knew she needed to be alone. She prayed to Athene for strength. As the time drew close for her to address hardened, cynical mercenaries, Lysandra wondered if she could really sway them. Despite her certainty that Athene was on her side, Illeana was living proof that not everyone gave the gods their due reverence.

Perhaps she should ask Kleandrias or even Euaristos to speak on her behalf. Like it or not, the soldiers would take the word of a man over hers. This was not the arena and Lysandra was not beloved here, despite what Euaristos had said about her fame among the men. She knew well that the Athenian was glib, silver-tongued and more than overt with his flattery.

Lysandra eyed the wine jug that Illeana had left, wondering if a cup or two would purge her of doubt.

No.

The voice of the goddess whispered at the back of her mind,

stilling her even as she rose to go to the table. It was plain, then, that this was a task she must undertake herself. Lysandra recalled Athene's words to her on the shore of the River Styx. '*I can promise you three things: firstly, that what remains of your life will be one of hardship, pain and loss; second, that you will raise your shield in defence of your homeland; and third, that the name of Lysandra will be lost to the sands of history – but that of Achillia will be known many thousands of years hence, when everything Rome has built is naught but ruin and men have themselves become as gods.*' Hardship, it seemed, came in many forms. A Spartan – and she still was Spartan, she reminded herself, despite what The Matriarch had said – would endure physical privation without compliant. But this was a different kind of trial in an arena of which she was unfamiliar.

She had become a leader amongst the women of Balbus's *ludus* because she was superior to all of them. She had led and commanded an army at Domitian's spectacle and the goddess had chosen her to lead this fight.

But as the door opened and Euaristos came in, she realised that all of that was small comfort.

XXXVI

Dacia

The IV Felix crossed over the border from Moesia to Dacia on the evening of the Saturnalia. The entire legion complained, of course, but then they would. Complaining was as essential to a legionary's morale as a cup of wine at the end of the day's march, but once the orders had been delivered, Valerian

228

was pleased that the holiday was forgotten and his men just got on with the task at hand.

The weather was horrendous. Cold rain lashed him as he rode at the head of the column, the icy droplets unerringly finding their way through his cloak to soak him to the skin. At least he was riding. Iulianus had 'gifted' the Felix the four *turmae* of cavalry that he had requested and these men he had thrown in a small screen to cover the line of march and reconnoitre the surrounding area.

Not that Dacia was any different to Moesia; endlessly green, which would, he imagined, in summer be lush and verdant. If Dacia even had a summer.

Valerian hated this place.

As soon as the Felix crossed the border, he was struck by the memories of the battle at Tapae and its horrific aftermath. The Dacians had destroyed the army and almost destroyed him in the process, stealing his pride, his dignity – his *virtus*: the very essence of his being.

With an army again at his back, he had a chance for vengeance; a gift, albeit a dubious one, from the wily Sextus Julius Frontinus. Valerian counted himself no fool; this mission was at best dangerous and he knew well that if Iulianus failed, he and his men would be food for the worms.

But he would not be captured again. He swore it once more to Jupiter and Pluto that he would fall on his sword or cut his own throat rather than suffer torture at the hands of the Dacians and their Amazons who delighted in emasculating Roman soldiers – an act, he reckoned, that was as symbolic as it was barbaric.

The pounding of horse's hooves broke his reverie as a young tribune rode up, ruddy faced from the rain.

'Sir. Scouts report a farmstead not far from here. They think they've not been seen.'

Valerian did not hesitate; they had their orders and they had to follow them. 'You know our orders, tribune,' he said. 'Take a century of men from the line of march and destroy the settlement. If they have livestock and grain, bring it back. Destroy everything else.'

The tribune looked him in the eye. 'Women? Children?'

Valerian hesitated and cursed himself for doing so; revenge was well and good, but giving the order to massacre civilians did not still sit well with him. He told himself to think of what the Dacians had done to him – so he could stomach what was necessary. 'Yes,' he said. 'Women and children too.'

The tribune saluted and dragged his horse's reins about, heading down the line, calling out for volunteers. There were of course none, so he selected a centurion at random and was insulted roundly by the officer and his men.

Valerian raised his arm and called a halt to the march. He looked around at the endless green, the grey forbidding sky and the forests that loomed in the distance. He recalled that Virgil had said that Tartarus was a place of fire; Virgil had clearly never been to Dacia.

Valerian warmed his hands over a brazier, cursing – like everyone else – the amount of time the marching camp was taking to construct. The severe weather was making progress slow, the rain driving and cold. Men cursed as shovels bruised hands and feet slipped in the mud. One third of the Felix stood to arms – standard procedure as the rest dug in, screamed at by hoarse throated centurions who also wanted the work done.

In the distance, he could see a red smudge – flames from the farmstead he had ordered destroyed. A fitting announcement to Roman presence in this area, he thought. Further north, Iulianus would be marching away from the River Olt, he too bringing fire and sword to the Dacians. The Roman army had been terrorised by Decabalus and his barbarians; now, Rome would terrorise all of Dacia.

'Happy fucking Saturnalia. Sir.' Valerian looked up to see a filthy, mud-caked Settus making his way towards him. 'Don't ask,' he said.

'I have to.'

'I fell in the fucking ditch,' Settus muttered, thrusting his hands out to warm them over the brazier. 'The lads got a right laugh out of it.'

'I'll bet.' Valerian could only imagine the choice use of language that mishap had caused. 'How's it going?'

'All but done,' Settus informed him. 'Your *praetorium* is up, so if you'd like to accompany me, sir, I'll escort you.'

'Very kind, centurion,' Valerian offered.

They made their way to the ditch and rampart – which was less than perfect, Valerian noted, but in the circumstances, it was as good as it could be.

'Good to see you're drying out, centurion!' one of the men called out as Settus marched past. Caballo, Valerian recalled.

'You're fucking hilarious, Caballo,' Settus shot back. 'Remind me how funny it is on mid-watch.'

'I'll be sure to wake you, then,' Caballo – apparently unruffled at pulling the worst guard duty – offered. First or last watches were always preferable as it only meant resting late or getting up early. Mid-watch meant interrupted sleep.

'You wake me for anything less than an emergency and I'll carve your fucking balls off and wear them round my neck as a reminder of how useless you really are.'

Settus's optio, the formidable Slainius had evidently decided the banter was at an end. 'Caballo, shut your fucking mouth and get your kit together . . . that goes for all of you . . .'

Valerian and Settus moved off, the liturgy of threats and counter-cursing fading into the patter of the rain.

'You know Caballo used to be a slave,' Settus said.

'Yes, I recall.'

'It's a funny world where a slave is manumitted and gets to

join the legions . . . but on Saturnalia still ends up doing the work.'

'You could have offered to swap places.'

Settus did not respond to that and the two made their way in silence to the *praetorium* at the centre of the marching camp. Two soldiers were already on guard, one informing them that the heating inside had been attended to – welcome news to Valerian.

'All right then, sir,' Settus said. 'I'll get back to my lads – make sure that they're all in order.'

Valerian wanted to invite him in for a cup of wine, but thought better of it – Settus had a reputation to maintain and being seen as the legate's pet would not serve him well. 'Very well,' he said. 'Thank you, centurion. See you at the morning briefing.'

'Very good, sir,' Settus said. 'Oh, my report.' He handed Valerian a mud-stained and very damp wax tablet.

Inside it was indeed warm – and Valerian was not above enjoying the privileges of command. He eyed his bunk, which looked inviting. However, the desk that had been placed in the centre of the room had neatly stacked reports that needed to be read and a centurions' meeting that needed preparing.

Valerian sat at his desk, poured a cup of wine and began his duties, knowing full well it would be less than entertaining work. But it needed to be done.

He opened the first report, seeing it was from the Third Century: an account of the day's march, soldiers injured or sick and the sortie to destroy the farmstead. A list of supplies seized and enemy killed with the epitaph that 'as per orders, no prisoners were taken'.

That was it then, he thought. First blood to Rome. And he did not doubt that there was plenty more to come.

XXXVII

Taenarum, Laconia

The night was chilly and there was rain in the air.

Despite herself, Lysandra was nervous. She should not be, of course; she was well schooled in oratory and had many times used words to encourage the women under care at the *ludus*. These men – these mercenaries – should be no different. They, like most others, were her intellectual inferiors.

Euaristos walked with her to the edge of the encampment. 'There is a podium set up,' he told her.

'You should not have gone to such effort,' she replied, glancing at the darkened barrack buildings; it was eerie in the silence, a ghost town.

'It's always there,' he grinned. 'You're not the first person to address the men – nor the last, I hope.' When she glanced at him, he expanded. 'War is our industry, Lysandra.'

She could hear them long before she caught sight of the throng. Talking, shouting, laughter – someone was playing the pipes while others sang a dirty song about a Priest of Hephaestus and his iron part. 'It seems as though they are in good spirits,' she observed.

'It's Saturnalia,' Euaristos said. 'I've had whores brought in from miles around, although I've rationed the booze till after your address. I want them in good spirits, not utterly plastered and fist happy.'

They rounded a corner and Lysandra caught her first sight of the men she hoped to command; dark silhouettes, moving in the gloom.

She swallowed and offered a silent prayer to Athene.

'Don't worry,' Euaristos seemed to pick up on her unseemly nervousness. 'You'll be fine. You're Lysandra of Sparta. Everyone's heard of you.'

She smiled tightly. 'You're a good man, Euaristos.'

'Gods save me from that,' the Athenian laughed. 'I'm a rogue, and an aging one at that. But I thank you, Lysandra. Now . . .' he paused as they came into view of the crowd, ' . . . Athene is with you.'

She was struck by his words, a sure sign that the goddess had heard her prayer. There was no time to respond; Euaristos quickened his pace and moved away from her to vanish into the throng.

Steeling herself, Lysandra climbed the short flight of steps that led her to the stout wooden podium; it was stout and had several lamps at its edge to illuminate her. She looked over the gathered soldiers; there were thousands of them, dimly lit by torches staked into the ground. It was too dark to make out individual features, but she recognised the shape of Illeana standing right at the front, flanked by Cappa and Murco. By their side was Kleandrias, shifting from foot to foot. Recalling Illeana's words to treat him kindly, she offered him a smile, which she hoped did not look more like a grimace. She saw him incline his head, but his expression was lost to her in the semi-darkness.

Lysandra stood and waited, the wind whipping through her hair. At length, the hubbub of chatter and laughter slowly died out as did the music and she felt the eyes of an army on her. Lysandra puffed out her cheeks, steeling herself before she began.

'Get on with it, love!' someone shouted. Instantly, there was more ruckus, some laughing and others telling those making noise to be quiet – all of which added to the clamour. This was not going to be easy – goddess or not.

'I am Lysandra!' she shouted, her voice cutting through the

commotion like a spear shaft. She was surprised herself at the clarity of her voice and how it seemed to carry. 'My friend, Euaristos, tells me that some of you know of me. That some have seen me fight in the arena both in Asia Minor and Rome itself. But I come to you not as a gladiatrix, but as a priestess. My words are Olympus-born, friends – or may Zeus Saviour strike me down if I speak false.'

She waited – as she sensed were the soldiers before her. No lighting bolt was forthcoming, so she pushed on.

'I was born of Sparta, chosen to be a Handmaiden of Athene from my earliest youth. From there, in an act of the gods, I was made slave to the Romans and forced to fight in their spectacles. At that time, I knew not why. I thought that the goddess had abandoned me to my fate and cursed me. In time I realised this was not her intent.

'My years in the arena honed me. I was schooled in the arts of war, yes . . . but only when sword meets sword and the bloody terror of the fight is on you do you truly know your mettle. I have my wounds – all of them in front.

'As the gladiatrix Achillia, I fought many times, friends, and always walked away. Until the last time.' Her eyes fell on Illeana and she wished she could see the Roman's expression. 'In Rome, I faced their greatest gladiatrix – we fought. I lost. She – Aemilia Illeana, called *Aesalon Nocturna* by the Romans – defeated me. And I fell hard, friends. Darkness took me.'

She paused, gathering herself – there was silence save for the crackling of the torches and hiss of the wind.

'I walked the banks of the River Styx, lost until Athene found me. The goddess herself came to me and gave me this prophesy: *You can return to the world from whence you came or you can take your place in Elysium.*

'She told me that if I returned, I would know hardship, pain and loss but that I would raise my shield in defence of my homeland and that my name, Achillia, would live for millennia thereafter.'

235

The image was still so strong in Lysandra's mind that, for a moment, she was overcome by the memory.

'Ever have I served Athene!' she shouted. 'Ever have I done her bidding. For now, I know I cannot augur all of her words, but I can tell you this much . . . All lives are full of hardship, pain and loss. That the name of Achillia will live on . . .? The Romans have made an image of me in stone – and stone long outlives flesh, my friends. As for men as gods – you all want to be gods!'

This drew some laughter from the men, breaking the tension in the air for a time.

'*And you shall lift your shield in defence of your homeland,*' she said again, letting the words hang. 'I did not know what this meant until recently. Many among you will have heard last year, the Romans fought in Dacia and were defeated.

'I will tell you the truth of the matter, friends. Rome suffered more than a defeat. She lost *five legions* to the Dacians. Five! Thirty thousand corpses left on the field, arms taken, supplies looted, Eagles lost.

'Even Rome, with all her great power, is reeling from the loss. And she has sent what men she has north to face the foe once again. If they lose this fight, friends, where do you think the barbarians will go? With no army to keep Moesia safe, the door to Hellas will be open!

'The goddess has spoken to me with winged words! She bade me come to you, men of Hellas, to entreat you to join me in this fight. I have warriors – they, like me, all once fought in the arena. But they . . . like me . . . are just women. And we have not the strength to win this fight alone.

'Hellas needs you. This goes beyond concern of our city states and ancient rivalries. Those days are gone. Now, it is time for all Hellenes who can fight to stand against the Dacians.

'Athene herself has entrusted me with this Mission. Will you honour the goddess, Men of Hellas? Will you fight for her! Will you lift your shields in defence of your homeland! The goddess calls upon you – I beseech you, do not let her cries fall on deaf ears . . .'

The men before her roared their approval, drowning her out in a cacophony of acclaim that was akin to the cheers of an arena crowd. Lysandra closed her eyes and let it wash over, drinking it in as she had done that first time in Halicarnassus so long ago.

Eventually, they stilled and allowed her to continue.

'The goddess smiles on you,' she said. 'But I know that that is not food and drink, house and home! Any man that serves me will earn one third more than standard pay for his rank and specialisation. Any man that serves me and falls can be sure his will will be honoured and his kin taken care of by me – and by the Romans. I have the word of Sextus Julius Frontinus himself on this. You will be honoured, friends. By me. By the Romans. And by the goddess herself!'

They cheered her then, and Lysandra knew that Athene was by her side. Her doubts were banished for now: this was the moment for which she had been reborn.

As the cheering died down, a voice rang out: 'This is blasphemy! Blasphemy and bullshit rolled into a pretty package!'

A chorus of disapproval threatened to drown him out, but Lysandra raised her arms. 'Peace, friends, peace. All must have their say.'

A big man shouldered his way to the front – he looked like Heracles, all that was missing was the lion's pelt and the club.

'What is your name?' Lysandra asked, her voice icy in the darkness.

'I am Glaukos of Delphi,' he replied, his baritone filling the air. 'I've heard some speeches in my time, woman, but that is the most fanciful of them all! You're lucky this lot are mostly pissed up or cunt-struck with their whores. I've never heard such shit in all my life!'

Lysandra frowned, wondering how best to deal with her detractor. Challenge him? Ridicule him? Or listen to him.

'The goddess *chose* you.' Glaukos mocked. 'That's a laugh. I've prayed many a time on the field of battle, woman, but the gods have done nothing but watch my friends die and none of the poor bastards ever come back from Hades after talking to a goddess. And women? You have women warriors? Even if that's true — which I doubt — how would they do in a real fight against real men? War is no place for a woman. Her place is at home, tending the family and being a good wife.'

He turned to the crowd. 'You lot are crazy to listen to this religious lunatic. Come on lads — its Saturnalia for fuck's sake. Let's get pissed, fuck some whores and wait till the spring — its four moons away and we'll be back in Persia earning some coin. Leave this Lysandra to her Athene and — '

The ground began to tremble — it was marked, a leap in the earth that knocked men sideways. Shouts of panic erupted from the grounds as it shook, rising in its fury. Behind her, Lysandra heard the crash of falling pottery and then the groan of wood as some of the barracks huts collapsed. She gripped the podium, hoping it too would not fall. Then the tremor quickly subsided and Lysandra looked to see Glaukos picking himself up off the ground.

'I rather think,' she shouted, 'that the gods have spoken!'

There was silence — fearful silence now. Inside, Lysandra thanked the Olympians — all of them — even Poseidon — for the gift of Glaukos and the tremors in the earth. 'I am Lysandra of Sparta and I do not lie. Those that will march with me march with the goddess at their side and the Olympians at their backs. Those that don't . . .' she gestured to where Glaukos stood . . . 'it is on their conscience. But for now, our friend Glaukos is right. It *is* Saturnalia. Celebrate this night with your wine and your whores. And on the morrow, we shall meet again.'

XXXVIII

Amagê's rest day seemed to be spent by most of the encampment sleeping off their hangovers.

Sorina wandered here and there, unwilling to return to her own tent and equally unwilling to visit Amagê because she knew well how it would end. The Clan Chief's words played in her head over and over again. And though she tried, Sorina could not find fault with them. Teuta was not formed from the same clay as she and Amagê and only circumstance had thrown them together in the *ludus*.

Sorina told herself that parting with Teuta would be fairer to the younger woman, but she knew that she lied even to herself. Loyal Teuta, who followed her everywhere and asked for nothing in return. Teuta who had given her strength when she needed it, an ear to which she poured out her heartache. Teuta who had borne her madness over Lysandra and Eirianwen with no complaint. Others would have walked away, but not her.

But what else to do? Sorina was too long in the tooth to think that she loved Amagê – she hardly knew her. But there was something intoxicating about the Sarmatian Clan Chief. She had the magic as had Eirianwen, but Sorina had never wanted Eirianwen that way, seeing her more as daughter than lover. But Amagê excited her in a way that Eirianwen ever had and Teuta no longer could.

She paused in her walk and laughed at herself, garnering a few looks from a small group of Getae who looked the worse for drink. She was acting like a lovestruck girl. Sorina of Dacia, the Right Hand of Decabalus mooning over a younger woman. And the truth of it was that Amagê would cast her aside as soon as she saw fit. She was Clan Chief and she'd want her bloodline to continue.

Be that as it may, Sorina knew she had to make a decision. She turned and made her way back through the encampment to her tent.

'You've been gone all day,' Teuta said as she crawled in through the flap.

'Yes.' She struggled out of her cloak and coat, and sat cross-legged. 'We need to talk, you and I.'

Teuta's face fell. 'I am sorry,' she said. 'About last night. I was drunk . . . Amagê gave me some of her brew and it . . .'

'Made your skin sing?' Sorina finished for her.

'Yes. I am sorry,' she said again.

'I am sorry too, Teuta. I have treated you badly.'

Teuta's eyes welled up with tears and Sorina despised herself for despising this show of weakness. 'You have done nothing wrong, it was I who . . .'

'No,' Sorina cut her short. 'I too lay with another last night.'

'Because you were angry with me,' Teuta wiped her nose on her forearm. 'I understand. Please forgive me.'

Sorina sighed. 'There is nothing for me to forgive. I have been less and less to you these past months. We are like branches on the river, Teuta, drifting away as the current around us changes.'

'What are you saying?'

Sorina steeled herself. 'I think that it is time for us to part.' She had not meant to say it so soon, but it was out before she could still her tongue.

'No!' Teuta went white with shock. 'Sorina, I love you. You can't mean this!' She went to embrace her but Sorina moved back.

It was as though she had slapped Teuta about the face.

'I have been unfair to you,' she said. Teuta broke down as she spoke and Sorina's heart went out to her. But she knew she spoke the truth. 'We are no longer slaves to Balbus. We are our own people now – and we have changed.'

'Sorina, please,' Teuta begged. 'I am sorry for what I did . . . I was not in control of myself and it just happened. I was out of my mind, you have to believe me . . .'

'I *do* believe you,' Sorina's tone was gentle. 'I do. This has nothing to do with last night.'

'What then? Why?'

Sorina looked at her once-lover, face ruddy and streaked with tears. She felt sorry for her; it saddened her to hit her with words hard as steel. But she did not love her. Perhaps it was the magic of Amagê. Or perhaps not. But the night with the Clan Chief had broken whatever tie she had to Teuta, despite what she had said.

Amagê had known her better than she had known herself.

'I cannot find it in my heart to live a lie with you, Teuta. It would not be fair to you. You are a good woman – the best I have ever known . . .'

'Then stay with me, please!'

'I cannot. It breaks my heart to say this to you. But this is how it must be.'

'Why . . . Why . . .' Teuta clutched herself like a child, swaying backwards and forwards. 'Please don't!'

'I must. What would you have me do, Teuta? Stay at your side as my heart grew colder and yours grew bitter. You know the truth as well as I. We have changed . . .'

'*I haven't changed*!' Teuta shrieked. 'I haven't! I still love you, Sorina!'

Sorina did not answer, but her eyes filled with tears. 'There is a place in my heart for you, Teuta . . .' She stopped as Teuta rolled onto her side, sobbing uncontrollably. There was nothing more to say. Sorina grabbed her coat and crawled from the tent, the sound of Teuta's cries loud in her ears.

The air outside was cold and Sorina breathed deeply as though it could cleanse her soul. She walked away from the tent so that she would no longer have to hear Teuta's anguish.

She needed a drink and now, somewhere to lay her head. Somewhere, she chided herself. Somewhere would only mean one place.

Of course, Amagê was there when she arrived, sitting on the floor, looking at a map. She glanced up as Sorina came in, a slight smile playing about her lips. 'I did not expect to see you so soon,' she said.

'I have thought about what you said. You were right.'

'I always am,' Amagê laughed. 'You look like you need a drink.'

'I do.'

Amagê indicated a jug on the floor. 'There's plenty,' she said as Sorina stooped to take it.

Beer. It was warm and tasted sweet as Sorina chugged it down. 'I have told Teuta,' she said.

'I will make sure she is entertained,' Amagê brushed this aside as though it were nothing.

'I have wounded her, Amagê. Deeply. I think that it will take more than a hard cock and a few nights of drunkenness for her to recover.'

'That's her look out,' Amagê dismissed. 'Sit by me,' she said, patting the rug. 'Look at this . . .'

Sorina did as she was bade, her mind still on Teuta. 'What?' she asked, peering at the map. The lines were blurred and she found she could only focus if she leant her head back.

'This is a Greek map,' Amagê explained. 'It is old now, but things don't change much, do they?'

Sorina grinned ruefully. 'No. I suppose not.'

'Here is where we are now – or hereabouts anyway,' Amagê tapped the map. 'There is the bridge across the River from Moesia into Dacia.'

'This was where the Romans crossed before. They will do so again – they are nothing if not consistent.'

'The main force, yes,' Amagê agreed. 'But our task is to defeat their rearguard, is it not? So, if I were a Roman general, where would I set my line of defence?'

Sorina studied the map for a time, trying to concentrate on the question whilst thinking of Teuta and the hurt she had caused her. But she had to bring the task at hand to mind: there was a battle to be fought. Lives depended on the decisions she and Amagê would make. 'Here,' she pointed at a mark on the map with Greek letters by it. 'Is this a river?' she traced a line on the map.

Amagê nodded. 'The Olt.'

Sorina grunted. 'The Romans will want to resupply and it is perfect for them. This is where they will head.' She tapped a town on the map. 'I am sure of it.'

'And I.' Amagê took the beer jug and tipped it back.

'What is this place called?'

'Durostorum.'

Teuta could not tell how many hours had passed, only that day had become night. Never before had she felt such pain; it was as though her soul had been ripped from her body leaving only emptiness where once her heart had been. She cried till no more tears would come, her throat raw, her cheeks chapped and stained.

She eyed her sword for a time, thinking to end her life to stop the pain. Taking the hilt, she pressed the tip of the blade to her chest, steeling herself.

Survive. She remembered Catuvolcos, the kindly trainer at Balbus's *ludus*. He had ingrained in all the women there never to give in, that pain could always be overcome. She cast the sword aside; it hit the floor of the tent with a thump and lay there, an accuser of her cowardice.

Bringing the Gaul's broad face to mind seemed to numb the anguish she felt. She recalled her first days in the *ludus*; the Parthian,

243

Stick, crude, vulgar and the one that humiliated the new girls. Teaching them that they were no longer as they once were. Nastasen, huge and ferocious, black as the night sky like a demon summoned by Zalmoxis, Titus the Roman, hard but fair and Catuvolcos, good and kind. Those, were happy days, despite their slavery. Eirianwen had often opined that they had more freedom than most women in the empire would ever know.

Balbus had freed them all in the end and, she heard, gave the *ludus* to the arrogant Spartan, Lysandra. Lysandra whom Sorina had hated and Eirianwen had loved. Sorina blamed Lysandra for the Briton's death – but the truth was that it was Sorina's blade that had taken her life.

Survive.

That was what Sorina always did, and she must too.

Teuta roused herself. It could not end this way between them. She had acted foolishly and taken a man to her bed. Sorina had responded from spite – lovers did these things and she would make it right between them. Not that it would be easy, she told herself; when Sorina had set her mind to something, she was hard to turn. But they had a shared history, ties that bound them. They had faced death in the arena, they had loved, they had taken the heads of Roman soldiers and danced to the music of their screams.

She crawled from the tent and breathed deep of the night air. It was tinged with the smoke from many cooking fires and the smell of roasting meat. Some voices were lifted in song and it somehow angered Teuta that others knew happiness while she had suffered such a blow.

She would make it right.

She wandered the camp for some hours, not knowing where to find Sorina, asking many but receiving no answers that would help, causing her to venture further abroad.

It was a strange place, she thought, in some ways like the *ludus*, with all different peoples making up the whole; yet as it was back in Asia Minor, those of kin stuck together, Getae with Getae, Sarmatian with Sarmatian and Scythian with Scythian.

Teuta made her way to a fire, where men and women were taking their meal. They were armed with curved swords and their small bows were within arm's reach.

'Greetings,' she offered in Getic, hoping they would understand.

They looked at her for a time, then one spoke, his voice guttural, a Scythian inflection to his accent. 'You lost?'

'No. Yes. I am seeking Sorina, the Right Hand of Decabalus. I cannot find her,' she gestured expansively to the camp. 'There are many thousands here, it's like seeking a single leaf in a forest.'

The Scythian grunted and barked out some words to his people. One of them who was drunk, answered. 'Ruga here says he saw the Dacian Queen a while back. Heading for the tents of the Sarmatians. Mind you, Ruga's been drinking all day.'

'You and Ruga have my thanks.'

Ruga said something else and the Scythians laughed, but the leader whacked him about the head. 'He's drunk,' he said again. 'Good luck, woman.'

It was a dismissal, and Teuta guessed that Ruga's comment was how she could repay him; such was the way of men.

Teuta made her way towards where she knew the Sarmatians had pitched their tents. Though the hour was late, they were still abroad and she was forced to thread her way through crowds of people, picking her way past campfires until she reached the centre where Amagê's tent set out, grand and huge, befitting her status.

The Clan Chief was there and, by her side, Sorina. With them, a group of chieftains from the Tribes. They would be discussing tactics, Teuta guessed. She would wait till they were done and then approach – it was not her place to interrupt such a meeting.

As she watched, she saw Amagê's arm curl around Sorina's waist. It was not a gesture of a friend. It was intimate. Then she saw it. The way that they stood, the glances they shared . . . this was why she had been cast aside. Not because they had drifted apart but because Sorina preferred another over her.

Teuta reeled away, almost sick with the realisation. Blind with despair she stumbled away, through the crowds, uncaring of their shouts of anger as she shoved them aside.

She made her way back to her tent and looked, once again at the sword where she had left it, lying on the floor.

Survive.

She sat down and picked up the beer sack, taking a long draught, gulping down the sweet liquid as though somehow it would wash the sight of Sorina and Amagê together. It would eventually, she knew.

Alone with the drink, she fantasied about killing them both. Then, that Sorina would come back to her. Then that she would ride from the camp and live her days alone like a hermit.

None of it was true. This was life – pain was part of life. But her heart began to harden then and she swore to Zalmoxis that one day she would hurt Sorina as she herself had been hurt.

She would survive. She would go on. She would find another. But she would not forget. She would never forget.

XXXIX

Taenarum, Laconia

Despite the ground tremors, the mercenaries were determined to enjoy Saturnalia and so the revelries had continued long into the night. There were no slaves in the encampment, so it seemed to Lysandra that the men just took turns pretending to be chattel until liberties were figuratively taken and, predictably, drunken fighting broke out.

Lysandra and Illeana endured the evening within the relative safety of the barracks hut whilst Cappa, Murco and even Kleandrias drank themselves into insensibility elsewhere in the encampment – probably under the auspices of Euaristos. They returned in the small hours, legless and loud, thinking their antics and pantomime shushing were hilarious. As it was, Lysandra showed no mercy the next morning, demanding they get up and attend her. She baulked, however, when even the iron-constitutioned Kleandrias threw up all over the floor.

'That is revolting.' She could hardly upbraid him for the cause of the vomiting; she had been a victim of Dionysus more than once. 'Clean it up.'

'Why are you so keen to be up and about?' Illeana sat up in her bunk and stretched.

'Because she hates us,' Murco said.

Lysandra looked at him, then at the sheepish Kleandrias trying to clean his own mess and finally at Cappa, who still snored. She shook her head. 'I am going for a run,' she said. She glanced at Illeana.

'Why not?' she said.

'I suppose you want to sleep?' Lysandra said to Murco, who fell back instantly on his bunk.

'I will accompany you.' Kleandrias looked pasty faced but resolute.

Lysandra bit down a caustic response and forced herself to smile. 'Peace, Kleandrias. We have all been where you are now. Rest. I will have need of you soon, my friend.'

'Take a weapon,' he advised her.

Outside, it looked as though the encampment had been the site of a major siege. Men lay everywhere, sleeping off the night's indulgences. Some could even have been corpses. There had been violence in the night due to drink – making Lysandra vow to herself that she would ration wine on the campaign. She could not afford to allow such lapses of discipline.

She and Illeana picked their way through the buildings; some of the men were aboard, either having just woken or, more likely, still going from the night before. It was unseemly, but that was the way of soldiers, Lysandra realised. She was glad she had heeded Kleandrias's advice and taken her sword – as had Illeana. She did not fear attack, but she reckoned that the weapons would discourage any over-amorous intentions.

Once free of the encampment, she and Illeana broke into an easy run, Lysandra setting the pace, the Roman content to run at her side. The day was cold and fresh and a light rain had begun to fall serving to both cool and invigorate.

'That was some speech last night,' Illeana commented as they ran.

'The goddess was with me,' Lysandra replied. 'She guided me – '

'Don't say *with winged words*. It's too early for quoting Homer.'

'It is never too early for Homer.'

They ran on in silence. Lysandra wanted to ask Illeana how she felt the speech had been received, but she felt that to do so would appear weak. She looked across at the *Gladiatrix Prima* and realised for the first time that the desire to test herself against her was waning. Nor did she think Illeana was being duplicitous by accompanying her. Her friendship seemed genuine, as was her contrition at playing mind games before their fight in Rome. The truth of it was that she was quite correct in her observation that they were similar creatures and Lysandra was finding herself growing increasingly fond of the woman who defeated her.

However, she vowed to herself that she could not let the loss go unavenged. That was not the Spartan way.

Whatever that was these days.

Lysandra could smell the sea in the air and pushed harder towards it till she could hear the surf. 'Not much further!' she shouted to Illeana who was now bathed in sweat, her hair plastered flat on her forehead.

They ran neck and neck, up a slight rise; as they crested it, the beach came into view. They exchanged a glance and ran harder towards the surf, both laughing as their sandaled feet dug into the sand. Illeana was not about to stop, so neither could Lysandra.

The Roman splashed into the sea, churning up water before she plunged headlong into an oncoming wave. Lysandra took a lungful of air and hurled herself into the cold water and surfaced a few moments later, coughing and spluttering, her hair hanging about her face. She swept it back in time to see Illeana come up for air.

'Jupiter!' she shouted. 'Colder than I thought!'

'It will be colder when we get out,' Lysandra told her, already regretting her impulsiveness. She sloughed towards the shore, Illeana in tow.

'But it was fun while it lasted,' Illeana commented, wringing out her hair as they walked back to the beach. 'It really was a good speech,' she added.

Lysandra glanced at her. 'Are you being sarcastic, Illeana?'

'No. Even I was caught up in it. I think you made them believe that by following you they would be part of something bigger. But . . .'

'But what?' Lysandra asked as they trudged away from the surf, the sand sticking to their feet and sandals.

'But do you really think women can stand in battle against men, Lysandra? Normal women, I mean? Not like us.'

'Any woman that fights for me will have fought before as a glad-iatrix,' Lysandra said. 'If not in the arena, then at the Spectacle for Domitian's birthday. They will stand, Illeana.'

The Roman turned her eyes to the sea. Through the mist on the horizon, the tip of a mast came into view, then the sail under it. 'You'll have to prove it, you know.'

Lysandra looked out to sea as well, seeing more and more sails appear in the distance, floating in from the sea mist as though they were vessels of Charon himself and the sea were the River Styx. 'Then prove it we shall,' she murmured.

'That's a lot of ships,' Illeana noted as more and more vessels blackened the horizon.

'We have a lot of people to carry.'

Illeana looked at her, genuine respect in her emerald coloured eyes. 'These are your ships?'

'I am hiring them, yes. I have kept this facet of my mission secret, Illeana.'

'Why? It's truly impressive!'

'The Dacians have spies in Rome – so Sextus Julius Frontinus told me. All of this – everything I have done – is to keep our enemies from knowing that Rome has a little more muscle than this Dacian rebel-king is expecting. That said, I doubt very much if even he would be expecting a legion comprising women and geriatric Hellene mercenaries.' She sounded rueful, even to herself.

'Ah yes, but the goddess is with us.' Illeana nudged her, which should have been irritating but somehow was not. She linked arms with Lysandra and led her to a small hillock in the sand. They sat down, bodies close together to ward off the chill, looking out to the oncoming ships. 'You know I don't have much truck with religion, Lysandra,' Illeana said after a moment. 'But last night . . . it almost made a believer out of me.'

'Almost?'

'The ground shook when you needed it to. I've read your Greek philosophy and I know that logic dictates that it was just a coincidence. But truly, Lysandra, when you spoke I was caught up in it. I said to you before that I know why people follow you – but to hold a crowd like that . . . it was truly amazing. It was as though the goddess was with you, as you say she is.'

Lysandra looked at her and smiled, genuinely touched by the

words. 'Thank you, Illeana.' They were silent for a moment and Lysandra found herself becoming lost in the Roman's emerald gaze. And, for once, there was no chiding joke, no words from Illeana – she simply reached up and touched Lysandra's face before turning her eyes away and looking out to sea as the ships drew closer to the shore.

'You are late,' Lysandra told Thebe as the Corinthian ran towards her. Thebe ignored that and threw her arms around her neck, holding her close. Lysandra thought that she should say something; it seemed that everyone was getting overly familiar these days. But then, along with Telemachus, Thebe was her oldest and dearest friend. She saw the priest coming down the beach, Titus at his side as Thebe broke away.

'It was a hard march,' she said.

'Was it?'

'It shouldn't have been, but it was. We toughened up on the way to Ceramos. The girls are fit and ready, Lysandra.'

'It is good to see you, Thebe,' Lysandra's gaze swept down the beach, looking at the Deiopolis going about their work of unloading necessary supplies. 'They move well,' she nodded appreciatively. 'Cohesive . . . a team.'

She could see Thebe glowing under this assessment as Titus and Telemachus drew near. 'They should be,' Titus rumbled. 'We've drilled them well enough.'

'Should we make camp along the beach?' Thebe asked.

Lysandra thought about that for a moment. 'No. We can billet the women at the mercenary encampment. But we must make it very clear, Thebe . . . no fraternisation with the men.'

'We threatened them with exclusion should that happen with Bedros's men,' Thebe said. 'No pay, no plot of land – we made it clear that spreading your legs for one night of pleasure just wasn't worth it.'

'Excellent work, Thebe. Although we might need sterner measures than that once we are in the field.'

'Do we have to discuss it here?' Telemachus looked around dismally. 'It's freezing cold and I need a cup of wine.'

'I told you!' She turned and saw Bedros stamping up the beach. He gestured expansively to his fleet. 'What do you think, Lysandra? Didn't I tell you I could do it?'

'You did indeed, my friend. I am most pleased.'

Bedros rubbed his hands together and eyed Illeana. 'Are you pleased too, eh, pretty one?'

'How could one not be, Bedros? You are a man who delivers, I can tell.'

'Always.' He winked at her. 'The priest is right though. You people get along, we'll finish the work here.'

'I'll brief the *lochagoi*,' Thebe said. 'Triple the guards. No frathernisation – nobody in nor out.'

'Very well,' Lysandra nodded. 'See to it. The encampment is that way,' she pointed.

It was a reunion of sorts and Lysandra found herself enjoying the sight of her friends together once again. They represented two parts of her life, she realised. Telemachus, Thebe and Titus from her days under as a gladiatrix, Cappa, Murco, Euaristos and Kleandrias from her time as Matriarch of the Deiopolis. Her happiness was tinged with sadness as she thought of Varia and then of Eirianwen; how different her life would have been had they lived.

Illeana sat off to one side, sipping wine as she watched the companions reacquaint themselves and, once again, Lysandra was struck by the similarity between herself and the Roman. Lysandra should have been the centre of attention here, but she was not. She was content to stand aside and let the others indulge in back-slap-and-catch-up. She realised that in her younger days she would have been irritated by this. But so much had changed.

Back then, she had not known defeat. Back then, she had not been marked as *xenos* by the Spartan High Priestess. Back then, she did not have the lives of thousands balanced on her shoulders. She tipped back her small cup of wine and pushed the thought aside, rereading once again the orders from Frontinus that Titus had delivered to her unopened.

'We should talk now . . .' she said, her voice cutting through the buzz of conversation, 'of how we will proceed.' She gestured to the table in the centre of the barrack-room, indicating that they should sit.

'I took the liberty,' Euaristos announced. With a flourish he produced a map from within his tunic. He rolled it across the table and Cappa and Murco weighted it with wine cups.

'Our mission is to support the Roman Army in their defence of this town,' Lysandra told them. 'Here.'

'Durostorum?' Kleandrias raised his eyebrows. 'Never heard of it.'

'Nor I,' Lysandra admitted. 'But that is by the by. Rome has no reason to believe the Dacians will change tactics in this campaign. Why would they? They have the advantage of being on home ground, they have local support and – Frontinus believes – Decabalus's crushing victory will have consolidated his power and, in all likelihood, brought fresh swords to his banner.'

'From where?' Euaristos asked.

'From the Northern Tribes,' Lysandra replied. 'Sarmatians. Getics. And whatever other barbarian scum live up there.'

'They might be scum, but there's enough of them, I've heard tell,' Euaristos said.

'Precisely. Clearly, they are inferior to us in every way. But a pack of mangy dogs can bring down a lion if there are enough of them. And like wild dogs the barbarian is cunning, ruthless and savage.' Thebe caught her eye and Lysandra looked away quickly. Of them all, the Corinthian knew how she had felt about Eirianwen – a Silurian from the misty island of Britannia. 'They are lesser creatures,' she pushed on, 'and all that stands between them and Hellas are the Legions of Tettius Iulianus . . . and us.'

'We have brought over half a legion,' Thebe said.

'And we have a little more than that here,' Euaristos affirmed. 'So, one slightly overstrength legion of old mercenaries and holy women. Not the greatest of hosts.'

Lysandra pressed her lips into a thin line, her ire rising at Euaristos's irritatingly correct observation. 'We will be acting as auxiliaries to the IV Felix Legion at Durostorum. The spearhead of the Roman attack will be led by Iulianus, as I have said. He will advance inland from the River Olt,' she pointed at the line on the map. 'His task is to bring Decabalus to battle and annihilate him. As such his orders – and ours – are to execute the *summa exstinctio*.'

Titus raised his eyebrows and looked at Cappa and Murco. 'That's virtually unheard of in modern times,' he said.

'And the Empire has not faced such a threat in modern times,' Lysandra snapped. 'The barbarian is a blight on humanity, Titus. You know this as well as I. As distasteful as it might be, a putre-fying sickness needs to be cut out and burned away. So it is with the Dacians. *Summa exstinctio* is the order.' She remained silent for a moment, allowing that to sink in. 'As I was saying. Iulianus will draw out and destroy Decabalus. The Dacian king will be expecting his allies to catch the Romans in a pincer movement – trapping them between two forces and annihilating *them*. Our job – along with the Felix – is to prevent that. So we will hold Durostorum and keep the trap from being sprung.

'Now, we have invested heavily in light infantry and artillery.

254

We Spartans are supposed to disdain such 'spindles' as weapons of women. Well, I bring women soldiers with women's weapons. I want to kill as many barbarians as I can without getting anyone in my command hurt. So range is critical. Of course, I have infantry. Frontinus said he thought the sight of women warriors ranged against the legionaries unmanned them. It is an unnatural thing for a civilised man, I am sure. So we will match the Dacian Amazons with – '

'Our Heronai,' Thebe interrupted. 'Frontinus named our soldiers so, and it is fitting, I think.'

'Agreed,' Euaristos put in. 'But whether the Romans were . . . *unmanned* or not, we may struggle to convince the common soldiery here that your priestesses are worthy. I can't put it delicately, Lysandra. Most soldiers think women are good for only one thing – and it isn't fighting.'

Lysandra smiled slightly. 'Then we shall have to show them otherwise.'

XLI

The Hellene mercenaries had gathered on the plains near the encampment at Lysandra's request. They were in good spirits, laughing and joking and shouting ribald comments at the assembled Heronai – the Women of the Temple. Lysandra felt a surge of pride at the sight of the three hundred *hypaspist* infantry in their full panoply of kit. She was grateful too: whilst she had forged this sisterhood, it was Thebe and Titus who had honed them.

The two forces were arrayed opposite each other, the Heronai with their backs to the mercenary camp, having marched up from the beach – in excellent order. The *hypaspistai* were the biggest and strongest of her troops: they had to be; their heavy round shields and long, single-handed thrusting spears were encumbering and strength sapping.

'They will not fail you, Lysandra,' Thebe said as Lysandra pulled herself onto her horse, Hades. He had made the journey in the care of Telemachus and, despite her dislike of horses in general she was pleased to see him.

'I am sure they will not, Thebe. They look fit and strong. But it is my hope that Illeana can deal with the situation herself.' She glanced at the Roman who gave her a stunning smile in response.

'I can help,' Thebe offered.

'As could I,' Lysandra agreed. 'But you are too valuable to me to be hurt in a useless – '

'Pissing contest,' Illeana put in, hauling herself into her own saddle. 'Don't worry. I'll put on a good show.' She winked at Thebe. 'It's what I do.'

Lysandra tapped Hades's flanks. When he didn't move she did it again, rocking forward in the saddle to get him moving. Naturally, Illeana's mount was grace itself and she seemed to flow along whilst Lysandra managed an ungainly bounce towards the mercenaries.

They looked good, Lysandra noted. Tough men, armed in Roman auxiliary fashion – long spear, oval shield and the *gladius* at their hips. Like her own troops, there was a hotchpotch of armour and helmets on display, which was only natural given the individual resources of each man.

A lone figure strode from the ranks – Euaristos. Grinning, he approached them as Lysandra hauled on the reins bringing Hades to a halt. 'So,' he said, nodding a greeting to Illeana. 'How do you want to play this?'

'Let me speak first,' she replied. 'And we will see.'

'Be my guest,' he said, gesturing expansively to the men before moving back to his troops.

'Hades,' Lysandra whispered. 'Play along.' Of course, the idiot creature did not understand, but it made her feel better. She nudged him forward and, for once, he obeyed, walking in a stately fashion adjacent to the front ranks. 'Men of Hellas!' she shouted, hoping her voice would carry. 'My ships – and your pay – have arrived!' This was greeted with a lusty cheer. 'When last we spoke, I told you of our mission – given to me by Athene herself. I told you that my priestesses would fight at your side.' She gestured at the *hypaspistai*. 'Here are some of their number. Just women, like myself – and my Champion . . . Illeana of Rome!

'I know that words are just that – words. It occurs to me that to fight at their side, you may need proof that my women – my Heronai – are not tremblers. That they – like you – are warriors. If any of you doubt this, now is the time to lay those fears to rest. My challenge, then. Pick a swordsman – your very best – Illeana will better him. Pick your squadron – my *hypaspistai* yonder will match them. Our squadrons will fight with staves, of course. I don't want to lose my best soldiers in an internecine brawl!' Some of them laughed, for which she was grateful. 'But anyone who crosses a blade with my Champion must be prepared to die – as is she.' She saw that sent a ripple through them. 'Why the hesitant looks?' she shouted. 'Why the indecision? This is precisely what undid the Romans in Dacia! Illeana is a woman – you hesitate to draw a blade against her? This will get you killed over there, my friends. This is what the barbarians are counting on!

'Who is your best warrior? Who will match Illeana?' Hades continued to pace up and down. Lysandra tried to meet the gaze of the men in the front ranks, but none would look into her eye. 'I will give you some time to chose!'

Illeana watched as the Spartan addressed the men. Lysandra was a fascinating woman. Illeana knew herself well enough to know that that was what attracted her to the former priestess – and it was more than just a desire to take the Spartan to her bed. As she had said – they were similar creatures in many ways. But Lysandra, with her utter belief in herself and her goddess, could do things like this where Illeana could not. What was more, these hard-bitten, cynical and aged men were taking her at face value – at least for now. They believed that she had been spared by their gods. Like them, she was Greek; their own Olympian champion. She was somewhat jealous.

Yet, for all that, Illeana could not deny that this had been a great adventure so far. But now, as she knew it must, it would turn dangerous. Lysandra rode her ungainly way towards her and dismounted with little elegance. Still, she looked like a general of old with her armour and red cloak whipping around her.

'Are you ready for this, Illeana?' she asked, her ice-coloured eyes glittering.

Illeana gave her an encouraging smile. 'Of course.'

'Whoever they chose, do not end him too quickly. I need these men to be in awe of you.'

That made her laugh. Lysandra was so staid she left herself open for wit almost all the time. 'Oh, Lysandra!' she said. 'They already are.'

The Spartan's brow crinkled, clearly unsure if Illeana was teasing her. It took a moment and she realised that she was. 'I am sure,' Lysandra said. 'Beat him. But be careful.'

'You worry too much.' Illeana swung her leg over her horse's head and dropped to the ground. Lysandra opened her mouth to speak, doubtless about to launch into a list of reasons as to why she had to worry, but Illeana moved away quickly.

There was much discussion among the assembled men, argument and counter argument no doubt, but Illeana shut it all out and concentrated on warming up her body. It had been a while, she thought as she swung arms about, loosening her shoulders. The wound where Lysandra had ended her arena career protested as she did so and with the pain came a tiny spark of doubt – that worry that today might be the day.

258

Good.

Fear was part of the game. Fear kept you sharp, as long as it was controlled.

Illeana squatted down on her haunches, stood, and squatted down again, the movement making the blood flow into her thighs and calves, stretching them, enlivening the muscles and tendons. At first it was easy – it always was – but she continued, counting from one to ten, ten to twenty and so on till she had completed a set of one hundred. Her breath coming fast now, she dropped into the press up position, her body perfectly straight, taking her weight on the balls of her feet and her shoulders. Again, the count – slow and precise to eke out the exercise, making it harder.

Sweating now, she rose, stretching her neck from side to side, shrugging her shoulders to keep the blood flowing. She looked over to the mercenaries to see Euaristos standing with several men; it seemed that they could not pick a champion.

No matter. The truth of it was that these were just soldiers, used to press of battle, the quick stab and hack to end the enemy as fast as possible. She was the *Gladiatrix Prima*.

She strode towards her would be opponents, loosening her baldric as she did so. Her eyes flicked towards the ranks of men as they watched her approach and she smiled at one of them – and all of them at the same time. Some of the men nudged one another, each sure that the gesture had been for him alone. All part of the theatre, she had done this so many times in the arena. She lifted her baldric and, keeping a grip on the handle of her sword, flicked it away to reveal the sharp metal of her blade. The men greeted the move with ironic cheers and applause.

She reached the handsome Athenian, Euaristos, and his chosen men – three of them along with two white-clad healers. 'Euaristos,' she said. '*These* are your champions?' She looked at them as though they were children, come to an instructor for the first lesson in combat. 'Do you need more time?' Her opponents laughed at this and she rewarded them with an indulgent glance.

'You're perfectly gorgeous,' one said. 'I don't know if I want to fight you –'

'Or fuck me, yes I know,' Illeana interrupted. 'As if I've never heard that one before. What's your name, soldier?'

He grinned at her, showing a gap between his front teeth. He had dark, wavy hair and a grey-flecked, badly shaven chin with a dimple. Not a looker, but his right arm had both fresh and faded scars – of course, he was a fighter, he would not have put himself forward otherwise. 'Krateros,' he answered.

'And you?' her eyes moved to the next man. Blond, green eyed, wiry and probably reliant on his speed, unlike Krateros who looked more of an all-rounder. 'Sophocles.'

Illeana could not resist. 'Tragic.'

Sophocles smiled, but there was only meanness in it. 'As if I've never heard that one before.'

Illeana turned her mouth down and nodded – this one was dangerous. 'And you, grandfather?' she looked at the final man. He was bluff, grey and bearded, thickset and all brute force. 'Are you here to add the benefit of your epic experience?'

'Aye,' he nodded, unfazed. 'I'm Bion. Are you sure about this?'

Illeana arched an eyebrow. 'Sure about what?'

'That you want this to end in death? The older I get – and I'm fifty now – the sweeter life is.'

'If that were true,' Illeana responded, 'why are you still a soldier? It's dangerous work.'

'It's all I know.'

Illeana smiled at him. 'Come then, Bion. Let us see if today is your day?'

'You want to fight the old man?' Sophocles put in. 'Not much of a challenge. If this farce is supposed to prove that whores can match blades with men, then you should be trying to make yourself look good, not taking the easy option.'

Illeana looked right at him, her eyes locking with his, willing him to look away. He held her gaze and so she shrugged. 'I'm fighting the old man *first*,' she answered. 'You'll have your chance, Sophocles.'

'That wasn't the agreement,' Euaristos sputtered. 'There's only to be one match, Illeana – '

'You worry too much,' she cut him off. 'Come on, Bion.'

She turned away without waiting for a response. The gathered soldiers began to shout and cheer, pleased that the talking was over and the action was about to begin. Just as it was in the arena.

Bion was armed with a longsword – a Roman *spatha*, a cavalryman's weapon; he swung it from side to side, the blade hissing as he did so. 'I don't want to kill you, girl,' he said.

'Don't worry,' she told him. 'You won't.'

Bion chuckled and raised his sword to indicate his readiness. Illeana stood stock still for a moment, examining him: the speed of his breathing, the clenching and unclenching of his fingers on the handle of his sword and, crucially, his stance. He favoured his front leg as would a soldier used to carrying a shield. He moved towards her and she shifted to her left, her *gladius* still held loose at her side.

The soldiers began to shout abuse, wanting to see some action. And Bion obliged, lunging forward with a roar, the *spatha* cutting downwards; there was no need to parry – she could see from the angle of his attack that this was a maiming strike – as he had said, he didn't want to kill her. Illeana tucked and rolled away, knowing that he would follow his initial cut with a swinging cross cut – it was the only move he could make.

'You are fast,' he said to her as she sprang to her feet.

'You have no idea. Ready?'

His eyes widened as she said it – warning him caught him off guard as she knew it would. Illeana stepped in to close with him, intercepting his thrust by angling her blade slightly to her right.

The watching soldiers heard the sharp retort of iron on iron and roared their encouragement, but Illeana was not done. Their blades still joined she rotated her wrist sharply, trying to loosen the old man's grip on his sword. He fought it as she knew he must. Her blade was the shorter; she withdrew it fast and brought it over the top of his hand, rapping the flat of the *gladius* down hard on his knuckles. He shouted in shock and the pain forced him to let go of the weapon — and, in less than a heartbeat, the tip of Illeana's sword was at his throat.

The cheering was cut short as the stunned crowd took in what had happened.

Illeana felt the familiar surge of ecstasy that only victory could provide. As she had always said, the rush was better than narcotics, better than wine; perhaps even better than sex. 'Yield?' she asked. Bion's nod was nervous and slight — he didn't want to move his head too much lest the sharp tip open his skin.

Illeana withdrew her blade and Bion stooped to pick up his sword. She watched him, hoping he would not try to take her out with a surprise attack and he must have noted her expression. 'I'm not that stupid,' he said with a wry grin. 'Gladiatrix?'

Illeana inclined her head. 'Gladiatrix *Prima*.'

'She's a canny one,' Bion jerked his head at the distant Lysandra. 'Not one of us will be able to match you.'

'She has a hard sell. Will you follow her?'

'Athene is with her.'

'Of course. Send Krateros over, would you.'

Bion nodded and moved off to the jeers of his comrades; Illeana reckoned that his thoughts were rueful, probably imagining that he would never live down his defeat at the hands of a woman. She would, however, prove to his detractors that victory over a woman would be something they would not take for granted again.

She saw Krateros approaching; by his confident swagger it was obvious that he thought his skills would be enough to put her in place, despite the ease at which she had bested Bion. He was grinning, gesturing to the soldiers, encouraging them to cheer him on. That he thought this was a huge joke was written all over his face.

'I'm doing this for a bet,' he told her as he drew near.

As with Bion, she studied him and found that he – unlike the old man – was relaxed and confident. Perhaps overly so. 'You're going to lose.'

Krateros shrugged. 'Maybe. But by the gods, woman, it'll be worth it. It'll be like crossing swords with a goddess! I've bedded plenty of women in my time but I've never seen your like. Not even close.'

'You're not going to bed me, Krateros.'

'You wouldn't want me to lose my bet, would you?'

Illeana laughed with genuine warmth. 'You're an arrogant bastard.'

'But an endearing one, don't you think?'

'Have you been taking lessons in flattery from Euaristos?'

'He learns from me.'

Illeana was about to reply when somebody in the ranks shouted at them to get on with it. The cry was soon taken up and there was a cacophony of spear butts being banged on shield backs. She raised her sword and Krateros's own *gladius* came up in response.

Illeana leapt to the attack, deciding this time to take the initiative and shatter the man's bravado before he got his tail up any more. She went in low, weight on her front leg to strike up hard through his stomach, but Krateros was swifter than she had given him credit for, swaying back and avoiding the thrust. Illeana had to roll forward – and this time there was no flashy entertainment to it. She was over-extended and had to get out of the way of his blade, which cut the air where her back had been. *Rusty*, she chided herself.

She rolled to her feet at speed and attacked again, a high cut to the head; Krateros parried and her sword was forced up by the impact. He did not execute a counter cross-cut as she had expected but rotated his wrist and struck at her face with the pommel of the

263

gladius. Her left hand lashed out, smacking into his wrist and deflecting the blow. She refused to execute another downwards strike lest she become entangled with him – his greater strength could overwhelm her. Instead, she stepped out to her left and kicked him in the thigh.

Krateros cursed and stumbled; Illeana knew she had hit the nerve and his leg would be numb for a moment. She attacked again, hard and fast, a series of chopping and stabbing blows that forced him back, giving him no chance to regain the initiative.

But Krateros was good. He kept moving back, eventually putting enough distance between them to disengage. Illeana sucked in air and, as she did so, it was Krateros's turn to wade in – and his comrades roared him on. It wasn't very sporting, but she was Roman, he was Greek and they wanted their man to win for them and, she surmised, for men in general after Bion had been dispatched with comparative ease.

Illeana was breathing hard now, sweat beading on her forehead and running down her back – she had kept herself fit these past months but the training was nothing like that which she put herself through when preparing for a bout in the arena. Krateros could sense her weakening and he came at her hard, forcing her onto the defensive.

He stepped in with a thrust and she was only able to partially deflect the blow; his blade thudded into her collarbone and she felt the white hot lance of pain as her skin split and the blood began to flow. He was still close and Illeana reacted instinctively, a low cross cut that scored a deep wound across her opponent's belly.

Krateros gasped in shock and pain; he wavered for a moment and Illeana knew that this was her chance. Pushing the pain aside she attacked – a lunge, then a feint – a downward strike. As his sword rose to parry, she rotated her wrist, turning the hacking blow to another cross cut, this time to his upper arm. Her blade crunched into his flesh – blood erupted from the wound and Krateros went down, rolling on the ground in pain, clutching his shoulder, his sword forgotten by his side.

Illeana stood over him, holding in her elation. 'Yield?' Krateros just gasped and she took it for a 'yes'. She beckoned to the healers and they came at a run, pulling a handcart behind them.

One of them went right to her – probably at Euaristos's orders, but she waved him away. The wound on her collarbone was painful but not too deep. Illeana rotated her shoulder. She bit her lip as the cut pulled but she knew that she could fight on.

The healers hauled up the cursing Krateros and he yelped as they hefted him into the cart. Then they bore him away.

The men were silent – disbelieving and shocked at the turn of events. It must have looked to them that Krateros was winning and now he – like Bion – was sent back to them in defeat.

But defeated or not, Krateros had put up a hard fight and Illeana was tired from it. She wiped sweat from her eyes with the arm of her tunic and looked over at Sophocles who was making his way towards her. She wanted to finish him quickly, but she knew that she could not rush the fight. Trying to end a contest too quickly nearly always worked against the one who was trying to force the ending. Part of Illeana was cursing her overconfidence. Three bouts, back to back – she would never have countenanced it when she was in her prime. It was vainglorious and dangerous – especially fighting opponents who were naturally bigger and stronger.

She laughed then. She was Illeana, the *Aesalon Nocturna* and *Gladiatrix Prima*. She had defeated everyone who had challenged her. And this would be no different.

Sophocles scowled as he drew near. 'You won't be laughing at me soon, bitch,' he said to her.

'You're very hostile,' Illeana observed.

'I usually am when I'm about to kill someone. That cut will slow you,' he pointed at her wound with his *gladius*. 'You beat the old man and Krateros, but you won't beat me.'

'If you say so,' Illeana forced mildness into her tone; something about the man irritated her. She raised her sword, still slick with the blood of Krateros. 'Let's see if your bite is as bad as your bark.'

Sophocles dropped into a fighting crouch, his eyes narrowed. He was studying her, she realised, as she was studying him. He unafraid and confident, circling her as she matched him, step for step. There was cheering from the men, but it was muted and unenthusiastic; either the soldiers were not confident or Sophocles was far from popular. Illeana was inclined to think it was the latter.

With awful suddenness, Sophocles leapt into the attack, a thrust which she was forced to parry followed up with a swinging left hook. Illeana ducked under it and speared her own blade toward his guts; Sophocles was too quick. He stepped back and lashed out with a kick that caught her on the brow.

Illeana's vison flashed white and she fell onto her back, stunned by the force of the blow. Sophocles was at her in less than a heart-beat and it was all she could do to roll aside as his blade scored the earth where she had been a moment before. Illeana rolled to her knee and parried as Sophocles swung his blade at her – more to ward off her counterstroke, she knew. She went with the attack, her blade absorbing the force and she surged to her feet, slamming into him.

He was side on and she had the centre line – he might be stronger but his balance was off and he fell back. She did not pursue, using the time he took to get up to try and clear her head, sucking in lungfuls of air.

'You Romans are all the same,' Sophocles taunted. 'Your arro-gance will be your downfall.'

Illeana didn't respond – she was grateful for the respite. Sophocles came on again, a circling cut to her head. She swayed back and executed her own slashing attack, her blade scoring the soldier's cheek. It was a deep cut and he cursed in pain as blood sluiced down his face. He was not undone and came back at her, a volley of attacks that forced her back.

The continued assault was taking its toll on her injured collar-bone and she could feel the wound weeping freely now. Sophocles saw that she was tiring – she read it in his eyes. They lit up as she knew her own must when she was close to victory.

Despite Lysandra's admonishments, the contests with both Bion and Krateros had been sporting, but Sophocles was trying to kill her. Sweat ran into Illeana's eyes and her heart was beating fast as the soldier waded in with thrusts and cuts that she was hard pressed to defend. The harsh ringing of iron on iron was loud in her ears, cutting through the distant shouts of the watching men.

Sophocles's blade lanced towards her chest; Illeana twisted slightly and allowed the edge of her *gladius* to guide his attack away. It had been close. Again he came in, this time a low, up-swinging cut that she had never seen before; Illeana blocked low and did not see the punch that smashed into her temple.

The world tilted as she crashed to the ground; she forced herself to roll as she hit, but she could hear him rushing in to finish her. Illeana turned as Sophocles reached her, his blade cutting down towards her skull. She hurled herself at him, crying out in pain as his *gladius* cut her back open. She took him around the waist and rammed her sword deep into his guts and up into his heart. His blood jetted out, splashing her face and neck as she fell with him in a heap.

Leaving her weapon embedded in his chest, Illeana rolled away onto her hands and knees. She puked, the pain of her wounds and exhaustion overcoming her. Illeana wretched bitter bile, cursing herself, dimly aware of the pounding of horses' hooves approaching and passing her by. She looked up through matted strands of hair to see Lysandra trying to make her horse stop.

The Spartan leapt out of the saddle and ran to her. 'Illeana!'

Illeana was touched; there was genuine concern in Lysandra's strange blue eyes. 'I'll be all right,' she said. 'That was stupid of me.'

Lysandra was peering at her, examining her to make sure she wasn't going to keel over — Illeana knew this because she had done it herself many times to other fighters. 'Yes, it was,' Lysandra agreed. 'But glorious. They cheered you after the kill.'

Illeana shrugged and winced at the pain it caused her. 'I missed that. I was . . .'

'I know.' Lysandra's smile was tight. 'Is it bad?'

'I've had worse, you know.'

'Come,' the Spartan said. 'Let me get you to a healer.'

Taenarum, Laconia

Lysandra looked across the field to where the mercenaries were dressing their lines. She had read the theorems of battle many times and, though she had fought in one herself, she had never faced real soldiers before. There was something in the way they moved that put fear into her. These were professionals, veterans well used to the press of battle. And though the contest to come would be bloodless, Lysandra was afraid that her *hypaspistai* would not be able to cope with the greater strength and cunning of the Hellene warriors.

That greater strength could have cost Illeana her life. It had been a gamble — but a necessary one. That did not assuage the guilt that she felt, however. She should have been the one to face the mercenaries; it had been her idea and she should have borne the danger. Even if Thebe had been right, that Lysandra was the stragegos and she could not risk herself, it still did not sit well with her.

Lysandra turned her attention to her own troops. They were stationed in grim, silent lines twenty-five across and twenty deep. Their large round shields were resting against their knees, each one decorated with a *heta* for 'Heronai' and their eight-foot staves planted in the earth, the blunted wooden tips pointing to the sky. The women's helmets were uniform in the Corinthian style, the famous plumed helmet of the hoplite soldier of old, but their armour was a hotchpotch of mail and modified Roman *segmentata*.

Lysandra nudged Hades forward and he plodded to the right of the line where the first *lochagos* stood. 'Laurenia, isn't it?' Lysandra asked her. The woman was tall, dark haired and formidable looking, her helmet resting at the top of her head, ready to pull down.

'Yes, strategos,' Laurenia replied.

'What do you think?' Lysandra jerked her chin at the men they were about to fight.

'I've fought in eleven arena bouts, strategos. I've asked the *missio* once and got it because I fought my guts out. Over there,' she raised her voice, 'are men who reckon they're hard. Easy to be hard when you're in a line like this one. Not many of them have fought like we've fought. One to one. On the sands. I'm not scared of them, strategos!' At her words, some of the women cheered and thumped the palms of their hands on their bowl-shaped *aspis* shields.

'They are going to come at us hard,' Lysandra said to her. 'Illeana has already humiliated their best – they are going to want to take it out on us and prove that they are still men.'

Laurenia laughed. 'Let them.'

'Pipers are to the rear?' Lysandra asked.

'Aye, strategos. You make us dance to your tune and we'll smash the smug grins from these bastards' faces and leave them puking on the field.' Laurenia looked up at Lysandra and met her eyes. 'Trust us. As we trust you.'

Lysandra tapped Hades's flanks with her heels and he plodded down the flank of her soldiers. To their credit, none looked at her, all had their eyes front, each of them probably wondering what combat would bring.

At the rear of the line were the pipers, the youngest girls of the temple, most of whom were still in their teens; girls too young to fight. There were ten of them – enough to make a cutting racket that would pierce the cacophony of battle. Lysandra remembered well the fight at Domitian's spectacle – the sound had been immense, screaming horses and women, cheering crowds, the pounding of hooves. There was nothing in the world quite like it.

'Greetings, Heronai,' she said to the girls; it was important to make each one of them feel as though they were as important as the rest. She did not doubt that the younger ones had been hazed for not being able to fight. 'On you, all depends. Because if those loud-shouters in front of you can't hear what dance I want, it will go wrong for us very quickly. I am counting on you most of all.'

Lysandra looked across the field once again. She could see a mounted Euaristos trotting up and down the front ranks, no doubt exhorting his men not to fail. There was no time for that now, she thought. She could sense that the *hypaspistai* were keen and tense – ready to get on with it.

She drew in a lungful of air. 'Helms!' she shouted. There was a pause: the women were not ready for the command and some were scrambling to dress their heads. Lysandra gave them time, then ordered, 'Shields!' This time, the transition was smooth as the troops hefted their *aspides* onto their shoulders. 'Spears!' From the rear, it looked as though the phalanx had taken a small jump as the weapons were plucked from the earth. Lysandra glanced at the pipers. 'By the right . . . One . . . two . . . one . . . two . . . one . . . two . . .' At this order the women began to march on the spot: cohesion was key and it made sense to give them a few steps to get into rhythm. Lysandra's heart beat fast in her breast as she looked across at the Hellene mercenaries, her mouth dry with fear and anticipation. 'Forward!'

The pipes wailed and the women took off at a measured step towards the line of mercenaries. Lysandra saw Euaristos jerk the reins of his horse, pulling her head about: clearly, he had not expected her to be the aggressor and that she would simply wait for his men to march on her. 'Shields . . . Port!' she shouted and the *hypaspistai* responded, bringing their *aspides* to bear, each woman interlocking her shield with a companion to her left. 'Spears . . . Ready!' The staves came up and swung down in perfect unison and Lysandra felt a surge of confidence – Thebe had done well; better than she could have hoped. Lysandra had not seen the manoeuvre performed so well since her youth in the Temple of Athene.

'Here they come!' Laurenia's voice rang out loud as the mercenaries began to meet the *hypaspistai* advance with their own. That too was encouraging; clearly Euaristos was not a commander who liked to fight a battle sitting on his backside.

The Hellene mercenaries came at them in an easy trot, their line thinning out from twenty-five shields across to fifty – and they were smooth in the change, their movements showing them to be long-practised and comfortable.

'Steady now,' Lysandra spoke to the pipers: 'Extend the line . . . fifty shields. Ten left and ten right – double the ranks.' This was a true test – and Lysandra's heart was in her mouth. If her women faltered now, it would all be over before it began.

But they did not.

She presented the same front to the enemy, but the ten shields to either flank were double-packed with *hypaspistai* – weakening her centre but giving her wings that she hoped would provide a massive punch. She dug her heels into Hades's flanks and urged him forward. 'Middle thirty!' she shouted. 'Give ground when we strike! Give ground when we strike!'

The women in the line cried out, indicating that they understood. Lysandra jerked the reins, causing a snort of protest from Hades. 'Stop your whining,' she muttered as they cantered back to the rear. 'Very well, ladies,' she said to the pipers. 'Ready . . . at the double . . .' the screeching wail upped in cadence and her women responded, the line phalanx speeding up, eating the distance between them and the mercenaries. Euaristos responded in kind, his own troops breaking into a run. The Roman auxiliary formation was quicker and more flexible than her own and Lysandra knew she could not match them for speed. But she prayed she could beat them all the same.

Now it was all a question of timing. The battle lines drew closer and closer, the harsh war cries of the Hellene men loud and raucous. She couldn't give her order too early, the phalanx could fall apart if she did. But too late and it would not have enough momentum. 'Athene,' she whispered. 'Guide me.' Lysandra puffed out air from her cheeks and raised her fist. 'Charge!'

The line exploded forward, the women's feet in good time as they ploughed towards the onrushing mercenaries. She looked over at Euaristos and could sense his surprise at this, but he had only moments to take it in before the *hypaspist* phalanx crashed into the auxiliary formation. Lysandra winced at the impact and at once a cacophony of male shouts and female screams erupted as the fight began.

The *hypaspistai* crouched low, sinking their shoulders in the bowls of their shields to take the weight of the mercenary charge. Their staves licked out, catching men in their faces and necks.

In the centre, the Hellene men poured through the weakened line, the women in the middle ranks backstepping frantically. They had to absorb the attack: they could not hold and if they tried, they would collapse and the game would be up. But even as they moved back, their staves licked out, hitting the men and disrupting their formation.

The heavy spears of the auxiliary men were not as long as the eight-footers of her *hypaspistai* and their oval shields were not as big – they were struggling to get at their foes and she could hear the

272

shouts and curses of frustration rising as they were hurt and not able to strike back.

On the wings, her women ploughed into their opposite numbers, the heavier flanks forcing the Hellene men into a funnel. Arms raised and staves rammed into flesh and armour as the *hypaspistai* shoved forward. 'Come on!' Lysandra shouted without intending to. 'Crush them in! Crush them in.'

This had been her stratagem – give ground in the centre and squeeze the mercenaries in a vice – praying that the big *aspides* and the long staves would do the work before the men got to grips with her troops. It was working, but the girls in the centre were hard pressed to hold them now. Euaristos's men were not green or rank amateurs and they fought back with savage ferocity, bearing the pain of a whack with a stave to close in on her women and even up the contest.

It got nasty then.

Up close, both *hypaspist* and auxiliary were forced to use the *rudis* – wooden training swords. They were heavy and they hurt when they cracked you on the head. For a moment, Lysandra recalled Hildreth and her sparring match at Balbus's *ludus*. Hildreth had schooled her that day and soon after she had become friendly with the loud German. Until the day she killed her.

Lysandra forced the memory away and concentrated on the fight at hand. On the flanks, her women had managed to turn the auxiliaries and they were closing in. But the cost was heavy, she could see many retiring hurt, clutching injured limbs, blood pouring from broken noses and teeth. In the centre, however, the men had gained the upper hand and Lysandra realised that they were going to push through and escape her trap.

She looked over at Euaristos and raised her hand. He responded and she called out to the pipers. 'Sound the halt!'

They responded and Lysandra could hear the shouts of Euaristos's centurions bawling at the men to disengage: it was pointless to continue the fight now lest more people be injured. The lines pulled apart, shoulders heaving with exertion, men and women dragging injured comrades away. Lysandra pressed her lips into a thin line, bitterly disappointed. There had been no obvious victory – but her women had held their ground for the most part and fought like the Furies. In a real battle, the eight-foot *doris* would have killed and maimed, not simply bruised and inconvenienced. In this case – there would have been carnage.

But it was not about that.

She looked over to the mercenary lines where aid was being administered in the form of cups of wine. Her own troops, too, were being given a drink by the younger girls – and they deserved it. She rode towards Euaristos whose grin she could see from afar. 'Well,' she asked as she drew closer to him.

'Magnificent,' he complimented. 'And your soldiers aren't too bad either.'

'Do not be insufferable, Euaristos.'

Typically, the rebuke left him unruffled. 'I thought they were excellent. But it is not me you have to convince,' he gestured to his men.

Lysandra nodded and steered Hades over to the lines sitting auxiliaries. 'Men of Hellas,' she shouted. 'You fought well. I think you would have carried the day in the end!' This was met by cheers and no little laughter – of course they would have thought thus. 'But still – you were hard pressed, were you not? You know why this match was drawn and you now know the calibre of my troops. I see many of you sporting a bloody nose and broken mouth. In battle, those wounds would be killers, my friends. So I ask you now. Will you fight with me?'

Silence.

So that was it then. Lysandra cursed inwardly, but she would not beg. She would take her soldiers and face the Dacians with fewer numbers.

'I'll fight with you, Lysandra!' She looked and a centurion – recognisable by his cross-crested helmet – rose to his feet. 'By the gods, your girls can fight!' He aimed a kick at the man nearest to him. 'On your feet, you idle bastards! Who will fight with Lysandra, Priestess of Athene!'

The men began to get up, thumping their shields. One fellow began to chant and it was picked up by the others, their voices raised in salute: 'Heronai . . . Heronai . . . Heronai!'

Across from them, her *hypaspistai* rose too and cheered their opposite numbers. Lysandra looked over at Euaristos who was wearing a look as though he'd known this would be the outcome all along.

It was a good beginning.

'How did it go?' Illeana was sitting on a bunk, doing her best not to look as though she was in pain.

'As planned,' Lysandra told her as her friends fussed around the beautiful Roman. Even Titus was charmed by her – so was Thebe for that matter. As for Telemachus, Lysandra was quite sure he would soon be composing bad Athenian poetry just so he could indulge in suffering unrequited love. 'It was a hard fight, but the Heronai gave as good as they got. We have casualties, of course, but nothing major.'

'It doesn't feel like nothing major to me,' Illeana said. 'My back's on fire.'

'You were only supposed to fight one of them,' Lysandra reminded her.

'*You* said you wanted them to be in awe of me,' Illeana was all sweetness. 'They are now, aren't they?'

There was no point in reprimanding her. Lysandra would have done the same thing herself. 'As is everyone, it seems,' she said, glancing at Telemachus who looked away from Illeana quickly.

'So what now,' he asked, pretending he hadn't been staring.

'We are done here,' Lysandra informed him. 'There are no more preparations to be made. Tomorrow we sail for Dacia.'

A quiet settled on them then and Lysandra felt the weight of the goddess on her shoulders. She had said the words and sail they would – to her destiny. This is what the goddess held in store for her. All her life, her sorrows, her training, every triumph and every catastrophe, it had all been in preparation for what was to come. For this fight she had given up her place in Elysium.

'The goddess is with us,' Kleandrias said. 'We shall win,'

'Or die,' muttered Telemachus.

'Win or die,' Lysandra smiled. 'That is the Spartan way.'

Durostorum, Dacia

They had laid waste to the surroundings. Villages, farmsteads and isolated communities had been wiped out. Slim pickings for the troops in terms of booty and, Mucius thought, it had taken far too long. That was the trouble with *summa extinctio*: you had to be thorough. As it was, the march to Durostorum had taken ten days – too many in his view.

The Felix was drawn up in a crescent, cutting the small town off by land – the only escape would be by river and those that could get away probably would have done so by now. Those that remained were in a hopeless position and they must now see it.

'Not much to look at, is it?' Valerian said.

Mucius had to agree. It was just like a thousand other barbarian towns – a ramshackle collection of stone and wooden houses surrounded by an unimpressive wall that the Felix would have to raise and reinforce once they had taken the town. But, unimpressive or not, the Dacians had men standing to arms on it waiting for the inevitable attack. 'We should get on with it, sir,' he advised.

'He's right,' Settus agreed. 'The boys are ready and these cunts will roll over as soon as we get anywhere near them. And there'll be women in there.'

Mucius saw the look of distaste on Valerian's aristocratic face. Well, war was not something for a man of delicate sensibilities. Men would kill, men would die and women would be raped – and then they would die too, as per the orders of the Emperor himself. A shame about the kids, though, but Mucius knew well that today's children were tomorrow's trouble and nothing made a more committed insurgent than slain parents.

'Hit them with some artillery, sir?' Mucius prompted.

Valerian nodded. 'Yes. You'd better get back to your men. I'll order you in as soon as we've cleared the walls.'

'Very good, sir.' Mucius saluted and made off, Settus at his side. 'He doesn't seem too keen now that we're at the business end,' he confided to the little man as soon as they were out of earshot.

'He's a gentleman. And a gentle man,' Settus replied. 'Not cut from the same cloth as us, mate. Saying that – he's a hard cunt when he has to be. But unlike myself, he's not a man of war. He doesn't like the work, you know what I mean? It's just a means to an end to him. Still, that's why he's the legate and has blokes like you and me to do the killing.'

Mucius laughed. 'You really do love it, don't you?'

'Fucking right I do. Frontinus gave me a second shot – this is the life I love, mate. Nothing like it when you're in the fight, eh? Speaking of which – I'll see you when it's over, all right?'

'Good luck, Settus.'

Mucius turned away and strode towards the First of the First where Livius was waiting. The men looked in good shape, Mucius thought and Settus was right – they were eager. The truth of it was that soldiers liked to fight – it was a welcome break in the endless toil of marching and building. 'Livius,' he greeted.

'*Primus*. Let me guess – a bombardment followed by a full assault.'

'Caesar must be sitting on your shoulder.'

'I hope so,' Livius said. 'I could use all the luck. I have a bad feeling about this.'

'If you get killed, I'll be sure to toast your shade,' Mucius offered.

'I'm just saying that we should be careful.'

'You're always careful, Livius. Ah,' he said, hearing harsh orders being shouted from the rear. 'Here we go then.'

No sooner had the words left his mouth when the familiar hiss-thunk of the Felix's onagers sounded. Everyone looked up as the stone shot arced skywards and fell with awful inevitability towards the men defending Durostorum.

Some of the shot fell short or landed within the town, but many hit the wall, sending stone shards and body parts flying. Even from here, Mucius could hear the screams of the injured. Nothing worse than having to stand there and take it without being able to get back at the enemy, he thought.

The second volley was on its way scant moments later – clearly the artillery boys were wound as tightly as their machines. Just like the legionaries, they wanted to prove that they could put their training into practice.

The shot they used was stone and about the size of a man's head. It was heavy and caused mayhem when dropped from on high – as the men of Durostorum were learning. Shot didn't discriminate – flesh or stone, whatever it hit it destroyed. The defenders had seen this up close and had – for now – fled the wall.

The bombardment continued and Mucius noted that Valerian was savvy enough to have ordered a focal point for the pounding once the range finding shots were complete. This would mean less work for them later as the entire wall wouldn't have to be repaired.

Shot rained down at the wall, merciless and unstoppable, pounding the shoddy building work to rubble, opening a widening breach that the men of the legions would soon pour through.

The *buccinas* – the military trumpets – rang out the orders to stand ready. This was it, then. 'Shields up and helmets on, boys!' Mucius shouted. 'Let's make short work of this and get in amongst the women and the wine!' The First of the First gave a small cheer, but they would be focussed now. Any man about to go into the fight knew he had to try and channel the fear he had in his guts into controlled aggression.

'This is it, this is it,' Livius said.

'Steady now, lads!' Mucius bawled. 'Remember your training.' The trumpets sounded again – the order for general advance. 'By the right! Forward . . . march!' The First of the First would lead the attack as was their right – and all would be looking to them now.

The IV Felix lumbered forward, a machine honed by many hours of practice. Perhaps not as smoothly as Mucius would have liked, but he had to admit that Valerian had done a good job with the men at his disposal. But manoevring was one thing: the real test of the legion would come once the bleeding began.

The wet grass underfoot trembled with the marching feet, a rhythmic thudding that brought comfort to Mucius and, he guessed, terror to the men preparing to face them. What must it be like to see the full might of Rome turned against you? How would those men be feeling now? That Nemesis, the Goddess of Vengeance was taking her due? Because it was more than likely that some of these men had been dancing on Roman bodies when Cornelius Fuscus and his lot had been wiped out the previous year.

Mucius could hear them now, shouting their defiance at the legion as it bore down on them, their faces twisted in rage, fear and hate. What few archers they had were loosing shafts at him and his men. Here and there, he heard the sharp pang of a spindle careening off a helmet or a curse as one found its mark. He wasn't going to order the *testudo* for these amateurs, he thought. 'All right,' he shouted. 'Double time boys, by the right . . . double . . . time!'

At his word, the First of the First broke into a trot, their easy strides eating up the distance between them and the breach. It was packed with men now, cursing and brandishing their weapons. Flanking them on the less damaged portions of the defence, he could see steaming pots being hefted into position. Boiling water or boiling oil, it made no difference when the stuff fell on you. 'Mind your step,' Mucius shouted out – needlessly as every man knew that the debris from the wall would make footing treacherous.

By the gods, the Dacians were *big*. Mucius had faced barbarians before but even so, nothing prepared a man for going up against a foe who towered over him. The only comfort was that these were probably blacksmiths, tanners and masons – amateurs who would do all right when things were going well and would cave in as soon as the going got tough. That was what he always told himself.

The ground began to rise and Mucius was forced to look down every so often as the debris from the wall threatened to trip him. He glanced along the line of legionaries – it was not as straight as it could be, undulating, bowing and curving as men struggled over the rough ground. 'Keep those fucking shields up!' he shouted as a fresh volley of missiles flew from the breach and the walls. He heard Roman voices cry out as, at closer range, the arrows and spears of the Dacians began to take their toll. The legionaries were not carrying their *pila* for the assault – the spears would only encumber them as they tried to take the breach.

Mucius ducked involuntarily as an arrow thudded into his shield. They were close now and his soldiers were bunching up behind him, forming a wedge that would slice through the breach. On either side, the rest of the legion was advancing, siege ladders to the fore. The First of the First's advance would have sucked in men to hold the breach – thus leaving the rest of the walls not so heavily defended. Good on Valerian, Mucius thought.

Mucius gripped his sword tight and his shield tighter, peaking over the top as he came closer to the breach. They were close enough now to hear the individual shouts and taunts of the Dacians. Mucius singled one out, their biggest, armed with their cursed *sica* – the strange, angled sword designed to cleave through Roman helmets that had spilled the brains of many of Fuscus's men. He steeled himself and ran forward, shouting incoherently. The barbarian screamed and hefted his weapon and then, in an instant, the battle was joined.

The Dacian hacked down with the *sica* but Mucius punched forward with a raised shield, catching the man under the arm to deflect the blow; at the same time, he stabbed out with his *gladius*, hard enough to cut through the Dacian's leather armour, not so hard the blade would become wedged. The Dacian fell and began screaming as he was trampled by the hobnailed boots of the First.

The momentum of the men behind him propelled Mucius forward – faster than he would have liked, but there was no stopping the First now. It was loud – the cacophony of battle, the screams, the clashing of iron on iron, the endless whump-whump-whump of shields colliding – so loud that a man couldn't hear his own shouts over the din. Off to the sides, though, the piercing wail of burned men cut through the clamour of war as the boiling pans ditched their deadly contents.

Mucius plunged his sword into the guts of an unarmoured man, feeling the hot spray of blood on his arm as the man screamed, but even as he fell, the centurion was staggered by a blow to the head. A man to his left was raising a sword to strike again but Livius was there, smashing the boss of his *scutum* into the Dacian's face before finishing him with a stab in the chest.

It was a melee now, men pressed in tight together – and it was here that the Roman superiority of armour and kit began to show its worth. The Dacians, with their bigger weapons could not easily bring them to bear in the crush. But the short, stabbing *gladius* was designed for this. You didn't have to spill a man's gizzards or split him from shoulder to neck to kill him – he died just as easily with finger's-worth of iron in him. Slower maybe, but dead was dead.

A big man grabbed at Mucius's shield, trying to wrench it from his grasp – the centurion let the man pull, surprising him and causing him to lose balance. Mucius did not give him the chance to regain it, slamming the *gladius* into his groin. Gouts of dark blood erupted from the wound as the man fell into the Tartarus that was the ground of any fight. A man standing had a chance, but a man on the ground was as good as dead – a slow, agonising way to go, trampled by friend and foe.

Mucius kept going, though his body was protesting, breath coming in short gasps. But he could feel the fight leeching out of the enemy as more and more of his men poured into the breach. He killed a man and risked a look up and behind him – the rest of the lads were on the walls and cleaving through the defenders and the First of the First continued to pour through the breach. His head whipped back to the front to see the man before him turn his back and run. He was not alone, the Dacians holding the breach were in full retreat, heading back to the warrens of the rathole town.

Though he was shattered, Mucius pursued. 'After them, lads!' he managed to shout, voice ragged with exhaustion. 'Kill them! Kill them all!'

The First of the First poured past him into Durostorum and he felt Livius's hand on his arm, steadying him before he'd known that he'd faltered. 'Fucking hell, centurion,' Livius enthused. 'You don't have to kill all of them on your own!'

Mucius was too tired to quip back. 'Come on,' he said. 'Let's finish this.'

So this was vengeance.

Valerian stood atop the walls of Durostorum, alone in the dark, listening to the song of victory. Begging. Screaming. Laughter. The crash of doors being broken in and the wailing of infants. It should have felt sweet. It should have been a cleansing fire, wiping away the shame of Tapae and the stealing of his *virtus* by the Dacians.

Should have. But did not.

He had never been involved in the sack of a city or town before. The Silurians had little villages and hillforts – nothing like this. This was a place with homes, business and families. No longer, though. Now it was Tartarus come to life with his men acting as the Furies to inflict tortures on the people of Durostorum. They were raping women in the street, dragging their babes from their arms and killing them before their eyes.

Valerian had stomached it as long as he could, but there was one moment he could not get out of his head. A soldier held a babe by the ankles whilst his mates gang raped its mother. It was screeching and the soldier had, casually, swung it against the wall of the house they had dragged them from. The screeches were cut short and the impact of the child's head had left an almost perfectly round disc of blood on the wall.

What was it Horace had said? *Wars . . . the horror of mothers.* Valerian drained his cup and tossed it into the darkness. The small mercy was that no mother or father would survive this night. But they would suffer before the dawn.

Dacia. Gods-cursed Dacia. It was his nemesis, he realised. He had come here before and it had broken him, taken everything from him and left him a burned out shell of a man until he had found love with Pyrrha – Varia as he had learned her name was, after she too was taken from him. Now he was back here again – a new man, a legate and a defender of Rome. *Virtus* and vengeance were his to regain. He had everything he wanted within his grasp.

'We should often be sorry if our prayers are answered,' he whispered to himself.

A raucous shout of greeting made him jump. Settus was striding along the wall towards him. Even in the darkness, he could see the little man beaming from ear to ear. 'What a night!' Settus enthused.

Valerian bit down a harsh retort. Settus was a soldier. This is what soldiers did. 'I want to call a halt to this soon,' he said.

'But . . .'

'We're here to do a job not have a fucking party. I can't have two thirds of the legion nursing hangovers tomorrow.'

'Too fucking late,' Settus said.

'Just get it done.'

Settus shrugged. 'I know you're not keen on all this, but anyone would think we lost the way you're acting.'

'Anyone would think we lost, *sir*,' Valerian snapped. 'And we've won nothing yet. The orders are to hold this ground.'

Settus shrugged, taking that on the chin. 'Very good, sir,' he said. 'I'll have the bodies slung in the river.'

'Burn them.'

'With respect, that'll stink this place out for days. If we sling them in the drink it'll shit the life out of the barbarians when they see a river full of corpses, sir. And also, piss them off. Bring them to us like flies to shit. Which is the plan.'

Valerian sighed. 'You're right of course.'

'Years of experience,' Settus acknowledged with a grin.

'I want work started on the wall at first light,' Valerian told him. 'We need to plug the gap between these rivers before the Dacians' allies get here.'

'Don't worry,' Settus was airy. 'The lads'll sort it.'

'See that they do.'

Settus saluted and turned to leave. He stopped and turned back. 'Permission to speak freely?'

Valerian nodded his acquiescence.

'Are you all right, mate?'

'I'm fine.'

'You know as well as I do that this is war, right? This is how it is. How it was. How it's always going to be. The thing is, we won, they lost. We're alive, they ain't. That's the important thing. I know you read a lot and that makes a man think too much. Well think on this. Those Dacian cunts fucked you over royally. And if this was Rome and they'd won and *we'd* lost, how do you think it'd go, eh? Eh? Fuck 'em. They're barbarians and they deserve to die. You keep in mind what happened to you before, all right. We can't show no mercy to them, Valerian. This is the way it has to be. The Emperor said so. We're soldiers – even you, legate. We do our duty. *Summa exstinctio.*'

Valerian was silent for a moment. 'Thank you, Settus,' he said.

Settus held his gaze for a moment before walking into the night and once again leaving Valerian alone with his thoughts.

XLIV

There was nothing here, Lysandra noted. Under a grey and roiling Dacian sky, endless fields of green undulated towards the horizon. Forests grew in great clumps with a cold mist as their skirting, mist that was brought by the river and the rain.

It was not real rain that came and went; rather it was an incessant cloud of moisture that seemed to have no substance but somehow soaked everything and everyone. And it was cold – though she could not admit feeling the discomfort of the harsh weather, Cappa, Murco and everyone else – save Kleandrias – made up for it with their continual carping. Indeed, Lysandra thought it impossible for one group of people to elicit such a volume of complaint on one subject for five days in a row, but her friends seemed determined to prove her wrong.

She had taken to steering the *Galene* – with Bedros's guidance – to get away from the chorus of disapproval and seize upon a little measure of peace. 'Rivers are different to the sea,' he told her – needlessly, but he was the captain after all. 'Slow and steady is the key,' he advised. 'More haste, less speed. We'll end up hitting the bottom and that lot,' he pointed to behind them where the flotilla followed on, 'will snarl up behind us. A good idea not to use warships, Lysandra,' Bedros added. 'Merchant ships were made with sea and river travel in mind.'

'You are ever an inspiration, Bedros,' she acknowledged making the seaman's weathered face split into a grin. She looked past him as Kleandrias approached, raising his hand in greeting. He and Bedros exchanged a glance and the captain stood around for a moment, clearly feeling a little uncomfortable – as though it were he and not her countryman that had interrupted. Mindful of Illeana's words to treat Kleandrias gently, she did not snap at him: she was steering so that she might find some peace.

Bedros coughed. 'Well – slow and steady like I said. I'll . . . err . . . you know,' he muttered and made off, acting as though he were checking up on his sailors – who, like everyone else – had nothing to do but watch the boring scenery roll past.

'A strange place,' Kleandrias rumbled. 'Eerie.'

Lysandra glanced at him. 'You are not scared, are you?'

'Spartans fear nothing.'

'Except boredom, maybe?'

Kleandrias did not reply; he looked into her eyes for a moment and she saw again what Illeana had seen. Lysandra looked away, turning her attention to the river.

'What do you think you will do when this is all over?' Kleandrias asked her.

'I had not thought,' she admitted. 'Perhaps I will return to Sparta.'

'That was my thought too. We will be rich,' he added.

'I am already rich. Well, I was until all of this. Domitian will reimburse me; though I have spent a mighty fortune, Kleandrias. Maybe he would prefer if we all died – that way he would not have to pay his debt.'

Kleandrias laughed. 'If we all die, he will not be far behind us. Rome cannot bear another defeat – and he would be the first to get the blame.'

'There is truth in that,' Lysandra agreed. She was about to say more when something caught her attention on the northern shore. A large group of locals had gathered on the bank; it was hard to make out their number, but she could afford to take no chances. 'Call Bedros,' she snapped. Kleandrias did not need to be told twice; he jumped down from the steering deck and rushed to the captain. Lysandra looked to the south bank where, here too, people were gathering.

As soon as Bedros had control of the ship, Lysandra took a deep breath. 'To arms! Archers and shield bearers!' she shouted. 'Contact on both banks! Pass the word!' Chaos erupted all down the flotilla, shouting, cursing, the thump of feet on the wood decks and the distinct clattering and ringing of weapons being brought to bear.

Something hit the *Galene* at the water line, a soft, thunking sound. One at first and then more. 'What is that, what is that?' Lysandra ran to the side and peered into the water. Even though the black surface was obscured by the omnipresent mist, she could see distended corpses wallowing in the river. The stench hit here then, foul and rancidly sweet.

The *Galene* drifted on and the strew of bodies became thicker. Lysandra could hear the sound of wailing and crying coming from the people gathered on the banks. There were children among them, but the majority were adults and thus could be considered a threat. Lysandra had no idea if she would find herself facing these people with sword in hand in the days to come – and she could take no chances.

'Archers will commence shooting once in range!' she shouted. 'Pass the word!' Bedros looked at her, the shock evident in his face. 'They are not like us, Bedros,' she said. 'They are lesser creatures. And our orders are clear.'

Thebe had taken control of the middle deck. 'You heard the strategos!' she walked up and down, making herself heard. 'Nock arrows!' Lysandra was proud that none of her Priestesses of Artemis looked behind themselves to question the order. These women had been with her for years – they placed their trust in her and the goddess they served. This mission was Olympus born, and they would not shirk from it.

The *Galene* came closer to the crowd and she saw that the river was utterly corrupt with the dead now. They stared up at her, eyes and mouths open, as though they were shouting at her. Accusing her. Let them, she thought. Better Dacian corpses than Hellene.

'Draw!' Thebe's voice made her head snap back around. 'Loose!'

The first flight of arrows spat out from either side of the ship arced towards the Dacians on the banks and, moments, later, shouts and screams of pain erupted. 'Draw . . . Loose!' Thebe cried out once again and the Priestesses of Artemis obeyed – but even now, the Dacians were gathering their children and fleeing, leaving only a few dead bodies on the ground. 'Cease!'

They drew back to a safe distance, watching the ships as they floated by. Even from here, Lysandra could feel the anger and hatred emanating from them. They shouted, shrieked and cursed the vessels, no doubt swearing all kinds of vengeance. Better empty words than action, she thought.

'I have to sail back this way,' Bedros told her. 'Now, everyone hates us.'

'You are being paid well,' Lysandra told him. 'You knew there would be risk.'

'I didn't except you to go out of your way to antagonise them!'

Lysandra regarded him coldly. 'You will bring us to Durostorum. And you will uphold our bargain to keep us supplied. That was the deal.'

'I am an honourable man,' he said. 'But these others will now know the danger that you have brought upon us.'

'If you renege on this, Rome will hear of it, Bedros. Make no mistake; I love you and count you as my friend, but do not cross me. It is more than our lives at stake. It is the lives of all Hellenes and the Empire itself.'

'So you say. But women and children?'

'What of your men's women and children, Bedros? Your own? If we fail here, they will know rape and slavery. Is that what you want?'

Bedros did not reply.

'Is it?'

'No. Of course not. I just . . . was that necessary?'

'Yes,' Lysandra said. 'It was.'

The corpses in the river grew thicker but there was no further incident with the locals. Lysandra kept her eyes ahead, peering through the mist. It had grown heavier now and she was glad that the encounter with the Dacians had happened before the clouds had fallen on them.

'Miserable, isn't it?' Illeana said as she came to stand by Lysandra. 'What a place. Have you ever seen anything like it?'

'It is like the River Styx,' Lysandra said. 'After we fought, I had a vision of myself there. It was much like this place, Illeana. Cold and grey.'

Illeana wrinkled her nose. 'And the stench of death?'

'That too. How is your back?'

'Painful.'

'You will live.'

Illeana laughed, the musical sound seeming out of place in the gloom. 'I have been reading your books again,' she offered. 'On tactics.'

'And they make sense now?'

'Not really. Well, perhaps a little.'

It was Lysandra's turn to smile. 'I rather think that your presence will inspire people, Illeana. You have that . . . way about you.'

Illeana was about to answer, but then stopped and held up her hand. 'Listen,' she said. 'Can you hear that?'

Lysandra could not. 'Silence on the deck!' she called and what little chat there was below died out at once. She cocked her head in the direction Illeana indicated. She picked up nothing at first, but then she heard it. Voices. The sound of men at work. As they drew closer, it became clearer − the language was Latin. As she realised it, the outline of Durostorum came into view and with it, the sight of many soldiers, all at work building a wall that extended from the periphery of the town till it was lost from sight in the fog.

As they saw the town, so they themselves were spotted by the Roman pickets, stood at arms to protect their compatriots. The alarm was raised at the sight of the ships − procedure, Lysandra guessed.

'I'll bring us closer,' Bedros said. 'Don't want to get us shot at.'

'Identify yourselves!' a Roman shouted from the north bank, his voice thin and reedy.

'Reinforcements for the IV Felix,' Bedros called back. 'Mercenary auxiliaries.'

'About fucking time!'

Illeana winked at Lysandra. 'Well,' she said. 'Here we go.'

Valerian was in his new *praetorium*, what had once been the biggest house in Durostorum and was now an empty shell thanks to the destructiveness of his men. He did not dwell on who had once lived here and what had become of them. It was two-storeyed and spacious – more space than he needed, but it was warm and better than a tent. It would have to go sooner or later, he knew. He had ordered the demolition of the houses in the town to strengthen the wall – and if the men were sleeping in tents, so would he.

Eventually.

He had despatched a *turmae* of his precious cavalry to Iulianus with a report of the battle and there was a small part of him that hoped that the word back would be that they had already crushed Decabalus and were on their way to re-enforce him.

That, however, was fantasy and the rest of the horsemen had been flung out in a reconnaissance mission to locate the Dacian allies and report back. Hopefully, they would be far away. The wall was taking too long to construct – the foul conditions and poor ground were proving a nightmare. And the wall *had* to be ready in time; if not, he and his men would face a torrid time.

There was pounding at his door, interrupting his train of thought. 'Come,' he said.

Settus barged in, grinning all over his face. 'You're going to want to see this,' he said.

'Can it wait?' The look Settus gave him told him it could not. 'All right, then,' he said and got to his feet. 'Throw me a cloak, will you?'

Settus looked around and saw an array of red capes hanging from hooks on the wall. 'The one with ermine trimming, sir,' he asked, all innocence and mockery at the same time.

'Just throw me the cloak.'

Settus did so and they left the warmth of the *praetorium*. The mist was thick as the centurion led him to the wall. Here it was strong at least and Valerian was pleased to see his redoubt was in full progress. The main wall would stretch between the rivers, but the defences around the town itself would also be augmented – just in case the legion was forced to retreat into Durostorum.

Valerian admitted to himself that this was more for morale than anything else – if it came to making a stand in the town proper, it would be all over bar the shouting. Silently, he reinforced his vow to fall on his sword rather than be taken again by the barbarians. He pushed the thought from his mind and followed Settus up the steps that led to the ramparts.

'What do you reckon?' Settus asked, pointing toward the river.

It was dark with merchant ships and soldiers were disembarking – thousands of soldiers. 'The auxiliaries,' he identified.

'Yeah, yeah. But look closer.'

Valerian squinted into the mist, but could not see what Settus was getting at. He lost patience. 'What?'

'Half of them are split-arses.'

'You're not serious.' But Valerian could hear his own men shouting at the troops as they marched by – and he'd never before heard one soldier ask another to suck his cock for him. 'This doesn't make any sense,' he said.

'We should get 'em inside, though.'

Valerian nodded. 'I agree. But keep them behind the wall and *out* of the town. I want distance between our lads and their . . . troops. Clear?'

'Yes, sir.'

'And have their commander sent to me. At once.'

Valerian admitted to himself that he was doing his utmost to appear the archetypal Roman legate, keeping his expression stern, his back straight in the seat, arms on the report scattered oak table, fingers clasped. He eyed the expensive looking Dacian wine jug on the table that had somehow survived the looting, but decided against it.

He had been kept waiting for some time, no doubt Settus had had trouble finding out who was in charge – disembarking was a chaotic business at any time – in this weather, it would be doubly

292

so. At length, however, someone rapped on his door. He re-stiffened his spine. 'Come!'

A man entered – he did not recognise him, but the woman at his side was all too familiar. Tall, pale-skinned and blue eyed, she was dressed in mail with a red tunic and cloak, her black hair plastered to her head by the rain. 'Lysandra . . .' he said slowly.

'And my colleague, Euaristos,' she introduced the effete looking fellow at her side. 'We are your re-enforcements, Valerian.'

Valerian was not quite sure what to say.

'You do not seem overwhelmed,' Lysandra observed. 'May we sit?' she indicated the chairs in front of his desk.

'Yes, yes, of course,' he stuttered, trying to get his thoughts in order. Some wine?' he gestured to the jug.

'No, thank you,' Lysandra replied – to the seeming chagrin of her 'colleague'. 'What is the current situation here?' she asked.

'Just hold on a moment,' Valerian decided that if they were not going to drink, he certainly needed one. 'Are you sure?' he eyed Euaristos and, without waiting for a reply, poured for them both, the gesture taken up enthusiastically by the man. 'How are you here, Lysandra? Why? I was expecting re-enforcements, yes, but my men tell me your force is comprising women as well as men. This is highly irregular.'

'By the looks of your men – the ones I saw – they are hardly elite legionary stock. Old men. Boys. Slaves too, I would guess. Hardly Caesar's glorious Tenth Legion, Valerian. But, to answer your question. I am here on the orders of Sextus Julius Frontinus . . .'

'That explains a lot,' Valerian muttered with feeling.

Clearly irked at being interrupted, Lysandra continued. 'You reported that your men baulked at fighting the Dacian women at Tapae. My troops have no such compunction. My soldiers are here specifically to combat that threat – and I would guess that it is Frontinus's hope that Dacian men will feel the same way as yours did – giving us a small advantage, I hope.'

'And you?' He looked at Euaristos.

'She hired me,' Euaristos said airily. 'I bring half a legion of quality veteran auxiliaries. We're armed, equipped and paid up for the winter.'

'Veteran?'

'We've seen our share, sir. More than our share, in fact. We're veteran veterans, if you will.'

Valerian let that go. 'And you?' he asked Lysandra.

'Half a legion. I have infantry to combat the Dacian women as I say, but my main strength is artillery and light troops. I have fought against men in the arena, Valerian. I won, of course, but not all women are Lysandra. Only the exceptional can really stand against a man in battle. Naturally, all my soldiers are exceptional – but only the best of the best will fight in the line.'

'You bring artillery?' Despite himself, Valerian's military interest was piqued. 'Do continue.'

Lysandra gave a slight smile – it reminded him of Pyrrha's half-grin and, he realised, she must have picked up this expression from Lysandra during her youth. 'Frontinus appraised me of the situation – and the tactics here are obvious. I hope you have learned something since we first met, Valerian?'

Valerian coloured, remembering their first encounter. He had been drunk and they had argued about the merits of Greek and Roman infantry. 'I hope so,' he waved it away. 'I am a legate now.'

'Indeed. Your mission is to sever the line between Decabalus and his allies. Durostorum is the perfect locale for this, situated as it is between two rivers. Frankly, I am amazed that this vaunted Dacian king has not seen this himself. But that is now his problem. Our problem is that we are few and they are many. Even with the wall, we would be hard pressed to hold. My thought was to use artillery and missile troops to bombard the Dacians as they come to us. And keep that bombardment going through each engagement – adjusting the elevation of course. Also, these barbarians are not professionals like your men and Euaristos's. Their morale could be questionable – they will be expecting one legion. We now have two – moreover, two equipped specially to combat them.'

'Yes – well, as I am sure you are aware, planning for battles and fighting them are often at opposite ends of the page. And I note you do not count your women as *professionals*.'

Lysandra arched a dark eyebrow. 'Of course. I thought that it would offend your ego.' Euaristos sniggered at that. 'My women are killers, Valerian. All of them. Can the same be said of your soldiers? Boys. Ex-slaves and so forth?'

The jibe hit home and Valerian felt his temper spark. 'My men will do their duty.'

'As will we,' Lysandra shot back. 'I do not expect you to believe me, Valerian, but this fight is ordained by Athene – Minerva – herself. All who stand with me believe this to be true. The *gods* are on our side.'

That, Valerian thought, was all he needed, an army of religious lunatics. He glanced at Euaristos who nodded slightly. Lysandra had made a believer out of him too. 'In my experience,' he said, 'the gods don't really help on the battlefield.'

'You are not a priest,' Lysandra shrugged. 'You have your beliefs. I have the truth.'

Valerian knew that there was no point in arguing with the god-addled. They couldn't be reasoned with, even when facts stared them in the face. He decided to move the conversation on. 'Your presence here is unusual,' he said, 'but far from unwelcome. However, the presence of so many women could be a . . . distraction . . . to my men.'

'I have thought of that too,' Lysandra said. 'Your . . . dim view of the gods might be true of the educated *equites*, Valerian, but most common men place great faith in them. I recall that Caligula's legions refused to march on Britannia because of the demons that lurked across the water. Have them swear oaths – terrible oaths – that fraternisation is forbidden. I shall do the same, as will Euaristos.'

Valerian got a laugh out of that. Lysandra might claim some technical knowledge but she clearly did not know soldiers. 'I rather think it won't be enough.'

The Spartan fixed him with her strange, ice-coloured eyes. 'It will be if the person caught is *not* punished but his – or her – tent-mates are crucified. Make it known that the fault of the one causes the punishment of the many. Besides,' she added. 'Soon, they will have more to think about than fornicating. The question is: how soon?'

Valerian sat back in his seat, trying to maintain his grip on the conversation. It was typical of Frontinus to gamble like this. But Valerian remembered the comments of his men before Tapae. How poorly they had fought against the Dacian 'amazons'. It was ingrained in men that women were weaker; they were wives, whores, home-makers and domestic slaves. Not warriors. So the wily Governor had concocted this scheme – and of course, placed the egomaniacal Lysandra at the forefront of his plan. Her Herculean arrogance coupled with her skill at arms, her military acumen, her utter faith that her mission was Olympian in its calling and her sex made her the perfect candidate for the job. He had to salute the old man.

'How soon indeed,' Valerian said after a moment. 'I do not know the answer to that. I have scouts in the field, looking for the enemy. The more immediate problem is the wall – it is taking longer to construct that we anticipated.'

'Lucky for you we arrived when we did,' Euaristos said. 'We have shovels and skill. And I know Lysandra's women – they are called the Heronai – the Women of the Temple . . .'

'I am fluent in your language,' Valerian interrupted. Something about the Greek irritated him. Valerian judged him to be a peacock and a ladies' man – and probably an adventurer to boot.

The interruption did not faze the man however. 'Of course,' he said. 'They can dig too. Trained by an ex-centurion. Ditch and rampart will be no issue to them, but I'd leave the stone work to your lads and mine.'

Valerian sighed. It was what it was and he had to deal with it. And, if he was honest with himself, it was more blessing than curse. 'Good,' he said. 'We'll ensure that there will be no fraternisation – and put them to work.' He turned his attention to Lysandra. 'Let us hope that toil is enough to keep their minds off . . . other matters. For now.'

The Dacian Plain

It was good to be free of the sprawling mass of the encampment. The rain fell in a fine mist, cleansing and life-giving and there was a bracing chill in the air that enlivened the flesh and made the heart beat stronger.

It was grand to be alive. Sorina glanced at Amagê who rode at her side at the head of a party of fifty riders, all good men and women, all heavily armed. Amagê looked back at her and winked, reminding Sorina of the previous night's passion. She was a fool, she chided herself, but love made fools of everyone and her feelings for the Sarmatian Clan Chief were growing deep.

Amagê had decided that a scouting mission was in order; all knew that they would soon encounter the Romans, the question was when. 'They will be searching for us too,' she had said. 'Better that we know where they are and they don't know we're coming.'

Sorina reckoned the truth of it was that Amagê was as keen as she to spend some time riding free of the responsibilities and mundane governance of the Tribes that had gathered to her banner. Always fractious and at times petty, there were many feuds and many fights. It was the way of things, but it could be draining when one constantly had judge and execute fines and punishments, rewards and boons.

'I don't like this ground,' Amagê said. 'Too soft.'

It was true – the rain had made the grasslands thick with mud. No real issue for a small band such as this, but Sorina knew well that the tread of many thousands would churn up the earth and make riding perilous. 'There's truth in that,' she replied.

'Amagê!' one of the riders called out – one of the Clan Chief's own Sarmatians by her accent. 'Look there!'

Sorina followed the line of the woman's spear to see a small farmstead – or what remained of it. As one, they turned the heads of their mounts, urging them gently towards the ruin. As they drew closer, Sorina saw a murder of crows as the approaching horses startled them and they exploded skywards, their harsh cawing ripping through the air. Sorina swung her leg over her horse's head and slid to the ground. She had seen this many times before in her youth.

Corpses lay bloated and stinking in the cool air; they had been so mutilated by the scavengers that only their clothing told her if the bodies were men or women. The children were all too obvious. 'Romans,' she spat.

Amagê leapt from her horse and joined her. 'Children? But why?'

'It is the way that they make war,' Sorina replied. 'No honour. No mercy. Their soldiers are like stone, Amagê. They feel nothing, care for nothing save that their orders are carried out. What kind of man can kill a child?'

'A Roman soldier.' The question was rhetorical, but Amagê answered anyway, her eyes cold with anger. 'They will pay for this. Zalmoxis will have their screams as music while he sups on their souls.'

'We should bury them,' the Sarmatian woman said. 'It's wrong for the carrion to get them.'

It was grim work. As they lifted the bodies from the ground, they fell apart, alive with maggots and other foulness; the stench was overpowering. But it had to be done. They made a cairn for the family and Sorina could see the hatred hardening on the faces of the riders. War was like that: it began as a grand adventure, something that you knew you would survive. You would be honoured and your grandchildren would sit on your knee and listen to your stories of valour. But those stories never told of the children killed, the women raped and the putrid corpses left on the field.

'Let's leave this place,' Amagê said.

They pushed on, leaving the cairn behind them. The rain grew heavier, coming down in thick droplets that pounded horse and rider, and Sorina hunched down in her cloak, the lightness of spirit she had felt long since fled. They continued west, following the line of the river. As they did, there was yet more evidence of the Romans and the destruction they had wrought. 'The people will hear of this,' Amagê said. 'When they see what we have seen, they will cry out for vengeance.'

Sorina did not reply. Something caught her eye, a movement to her right. She slowed her mount, raising her hand that the others might do the same and peered into the distance.

'Riders,' she murmured.

'Where?'

Sorina raised her spear and pointed. 'See them? Heading east.'

'Aye, but they've not seen us, I'll guess.' Both women looked at each other and, as one, they slid from their mounts. 'Down, down,' Amagê hissed. The others dismounted, gripped their horses by their necks, lowered them gently to the ground and lay across them to keep them still.

Sorina counted thirty horses. 'Romans,' she said to Amagê. 'A cavalry squadron. They are looking for us, Amagê.'

'Good,' the Clan Chief replied. 'Let them. We'll follow them. And finish them.'

'They're a long way ahead,' Sorina cautioned. 'I want them, but we could lose them in this weather.'

'They won't know we're coming,' Amagê insisted. 'We'll ambush them.'

As she spoke, thunder rolled above them and the rain fell hard in thick icy droplets. Sorina did not need to say that the going would be hard: all knew it – but all hungered for vengeance.

The Romans disappeared from view and, after giving it some time to be sure that they could not be spotted, they allowed their mounts to rise. 'Let's get them,' Amagê said as she mounted. 'Let's make them pay.'

All knew that they had much ground to make up on the cavalrymen. They rode as hard as they dared, but the going was treacherous and all of them were worried for their mounts' safety. A horse could break her leg easily or fall and throw her rider and with the Romans laying waste to everything for miles around, there would be no safe haven for an injured warrior – most of the locals had fled and would soon become attached to the war band. But at least the weather would make it equally perilous for the Romans. If they fell here, sooner or later, they died here.

The weather worsened, rain falling in thick, blinding sheets, thunder rolling in the sky above. No one complained, but Sorina guessed that all must be thinking they would not find the Romans in this deluge. But none put voice to it, so they carried on, eyes trying to pierce the gloom, ears straining to pick out the sound of voices or the whinny of other horses through the heavy, omniscient patter of the rain.

The hours crawled by, miserable afternoon turning to dark early evening. Sorina's fingers were numb on the leather, her feet so cold she could no longer feel them. She needed to rest – they all needed to rest, and well they knew it. 'We should head back,' she shouted to Amagê.

'We must keep searching!'

'We've lost them!' Sorina reached out and gripped Amagê's arm. 'And if we stay out here all night, it could be *us* that gets ambushed!'

Amagê gritted her teeth, but Sorina could see in her eyes that she knew she was right. The Sarmatian cursed. 'All right,' she said at length.

Sullen, they angled back in the direction of the encampment, cold, soaked and frustrated. The rain eased off but with that came the biting chill of evening and Sorina bit down hard to stop her teeth from chattering. Nobody spoke, heads bowed low as their weary horses plodded on.

'I am looking forward to the tent and something hot to drink,' Sorina offered, hoping to break the tension.

Amagê wiped her nose on her sleeve and looked over. 'Feeling it?' she asked, her lips lifting in a grin.

That was the way of her, Sorina thought; fiery and quick-mooded. 'Aye,' she admitted. 'I am . . .' She stopped as she saw horsemen approaching in the half-light – directly ahead of them. For a moment she hesitated – but they did not.

'Fuck!' A man's voice. A Latin curse. The sound of a sword being dragged from its scabbard. 'Third *Turma*, on me! On me!'

'Romans!' Amagê's voice rang out. 'At them!'

Sorina dug her heels into her horse's flanks and she shot forwards, an arrow from a bow. Her heart rose to her throat as she sped towards the on-rushing Roman cavalry, spear levelled. Risking a glance over her shoulder, she saw the tribespeople thundering headlong in a mad rush to wreak vengeance on the hated enemy. In sharp contrast, the Roman's had formed behind their decurion, a ballista bolt formation with him at its head.

Sorina raised her spear, as did the decurion: they had marked each other out, it was clear – but he had the small shield and armour with which the Romans equipped their troopers. Sorina wore mail – but no shield with which to deflect the man's attack.

Screaming her battle cry, Sorina drew her arm back as the two forces hammered towards each other, each heartbeat bringing them closer. Behind her she could hear the wild shouts of the tribespeople, in front the harsh calls of the decurion to his men to stay in formation, beneath her the laboured breathing and snorting of her horse, the dull pounding of her hooves on the earth.

She hurled her spear with all her strength and it flew true, the warhead sawing into the man's throat before he could bring up his shield. Bright blood flew in the chill air and the decurion fell from the saddle. But before he had even hit the ground the forces collided in a screaming mass of flesh, iron and steel. Horses shrieked in terror, rearing and plunging as sword and spear flashed about them in the melee.

Sorina ducked as a Roman *spatha* cut the air above her head and she heard the choking wail of agony as it took the woman behind her. She scrabbled for her sword and had it loose just in time to deflect a spear thrust from a big cavalryman – a Gaul if she was any judge. She lashed out at him, but he was gone, plunging past her into the fight. The man behind him was not so fortunate and she felt the satisfying judder up her arm as her blade bit deep into his shoulder, cutting down into the bone. His harsh shout of pain cut through the mad cacophony of battle, music to her ears.

Age fell away from Sorina at that moment, the weight of years lifting from her as they always did in the eye of the battle's storm. Another rider flew past her and she cut sideways and high, over his shield and into his neck. The man's horse pounded on as his headless body jetted a crimson geyser, a blood offering to Zalmoxis.

By her side, Amagê had wrested her axe from her saddle and she looked in time to see her deliver a huge blow to a Roman – it split his shield and must have broken his arm in the process; the soldier did not stay to trade blows but ducked his head low and kicked hard at his horse, sending it darting forward.

Then she was free, with no men to kill in front of her. Sorina urged her horse to turn and turn fast lest she be caught in the back.

But the Romans had not stayed to fight. They had used the arrow-head of their wedge to punch through the Sarmatian cavalry and were making a break for it, leaving their dead littered on the field.

'After them!' Amagê screamed, waving her axe about her head. 'Kill them! Kill them all!'

'No!' Sorina shouted. 'Wait! Hold!' The Sarmatians milled in confusion as she countered the order of their Clan Chief.

'You dare . . .!' Amagê urged her horse forward so she could scream into Sorina's face, fury etched on her beautiful broad features.

'There will be more out there,' Sorina shouted back. 'If we give chase, we could end up with blown horses and half the Roman army on our backs. You're too important to risk, Amagê . . .'

The Clan Chief's impotent howl of fury cut her off, rending the air with its hate. 'Check the bodies,' she ranted. 'See if any are alive – we will have our sport with them, the bastards!' Her grey eyes turned to the backs of the fleeing Romans. 'Soon,' she said. 'Soon we will have our sport with all of you.'

Durostorum

'They are like worker bees,' Lysandra observed.

'I've never seen anything like it,' Telemachus marvelled. They stood on top of Durostorum's town wall looking north as the ditch and rampart trailed into the mist. Thousands of men – and now women – toiled in the cool air, shifting tons of earth with only their shovels and the strength of their backs.

Titus cleared his throat. 'To be fair,' he said, 'we drilled for this back in Asia Minor.'

'But not on such *scale*,' the priest said, clearly unaware he was wiping his sandals on Titus's professional pride.

'It is obvious that you did,' Lysandra decided to offer balm before the centurion could take offence. 'The Heronai are fine soldiers, Titus. Thebe, you have done a better job than I ever could have,' she finished with a lie.

'Oh, no Lysandra, everything I did, I learned from you,' Thebe said. That was the truth of course, but there was no need to point it out.

They *had* done well, the women were fit, in good spirits and clearly working as one to their purpose. Behind the walls, Lysandra could see her artillery pieces taking shape at regular intervals, fearsome onagers, ballistae and scorpions. It was an impressive array — and a continuous bombardment from these beasts would be demoralising — not to mention lethal — in the extreme.

'The poor weather works against us,' Kleandrias observed. 'The ropes on the war machines must be kept covered in tallow in this,' he opened his palm to the omnipresent drizzle.

'And the wood oiled, we know,' Titus gritted. 'Priest . . .'

Telemachus looked rather smug as he answered. 'Everyone knows that the weather in the north is foul. So I overstocked. All is in order.'

'I bet you didn't anticipate it being this foul,' Murco complained. He and Cappa had accompanied Lysandra, despite her strong suggestion that they could assist with the construction of the wall. Cappa claimed that, as an ex-Praetorian and now her bodyguard, his pace was close to his strategos. It was the basest and most obvious flattery and Lysandra admitted to herself that it had worked like a charm. But he had then been acutely embarrassed when Illeana had volunteered herself for the work.

'Look there,' Thebe pointed.

'What?' Lysandra squinted into this mist.

'A rider,' the Corinthian said. '*There*.' She leaned closer to Lysandra. 'See him?'

'Yes. Valerian's scouts – some of them at any rate.' She had to know what their news was. 'Cappa . . . Murco . . .'

'Yes, strategos,' Cappa said, as Murco rolled his eyes.

'Find Euaristos. I will be at Valerian's *praetorium*. Tell him to meet me there.'

The cavalryman was young – perhaps still in his teens. He had a stoat-like face and eyes that were too close together, dark and wet with fear and shock. His face was ashen, coated with a thin sheen of sweat and his hands trembled on the cup as he held it. His shield arm was pressed close to his chest, broken or badly sprained.

Valerian was not sitting behind his desk; rather he placed himself next to the lad on a bench, which, Lysandra thought overly familiar. But then, Valerian was a Roman. 'Thank you for coming,' the legate said as she entered, Euaristos in tow. She did miss the irony in his tone.

'I saw the rider approach,' Lysandra said. 'What news?'

'Take a seat,' Valerian offered. 'And help yourself to wine.'

Euaristos needed no second invitation, but Lysandra hesitated. She did not want to drink lest it fog her mind and there was always the temptation that she would want more. 'I will have water,' she said to the Athenian.

'This is Marcellus,' Valerian said, his voice gentle. 'Tell us what happened.'

Marcellus finished his cup and, ever the gentleman, Euaristos was there with the jug, giving the lad an encouraging wink as he did so. 'We were on patrol,' Marcellus began. 'The weather was shite . . .' He looked over to Lysandra who waved away the obscenity. '. . . Really bad,' Marcellus went on. 'Visibility is poor out there. Not

305

that there's much to see after the legions have been at work. Anything standing ain't standing anymore.'

'*Summa exstinctio*,' Euaristos said.

'Yeah, that's right,' Marcellus nodded. 'We've been out in the field what . . . five days now? Something like that. You lose track, you know. We were due to head back here, but the decurion — Arius — he wanted to push on. So we pushed on.'

'Go on,' Valerian encouraged.

'Sir, we found the enemy camp,' Marcellus blurted.

'Good! Good lad,' Valerian patted his shoulder. 'Well done.'

'But, sir . . .' Marcellus looked at his commander as though fearing he would be in trouble. 'You've never seen anything like it! It was early evening. Dinner time. Sir, we saw their campfires. There were more of them than stars in the sky.'

Valerian's eyes flicked over to Lysandra who raised an eyebrow in response.

'How many do you think?'

'Beyond counting.'

'I need a number, lad.'

'Tens of thousands. Sir, I can't be sure — there were so many. Like ten Flavian amphitheatres.'

Lysandra thought that had to be gross exaggeration, but it was nonetheless clear that a huge force was descending on them. 'Where are the rest of your men?' she asked. Marcellus looked at Valerian for approval before answering, which irritated her.

'It's all right,' Valerian said. 'She's a soldier too.'

Marcellus had the look of a man that didn't believe what he'd heard, but he did as he was told. 'We scarpered after we saw it. On our way back here, we ran into a barbarian patrol,' he met her gaze. 'Men — and women warriors like you, miss — '

'Address me as Lady or strategos, boy,'

'Yes . . . Lady. Sorry. We ran into a barbarian patrol,' he said again. 'Arius had given orders that if that happened, we were to punch through and make a break for it. On no account were we to stick around and fight. The information we had was too important, that's what he said. Priority was to get back to Durostorum and report.

'So that's what we did. I saw Arius go down in the first contact, a woman took him out with a spear. I was lucky to get away with my life,' he added. 'Some of us got through – there must have been fifty of them against our thirty – and we legged it. Oppius – he's the oldest – took command after Arius got killed. He said we should split up. We'd be harder to track that way and someone was bound to make it home.'

'You are the first,' Lysandra informed him. 'As your legate says, you have done well.'

'These barbarians,' Euaristos said. 'How far away are they?'

'Two days march,' Marcellus replied. 'Look, I know how long it takes to get a legion moving. It is like the barbarians have ten legions . . . I reckon two days.'

As he spoke, Lysandra saw Valerian's face go white; fear, she recognised. She recognised it because she had felt it herself. Not the fear of losing one's own life but the fear that the thousands of souls you were responsible for lived or died on your decisions. 'Thank you, Marcellus,' Valerian said, surprising Lysandra with the steady timbre of his voice. 'You get on back to the *medicus*. Rest up. You've done well, son.' Marcellus got to his feet, saluted and made his way out.

'What is it?' Lysandra asked as soon as the boy closed the door behind him.

'The wall,' Euaristos answered for the legate. 'It won't be finished in two days. Even if we dug all day and all night.'

The realisation almost made Lysandra sick. If the boy Marcellus was even half correct on the numbers, they could not hold off the barbarians without adequate defences. 'How long?'

Valerian stood and poured himself wine, which he drained in

one go. Wincing on the bitter taste, he replied: 'Four days. At least.'

'If that wall isn't ready, we've had it,' Euaristos said – needlessly in Lysandra's judgement.

'Options?' She ignored him and spoke to Valerian.

'We had no idea that they would move so fast,' Valerian replied. 'I need time to think. To plan.'

'Sadly, that is one option not availed to you, Valerian,' Lysandra said. 'Time. We have none.'

'Get out!' Valerian snapped. 'I will think on this and give you your orders presently.' Well used to taking orders, Euaristos rose and saluted, but Lysandra stayed put – which threw her Athenian companion entirely; he did not know whether to sit back down or head for the door. 'I just issued – '

'Valerian,' Lysandra interrupted. 'There is only one answer to this.' Lysandra felt the familiar and comforting warmth of the goddess with her as she spoke. She knew she was right – Athene whispered at the back of her mind, urging her, encouraging her to speak.

'Make it good, Spartan,' Valerian said.

'We attack.'

'Don't be absurd,' the legate snorted with derision. 'The boy said ten legions. We have one, supplemented by women and auxiliaries. No offence,' he glanced at Euaristos who opted to sit back down. 'Even if Marcellus has exaggerated twofold – two legions against five – we'd be obliterated. And if he is right, the result is the same – we do not have the numbers. And think on this – we're holding the line for Iulianus. If we fail, the Dacian allies will fall on him and it will all be over!'

'I do not intend to annihilate their entire host,' Lysandra felt her cheeks colour with anger at the audacity of the man's dismissal of her suggestion. 'You need time to build the wall. You do not have it. *I* can give it to you.'

'Just a moment,' Euaristos broke in. 'Lysandra, you are an inspiration and I believe in my heart that Athene is with you – just as all my men do. But Valerian is right . . .' He trailed off. 'I didn't sign up to throw my life away. Or the lives of my men.'

'Nor I,' Lysandra replied. 'But hear me out. My . . . legion . . . can march out into the field. We can take a strong position and hold it – to delay the enemy while you, Valerian, and your 'real' soldiers can finish the fortifications.'

'There are no "strong positions",' Valerian answered. 'This is grassland, forest, and a few hills. But even taking a position on the high ground isn't going to help you. And it's not as though you can bring your artillery with you if you want to move at speed. And you'd need to.'

'We know that they are strong in cavalry,' Euaristos said. 'We have none to combat it. And if we build a marching camp, they'd just surround and overwhelm us. It's not as if we can make another wall between the two rivers further down. Look what happened here.'

'That is true,' Lysandra smiled. 'But we can bring a wall with us.'

XLVIII

The Dacian Plain

'You have done well!' Lysandra's voice rang out over the assembled troops, mercenary and Heronai both. She stood on a small platform outside the growing wall. Behind her, the Romans had paused in their work, Valerian among them, to watch their new allies leave. 'Men of Hellas. Heronai . . .' She pointed. 'Out there, the enemy comes upon us. Here, our defences are not yet ready. So it falls to us, brothers and sisters, to hold the barbarian at bay.' She saw them, men and women both, glancing at each other – some faces full of fear, some full of excitement and others merely resigned.

'We should not underestimate the size of the enemy force,' she said. 'It is vast – many times our own number. Our mission is simply to delay their host by a few days – we can do that with a single strike and be back here before they gather themselves in time to march to their imminent annihilation. On this wall!'

Telemachus approached, leading a well-drugged ox. It was a fine animal, young and strong – a fitting offering to the goddess. 'Men of Hellas,' Lysandra said as she drew her sword. 'Heronai. I make this offering to the Goddess Athene. Into her hands we entrust our lives – as in ours she puts the fate of Hellas. Hear me, Athene! Lend us your strength that we may cut down the barbarian as the farmer scythes the wheat. May we drench the ground in their blood! Athene, bring us victory!' Lysandra swung the sword down with all her strength, the blade cutting deep into the ox's neck. The beast collapsed without making a sound, its blood spraying Lysandra, drenching her in the viscous crimson fluid.

Her soldiers cheered and banged their weapons on their shields. Even the watching Romans joined in. 'We march with the goddess at our side, the Romans at our backs and our swords to the front!' At this, they roared louder. Lysandra looked out at the ranks and saw Kleandrias standing at the front. He smiled at her and she returned it, imagining that it must look to him like a rictus grin, her face and hair sticky with ox blood.

'That was nicely done,' Telemachus said to her, glancing down at his robe. It too was soaked in gore. 'I recall your speeches at my shrine. You're more colloquial these days, Lysandra.'

'I was young then.'

'But endearing,' he mocked, gently. Then he sobered. 'She is here,' he said. 'Even I can feel her presence.'

'Athene called us to this fight, Telemachus,' Lysandra said. 'It would not be fitting if she did not accept her offering,' she gestured to the fallen ox. 'Have it burned so the hecatombs might please her.'

He bowed his head slightly. 'As you wish.' He turned to go, but then stopped. 'I could march with you,' he offered, all earnest intent. 'We should see it through together.'

'You are a brave man, Athenian,' Lysandra said.

'Believe me, I'd rather not,' Telemachus replied. 'But it would be cowardly not to.'

'Courage, Telemachus, is not the absence of fear, but the facing of it. I see in your eyes that you would march if you were called to. But that would only serve my comfort and there would be no point to it. I need you here.'

'But . . .'

'No,' she cut him off. 'Your offer is well received, my friend. By the goddess, it would be a balm to my soul if you were by my side. But that does not serve our purpose. Marshall them here – make sure there are supplies. Make sure Bedros and his men are paid so they stay loyal. The coming fight is only the smallest part of the war, Telemachus – you know that as well as I. Without the logisticians, the soldiers are nothing. You are too important to me. To us. To Hellas. Stay and do your job. And I will go and do mine.'

They set out soon after to the cheers of the Romans – something that Lysandra had not expected and was touched by. The non-fraternisation order had gone out days previously, but the truth of it was Lysandra felt that the tough men of the Felix had come to respect her mercenaries and her Heronai simply because they had shouldered their share of the work and done it well. Many of the Heronai remained along with Telemachus – those women tasked with looking after the siege weapons.

They marched in two columns, the mercenaries to the north, Heronai to the south with the meagre supply of pack animals bringing

311

up the rear. They headed directly east – the direction in which the enemy had been sighted. Several other men from Marcellus's *turma* had drifted in and confirmed the boy's tale, so Lysandra was confident that no host of the size reported could pull an out-flanking manoeuvre without being seen from miles around.

The weather was predictably poor, the clouds above them iron grey and angry looking, the rain cold and all pervasive. Rather than the crunch-crunch of many marching feet, the army advanced with more of a plodding squelch. The terrain was not good for armoured troops; it sapped both strength and morale. Lysandra was thankful that Thebe and Titus had trained her women well – they were fit and strong, able to keep up with Euaristos's auxiliaries. She said as much to Thebe who, along with Illeana, marched at the head of their column.

'They were already fit, Lysandra.' Thebe brushed the praise aside. 'We merely sharpened them. But none of them are going to thank you for the extra load.'

Lysandra grinned. 'They will when we fight,' she said, shifting the heavy wooden stake on her shoulder. It was thick and unwieldy, but these staves would make up the 'wall' she spoke of to Valerian.

'You really think a few posts are going to hold back an army?' Murco asked from behind her. He and Cappa marched with Kleandrias to ensure her safety.

'Yes I do,' Lysandra said over her shoulder, 'At least for a while. We just need to find the right place to deploy.'

'Where's that, then?'

'The rivers draw closer a day or so to the east,' Illeana put in. When Lysandra glanced at her, impressed, she added: 'I remember from the maps.'

'So we shall stop at the narrowest point and make our wall. I pray we have time to either make a ditch and rampart or at least find some high ground.'

'And if we can't find either of those things?' Thebe asked.

'Then we deploy as we are.'

The Corinthian grinned. 'Famous Spartan pragmatism.'

Lysandra glanced at her. 'It has worked in the past,' she said with a hint of self-mockery.

'We could have left these staves on a ship,' Murco was determined to continue the complaining. If we're heading for a spot between rivers, it would have been much quicker and easier that way.'

'Yes it would,' Lysandra agreed. But it takes a long time to form up our people when they're disembarking a ship. This way, we are marching to our destination in formation so if the enemy comes upon us before the choke point, we will be able to stand and fight. If they do not, we make our wall when we arrive and that will be that. Otherwise we risk the chaos of unloading and extending our lines. We would be asking for trouble.'

'You see,' Cappa said. 'That is why she is the strategos and you are a lowly bodyguard. And not a very good one.'

'Bollocks. And why have you gone all Greek? *Strategos* my arse. You hoping for a raise in pay or something?'

'Maybe,' Cappa admitted.

'At least we get to go on the ships on our way back to Durostorum,' Thebe offered, trying to lift the man's spirits. 'We will strike a blow against the enemy and retreat fast back to the ships and escape. Each unit had been assigned a vessel, so all will be well.'

'Unless it's a rout and we're in full retreat,' Murco said mournfully.

'Just shut the fuck up,' Cappa said.

There was little more said after that, the army slogging onwards into the miserable weather. Heads bowed and cloaks wrapped tight, they concentrated on putting one foot in front of the other. The only vocal contingent of the forces were the centurions and *lochagoi* who prowled the respective lines of auxiliary and Heronai, shouting orders and generally haranguing their charges. Morning crawled

313

into afternoon and the conditions ensured that there would be a break in the march. Still, Lysandra posted a strong guard whilst the majority sat in the wet and ate their food lest they be caught unawares, but the enemy was not forthcoming.

Lysandra moved away from her group walking past the guard's perimeter that she had set and gazed into the mist. This was a foul place, she thought. Wet, green and cold, it was alien to her. This was not the verdant heartland of Lakedaimonia that was her home, it was a vast plain of nothingness, at once awe inspiring and depressing.

Somewhere out there, thousands of savages were heading towards Durostorum with a singular intent: massacre the defenders as its citizens had been massacred by them. Somewhere out there too was Sorina. This was her land, the land she fought and bled to protect. With her, came an army of barbarians, bent on destruction; an army that, if victorious, would be unleashed upon Hellas. She must stop them, she affirmed to herself. With the help of the goddess, she would.

Or at least delay them, Athene's voice echoed in her mind. Lysandra turned to look back at the force she had assembled and part of her wondered if it would be enough to do even that.

It would have to be.

She heard the distant shouts of her *lochagoi* kicking their charges into life and made her way back, preparing herself for the long slog ahead.

They marched hard for the rest of the day, Lysandra insisting on pressing on until it was almost too dark to see. Titus was furious that she contradicted him – there would be no marching camp that night, she decreed. Instead, she posted a strong guard and ordered that everyone slept in their tents under arms. The hours it would take to build the camp meant fewer miles travelled – something she could not countenance.

As it was, there was no attack forthcoming and she had the troops roused before dawn to push on. Those that had stood guard had to accept the weariness and go with the rest — and Lysandra set a punishing pace, urgency gripping her, until two hours before noon, she called a halt.

'This is it,' Illeana identified. 'The narrowest land between the two rivers.'

'A natural choke point,' Thebe said.

'No high ground, though,' Cappa glanced around.

'Get them to work!' Lysandra ordered Titus. 'Two thirds digging the ditch and rampart, one third stood to arms. I will meet with Euaristos and organise them — you see to the diggers.'

'At once,' Titus nodded.

'And get those stakes honed and planted!' She called after him as he trotted off, shouting orders. She turned to Thebe. 'I want the archers stationed now. All along this line,' she pointed between the two rivers.'

'Slingers too?'

'No — get them digging.'

Thebe winked. 'Yes, strategos.'

It was all frenzied activity now, Lysandra noted. The march had been laborious and the weather hadn't helped. It was still bad, chilly and damp with spots of rain. But there was no deluge to hamper their work — at least for now. And the Romans, she thought — the break in the wet weather would augment their progress too. The men of the auxiliaries and women of the Heronai set to their task, spades working frantically in the wet, muddy ground, throwing up clods of earth that would form the rampart. Lysandra silently thanked Titus — he was a hard taskmaster but his interminable drilling paid dividends. She had experienced it as a gladiatrix and saw now with her own eyes as her troops worked cohesively and without fuss. She promised herself that one day she would allow him to finish one of his wearied-voice-of-experience stories.

'I'll go and pitch in,' Illeana said.

Lysandra arched an eyebrow.

'I know.' The Roman shrugged. 'I'm getting to quite enjoy the work. I don't know why.'

'Because you have the option,' Kleandrias offered. 'I would not like to dig. I did it for years in the legions.'

'A shame then that you will have to join her,' Lysandra said. Cappa and Murco laughed until she turned her gaze on them.

'But . . . we're your bodyguards,' Cappa protested.

'I rather think that a speedy construction of ditch and rampart will protect me as well, do you not, Cappa?'

'If it's all the same, I'd just rather do the job I was employed to do.

'What happened to "yes, strategos"?' Murco wanted to know.

'Fuck off!' Cappa looked back to Lysandra. 'Dig?'

'Dig.'

They made off, Illeana teasing them all about their laziness and how she, a woman, would show them how to work, fight and kill. It made Lysandra smile and she went to help Euaristos with the deployment of the forward troops.

XLIX

Two men had survived the brief clash in the wilderness – and were cursed for their luck. They were dragged to the encampment where news of their arrival spread like wildfire. Soon, hundreds of baying tribespeople converged, screaming for Roman blood.

They herded the prisoners to the centre of the camp. They were terrified, one literally soiling himself with fear – with good reason, Sorina thought: his death would be long and excruciating. She would wish such suffering only on Romans. 'We should question them,' Sorina said to Amagê – who was still seething at the atrocities she had seen.

'I am anxious to hear them scream,' the Clan Chief replied. She noted the two cavalrymen looking at her. 'I said I want to hear you scream,' she said again, this time in Latin.

'Please,' one of them fell to his knees, imploring, eyes wet with tears. 'Please . . .'

'Is that what the Dacians said to you, Roman?' Amagê snarled. 'How many did you kill or rape. How many?'

'No one, I swear by all the gods!' the man started crying. 'That was the infantry, not us . . . we're just scouts . . .'

'He's right,' the other soldier said, he too falling to his knees. 'We weren't involved in any of that. Please, lady, you must believe us.'

Amagê slid out of the saddle. 'I do believe you.'

Sorina dismounted too, surprised at this. Amagê would hardly disappoint the assembled throng for the sake of a couple of Romans.

'I heard how ruthless your legions could be. Now, I have seen it with my own eyes.'

'They are animals, lady,' the first man said. 'We have only been seconded to this force – we're nothing to do with them.'

Amagê smiled. 'You are going a long way to saving your lives,' she told him. 'What's your name?'

'Brandus,' he replied. 'This is Priscus. We're – '

'Scouts. Yes you said.'

The crowd began to jeer, becoming agitated – causing the cavalrymen to shrink in terror. 'She's questioning them!' Sorina shouted out. 'Be still!'

'Very well,' Amagê said. 'Very well. We are not the savages you have been led to believe, Brandus. 'I am sure you have heard tell of all sorts of vile tortures we inflict on our captives.'

Brandus and Priscus exchanged a glance – clearly they had heard, but did not want to admit it. It was Priscus who spoke first. 'Just rumours, lady,' he said. 'People make things up at times of war.'

'Those bastards in Rome,' Brandus said. 'Sending us here – I don't even know where here is,' he added. 'They just send us to these places – we're just scouts.'

'Well, that's lucky for you,' Amagê smiled. 'And lucky for me too. Now Brandus . . . Priscus . . . I'm not going to have you hung over a slow burning fire and slowly cook you to death . . .'

At this, both men began to weep, shaking their heads reaching out imploringly, saying 'please don't kill me, please don't kill me,' over and over again.

Amagê silenced them with a wave of her hand. 'But you need to answer some questions. Then, you'll be made slaves. Trust me, it's better than what I'd do to you if you were legionaries.'

'We don't know anything!' Brandus cried.

'Of course you do,' Amagê squatted down so she was eye-level with him. 'How many men are facing us?'

Priscus didn't even hesitate. 'It's one legion,' he said. 'Nothing – we've seen the size of your army. And they're poor quality troops – old men, young boys and manumitted slaves. You'll roll over them in a single day. When we left, they hadn't even finished building the wall.'

'What wall? Where are they?'

'They took a town called Durostorum.' Brandus had evidently decided if Priscus was going to talk then he would as well. 'The soldiers killed everyone there – we had nothing to do with it. They are building a wall from river to river, but the going is slow.'

'I see. Only one legion?'

'Yes,' Priscus said. 'There is talk of re-enforcement. But there is always talk of that – we don't know if we'll get them.'

'Why Durostorum? There are narrower points between the two rivers.' Her slate-coloured eyes flicked towards Sorina; they had already guessed at Durostorum, but confirmation was always reassuring.

'I don't know, lady,' Brandus held up his hands. 'My guess would be that it's easier to supply a town – safer for the ships. Easier to defend too.'

'Not for the people of Durostorum it appears.'

'We had – '

'Nothing to do with it, I know.' She turned to Sorina and spoke in her own tongue. 'Come. I am weary of these two. I need a drink. More than a drink.' She walked off in the direction of her tent, ignoring the angry mutterings of the crowd.

Sorina shrugged. 'As you wish. What about them?' She turned her eyes to the Romans who were now weeping again – this time with relief.

Amagê stopped and turned. 'Brandus . . . Priscus . . .'

'Thank you, thank you for our lives . . .' Priscus babbled.

'Remember when I told you I wouldn't have you tortured?' she asked in Latin. 'I lied.'

'Take them!' Sorina shouted. The scream of both men was loud as the people descended on them. 'An offering for Zalmoxis. Burn them. Burn them alive!' The cavalrymen were dragged up, wailing in terror as they were born away, begging and pleading, lying and weeping.

'You're enthusiastic,' Amagê said as they walked away. It warmed Sorina that she linked arms with her.

'I hate Romans,' she said. 'I can find no pity in my heart for them. They took my lands, made war on my people, made me a slave. And you saw what they did to those families out there. And you put on a good act,' she added pointedly.

'I don't want defiance when I'm after information.' Amagê was blithe. 'Better to let them think there's hope . . .' she stopped as a high-pitched wail followed by a cheer rolled across the night. 'Someone's lost his balls already. Where was I? Doomed men can be stubborn – I don't need to waste hours with torture with what I can get with a smile in a few moments.'

'They didn't tell us much.'

'They told me enough to know that stepping up the pace was the right idea. Durostorum isn't far from here – a few days at most. They won't have finished their wall. And the Roman was right . . . We'll run over them in a single day.'

They had reached her tent and it looked warm inside. 'And their re-enforcements?'

'Won't matter one way or the other. Come inside, Sorina – the night is cold. We'll warm each other.'

Her words not only sent heat to Sorina's loins but also warmth to her heart.

They rode out at mid-morning, despite Amagê's urging to pick up the pace. But the tribes warriors were not soldiers like the Romans. There was no real military discipline here; rousing them and getting them moving took time.

The wind whipped across the grasslands from the river, bringing with it a biting chill – but the rain had stopped and Sorina found it more bracing than discomforting. She rode at the head of the tribespeople, Amagê at her side. The Sarmatian's fit of pique over their slow start soon evaporated with the mist. 'A finer day,' Sorina said to her.

'No rain, either, Amagê grinned. 'Makes a change.'

'Let us hope it stays this way. Horses or no, our feet will still leave a bog in our wake.'

'Zalmoxis smiles on us, perhaps?'

'Perhaps. Or the Earth Mother. Either way – harder ground would be better.'

'With no mist, the Romans will see us coming from miles away,' Amagê noted. 'The sight of us will terrify them. Unman them.'

'We have enough numbers to swallow their legion,' Sorina said.

'But we must not underestimate them, Amagê. As I have said – the Romans did not conquer the world by being foolish or cowards.'

Amagê laughed. 'You worry too much.'

'I just don't want to lose more people than we have to.'

Amagê looked at her, her eyes glinting. 'Unlike Decabalus.'

Sorina shrugged. 'He has become a king. They do as they will, Amagê. His world and his view on it has changed – yours doesn't have to.'

'But when Rome is gone, the world *will* have changed. It will need new kings. And queens. Like us,' she leaned across in the saddle and punched Sorina on the arm to take the weight from her words. But Sorina knew she spoke from the heart; Amagê was young – she still had ambition whereas all Sorina wanted was an end to Rome and peace. Peace by Amagê's side for as long as she wanted her to be there. But she knew well that if that was her desire, she would have to play in the game of power alongside her.

They rode without speaking for a time, but it was far from silent around them, the braying of pack animals, the song of the horses, the sound of the earth sucking at the feet of the tribes as they marched on. There was music too, laughter, song and conversation: these were things that truly mattered in life. But always in the warrior was the need to test him or herself against death. The music of battle was a crueller sound than this.

Sorina looked into the distance and squinted. There was a dark smudge on the horizon, dark against the beautiful green of the plains, stretching from bank to bank of both rivers. 'What is that?' she said to Amagê.

The Clan Chief craned her neck, she too narrowing her eyes. 'I don't know,' she murmured. 'Let us find out!' Without waiting for a response, she cried out and slapped the rump of her horse, sending her flying forward. Sorina cursed and dug her heels into her own mare, calling Amagê's bodyguards to follow her.

They ran over the wet ground as fast as they dared, but they were not long at the gallop before it became clear what they were looking at. Amagê pulled her mount to a halt and Sorina was by her side a moment later.

The rampart stretched from shore to shore with sharpened stakes for its teeth. Below it was a deep ditch and, behind the uniform line of wooden obstacles were the Romans.

'They were supposed to be at Durostorum,' Amagê snarled. 'That rampart is complete . . .'

'Those aren't legionaries,' Sorina said. 'Auxiliaries on the right flank. Mercenaries, by the looks of them, on the left. These must be the re-enforcements.'

'Unless the prisoners lied.'

'Unless they lied.'

'It matters not,' Amagê turned her horse.

'When do we attack?'

'Now. We attack now.'

Lysandra watched as the horizon began to turn black with bodies, thousands and thousands of them, cavalry and infantry. She turned to Kleandrias. 'This is it, then.'

'Aye.' He was quiet, he too staring into the distance.

Lysandra swallowed, feeling nerves and no little fear well up in her stomach. She had faced a battle before – but that had been a fair fight and a spectacle. This was horribly different. She knew the goddess was with her, knew that this was the moment she had been born for – and perhaps yearned for. Yet, now that it was upon her, the sickening reality of the odds marching towards her, she almost baulked.

But she had marched her army to a fight from which they could not easily run; they had no cavalry so they could not outrace the Dacian allies. Nor were Bedros's transports anywhere nearby to evacuate the troops. Here they must stand.

'This is it, then!' Illeana unwittingly repeated Lysandra's words. She strode towards them, her peerless green eyes alive with excitement. 'There's enough of them, isn't there?' she added as the blackness on the horizon grew even thicker.

'There is,' Lysandra agreed.

'Good thing you have a plan then,' Illeana said. Then she turned away, looking at the oncoming horde and spoke in a quiet voice. 'I can't wait for this.' She took a moment, seemingly in quiet contemplation; then she laughed. 'Where do you want me, Lysandra? Where shall I fight?'

'You should stay back at first,' Lysandra advised. 'They will be fresh and eager . . .'

Of course, Illeana would not hear of it. 'In the front, then?'

Lysandra smiled. 'In the front. But behind the stakes!'

Illeana slammed a fist over her heart, a flawed attempt at a military salute, and then made her way forward.

'I'll have what she's had.' Cappa approached with Murco in tow. He spat on the floor. 'This is it, then . . .'

Kleandrias and Lysandra chuckled. 'So it would seem,' she said.

'I don't think it's funny,' Murco said. 'There's a load of people over there that definitely want to separate my head from my body.'

'Make sure that they don't,' Kleandrias advised.

'I've got your back, brother,' Cappa said, surprising Lysandra. There was no jocularity, no banter. Not this time. He turned to Lysandra, 'And you stay close to us. Let us do our jobs.'

Lysandra nodded and looked around for the *hypaspistai*; they were making their way forward to the centre of her line. Across the field, she could see Euaristos's men moving into position, the brazen crow of their *buccinas* contrasting with the shrill wail of her own pipers.

She peered into the throngs assembling behind the vicious rows of sharpened stakes and saw Thebe's white-crested helmet and cloak weaving in and out of her heavy infantry. Behind them, were her *peltasts*, armed with javelin and sling and, bringing up the rear, the Priestesses of Artemis. Aloof and secure in their élan, these women knew well that many lives depended on their speed and accuracy. Lysandra wished that she could have brought the full force of her artillery to bear on the enemy at this point – squeezed between the two rivers, the onagers would have devastated them. But she may as well have wished for Athene to appear and strike down the barbarians herself. The line of Artemisian archers spanned both contingents – thinner than Lysandra would have liked but it was her opinion that concentrating missile attack on a single segment of the enemy would cause pressure elsewhere on her front as the barbarians bunched up to avoid the arrows. Better to keep an even spread of death.

Beyond the archers were the pack animals, medics, cooks and other personnel. The carts, which carried the medical supplies and wine, were being emptied – these would now be used to ferry the wounded from the front. Lysandra turned and looked back from where they had marched – hoping that Bedros and his ships would not let them down.

'We should be about it, then,' she said to Kleandrias. He was looking at her strangely. 'What?'

'You resemble Athene herself,' he said – which, Lysandra fancied was true, given her red cloak and armour.

'Not quite,' she commented with a smile – a smile that hid the churning worry in her belly. She placed the heavy, open-faced helm with its red crest on her head. 'Now?'

Kleandrias laughed. 'Perhaps another statue of you is due, Lysandra.'

'Let us see what happens here first, Kleandrias.'

The big man swallowed and glanced at Cappa and Murco; the latter caught the look and developed a sudden interest in the deployment of the troops – and needed Cappa's opinion on it. 'Lysandra,' Kleandrias rumbled. 'If something happens to me today . . .' he hesitated as she looked at his plain, honest face. 'I mean to say that . . . I struggle with these words . . . if I fall . . . I want you to know . . .'

'I do,' she cut him off. 'Just make sure you do not fall.' His eyes filled with hope and Lysandra felt mean spirited that she did not return his affections; but what else could she say to him? Now was not the time. 'Let us be about it,' she said.

'I was wondering when you'd turn up,' Thebe said as Illeana shoved her way to the front. The *Gladiatrix Prima* looked primed and ready – her green eyes alight with anticipation. 'You want to be in the Emperor's Box for the games,' she added.

'I've never fought in a war before,' Illeana said, turning her gaze towards the enemy. She hefted her shield – as with the rest of the heavy infantry, Illeana had the *secutrix scutum* – not as large as its military cousin, it still afforded a good deal of protection. And Thebe knew that, like the rest of the women, Illeana would be well used to wielding it.

'Stay close to me,' Thebe advised. 'You've not had the training the other girls have had.'

'I understand,' Illeana replied, surprising Thebe at her willingness to do as she was told. But then, Illeana was a surprising woman. Thebe had expected to hate her. After all, Lysandra had nearly died at her hand. But Illeana had no malice in her; it was all about professional pride for the Roman. Fighting was her job and she was the best – nobody could dispute that now. The thought brought a wry smile to Thebe's face: Lysandra would dispute it.

'Are you afraid?' Illeana asked, catching her off guard.

'No,' Thebe lied quickly.

'I'm shitting myself,' a woman nearby piped up, causing a ripple of giggles around her.

'This'll be easy compared to the arena!' Thebe shouted. 'We've all fought – and not with friends at our sides and at our backs. And not protected by a wooden wall of spikes. Think on this, girls. Some of those bastards out there will have killed before, but most of them won't. They'll be serving their chiefs, that lot – duty bound. Not professionals. Not like us. Every single one of us has had blood on their *gladius*. We'll put the fear of the gods into them!' The cheer she got in response was shrill and reedy – not a little fearful itself. 'Just stay in formation,' she added. 'No one's getting the *missio* for a flashy performance. Shields close. Strike true. Hold them off. That's all we have to do. *Hold them off.* A wound is as good as a kill – we'll be back on the boats before we know it.'

She looked across the field as the Dacian allies advanced – infantry to the front, horse soldiers behind. Her heart beat fast in her chest now and she realised that the comparison with the arena was apt. She was always afraid before the fight. Everyone was. But with that knowledge came the comfort that as soon as it began, the fear would fall away. She glanced at Illeana. 'A little,' she admitted.

'A little what?' Illeana did not look at her, her eyes fixed to the front.

'Afraid,' Thebe murmured.

'As am I, all of a sudden.'

'You'll be fine.'

'Oh, I know,' Illeana looked over to her and winked. 'It's no fun if you're not a bit afraid, is it? You can't fully appreciate life unless you've stared death in the face a few times. I will miss the thrill in later life. It's a shame we have to get old, Thebe.'

'If I'm a day older by tomorrow, I'll be happy,' she replied. She could feel the change in the women around her. Illeana's banter was having some effect on them, as though they were drawing courage from her.

'They're taking their time,' Illeana observed of the barbarians.

It was true – as the land between the rivers narrowed, the advance

326

was becoming slow and congested. Now that they were closer, Thebe could see them struggling in the muddy fields – not the first few ranks but those behind, as their feet churned up the sodden Dacian ground. But they were determined and pushed on, and she could make out individual forms as they drew nearer, the tall, bulky shapes of men making up the vast majority, but there were females among them too – as Sorina had told them all once, back in Balbus's *ludus*.

'I don't think a few sharp sticks are going to stop this lot,' the woman who had admitted to her fear earlier prophesised.

'Good!' Illeana shouted. 'I'd hate to have come all this way, leaving blessed Apollo's sun on the other side of the world and not have a fight at the end of it. I want to kill these bastards for their weather alone!'

That got some laughs and Thebe was relieved because of it, especially as she knew Illeana had only invoked the name of the god because she was with believers. Then, there was more hilarity as, as though on cue, thunder rolled across the sky and the first drops of rain began to fall. It was light at first and then, with Dacian typicality, it grew heavier and heavier until the familiar thick, blinding sheets came down.

It was hard going for the Dacian allies as they slogged towards the lines of stakes, but there was a palpable feeling of hatred rolling across the field to the Heronai lines. Thebe could imagine no mercy from these people – they were there to wipe out the thin line of humanity that stood between them and their ultimate goal of Durostorum and the last line of Roman defence.

The wailing of pipes floated to them from the rear and then, moments later, what sounded like the clap of a giant's hand followed by the hiss of a thousand hydras. Thebe looked up and saw the black shafts of arrows arcing overhead, disappearing into dark skies before falling. Screams erupted from the barbarians as the first barbs found their marks, but there was no respite – again the Artemisian Priestesses spat death at the enemy.

'Swords!' Thebe screamed at the top of her lungs. All down the line, the harsh scrape of metal followed by the 'thunk-thunk' of the women's *gladius* blades banging on the right edges of their shields.

The barbarians were galvanised by the arrows and they sped up as best they could in the muck, heaving themselves towards the Heronai line. 'Here they come!' Thebe shouted. 'Here they come, girls! Stay steady . . . stay in formation!' As if in answer to her, the enemy roared a battle cry and came on, swords and axes glinting dully in the rain. Arrows began to fall among the Heronai now, the barbarians bringing their own missile troops to the fight. But unlike the Priestesses of Artemis, there was no cold order to their attack, no cohesion. But still, there were enough of them out there and their barbs carried death as well as the Artemisians. Thebe could hear the careening impact of metal warheads on the shields and armour and the odd cry as one found flesh.

Thebe's grip tightened on her sword and she licked her lips: she could see faces now as the barbarians ran towards her: big, bearded men, eyes and mouths wide as they screamed at them, bolstering their courage; the warrior women, faces twisted in fury, fear and hate.

And then they were at the ditch, flowing into it like a river of armoured flesh, fingers scrabbling at the mud on which they could gain no purchase. It was chaos a few feet below their feet, the furious war cries now becoming screams of fear and panic as the warriors behind piled in, trampling the fallen as they were unable to halt the momentum of the thousands of bodies committed to the rush.

Above them, the arrows continued to rain down on the barbarians, an unmerciful torrent that tore flesh and snuffed out lives with impunity. In the ditch below, the bodies piled up, the living and the dead filling the ghastly pit with flesh.

Thebe was shoved from the side – one of the *peltasts* was there, and she saw more of them, pushing their sister soldiers out of the way, hurling javelins and slingshot down at the helpless warriors in the pit. She could not count the kills, but many hundreds must have died in the first few moments without getting to grips with them. But that, she knew, would change.

The barbarians were clambering over their own dead and wounded, the bodies providing more purchase than the mud, and they were gaining height now, pulling themselves closer to the top. Pipes wailed and the *peltasts* shoved their way out again, running to the rear to replenish their arms.

A helmeted head and armoured shoulders heaved into view at the lip of the ditch – a few scant yards from the wall of stakes. All along the line, bloodied, mud-covered shapes were rising from it like Furies from Tartarus. Thebe steeled herself as the first man, wielding a massive, curiously-angled sword came rushing at her. Behind him, more and more of them clambered up, filling the narrow ground, forcing their first rankers onwards by the press of bodies alone.

Thebe tried to stay relaxed as he charged her, waiting to see how to counter him – but the man was forced off course by the crush and was propelled, shrieking towards the tip of a stake. Unable to stop, he was forced onto it, the wooden shaft piercing his chest. His blood burst out in great gouts as he screamed and writhed in agony.

There was no time to think as more warriors hurled themselves forward with spectacular disregard for their own safety; like ravening beasts, they surged against the barricade, desperate to get at the Heronai – but the women of the temple held them off with shield and sword, striking back at faces and limbs sending their foes screaming to the earth.

By Thebe's side, Illeana moved with speed and economy of motion, her sword licking out with deadly efficiency. A wild-haired woman tried to weave her way through the stakes, but Illeana stepped forward, ramming the *gladius* into her neck; she fell with a gurgling cry to lay on the ground, legs kicking in mute agony as her ruined throat tried to suck air into her lungs.

Thebe smashed her shield-boss into the face of another man, sending him reeling away, but the instant he was gone, he was replaced by another warrior — this one wielding an axe. He swung it at the staves that protected her, smashing them to splinters. With a roar he leapt forward — onto her blade as she rammed it into his groin. His blood was hot on her wrist as she twisted her blade, trying to free it. The warrior was heavy and he tipped back, dragging her with him. Thebe screamed in panic as she over-balanced and fell, her shield thudding to the earth.

Frantic, she tried to rise and could hear the barbarians screaming as one of their foes came to within their grasp. A woman flew at her, sword raised; Thebe's arms flew up in self-preservation, eyes closed. But the blow never fell; Illeana had leapt from the lines, sword whirling as she hacked the woman from her feet. Thebe pushed herself back on her backside, legs flailing to propel herself backwards as Illeana moved with incomparable grace amongst the enemy; so swift and precise were her movements that it seemed to Thebe that the goddess herself had come from Olympus to aid them.

Rough hands hauled Thebe back into the relative safety of her line. 'Illeana!' she screamed, as the Roman ducked under an attack and, on rising, cut upwards with her sword, severing the man's hand at the wrist. He fell to his knees, clutching the bloody stump as it geysered blood. Illeana spun around, her shield knocking the teeth from another warrior — a thrust took another in the guts as she fought her way backwards, each movement of her blade stealing another life. The Heronai surged forward to the small breach as she reached it, barging their shields into the faces of the enemy so that Illeana might reach safety. The Roman dived to the ground and squirmed under her protectors, escaping the horde as the defence closed around her.

She was laughing.

LI

It was war.

People died, that was the way of it. But in a war of honour, there was pride; a feud might go on for generations as sons took vengeance for their fathers and grow their reputation by the strength of their sword arm. They would be respected by friend and enemy both.

There was no honour in this.

Philip of Macedonia, had invented total war. His son, Alexander, had mastered it and Alexander's military heirs, the Romans, had perfected it. Though it went against her grain, she knew in her heart that Decabalus had the rights of it by imitating them; like the metals mixed to make a strong sword, the Dacian King hoped to temper the natural ferocity of his people with Roman discipline.

But the Tribes, Sarmatian, Scythian and Getae had no such tactics or strategy. They fought in the old way – close with the enemy and defeat him eye to eye. They had courage, good weapons and numbers. This last was the key, she knew. No matter how good the position, how well trained and disciplined the soldiers were, they could not fight overwhelming odds forever. It was all a matter of time. Time and toll.

She rode at the front of the cavalry, Amagê at her side. Both of them knew that horses would be useless in this weather and on this ground, but the height afforded them a good view of the battle. Sorina struggled to remain dispassionate; she had fought countless times, but it pained her to see so many people fall in the first rush, struck down by arrows that fell with a rapidity she had not seen before. Mercenary archers, she guessed: Rome's strength was her infantry, but she had no qualms about hiring specialists for a job. Few in number they might be, but they were already paying for themselves.

Amagê, she could tell, was living and dying with each man and woman; it was like watching a spectator at a gladiatorial show. The Clan Chief hissed, groaned and cheered as the battle ebbed and flowed. The Roman ditch causing her the most distress; hundreds died in it, most crushed by their own kin. She turned to Sorina. 'These Romans fight battles sitting on their arses,' she spat.

'You know as well as I – they fight to win and they don't care that they shame themselves doing it.'

'They can't win,' Amagê declared.

'No,' Sorina agreed. 'They can't. But they will take a bloody price, my love.'

They were quiet then as the first wave of warriors reached the Roman barricades and battle was joined in full. Behind them, countless others, heading towards the fray, an endless sea of bobbing heads, glinting weapons and shields. Arrows from the Roman lines rained down, sharp metal mingled with the downpour.

Sorina's gaze swept along the front: the auxiliaries to the north were holding off the assault, using their spears to devastating effect. The hotchpotch of mercenaries were faring less well to the south – the centre of their line comprising strangely-clad warriors with round shields, heavy armour and long spears that caused most of the damage. They looked like *hoplomachus* gladiators, she realised, those clad like the Ancient Greeks. On either flank of the spear wielders were heavy infantry, faux legionaries with smaller shields . . . a chill going through her. They resembled *secutors* from the arena.

'Gladiators,' she said to Amagê. 'On the southern wing. Those are *arena* fighters.'

Amagê peered into the distance. 'They seem a bit small to be gladiators – I thought they were all huge.'

'Not all,' Sorina murmured, thinking of her old trainer, the Parthian known only as 'Stick'. She was about to speak again when she heard a roar erupting from the fight in the south – and then she saw it: the line closest to the river was beginning to bow. 'There,' she pointed with her spear. 'Amagê, there!'

'They're breaking through!' the Clan Chief snarled. 'They're breaking through!'

'They are breaking through,' Lysandra said. She pressed her lips into a thin line as the barbarians pressed their assault close to the river. 'The stakes aren't holding. I had not anticipated this.'

'Soft ground?' Kleandrias guessed. 'The stakes will be easier to drag out.'

'Perhaps,' Lysandra could say no more, her voice caught in her throat.

'What are we going to do?' Cappa said.

Lysandra puffed out a breath. 'Inspire them.'

'You can't,' Murco stepped forward. 'It's too dangerous.'

'If we do not stem them, we are all finished, Murco. Kleandrias – go to the *peltasts* and bring them to that flank in support.'

'What about the Artemisians?'

'No. Keep them going as they are. Titus will marshal them as needed.'

'As you command,' he said. 'But you should – '

'I am the strategos!' she snapped, anger, disappointment and no little shame boiling to the fore. 'This error is mine – I will right it. You will obey me. Go! Now!' Kleandrias snapped a salute and ran off, his armour clattering as he did so.

'You're going to get us killed,' Cappa told her, but he had a grin on his face and a glint in his eye.

'We shall see. Come, Cappa. Murco. Let us add our weight to the fight.'

Lysandra drew her sword and strode away, leaving the Romans

in her wake, her scarlet cloak flying out behind her as the wind whipped across the ground. She could hear them following on and pretending to argue about who was going to be first into the fray and who would stand by her side. They were good men. She offered a prayer to Athene that they might live, even if she did not.

That all of them might live if she did not.

It did not take her long to reach the rear ranks and the steady stream of injured and dying being ferried to the medical carts. The screams of her injured were loud in her ears, as were the battle cries of those at the front. 'Make way!' she shouted, barging her way through the throng of Heronai. 'Make way!'

'Lysandra!' one woman shouted. 'Lysandra is here!' Soon, the cry was taken up by others.

Lysandra pushed and shoved her way to the front, bearing many slaps on the back and helmet as she did so. The closer she got, the easier the going became because the press of bodies was less as her troops wavered. But she could hear her name being shouted over and over by the women behind her.

She now saw the full throng of the enemy: men and women, tall and fearsome in aspect, coated in mud and filth, their weapons red with the blood of her Heronai. The stakes that were supposed to hold them at bay were in ruins, lying like so many dead men in the Dacian mud.

Lysandra ran forward as a barbarian spearman took down a girl in the foremost rank. She blocked his leaf-bladed weapon with her shield as he struck out at her and rammed her *gladius* into his throat. Another warrior, a woman this time, hacking at her with a longsword: Lysandra parried and struck low, the *gladius* plunging into her meaty thigh, sending red ichor flying. Behind her, she could feel Cappa, Murco and the Heronai surging forward.

A huge warrior, armed with an axe – its haft almost as tall as a man – lunged at her from the side – it was all she could do to raise her shield in time and the impact of the axe blade onto the wooden surface nearly broke her arm. The barbarian dragged the weapon away, and with it the shattered remnants of her *scutum*. He roared in triumph and raised the weapon aiming to split her in two, a move she countered by kicking him in the testicles. He fell, clutching himself and she swung the *gladius* hard at his neck. Her arm jarred as the blade sunk in, cutting through flesh, bone and gristle; his head tipped sideways at an obscene angle, blood fountaining skywards.

Lysandra tore the weapon free and turned to see an amazon hurtling towards her, sword raised. There was no time to react and time seemed to slow as the weapon fell – but no blow landed. Murco dived at the woman, tackling her and taking her down into the mud. The two rolled away, lost in the surging scrum of the battle – she wanted to go after him but could not as more enemy pressed her. But now, her Heronai had found their strength and they rallied around her, screaming her name as they threw themselves at their foes.

Lysandra stooped and picked up a fallen *gladius*, grateful of the respite. She stretched her neck from side to side, spun both blades twice and breathed out sharply through her nose before hurling herself back into the fight.

All was chaos now as the Heronai regained the ground they had lost, screaming the names of the gods that they served so loud that the Olympians must have heard. Lysandra slashed and hacked her way forward, her blades moving with remembered ease as they stole the lives of her enemies. She had seen death up close before and she could see in the eyes of many she killed that they had not – and those around them began to fear her. She had no breath to shout encouragement, she simply killed and killed, her arm never wearing of it.

It was a nightmarish tableau, the screams of the wounded, the sight of the their guts spewing onto the churned ground, limbs fallen, severed arms still clutching weapons with shattered bone protruding from them, the endless cacophony of iron on iron, the thud of weapon meeting shield. If Athene was the goddess of strategic warfare, Lysandra knew well that she was dancing on Ares's field now and he would be revelling in the craft that she, his wiser sister's handmaiden, was displaying.

She took a blow to the side of the head and stumbled, her helmet falling away; it was Cappa this time who came to her aid and with him – impossibly – Murco, bloodied, mud-spattered but still alive and fighting ferociously. Both men stood before her, shields locked, their swords stabbing out at the wall of flesh before them, buying her precious moments to gather her senses.

Heronai flooded past her, taking the fight to Dacian allies and Lysandra sucked in a huge lungful of air, held it and let it out, trying to recover her breath. Sweat, blood and rain drenched her hair and it hung about her face in greasy hanks; her hands were coated in gore, her armour spattered in filth, her cloak ripped into tatters.

For a moment she thought they could win out; but then she saw the mass of enemy bearing down on them. Their cavalry had dismounted and were now throwing the weight of their swords into this fight. The rush of the Heronai was stemmed and she saw many fall as the counter shove of the barbarians drove them back.

'You all right?' Murco asked as he ran to her, Cappa in tow. 'We lost you there for a moment.'

There was no time to wonder at Murco's survival. She put her hand on his shoulder. 'Murco – find Thebe,' she gasped. Tell her . . . refuse the front and fight on an echelon. I will hold here until they can redeploy.'

'You can't do that,' Murco said in his doleful tone. 'You'll be cut off – '

'And we will be outflanked if I do not! Murco, we can still win this,' she lied. 'We can! I can feel the fight leeching out of them.' That much, she thought was true – but there was no power that could stop the barbarians from overrunning the south flank now.

The Heronai did not have the numbers to press home their advantage before the barbarian re-enforcements overwhelmed them.

'But – '

'Murco, you must tell the surgeons to move to behind the lines – the barbarians will not spare them or our wounded if we are overrun.'

'We can't leave you. You're the strategos. We need you!'

'This was my fault!' Lysandra shouted. 'My mistake! I have led us to this.'

'Throwing your life away won't help,' Murco's mournful face was full of purpose.

'And how long do you think these women will stand if I turn and run? The rest of the army needs time. I will ensure they have it. And we are wasting it here.'

'Lysandra –'

'Murco!' Cappa grabbed his friend by the shoulder. 'Come on. She's told us. Let's go!' He shoved the man forward and turned to Lysandra, his grizzled face set, his eyes alive with fury. 'We'll deliver the messages and then we'll be back for you.'

Lysandra nodded and gave him a tight smile. They both knew it would likely be the last time they would see each other this side of the Styx. 'Goodbye, Cappa,' she said and ran back into the fray before he could answer.

The fighting was frantic now – the only reason the Heronai were still holding was the ditch – and it was so full of bodies that the barbarians were stumbling across a grisly carpet of twisted limbs and shattered bodies. The women of the Heronai continued to rotate the front rankers, but with each passing moment they were being pushed back as exhaustion and wounds took their toll. Lysandra's hands and arms became numb from killing and still they fought on. The rain ceased, and soon after, a putrid mist began to rise from the sweat-drenched bodies of the combatants and the exposed organs of the dead. The day began to turn dark, but she

337

had lost all sense of time, aware only of the need to survive.

Lysandra found herself facing another axe man – she took him high and low at the same time, both blades licking past his guard and striking him simultaneously under the chin and in the side. She felt a thudding blow under her ribs and staggered – her armour held but it hurt her badly. The man delivering the blow was struck down by a woman to her right and he collapsed still living, his screams muffled by the hundreds of booted feet that crushed him to a bloody pulp.

The barbarians surged forwards, pressed by the weight of the masses from behind them – and there was nothing Lysandra or any of the others could do. They were borne along by the tide, carried backwards, still lashing out with their weapons as all cohesion broke down.

A snarling woman with blonde hair swung her sword at Lysandra; she parried with her left blade and shifted her weight giving her the angle to open the barbarian's throat with the *gladius* in her right hand. As she did so, she saw a huge warrior swinging for her head, his sword bright in the gloom.

Bright light flashed before her eyes and Lysandra found herself looking up at a grey sky through a bloody veil that fell into blackness. And there was no more pain.

Illeana saw a barbarian preparing to cut down at a woman to her right – she reached out and grabbed him by his long hair and pulled hard, sending him off balance and exposing his throat to the sky. Her blade sunk into the gristle of his larynx, which spewed blood as he fell. She was weary now, but she saw that the barbarians too were weakening, backing away across a stinking carpet of their own dead.

'They're backing off!' she shouted, which caused the women around her to cheer. She saw a black shape speeding towards her and raised her shield: the arrow careened off it with a metallic *pang*. 'Bastard,' she muttered.

Illeana looked down the line towards the southern bank: she knew nothing of military matters, but it looked to her that things had gone badly wrong. Indeed, the pressure on her part of the army was lessening as the chaos and easier pickings down there were siphoning the enemy away. 'They're losing down there,' she said aloud. 'Thebe, we have to help them!'

'We can't!' the Corinthian said. 'I can see what is happening here. Lysandra's orders are to form an echelon —'

'A what?'

'A . . . diagonal. We need to turn on an axis and keep our extreme right close to the river. And hope that Bedros arrives on time.'

'What about the wall?'

'It has done its job,' Thebe looked over to the retreating barbarians. 'Look how many we've killed.'

'A drop in the ocean,' Illeana said with a grin. She was enjoying the carnage — it was nothing like the arena but no less exhilarating. She understood now why old soldiers kept telling stories of their younger days: there were fights in the Flavian that she could barely recall, but this day would be scorched indelibly in her memory.

'We've plenty dead of our own,' Thebe was taut; it wasn't a game to her. Illeana realised this and forced away her grin. 'And you're right — they are losing down there. Lysandra is losing down there. She's being cut off! We have to move now!' Thebe looked around for a runner. 'Get the pipers to sound the refusal.' The girl saluted and ran away. 'Illeana, pass the word to your right and left — we back up the *hypaspistai*. We take it slow and we keep in formation. Understand?'

Illeana was going to salute but thought better of it. 'All right,' she replied. 'You hear her?' she asked the woman to her right. 'The pipes are going to sound a refusal – and we are to back up the *hypaspistai*. Keep it slow and keep in formation.' She repeated the same words to her left and soon after, the wailing of the Greek pipes signalled that they start moving. As they did so, the arrows of the Artemisian Priestesses began to fall with increasing rapidity, covering them. Everyone around Illeana started to march on the spot, so she did the same, feeling faintly ridiculos.

'It's to stay in time,' Thebe told her. 'Cohesion is the key – if we fall apart, they'll be on us like wolves.'

'I don't know about that,' Illeana glanced across at the Dacian allies who had backed away to the other side of the now almost filled ditch. 'They look like they've had enough to me.'

'Have you ever met a barbarian before, Illeana?'

'Only in the arena. So yes. But briefly. Obviously.'

'Ever known one to give in?'

There was no answer to that so Illeana continued to march on the spot, willing to admit to herself that she was grateful for the rest.

After what seemed like an eternity, she felt a shifting in the line to her left and little by little, the front began to turn on a very slight axis. It seemed as nothing to Illeana, but after some time, when she looked to her right she saw that there was wide space of churned up field becoming visible – they were moving away from the river on the straight line and lengthening to the diagonal – just as Thebe had said.

But now she was looking almost straight ahead she could see that the southern wing of the army was in dire straits. The barbarians were leaving Thebe's section alone – so they could concentrate on wiping out the stubborn resistance close to the river.

It had ceased to be a game for Illeana because the truth of it was that it was only fun when you were doing the killing, when it was test of skill at arms, a contest of wits, guile and strength. But this was a vision from Tartarus.

Even though they were far away, Illeana could see men hurling the Heronai to the ground, falling upon them like animals and raping them whilst the battle raged around them. Heads were cut from necks and raised up on spears, bodies hacked to pieces where they lay.

And those were the lucky ones. Other women were being dragged away, screaming and begging, passed back into the horde for the gods only knew what torments to be inflicted upon them. Illeana vowed that she would die before that happened to her. She looked to Thebe. 'We have to help them,' she said. 'Thebe . . .'

'You shut your mouth!' Thebe said, her eyes wet with tears. 'We have orders — and I'm not getting everyone killed — which will happen if we break formation and charge down there. It's over, Illeana. It's our job to take vengeance.'

Illeana nodded. 'I'll kill them,' she said softly. Then louder: 'I'll kill so many that my name will be told as a nightmare to their grandchildren. Do you hear me, barbarians!' she screamed, tears springing to her own eyes. 'Do you hear me! Face me, you bastards! I'll fucking kill you! I'll kill you all. You're all going to die!' She looked to her left and to her right. She did not know these women: they were Lysandra's and Thebe's people from their Temple in Asia Minor. They had nothing in common save for one thing. Each one of them had walked naked onto the sands of the arena and survived.

Each one a gladiatrix.

'*Fortuna!*' she shouted. '*Contemptio mortis! Cupido victoriae!*' Good fortune. Contempt of death. Love victory. She shouted it again, and then again, banging her sword onto her shield until the cry was taken up by the Heronai and beyond, the rough baritone of Euaristos's men. They shouted it, their challenge rolling across the field to the barbarians and beyond, she prayed, to Lysandra's goddess on High Olympus.

★

341

'They're all women.' Amagê had dismounted and was lifting back a corpse's head. The head almost came away in her hand, a livid and now bloodless wound carved deep into her throat. 'The Romans must indeed be desperate.' She grinned.

Sorina's mouth was dry as she surveyed the carnage. Up ahead, the battle still raged as the female defenders fought on, but it was in a lost cause. She too dismounted and walked amongst the long-haired dead. Red. Blonde. Raven. Mostly raven – Greeks by the look of them.

She too squatted down by a body, a young girl in a foetal position, crying soundlessly, her guts spilling out over her fingers as she pathetically tried to hold them in and cling to life. There was a part of Sorina that felt she should end the girl's suffering but then she looked again at the dead: hundreds, *thousands* of the plainspeople, littered on the field. A ditch full of them and it moved, undulating as those still alive shuddered in unknowable pain. How many had this one killed, she asked herself. Let her suffer.

She stood and walked closer to the fighting, her sword held loosely by her side.

It was simple butchery now, but still these women fought on, falling one by one – the lucky ones. She walked by a man atop an enemy, ploughing her. The woman was not fighting back – she may have even been dead. Another was dragged down by a group, screeching like a harpy, punching and kicking till a meaty fist smashed into her face and sent her to the filthy earth. They started kicking her then, laughing as she tried to escape.

The Greeks had lost their cohesion and fought now as individuals – and Sorina recognised them for what they were – arena fighters and, in or out of formation, they were still dangerous. She glanced across to the other side of the field where the rest of them were redeploying – they were most vulnerable now, but she could tell that the tribespeople were all but spent too. They had paid a heavy toll for so little gained. They had the numbers yes, but these Greeks had priced their lives dear.

One of them – an officer if her tattered red cloak was anything to go by, was about to be mounted by a Getic warrior – he struggled to get beneath the tunic under her mail shirt. She had long, black hair and her face was swathed in blood from a bad cut on her head. Her eyes flew open and she clamped her thumbs into his eyes. The man screamed and the woman struggled to her feet and kicked him in the side of his head. She stooped and grabbed his sword and without hesitation brought it down hard, severing his head from his neck.

Sorina's heart nearly burst in shock. 'Take her!' she screamed, a thousand memories buffeting her mind at once. 'Take that one! Take her alive!' Those nearby heard her and they ran at the raven-haired warrior. She was injured and dazed – and killed three more before they brought her low.

Sorina offered a silent prayer of thanks to the Earth Mother, a feeling of bliss flooding through her despite the ruin of corpses around her. The warriors kicked and punched the Greek into submission, nearly knocking her unconscious and they dragged her before Sorina, forcing her to her knees. One man put his gnarled, knotted fingers into her hair, dragging her head back and forcing her to look up into Sorina's face.

Lysandra's eyes. Those hated, ice blue eyes, stared up at her.

'No barbarian army can stand against disciplined troops? Isn't that what you said to me?' Sorina raised her sword, wanting desperately to hack down and end it. To take her revenge for what this woman had done to her. To Eirianwen. To her people. But to do so would be to deny herself proper vengeance. 'What? No lecture from you, Lysandra? No quotation of great learning? I have defeated you . . . I, Sorina of Dacia –'

'You have not won yet,' Lysandra said.

As she spoke, voices floated to her from across the field mingled with the sound of thousands of swords clattering on their shields: '*Fortuna! Contemptio mortis. Cupido victoriae.*' Fury rushed through

Sorina and she backhanded the hated Spartan's face. Lysandra's head hung low and she spat out a gob of blood.

'It would seem that age has robbed you of your vigour, Sorina,' Lysandra said, her teeth pink and bloodied. 'You had best kill me now. If you do not, you will regret it.'

Sorina was tempted and her fingers gripped tight on the hilt of her sword. Every part of her screamed out to do it.

'Who's this?' Amagê approached, her voice pulling Sorina back from the brink.

'Lysandra the Spartan,' Sorina replied, her voice shaking with emotion. 'I want her to suffer. She is their leader – she is the enemy of blood. I want her end to be terrible.'

Amagê looked down at the arrogant face. 'This is their leader?'

'Are you deaf or just stupid, fat one?' Lysandra laughed, a choking hacking sound. Amagê said something to Lysandra that Sorina didn't understand, but Lysandra simply sneered. 'An ape that speaks Hellenic,' she said in Latin. 'Did you train it, Sorina? Does it do other tricks –'

Amagê punched Lysandra full in the face, a mighty blow that snapped the Spartan's head back. Her eyes rolled and she slumped down unconscious. 'Talks a lot, doesn't she,' Amagê said, shaking her hand to wave away the pain in her knuckles. 'We'll have our sport with this one later.'

'I will interrogate her now,' Sorina spat on the prone Spartan. 'I'll make her sing and tell us their plans.'

'We already know their plans,' Amagê said.

'I hate her, Amagê, but she is a cunning bitch – who knows what tricks she has up her sleeve? Better that we get the information now.'

Before she spoke, Sorina knew the Clan Chief would not be moved. 'I need you with me, Sorina. You will have your revenge on this one.' She gestured to the warriors nearby. 'Take her!' she ordered. 'Keep her in one piece. If she gives you trouble, teach her a lesson. But I want her alive and unmolested – for now.'

Amagê turned her eyes to the reformed Greek line. 'We have to deal with them first,' she said to Sorina. 'But our people are weary. One last push – we'll see if we can knock them over today.'

'And if not?'

'Time is our friend, not theirs.'

They were worse than animals, Illeana thought, for beasts killed for a purpose. These savages were the sum of everything that was wrong with the human condition. Lysandra was famous in her condemnation of them and their ilk and now Illeana could see why. In Rome, a barbarian was away from his heartland and was cowed by the empire. But here, in the wilderness, he was unchecked and, played out before them in stark relief, was the fate that awaited the civilised peoples of Rome, Greece and beyond.

'I can't stand it,' Illeana said to Thebe as the barbarians went about their grisly work of butchery, rape and mutilation. 'Both what they are doing and the fact that I must stand here and let it happen. I have never felt so . . . powerless.'

Thebe glanced at her. 'Not a feeling you're used to, I imagine.'

Illeana nodded; it was true. She lived as she chose because her skill had earned her that right. But the horrors she was witnessing made everything she had done seem somehow petty and insignificant. The arena truly was a game compared to this carnage; it sickened and angered her in equal measure.

Illeana could not tell how long it went on only that the air grew colder and the sky greyer. Then, from behind, she heard shouts and the clash of weapons. Battle had resumed on Euaristos's front and, before them, the barbarians were now massing once again.

'I didn't think they'd try again today,' Thebe admitted, tilting her head skywards. 'It must be late in the day. But who can tell,' she added. 'As you said before, Apollo turned his face from here, Illeana.'

Illeana heard defeat in her tone. They were outnumbered and in all likelihood, the cornerstone of their enterprise, Lysandra, was already dead in the carnage on the southern bank. Illeana had a place in her heart for the uptight Spartan. Though they had not known each other long, she realised that all these women had come to this place because Lysandra had asked them. She had given them everything – and they believed in her and her goddess. If Lysandra's claim that Athene was with them and she had fallen – what fate lay in store for the rest of them?

The answer lay in bloody, tattered ribbons across the field.

'Let them come,' she said, a little too loud, making heads turn. 'I want them over here, in front of me so I can kill them. All we need to do is stand. It isn't about numbers any more, it's about will. We've all survived the arena. We'll survive this. Bedros won't let us down.' Not much of a speech, she thought to herself. Lysandra would have done better. But Lysandra couldn't help them now.

Thebe smiled tightly in thanks. 'She's right, girls!' she shouted. 'Stand fast. Keep killing until they give up or we're all dead. Hold the line – above all, hold the line! If we don't run – we win. It's as simple as that.'

'Here they come, then,' Illeana said as a girl shouldered her way through the ranks, one of several who were offering bread and water to the fighters. She refused neither; though she felt neither hunger nor thirst, she knew that she'd need the strength it gave her to fight on.

The Dacian allies came at a measured pace this time – no mad, ravening charge but a slow trot. 'They're tired too,' she said to no

346

one in particular. As she spoke, the first flight of arrows from the Artemisian Priestesses flew overhead and landed in the throng. Screams floated across the field to the Heronai lines and its sound seemed to lift them. Backs were straightened. Shields raised. Heads nodded.

More shafts were loosed from the rear, but not with the intensity of earlier in the day: they were running low on ammunition, Illeana guessed. It was a good and bad thing – good because when they were out of shafts, they would add their weight to the defence. But she reckoned that they had killed more with their arrows than the infantry had done all day.

She lifted her shield as the barbarians loosed their own arrows in response. They fell like ragged rain and there were a few cries of pain from the Heronai ranks as some of the barbs found their mark.

Thebe grabbed her shoulder and pointed. 'Look!'

Illeana looked towards the river and saw ships speeding west, oars dipping in and out of the river like so many wings. 'Supply boats?' she guessed as she counted them. 'There's only ten. Not enough to evacuate us. And besides – they're going the wrong way. Bedros will be coming from Durostorum. Look out,' she added as more arrows came their way, the clatter of iron on shield louder this time as the enemy drew closer. She looked in vain for a response from the Artemisians, but none came.

The barbarians began to shout and scream, brandishing their weapons, most still clotted and red with the blood of the Heronai. They made obscene gestures and taunts – Illeana was reminded of the mob at the Flavian.

'They're getting their blood up,' Thebe murmured. No sooner had the words left her mouth when the barbarians began to run at them.

Missiles were hurled at the Heronai lines, spears, axes and even stones as Illeana learned to her cost, one careening off her helmet stunning her for an instant. She took a step back and the woman behind her shoved her back into place. Illeana glanced over her shoulder and gave her a smile in thanks.

'Here we go!' Thebe shouted. 'Hold the line! Just hold the line!'

There was no more time for words as the lines collided and the sound of individual voices were lost to the hellish cacophony of battle.

'Go on!' Amagê screamed. 'Go on!'

The tribespeople crashed into the Roman lines first on the east-facing front, then to the corps of Lysandra's gladiatrices. The line bowed at the impact, the cause of Amagê's exhortations. She knew as well as Sorina that if they could break them on either side the battle would be over and the slaughter would be great and just.

'I must get up there!' Amagê said to her. '*We* must. We will lead them to victory.'

Sorina nodded – though she could not get thoughts of Lysandra from her mind. She recalled that Eirianwen had once prophesised that the Morrighan – the goddess of dark fates had her hands on the three of them when their paths crossed. And so it was again: Lysandra was in her power; she was so close to vengeance that she could not yet take. Not till the battle was won. The Old Crow would be laughing.

She drew her sword, hefted her shield and walked forward with Amagê who had her axe clasped in her hands. Behind them, Roman supply ships raced past the carnage, unable to do anything to help their beleaguered warriors. Good, Sorina thought. Let them flee. They would meet their fate at Durostorum when Lysandra's bitches and their Roman friends had been put to the sword.

Amagê forced them a path, pushing Sarmatian, Scythian and Getae alike from her path as she surged to the front. It was clear that she wanted to carry the day and soak herself in the blood of the invaders. So much so that she could not see the toll the battle was taking on her warriors.

Men and women were being carried past them, all of them bloodied and crying out from grievous wounds. Sorina knew that Lysandra would have prepared her women well for this fight – she hated the Spartan, but she would not allow herself to underestimate her. And the proof was plain – her gladiatrices were inflicting far more losses than they were taking.

Sorina thought to call Amagê back – to regroup and make their enemies wait out a night of ice and terror. Finish them in the cold light of day when the plains warriors' morale and strength were replenished. But it worked both ways – giving the Greeks some respite might make the price in lives even greater; Amagê was right – they had the numbers to break them and they had to do it soon.

Sorina could hear the sound of Greek curses and, through the throng, could see they were close to the front line now. She hated herself, but a part of her admired the courage of Lysandra's women. They stood in their civilised lines, fighting like ants – no honour, no glory – but they stood in the face of massive odds and did not turn their backs.

Amagê screamed a war cry and burst to the fore, her axe swinging, sighting an officer with a dirty white cloak in the front line. The woman was engaged with another warrior and didn't even see the blow that struck her head from her body. Blood fountained, drenching Amagê and everyone around her with its warmth. Like a goddess, the Clan Chief ploughed into their lines, hacking and slashing – so intent on killing that she did not see the gladiatrix coming for her.

Sorina leapt to defend Amagê, taking the gladiatrix's attack on her shield and striking back with venom. The warrior parried with her *scutum* and Sorina could see that – despite the blood and the filth – she was a great beauty. She had little time to admire her as the swirling tide of battle dragged them apart.

'Kill them!' she heard the woman shout in Latin. 'Kill them all!'

The gladiatrices rallied to her call and they surged back at the tribespeople, their short blades stabbing, shields punching, feet churning forward. They could not win. But they could hold and they were forcing the tribespeople back.

And Sorina could feel the fear and frustration beginning to build. 'At them!' she screamed. 'For our lands and our people! For freedom!' She hurled herself into the fray, cutting and hacking with her longsword, but in the closely packed ranks, she had little room to strike. Furious, she dropped the longsword and stooped to grab a *gladius* from the hand of a dead Greek. It was better for close quarters killing.

It shocked Sorina how comfortable the Roman weapon felt in her hand. So many years at the *ludus*, so many years of practising with one, her body could not forget it. She ploughed forward, shield up, head low, stabbing out into the enemy lines. Thrust met counter thrust, blade met board, iron sank into flesh.

She could hear Amagê laughing and exhorting the gods as she killed – and for her part, Sorina found once again the thrill of battle – as familiar to her as the Roman sword in her hand. Here was the place where fear fled. Here, in the eye of the storm, she was striking down her enemies and defending her lands and those of others against a threat that would devour them all.

To her left a man fell, taken down with a stab to the groin. A boy leapt to fill his space and he too was killed. To her right, a woman took the boss of a shield to the face and two thumbs of iron to the throat. The man behind her – a Scythian by the look of him went down moments later. Then there was nobody and she too backed away, chest heaving from exertion. Likewise, the women facing them stopped, exhausted by the savagery of the fight. Cutting over the gasping and puking of those still on their feet were the screams of the wounded and dying, some crawling away, others unable to move from their wounds. The stench was ripe, shit and the coppery reek of blood.

Sorina knew that the moment was now. If they did not attack again now, morale would flee and the Greeks would have the day. She filled her lungs, about to cry out for them to charge again when she heard the sound of singing coming from the west.

She turned and saw soldiers advancing. They too looked like the *hoplomachus* gladiators from the centre of the gladiatrix line. But these ones were different. They were uniform, each one wearing a red cloak. Each one with a large round shield – on it painted an inverse V. Each one holding a heavy, iron tipped spear. There could only have been a thousand of them, but they moved *fast*, their feet flying over the muddy ground. They sang – women's voices too – in Greek. Sorina's eyes widened in horror as she recalled the inverted V on their shields: it was the *lambda*, the symbol of Lysandra's beloved Sparta. Sorina remembered the time she shared with Lysandra in the *ludus*: the Spartan's boasting of her upbringing in a temple where they trained young girls for prayer and war. Lysandra had been forged in that place and now her sisters had come to the battle, borne on the ships that had just passed by.

As if they were a single bronze-clad warrior, they smashed into the flank of the tribespeople and a great groan erupted from them. The Spartan Priestesses ploughed a bloody furrow, thousands deep in less time than it took for the full horror of what was happening to impress itself on Sorina. And at the sight of them, Lysandra's gladiatrices counter attacked, throwing themselves into the fight with renewed vigour.

Sorina – like the rest – turned and ran. There would be time enough to kill them all on the morrow. But this day was lost.

As they fled back towards their encampment, the mocking shouts of the Greeks shamed them. Sorina comforted herself with the thought that, come first light, she would drag out their beloved Lysandra. She would be raped and tortured before their eyes before being set afire to honour Zalmoxis. Sorina would smear herself in

the Spartan's ashes and then put an end to her gladiatrices and her
Sisterhood in a single day.

LIV

At the point of a sword, they had made Lysandra disrobe. Now,
with a rope around her neck and her wrists bound, three
burly guards dragged her naked through the barbarian
encampment as the tribes hurled mud and abuse as she passed by.

She counted herself lucky; other women were now being raped
by these animals who, when they were done, would kill them in
the most vile way they could think of. That would happen to her
too. She deserved it — she had led the others to this end.

A clod of earth hit her in the face and she stumbled, falling to
cold, muddy ground. They laughed at her as the guards kicked her
till the one with her leash dragged her to her feet by her hair, pulling
her face close to his. He screamed at her, shouting orders or threats.

They were going to kill her anyway. With what little strength
she had left, she lunged forward and smashed her forehead into the
warrior's nose. Down he went, but she had no chance to savour her
moment, as one of the others punched her on the side of the head.

She fell again, the pain from the wound in her skull blinding her
and bile rushed from her throat. A kick to the ribs sent her over
again and she had no strength to rise. The one she had head butted
stood over her, eyes blazing with fury. His cohorts shouted at him,
gesticulating wildly — the message was clear: 'we cannot kill her.'
Instead, he put his foot on her chest and fished around inside his
trews. Moments later, piss spattered onto her face and neck as he
relieved himself while the crowd laughed and jeered.

Lysandra turned her face away from the hot, stinking liquid as it ran over her head, stinging her wound, trickling into her ear and nose. She didn't give them the satisfaction of cringing away, concentrating on keeping her face a stoic mask, eyes closed. The other two took a turn after that.

They dragged her then, forcing her to grip the rope fastened to her neck to save herself from choking until she was able to lurch to her feet and stagger along. She tried to make out details of the camp, picking out landmarks in case she had a chance to get away. But, with barbarian typicality, there was no order to it. It was simply an endless sea of tents, thrown up with no thought behind it.

At length, they arrived at a bigger shelter; smaller than a Roman general's *praetorium*, but big nevertheless. The men shoved her inside and bound her tightly to the central pole of the tent. The one whose nose she had bloodied punched her in the stomach. It was excruciating, since her bonds didn't allow her to bend. She coughed and gagged, making him laugh. He slapped her in the face and, along with the others, left her alone.

She struggled in her bonds, but her hands, feet and neck were bound fast to the posting and she had no leverage. After a few moments of trying fruitlessly to snap the ropes at her wrists, she gave up.

Despair opened like a pit inside her. She had failed so utterly she could barely comprehend it. In that moment, she realised that she had been deluding herself: the goddess did not speak to her. Rather, it was her own mind, her own ego – her subconscious telling her what she wanted to hear.

Strategos.

The word mocked her now. What was she other than a failed priestess and an arena fighter? A pawn in Sextus Julius Frontinus's grand plan; she saw it all, as plain as day. Why would a Roman senator entrust a former slave with an army? The answer was, of course, to buy the Romans time with their lives.

Lysandra knew she was going to die here. Sorina would inflict terrible torture on her and the thought of it terrified her. The pain was one thing, but the knowledge that she would be broken and humiliated filled her with dread. She told herself she would not beg for her death, but she knew she was lying. Sorina had all the time in the world to eke out her suffering. And Lysandra was strong; she had been trained to endure, her body fit and hard; she would last, and each moment would be filled with excruciating agony.

Tears filled her eyes. She sobbed, her body shaking with grief not only for herself but for those she had brought to the same end: Thebe, Kleandrias, Cappa and Murco, Illeana; they would all die, along with the thousands of trusting fools who had answered her call to arms.

Those that would fall in battle would be the lucky ones and Lysandra counted herself doubly a fool for bringing women to the man's world of war. Only now, at the end, did she realise that the Matriarch of the Temple had been right to cast her out; wise, like the goddess they served, not to throw Spartan lives away on Lysandra's vanity.

At least she and Kleandrias would be the only Spartans to die here. And die they would. Lysandra knew that even if the Heronai and the mercenaries escaped on Bedros's ships, he and the others would stand and fall at Durostorum – obedient to her word.

Indeterminate hours crawled by and Lysandra thought she must have slept. There was shouting from outside the tent, the sound of many voices over which she could hear the cries of the injured. The day was over, then, and she could hear no victory songs from the barbarians.

They had held. Thebe and Euaristos had held.

The flap of the tent parted and Sorina stepped in. She said nothing for a time, lighting a brazier, which flooded the interior with light. Lysandra watched her from behind matted hanks of hair. Sorina would break her in the end, she knew that. But she would resist as long as she could. She would show no fear, even if it churned inside her like the roiling sea.

'Warm enough for you, Lysandra?' Sorina asked, coming close to her. 'It will be warmer tomorrow.'

'Good. The weather here is vile.'

Sorina chuckled. 'You are afraid, Lysandra. I can see it in your eyes and the stains of your tears have cracked the blood on your face.'

'I was weeping at the stench. I am unused to being around so many barbarians.'

'Barbarians have bettered you.'

Lysandra looked Sorina in the eyes. 'I hear no victory songs. No laughter. You have failed, Sorina. Even with these great numbers . . .'

Sorina slapped her in the face, delivering a sharp, stinging pain.

'Truth hurts.' Lysandra saw the Dacian's cheeks colour as the barb found its mark.

'You're going to scream tomorrow, Lysandra,' Sorina's grin was feral in the half-light. 'You are right, though. Your people did stand. There are many dead and tomorrow we will finish them. But before that, I will have you dragged out before them. You will pleasure our best warriors. Your eyes will be put out. And then we will burn you. It will take hours, but we have time. And we'll see how much you have to say then.'

'Quite a bit, I imagine.' Lysandra willed her voice not to tremble. 'Poor Sorina! Too old to fight me even as I am now . . .'

'Why give you a chance, Lysandra? Even a small one? You're mine. You're in my power and there's nothing you can do. I will make you pay for what you did to Eirianwen.'

The mention of her name sent a shock through Lysandra and bringing her face to mind gave her strength. 'I loved her, Sorina – as she loved me. It was *you*! You drove her to her death. Your pride did it. Your rage did it! You could not bear that she was happy with me!'

'Shut up!' Sorina screamed at her. 'Shut up! Because of you, she is dead!'

'You killed her! *You!* With her own sword! By the gods, I wish I could have struck you down in the arena!' Lysandra surged against her bonds to no avail.

'But you couldn't! You failed then as you have failed now! I will burn you alive as an offering to her shade, Lysandra. Your screams will be as music to my ears. I will have my vengeance and with it my peace.'

'You will never have peace,' Lysandra hissed. 'I will haunt you in death as I have in life. I curse you in the names of all the gods . . .'

'Your gods have no sway here, you arrogant bitch.'

'Is that what you think, Sorina?' Lysandra stared into the light brown eyes of her hated enemy. 'Comfort yourself with that, then. But know that I will be the Fury in your dreams. You will fear sleep, because I will be your bringer of nightmares.'

'Words. The empty, desperate words of a woman whose fate is sealed. Your nightmare begins tomorrow. Let us see if you are as bold when your legs are splayed and your body is spewing out the seed of *barbarians* because there is no room in you to hold it. Let us see if you are as bold when your skin falls melting from your flesh – for I will burn you slowly, Spartan.'

Lysandra swallowed. Sorina saw it and Lysandra registered the triumph in her eyes. 'We will see, then,' she said.

'*You* won't,' Sorina told her. 'I'm having your eyes out, remember? Think on that, Spartan. But you'll still be able to hear yourself begging to die.' Sorina drew a dagger from her hip. 'Something to remember me by till then,' she said. She raised the blade and Lysandra refused to baulk. She would not flinch. She was still a Spartan.

Slowly and very deliberately, Sorina dragged the blade down the left side of Lysandra's face beginning at her forehead. It was excruciating; white-hot pain burned as the tip of the knife sliced through her flesh. It slipped at her eye socket, digging into her nose by her tear-ducts before continuing on to her chin. Blood sluiced down her face and onto her neck and chest. 'You still have your eyes,' she said. 'For now. And your ears. Later, when we have finished with our prisoners, I'll make sure that you can hear them die. Think on it, Lysandra. Imagine their suffering. This is what you have brought them to. Your pride brought suffering to many. And their agony will soon be yours.'

Sorina turned and extinguished the brazier, plunging the tent into darkness. She left Lysandra with only black thoughts for comfort until the screams of the burning began.

LV

Illeana knelt and covered Thebe's headless corpse with the remnants of her cloak. It had happened so fast – too fast for even she to intervene. The woman with the axe had taken Thebe's life in the blinking of an eye. One moment she had been fighting at Illeana's side, the next, struck down.

Like so many others.

Illeana surveyed the carnage. The field was littered with dead bodies, mostly barbarians, but there were enough Heronai and merce-naries among them. Too many, she knew.

'Come on, love!' She looked up to see Cappa and a bloodied Murco in tow. 'She's gone.' He held out his hand and pulled her to her feet.

'Now what?' Illeana asked. 'What are we going to do now?'

'A good question.' They turned to see a tall woman of middling years striding towards them. She had the same weird accent as

Lysandra and Kleandrias – the armour she wore marking her a Priestess of Lysandra's Spartan Temple. With her were two others, one gaunt and red haired, the other blonde and fair. 'Who commands here?' the woman asked.

Illeana looked around. 'We don't know. Not anymore. Does Euaristos still live? Titus?'

'Both still kicking last I saw them,' Murco said.

'Then they are now in command,' Illeana said to the woman. 'Who are you? We thank you for our lives. Without your help . . .'

'I am Halkyone,' the Spartan interrupted. 'We are aware that our intervention saved you. Where is Lysandra? It is at her behest that we have come.'

'Lysandra is dead.'

'Unfortunate.' The woman pressed her lips into a thin line and Illeana saw – just for a moment – a flicker of sadness on her granite features. 'These men – Titus and Euaristos. They took orders from Lysandra?'

Illeana looked at Cappa and Murco for support but none was forthcoming. 'Euaristos commands the mercenaries down the line. Titus was one of Lysandra's chosen men – A Roman centurion. But Lysandra was in command of this legion – we're the Heronai . . .'

'No longer. I am in command now, as there are no others fit to lead.'

'Now hang on a moment. I don't know about that,' Cappa finally cut in. 'I mean, we need to call the roll and . . .'

'Are there other Spartans here?'

'Only Kleandrias.' Illeana said.

'And he does not command?'

'No.'

'Then there are no others fit to lead. Bring these men to me. Now. We must make haste and the barbarians will not afford us much time.'

Illeana looked at Cappa and Murco but the woman's demeanour seemed to have knocked the fight out of them. 'We'll go,' Cappa said. 'See if we can find Kleandrias too. He's less up himself than most Spartans, if you take my meaning, lady.'

'I do not,' Halkyone said. 'And I do not care for an explanation.' She looked Cappa in the eye and he bristled, clearly preparing to argue. 'You are still here,' she observed.

'Come on,' Murco pulled him away. 'The last thing we need is internecine bickering.'

'Internecine,' Cappa allowed himself to be drawn away. 'What does that mean?'

Illeana saw Halkyone shake her head slightly as the two Romans walked off, her eyes cold and hard.

Fires burned and the tang of cooking meat hung heavy in the air. Both Heronai and mercenary ate in their positions, fearing an attack. The cries of the wounded were close, and from time to time the agonised shrieking of the captured women floated to them from the distant barbarian camp. Illeana felt both grateful and guilty: grateful to have lived and not be in the hands of the barbarians; guilty for feeling relieved about it. It was shameful.

It had not been as she had expected. It had been thrilling enough at first but, as the fight wore on and intensified, she realised the truth of it: there was no honour or glory here. No slaughter of men and beasts in the arena could compare to this. This was utterly different. It was truly horrific, and it was all she could do to stop her hands from shaking as the memories of the battle buffeted her mind.

She was grateful to be included in the meeting of Titus, Euaristos and the Spartan commander – she hoped it would take her mind off what had gone before. Not that the council was anything grand. They sat around a fire – Halkyone and her two seconds, the red-haired Melantha and the blonde Deianara, an inconsolable Kleandrias, eyes red-rimmed from tears and Euaristos – blood spattered, wounded and nearly out on his feet. Titus looked as if he had aged twenty years in one day. She had told him of Thebe's death and she could see in his face that this news – coupled with the loss of Lysandra, had cut him to the quick.

'That you cry for the fallen cheapens you, brother,' Halkyone said to Kleandrias. 'It is not the Spartan way.'

'Easy words for the latecomer, who has not shed her blood,' he shot back.

'Latecomers who saved your life, friend.' This from the pretty Deianara.

Euaristos coughed. 'Now that the pleasantries are all done with, can someone tell me what in the name of the gods is going on?'

'You are defeated here,' Halkyone stated. 'You must evacuate. But our ships will not be able to hold all of you.'

'We're excepting to be evacuated by our own ships,' Titus said. 'Due the day after tomorrow.'

'You will all be dead by them,' Halkyone said. 'Even with our help.'

'Our ships are at Durostorum,' Euaristos seemed to Illeana to be bone weary, barely able to continue the conversation. 'One of your vessels could row upriver – bring them to us early. Then we can hold at the town.'

Halkyone seemed to weigh that up for a moment. 'Agreed. We will march. Tonight.

'We can't,' Titus spoke finally. 'If the barbarians attack, we'll be strung out on the march and easy meat for them.'

'The barbarians will not attack,' Halkyone told him. The former centurion simply shrugged in response. To Illeana he looked to have aged twenty years in one day.

'Are you an oracle as well as a priestess?' Kleandrias snapped.

'No, just a competent commander. Speaking of which, we are agreed that I will command these Heronai now that Lysandra is dead.' Her gaze challenged Titus and Euaristos – and neither man seemed to have the energy to fight back.

'The Heronai should have a voice in that,' Illeana put in. 'You can't just turn up and take over. That wouldn't be right.'

'What is not right is to think war has a place for democracy. You, pretty one, can break the news to your sisters as you please.'

'I haven't agreed yet,' Euaristos said tiredly. 'And, even if I do, you've not yet told us how you can predict the barbarians will not attack. There's nothing to stop them.'

'That is where you are quite mistaken,' Halkyone said. 'We are done here. Muster your people. Get them ready to march. You, pretty one,' she said to Illeana.

'Illeana. I'm called Illeana.'

Halkyone didn't seem to care much for the information. 'And you . . . Centurion Titus . . . inform your Heronai of the change in the command. My Spartans will help you muster them. Get ready. And tell your healers to kill anyone that can't be moved.'

'What! We cannot do that!' Kleandrias rose to his feet, eyes blazing. 'Those people fought hard. We will not abandon them.'

'*E tan, e epi tan,*' Halkyone said.

'This is not Sparta, woman!' Kleandrias blazed. 'These are not Spartans – they cannot be treated as – '

'Now I know why you weep so easily. You have spent far too much time with these *xenoi*.'

'What about your ships?' Titus asked. 'You can carry the wounded, can't you?'

Halkyone regarded him. 'Those ships are for my priestesses. We came here to help you, not throw our lives away.'

'If you came here at Lysandra's behest . . . she would not countenance this thing you suggest.'

Halkyone folded her arms, index finger tapping her chin – a habit, Illeana noted, that Lysandra had as well. The priestess rose to her feet. 'Lysandra has also clearly spent too much time with

361

xenoi and lesser Hellenes. For her sake, however, we will slog through the mud with you. Get those that you can onto our ships. The rest . . . use mercy. We will have to march at speed and those left behind . . .' she jerked her chin in the direction of the barbarian encampment, 'what fate do you think will befall them?'

'And you?' Kleandrias said. 'What will you do?'

Halkyone smiled and it was as cold and bleak as the night that was falling. 'Start a fire.'

LVI

Sorina was drunk, lurching between feelings of anger, hurt, satisfaction and melancholy. The fires that had consumed the gladiatrices were dying out. Sorina could still hear their screams and though she had hardened her heart against them, she could not escape the thought that she had probably known some of those women. She reminded herself of what the Romans had done to the people of Dacia. She knew these women had no part of that – but they were with Lysandra, and they had come to kill her people.

And they had done just that, she thought bitterly. Thousands of them had fallen to their swords, to their spears to their *discipline*.

Discipline. It made her think of Lysandra again.

She had the hated Spartan in her grasp; Sorina's heart burned with the desire to torture her further, to hurt her, to strip the flesh from her body. But she could not.

She knew it would destroy Lysandra's followers to see her brought low before them. And for Lysandra herself, far beyond the pain of the physical agonies she would endure, she would go to the under- world humiliated by the knowledge that Sorina had bested her. Had ruined her. That was a wine too exquisite to swallow in one draught; she must eke it out, make it last and savour it.

The hour was late, most of the tribespeople slept off the drink they had consumed to dull the bitter sting of defeat – for a defeat it was, whichever way one turned it. They should have overwhelmed Lysandra's forces earlier. They would tomorrow, she knew. There would be no way the little force could stand against them. Not again. They would be exhausted, cold and utterly demoralised; they had lost their leader and a good many of their number.

She weaved her way through the sleeping encampment, towards the pickets her eyes on the not-so-distant fires of the enemy, swigging from her sack of beer to ward off the cold. The ground was beginning to harden, a frost descending across the field, and she pulled her cloak tighter around her, wondering if it would be firm enough for horses come the dawn. If that were so, the battle would be over before mid-morning. She would make her way onto the killing field proper and make an assessment.

She bridled when she came to the sleeping picket. He was sat on his arse, his head resting on his chest. He was probably drunker than herself, but even though there was little danger from the enemy, sleeping on picket duty put them all at risk. She reached out and shook him.

He toppled over and lay unmoving, so she kicked him hard in the ribs.

He did not move.

Sorina crouched down and put her fingers to his throat; they came away wet and her heart lurched with shock and fear. She turned back to the encampment and saw flames beginning to lick at the tents and the shouts and curses of the warriors. 'We are under attack!' she shouted, casting her beer sack aside, racing back towards the camp. 'We are under attack!'

But no guards answered her call.

She ran hard, now cursing the drink she had consumed as it

slowed her and made her stumble more than once. With every heartbeat that passed, the more pandemonium seemed to descend on the encampment, the shouts and screams of men and women now mingling with the shrill whinny of horses: the attackers had opened the corrals and the horses were stampeding, terrified by the chaos and the fires that were spreading everywhere.

Warriors stumbled from their tents, looking for someone to fight. But in the bouncing, hellish glare of the fires and shadow it was impossible to tell who was attacking and from where.

Lysandra.

The realisation hit Sorina like a hammer blow. They had come to rescue Lysandra. Screaming in fury, she tried to run towards her tent, but the milling throng slowed her at every step, cursing her as she tried to shove her way through. Every so often, she caught sight of an enemy: dark, lithe figures skipping through the chaos, striking out with short swords before disappearing again into the turmoil.

She had to get to Lysandra and finish her before she could be saved. Weeping with frustration, she pushed on, praying to the Earth Mother that she would get there in time.

The screams of the dying still haunted Lysandra. It had gone on for hours as the barbarians roasted her priestesses alive, torturing them for no reason other than to make them suffer. Sorina would be savouring her vengeance; the Dacian knew well what she was doing, every savage act designed to distress her. To fill her full of fear and regret.

And it was working. Lysandra had never before felt such terror. She was bound and helpless and, on the morrow, it would be her turn to shriek in agony as the flames consumed her. She would not beg for her life, she told herself. No matter what, she would not give them the satisfaction. But she would scream, of that she was certain. The pain would be unendurable.

When they were done torturing their prisoners, the barbarians had set about drinking and carousing, before a partial silence eventually descended on the encampment as most put their heads down to rest. The quiet was more terrifying, as it meant that for Lysandra, the sands of time were slipping away and each passing moment brought the dawn closer.

She prayed to Athene constantly for deliverance, hoping against hope that the goddess would answer her prayers. She begged forgiveness for doubting her Mission, but even as she brought the words to mind, she knew that they were borne from her own desperation and fear.

Lysandra realised in that moment that she had never countenanced the thought that she might die obeying the word of the goddess. She had been so confident, so sure of herself, safe in the knowledge that her victory was ordained.

Hubris.

She could see it now, in her last hours: Spartan pride, the superiority of the blood that ran in her veins, her conceit, her arrogance. She had always told herself that she was the best, that the gods had favoured the Spartans above all others and in her heart she fancied herself favoured above all Spartans. But the truth of it was that her vanity had brought both herself and others more pain than joy, and her supposed superiority had been illusory.

If not for her harsh words to Sorina those years ago, they might have made peace and put the ghost of Eirianwen to rest. There could have been a healing between them; for was not Eirianwen, like Sorina herself, of barbarian stock? Eirianwen who had represented all that was pure and good in her life was dead because Lysandra could not swallow her pride and accept the apology offered to her by another woman who simply had as much pride as she did.

Yet, she had spat it back in Sorina's face and so the *Morai* – the Fates – had spun a new tale for her life: Lysandra of Sparta would die at the hands of the woman she hated more than any other and to whom she had given the cause to hate her.

And what of her vaunted superiority? She had had the chance

to kill Sorina and failed. She had faced Illeana and had been defeated. She had marshalled an army and seen it beaten.

Of it all, this is what sickened her the most. She had sheltered those women, given them a life they could not have dreamed of in the modern world; they had trusted her. Believed in her. And she had led them here to where they would all end up as those others: raped, tortured and burned alive. As would she be, all too soon.

The bindings at her wrists parted and Lysandra fell forward.

Moments later the ones at her feet were sliced away, and then the ropes at her waist. She fell to the ground, her legs unable to hold her. She wondered if she was asleep in a dream when a dirty hand clamped over her mouth.

'Don't make a sound!' The voice was thickly accented Latin. A voice she knew well.

Lysandra turned, not daring to believe. 'Teuta?' she whispered.

'Put these on!' Teuta dropped a pile of clothing at her feet. 'And be swift!'

Lysandra nodded and dressed in the barbarian clothes as fast as she could: trews, boots, a tunic and a hooded woollen cloak.

'Hood up!' Teuta ordered. 'And follow me! Anyone speaks to us, act drunk and stupid. I've seen you like that once before,' she added with a quick smile. 'I will talk, you say nothing.' She turned and went to the back of the tent and dropped to her knees, crawling through a slit she must have carved with a dagger.

Lysandra followed Teuta on unsteady legs and the cold night air was almost as much of a blessing as the overwhelming relief that flooded through her, so that tears once again welled in her eyes. Teuta beckoned in the darkness and she went to her, head bowed low. The camp was quiet, most were asleep and the others too drunk to care who else was abroad. Teuta led her unerringly through the blackness, picking her way through the encampment. As they went on, Lysandra felt the numbness leaving her legs as the blood began to flow freely once again.

The sudden shouting stopped them both cold as though Hades himself had clamped his hand around their hearts. Then, fires began to burn and warriors fell from their tents, roused by the chaos. There was a phrase being shouted over and over by many different voices, and Lysandra needed no translator as the chaos spread.

'The camp is under attack,' she said to Teuta.

'We must go!' Teuta replied and pulled Lysandra along. 'Keep your head down and your mouth shut!'

They pressed on, but the attackers were spreading pandemonium in the encampment and it was soon thick with warriors and then horses as the beasts were freed from their paddocks and they too ran amok, adding to the chaos. It was, Lysandra thought, a raid of which Leonidas would have been proud.

Teuta gripped her arm tightly and led her through the thickening crowds, each heartbeat more terrifying than the last. But no one harassed them; all were more concerned with identifying attackers than unarmed friends.

It seemed to take hours, but they were finally free of the press of people – the horses, had clearly bolted for the freedom of the battlefield, leaving the burning encampment behind them. The picket posts were deserted or manned by corpses – evidence of the raiders' passage. In the distance, Lysandra could see the fires of her own camp, beckoning to her, warm with the promise of safety and the embrace of friends.

A horse cantered past and Teuta sprinted forward and grabbed its mane, vaulting onto its back. The beast was clearly distressed but it took her scant moments to get it under control. She slid from it and led it to Lysandra.

'Can you ride?'

'Not well.'

'Your life depends on it, Spartan.'

Lysandra did not need to be told twice; with Teuta's help, she struggled onto the horse's back and gripped its mane tight. 'Why?' she asked Teuta. 'Why help me?'

'You're religious, aren't you?' Teuta asked. 'Maybe your gods helped you. Or maybe I hate Sorina more than you do. Saving you hurts her. As she hurt me.'

'Come with me, Teuta.' Lysandra held out her hand. 'She will take her revenge if she discovers you.'

Teuta smiled. 'She won't. You don't think I'm staying here, do you? I'm going to find another horse and get out of here. I'm going home. As should you.' She nodded. '*Vale, Gladiatrix.*'

Lysandra smiled tightly, refusing to wince as the cut on her face pulled. There was nothing else to say, so she dragged the horse's head around and kicked its flanks aiming its head in the direction of her camp.

Sorina reached her tent, relieved that the chaos had not yet reached the centre of the camp. She ripped the dagger from the scabbard at her hip and threw open the flap, ready to carve Lysandra's heart out.

The cut ropes that lay on the floor mocked her. Sorina fell to her knees and opened her throat in a scream of anguish that rended the black night sky.

Somewhere the Morrighan was laughing.

LVII

The Spartans set a blistering pace and, Illeana fancied, it was only pride that kept the Heronai and the mercenaries going. They all counted themselves fit, but the women of Athene's Temple were conditioned like athletes, pounding along and putting as much distance between them and the barbarians as they could before the dawn.

It was, Halkyone had told them, a precaution. Her plan was a simple one: to leave their campfires burning and march out at speed whilst a detachment of her priestesses raided the barbarian encampment and wreaked as much havoc as they could before they were discovered. If things went as they should, the disruption would hold up the enemy – and allow them more time to flee.

They left everything that could not easily be carried, including the mortally wounded. It was little comfort to those healers tasked with administering their lethal draught of medicine that the fighters in their care would have crossed the Styx anyway; Illeana had seen many of them weeping as they mustered for the march. The rest of the wounded that could not walk had been loaded onto the Spartan ships and borne away to the tenuous safety of Durostorum.

They rushed through the night and the sky began to turn grey with light as the sun tried – and failed – to break through the clouds. It seemed that Halkyone's plan had worked, for there was no sign nor sound of pursuit.

Illeana marched by Titus and Kleandrias. Neither man spoke, both walked with their heads down, both wrapped in their grief, and Illeana felt a bitter swell of guilt that she had not been able to save Thebe. She wanted to tell Titus that had she seen the blow coming she would have stopped it if she could.

But to what end?

What could she, *Gladiatrix Prima*, the one person here for herself and not for a cause say to him? She had come because she wanted to experience something new, something that few women – and men for that matter – in the civilised world would ever know: the thrill and exhalation of pitched battle. In her imaginings, Illeana had reckoned it would be far sweeter than the rush of victory in the arena. She believed that war would be the ultimate thrill.

She had been gravely mistaken. Words from the *Aeneid* came to mind: *Wars. Horrid wars.*

'What did you say?' Titus glanced at her and she realised she had let the words in mind slip out of her mouth.

'Just thinking aloud,' she replied.

'Virgil, isn't it?'

'Yes.'

'He's right. I'd forgotten all of this,' the former centurion admitted. 'Old men only remember the glory days,' he added, his voice thick.

'You're not old, Titus.'

'I am now,' he said. 'I'd known Lysandra since she was not yet out of her teens – nearly ten years, Illeana. And Thebe longer than that. They're all gone now. All of them. Hildreth. Penelope. Eirianwen. And now Lysandra and Thebe too. Back then, it was business. They were fighters and I was their trainer. They went to the arena and, more often than not, they'd come back – if not unharmed, in one piece. But this is different. I should not have let them come here, Illeana. I should have been more of a man and stopped them.'

Illeana was about to reply, to offer a word of conciliation, but the deep rumble of Kleandrias stopped her. 'I think, my friend, that Lysandra would not be dissuaded by anyone. She was . . . unique.'

Titus looked over to him. 'You loved her, didn't you? For a long time.'

Kleandrias kept his eyes down and his voice steady. 'Aye. That I did. Who that knew her could not?'

Titus's smile was a ghost. 'Plenty. She was, as you say . . . unique.'

'I should have told her,' Kleandrias said. 'Perhaps if I had, all of this would not have come to pass. Perhaps she would have had me and her fate would not have been so dark.'

Illeana shook her head. 'I have not known her as long as you both. And, Kleandrias, I believe she loved you in her own way,' she added the lie. 'But I know her well enough to know that hearth and home, wife and child would not be a path Lysandra would have chosen. Not when her goddess called her to this . . . Mission.'

'A call I wish she had not answered,' Kleandrias replied. 'I do not wish to be impious, but I fear that Athene's words could have been misinterpreted. Things run hard against us and Lysandra has fallen.'

'She fell in battle, her sword in her hand. She was a Spartan — isn't this the way you people look forward to going out?'

'Yes, but . . .'

'And we are not done yet,' Illeana pressed on. 'We still live, the barbarians are in disarray and we have allies waiting for us behind a strong wall. Maybe Athene's message was that she would die so the Empire — and Greece — would live. Like Leonidas.'

'You believe that to be true?' Kleandrias lifted his gaze from the ground.

'Yes I do,' she lied. 'What else could it be? Think about it — poems will be written about all of this and recited long after we're all ashes. Lysandra's fame will endure — she fought and died for her goddess and her land. A fitting epitaph for her, Kleandrias, and I think she would have it no other way.'

His smile was tight. 'Aye. But I wish with all my heart it could have been otherwise.'

'All of us do,' Titus said.

'That and a few sesterces will get you a bowl of soup,' Illeana said. 'Harden your hearts and don't fall victim to despair. Remember, if there's no cause to fight for, there's always revenge. Think on that. We did our job back there — we held them and your Athene came and rescued us with her priestesses, didn't she? We killed enough of the bastards and with a Roman legion standing with us . . . we will win this thing. I'm sure of it.'

Both men looked at her and she saw the kindling of a cold anger behind the grief in their eyes. Good, she thought. They'd need it. Because what she'd just spouted was all hot air. There were too

371

many barbarians and not enough of them to hold out for long. Sooner or later, they'd be over whatever defences Valerian and his soldiers had built and that would be the end of it.

For her part, Illeana would take as many of the bastards with her as she could, and she swore before Venus, Fortuna and Jupiter Best and Greatest – if they would hear her and if they were real – that she would not be captured alive. But she promised herself that, like Lysandra, she would die with a sword in her hand and the blood of her enemies upon it.

'That true, what you said?' a woman asked her – one of Lysandra's *hypaspistai* judging by her gear.

'Yes, it's true,' Illeana replied, a little embarrassed that she'd been overheard.

'Good, because most of the girls are close to having had enough,' the woman said. 'Me too, for that matter.'

'I thought you were priestesses. And former gladiatrices? In Rome, a gladiatrix fights on to the last. You Greek girls are different, I take it?'

'I'm not Greek,' the woman shot back. 'I'm from Halicarnassus.'

'There's a difference?'

'Fuck you.'

'In your dreams. But really – are the Heronai, the women of Lysandra's temple, servants of the Olympians going to roll over and give in because they've had a kicking?' Illeana found her voice rising as she spoke and she could feel the eyes of many in the ranks on her. She took a breath.

'By the gods, girls,' she said. 'I'd expected better. On my left a geriatric trainer of fighters and on my right greybeard Spartan and me, a Roman – albeit a pretty one, I'll grant you.' That raised a few chuckles and she pushed on. 'We're still here to fight. Now listen and pass the word . . . Lysandra and Thebe may have fallen and I know all of you have lost friends. But we're still alive. The IV Felix awaits us – they have supplies and a wall – a proper wall

– to fight behind. Your onagers and scorpions will be set by now and they'll give the barbarians a warm welcome when they come. Let's send them all to Hades, Heronai. Let's kill them all.'

It wasn't much of a speech – Lysandra was so much better at it, as was Thebe for that matter. Illeana didn't like the taste of the words on her tongue, either. The war sickened her and she wanted nothing more than to get away, return home and count herself lucky to have survived one day of it.

But her words seemed to have some effect and Illeana could feel the mood around her change. It had not lifted – but it had gone as cold and hard as the frosted mud beneath their feet. And that would have to do, she thought.

It kept them strong until at last, they saw the first of Bedros's ships coming towards them from the west and knew that, for now, they were safe.

Many of the Heronai patted her arm or nodded at her as they marched by, eager now to be aboard and free from danger. They were looking to her for leadership – because no one yet trusted or even liked the aloof Spartans who claimed command. But leadership was a thing she could not provide.

It came to her then. Was she not the *Aesalon Nocturna*? The most beautiful and deadly gladiatrix in the Empire? Her name caused fear and love in equal measure, no man or woman could resist her – or so it was written on the walls of the Flavian Amphitheatre. If she could inspire the Heronai as she inspired the crowds in Rome, she would. If she could lead by example – by killing – she would. If this would make them fight harder, she would do it.

As the thought came to her she watched Bedros's ships rowing fast upriver. And, for a moment, she believed her own lies that they might just survive this.

LVIII

Durostorum

There was no time to rest. No sooner had their feet touched dry land, Halkyone marshalled the surviving commanders of the Heronai and demanded that they be taken at once to 'the Roman Commander'.

As they rushed through the town – it seemed to Illeana that the Spartans went everywhere at a half-trot – she was struck by the work that had been done in the short time they had been in the field. Houses had been knocked down, their remains protruding from the ground like the ruins of a long since vanished civilisation.

Settus escorted the Heronai commanders to Valerian's *praetorium,* which had yet to be demolished. He ushered them inside and then left in haste.

Illeana was shocked at Valerian's appearance. He was unshaven, his eyes rimmed with exhaustion, his skin a grey pallor. She had always liked the man: he had been a worker at the Flavian when he had fallen on hard times; he and Settus had made their fortune selling fertilizer for the gardens of Rome, she recalled. And now, here he was, a legate of his own legion. A sweet poison, she reckoned. He rose as they entered, but did not get a chance to speak.

'I am Halkyone of Sparta,' the priestess told him. 'I command the Heronai now.'

What little colour was left in Valerian's face drained away. 'Lysandra?'

'Dead,' Halkyone said.

'And Thebe,' Titus put in. 'And many others.'

Valerian sat down slowly. 'Your priestesses brought the wounded,' he said. 'They are being cared for by their own.'

'Your wall does not look ready,' Euaristos observed. 'Not from what I saw as we sailed in.'

'We are working as hard as we can,' Valerian spread his hands. 'But the conditions are making life difficult. The rain has made the ground soft, we have to dig deeper foundations . . . then it freezes, making the digging harder work. It seems to me that the Dacian gods are throwing their weight into this fight.'

'I spit on barbarian gods,' Halkyone said. 'Divine Athene is with you now. We, her Handmaidens, will fight at your side.'

Valerian gave her the ghost of a smile. 'We'll take all the help we can get.'

'Is there any news from Iulianus?' Titus asked.

'Yes, but if you're asking if he can help us, the answer is no. He pursues Decabalus inland. Our orders are to hold until we are relieved.'

Titus chuckled. 'I see.'

'What happened?' Valerian asked. 'Lysandra's plan was sound. I expected that you would have held longer.'

'Her flank collapsed,' Kleandrias said. 'The terrain was too soft for the stakes that defended her wing . . . the barbarians saw this and concentrated their efforts there. Lysandra gave orders that we fight on the echelon – we redeployed, but she was lost to us.

'We fought on. But, Valerian, you have never seen numbers like them. So many warriors – we could kill ten each and there would still be more of them.'

'But they lack discipline,' Euaristos said. 'Their morale is fragile. When the Lady Halkyone and her troops counter attacked, they broke. It was like giving them a kick in the stones,' he extrapolated.

'They didn't come again?'

'They were unable to,' Halkyone said. 'I sent raiders into their camp. Burned their tents and let loose their horses. It slowed them enough for us to slip away in the night.'

'The first good news I've heard in a while,' Valerian said. He was about to speak again when something seemed to attract his attention. He held up his hand. 'Listen.'

Illeana heard it then, the sound of shouting from outside. Distant at first, but then it swelled in volume, many thousands of voices lifted as one. They all rose to their feet. 'They got here fast,' she muttered.

Valerian in the lead, they rushed outside, hands scrabbling for weapons.

But the soldiers were not shouting in fear or anger. Rather, they were cheering. For a moment, Illeana dared to hope that the Roman Army led by Iulianus had arrived, but it was clear that was not the case. The men of the IV Felix and, further down the line, the women of the Heronai were on the wall, shouting and banging their weapons on their shields. She, along with the others, rushed to the steps that led to Durostorum's wall.

A lone rider was at the ditch. She was clad like a barbarian, but there was no mistaking her. Illeana found herself cheering with the rest.

Lysandra had returned.

Even Halkyone cracked a smile. 'I told you,' she said to Valerian. 'The goddess is with us.'

From below, a man was running toward Lysandra, clad in a white robe. Illeana saw that the hem was filthy with mud. He sprinted across a gangplank that had been placed over the ditch and rushed towards her.

Lysandra slid from her horse and almost fell into the arms of Telemachus. Even from here, Illeana could see that the priest was weeping.

★

Lysandra felt like kissing the ground when she finally stepped inside the relative safety of Durostorum's walls. She was exhausted, saddle sore and frozen to the core – Telemachus was holding her up as her friends rushed to her: Kleandrias, Titus, Illeana, Cappa, Murco and Euaristos – all wanted to embrace her, their disbelieve at her survival writ clear on their faces. They took her to her quarters where she waited while they fussed around, ordering water to be heated, food to be brought and a healer summoned.

Later, having bathed and supped, she sat with them – knowing all too well that she would have to tell them her tale. 'It will heal,' Illeana told her, referring to the cut on her face. 'It's deep enough, mind.'

'It is of no consequence,' Lysandra said. 'It will scar or it won't. Illeana, I am fortunate to be here, Athene's strength be praised for it. I will trade a scar for my life on any given day.'

'You must tell us what happened,' Kleandrias said. 'We feared the worst.'

'In good time,' Lysandra replied. 'Send for Thebe, or I will only have to tell her a second time.' No one spoke, but all shared a look – it was one of guilt and sadness, and Lysandra did not have to ask to know what had happened. 'Ah,' she said after a moment. 'Poor Thebe.' Lysandra swallowed, unwilling to say more lest her voice crack and she fell into crying. It would be unseemly to show weakness now, even if these were her friends.

But still, the news hurt her to the core – as it did Titus, she could tell. Thebe was a good soul, kind and fair. Her oldest friend, she realised. Titus, after all, had been slave master and trainer for her first years in the *ludus*. But Thebe – Thebe had always been with her.

But not anymore.

'I am sorry,' Illeana said. 'I could not save her. I tried, but the woman struck too fast.'

'It was a battle,' Lysandra said. 'All is chaos.' Then she added: 'I

377

will miss her. Her death – and that of all those others – weighs heavily on me.'

'This fight has to be fought,' Kleandrias said, earnestly. 'We knew this would happen – we almost lost you as well, Lysandra.'

'I was lucky,' Lysandra said. She looked at Titus. 'Teuta rides with them. As does Sorina.'

Titus grunted. 'I'm not surprised. She was taken fighting against Rome. It is no surprise to find her fighting us again.'

'It would seem that she and Teuta have had a falling out. It was Teuta who freed me – just to spite Sorina. If not for her, I would have faced the same fate as those others. She would not come with me,' Lysandra added. 'She has fled this war – and who could blame her for that?'

'She led you away?' Titus asked.

'No. During the raid on the barbarian camp, their horses were set loose. Teuta captured one and bade me ride for it. I did, but when I got to our lines, you had already marched. I took to the forests and then made my way here. The raid was artfully done. I suspect it has bought us a day or more to prepare. Who ordered it?'

Kleandrias smiled. 'I suppose you will want to commend the instigator in person, strategos.'

Lysandra felt a jolt of shame and inadequacy when he used the rank to address her. 'Is that your way of saying it was your idea?' she asked, making light of the suggestion to hide her ignominy.

'I am just a simple soldier,' he replied. 'But, if you are up to it, I will take you to her.'

'You should rest,' Telemachus said to her. 'Lysandra, you have been through a lot – more than you've told us, if I know you.'

'Only up here,' she tapped her forehead. 'They did not hurt me, save for this scratch on my face. But I was afraid – for a long time, though it shames me to admit it.'

'Anyone would have been,' Euaristos said. 'They say that the anticipation of death is worse than death itself. I cannot imagine what it must have been like.'

'All the same,' Telemachus tried again, 'mental stress takes its toll on the body. You should rest – immediately.'

'Good Telemachus . . . Where would I be without you, my friend?'

'Not resting when you're supposed to,' he sniffed. 'Go on, then.'

Kleandrias needed no further bidding and had her out of the door before the Athenian could protest. He led her through what had once been the streets of Durostorum, holding her arm the entire time, walking close to her as though if he let her go, she would vanish.

'My heart broke when I thought you dead,' he said to her. 'It would be hard to go on without you, Lysandra.'

'My constant complaining will soon have you thinking differently,' she offered with a smile. He grinned, but she knew it was not the response he craved. Poor Kleandrias, she thought. The relief on his face when he had seen her alive was keener than all the others combined. He was in love with her – Illeana had said it and she knew it was the truth. He was a good man and she wished she could reciprocate his feelings, but there was nothing in her heart for him save friendship. She wished it could be otherwise, but what she had said to him in Rome was the truth: she was for women and men did not appeal to her. And even if they did, she had sworn that her heart would remain her own; the pain of Eirianwen's death was still with her.

They passed on through the Roman lines to those of the Heronai and Lysandra was pleased to see that a strong guard had been posted on both sides of the divide; clearly, the warnings and penalties for fraternisation were still being heeded.

The guards on the Heronai side caught her attention as she drew nearer; they were being addressed by a commander, tall women, clad in hoplite armour. Red cloaked. And their shields bore the

Spartan *lambda*. 'By the gods,' she murmured. She looked at Kleandrias, who was now grinning from ear to ear, the smile this time in his eyes as well as on his face.

The commander finished addressing her troops and looked over as Lysandra approached. She would recognise the red hair and pock-marked face anywhere.

'Greetings, worm,' Melantha said. 'Welcome back from the grave.'

LIX

The Dacian Plain

'Bastards!' Amagê was raging with all the fury of the help-less. The encampment was in utter chaos, tents wrecked, people killed, horses scattered. 'I'll kill every last one of them! All of them!' She kicked a fallen cauldron across the ground, the metal chiming as she did so.

Sorina watched her, tight lipped, her heart full of regret and a cold anger of her own. 'We were foolish,' she said. 'Over confident.'

'I posted pickets! The stupid, dead, idle bastards! Fuck! Look at this place!' She stooped and picked up a fallen lamellar cuirass and then hurled it away. A longhaired Scythian skipped aside as the armour whizzed past him.

'Whoever conducted the raid knew their business,' Sorina said. 'Idle or stupid some of the pickets may have been. But all of them?' She shook her head. 'No. They caught us out, Amagê.'

'Yes,' the Clan Chief turned around. 'And their commander escapes in the chaos. You should have killed her!'

'Yes,' Sorina admitted. 'I should have.'

'They're laughing at us,' Amagê spat. 'At me! Fucking Romans . . . Greeks . . . whatever they are. Look at the field out there!' She gestured at the battleground. 'Look at it. Hundreds of theirs; thousands of ours. How could this happen? How?'

'I warned you about the Roman way of war.' Sorina said. 'And those that we faced – Lysandra's gladiatrices and her mercenaries. They weren't even a real legion. The real one waits for us at Durostorum – along with those we were unable to best.'

Amagê calmed herself with visible effort. 'It is supposed to be a substandard legion.'

Sorina raised an eyebrow; there was no need to answer that: if this was what a bunch of arena fighters and mercenaries could do, even a 'substandard' legion would cause problems. 'We were overconfident. The ditch did for us. Rest assured they will have one at Durostorum. Wider and deeper.'

Amagê came to her and caressed her face briefly which, for an instant, melted the cold desolation of Lysandra's escape away from Sorina's heart. 'That it did,' Amagê said. 'That it did. Look out there,' she pointed at the battlefield. 'The stakes – they did for us too. You know that wood must have come from Dacian trees. They turned this land against us – so we will turn the land against them.'

'How?'

Amagê smiled. 'Have an advance party sent out to Durostorum. I want to know what the defences are before we go up against them.'

'And now?'

'Now we clean this mess up,' Amagê gestured expansively to the wreckage around them. 'Get ready to move. We will gather the dead so we might burn their bodies for Zalmoxis. And then, Sorina, we will fell trees. Hundreds of trees.'

'The worm returns!' Melantha threw her arm around Lysandra's shoulder as she led her to the heart of the Spartan section of the camp. There, Halkyone sat at a fire, Deianara next to her and, around them, the senior priestesses of their order. She had seen them all not half a year ago, but Lysandra could sense the difference this time. There was no coldness in their eyes – it was as though a weight had been lifted from them.

Halkyone rose, as did Deianara. They both embraced her, but it was to Deianara, her childhood friend, to whom she clung the longest. 'I am sorry for what happened in Sparta,' she said.

'I too, Lysandra,' Deianara said. 'I was hardly trying, as I feared I would embarrass you. After all, we all knew you had spent years with the *xenoi* – why heap further shame on your already shameful head?'

'Then your performance was of Athenian expertise.' Lysandra shot back. 'The deception was truly artful.'

'You always were easy to deceive.'

Lysandra laughed, though it hurt the wound on her face. Thebe's death was still a black poison on her soul, but seeing her sisters again lifted her and filled her with joy.

Kleandrias coughed. 'I will make my back,' he said, clearly a little embarrassed by the familiarity between the women. He bowed his head to Halkyone and made off.

'It would seem my command of the Heronai was short-lived,' Halkyone said, indicating that the others take their places by the fire. 'Athene be thanked for it. These *xenoi* and lesser Hellenes you associate with are strange, Lysandra.'

'However we may wish it so, the world is not Sparta, Halkyone. Different peoples have different ways. Of course, they are inferior, but they are none the worse for it.'

'Your lover is likewise corrupted,' Deianara jerked her chin at the departing Kleandrias. 'Bawling like an infant at your reported demise. We mocked him for it, of course.'

'He is not my lover.'

'Then he wishes it so. But I guess you are still too high and mighty to even touch your own bean, let alone allow another anywhere near it.' Halkyone and Melantha laughed and Lysandra felt a flush of embarrassment: Deianara was still too earthy to be a priestess, she reckoned.

'My bean is my business,' Lysandra said mildly. She sobered then. 'How are you here? The Matriarch made it clear — '

'The Matriarch is dead,' Halkyone said. 'And the temple has fallen.'

The warmth in Lysandra's heart was quickly doused at her words. 'Fallen? How? By the sword? The Romans . . .'

'By the hand of Athene herself, worm,' Melantha said. 'Soon after you were cast out, the earth trembled. Nothing unusual in that because Poseidon is a moody bastard. But this was different. The tremors went on for days.'

Lysandra nodded. 'We felt them in Taenarum.'

'Imagine what it was like at home, then,' Deianara said. 'The real quake came suddenly and with fury. Sparta is badly damaged — your statue fell over, by the way, smashed to pieces, I heard tell. It looked nothing like you, so it is for the best.'

'Statues have a way of doing that,' Halkyone said. 'Our temple is gone. Devastated. We found the Matriarch . . . crushed under the head and breast of the goddess herself. The message was clear. She had angered Athene when she cast you out, Lysandra. The Matriarch cursed you — and you cursed her back. Soon after, the earth shook, the temple fell and Athene's statue killed the Matriarch . . .' Halkyone shrugged. 'It does not take a skilled augur to see the meaning in that.'

'So you are Matriarch now?' Lysandra observed.

'Matriarch of what?' Halkyone asked. 'Ruins?'

'Temples can be rebuilt. I raised one with my own hands. We can do so again.'

'If we survive,' Halkyone replied. 'Lysandra, you have seen the enemy as well as I. Do you think – even with a wall and your cata-pults – that we can hold them? A day? Two? Three maybe? They will find a weak point sooner or later and then they'll be in among us.'

'And then we will die,' Melantha said, poking the fire with a stick. 'Like Leonidas. Only we won't send the *xenoi* away like he did.'

'Ah, yes,' Halkyone said. 'Leonidas. Idiot King of Sparta who did not think to his rearguard. Perhaps you are mistaken, Melantha – for now we have Lysandra, *Gladiatrix Prima,* the Lioness of Sparta to lead us, the strategos who rivals the Macedonian himself. The woman who, if Caesar had her at his side, would have laid low the Parthians and brought their empire under Roman sway.'

'Are you making fun of me, Halkyone?' Lysandra said, keeping her face straight with difficulty.

'No,' Deianara said. 'She believes that shit.'

Halkyone smiled, but it was brittle. 'This is a holding action. One that relies on your Roman General – Iulianus. If he fails, so do we.'

'He will not. We can win this,' Lysandra said. 'That you are here . . . that *I* am here tells me that we can win this. The goddess brought you here. The goddess had a hand in saving me, Halkyone. I was sure I was going to die – but I escaped and here I am. Scarred, but alive.'

'All the same . . . they are many; we are few.'

'Spartans ask not how many, but where,' Lysandra replied. 'We are not going to die here,' she looked around. 'Not here. Not in this place.'

'We have made our peace, worm,' Melantha tossed the stick onto the flames. 'All the women here came of their own free will – we asked for volunteers, not one of them trembled. Even the young ones wanted to come – those we gave back to their kin. But all of them saw the Matriarch denounce you and all of them saw her corpse. Athene is with you. And so are we. From these walls, we will not retreat.'

'Maybe the barbarians will give us a chance to surrender,' Deianara grinned. 'Demand our weapons in exchange for the chance to leave on our ships.'

'And what would we say to such an offer?' Halkyone asked, her eyes dancing with mirth in the firelight.

As one they spoke: '*Molon labe.*' They laughed then. They laughed because it was absurd, because Halkyone was probably right, but most of all because if they were to die, it would be a good death.

In the Spartan way.

'**W**hat do you reckon?' Settus asked.

Valerian looked over to him and Mucius who were debating the merits of the wall. Settus was pushing against it, hands spread wide, legs straining. 'If it falls over, I'll buy you a skin of wine,' he said. He could not deny the sense of relief that he felt at the completion of the wall. Lysandra had bought him the time he needed – more in fact as it had been four days now and there was no sign of the barbarian horde that she, Euaristos and the Spartan women had described. His scouts reported the same – they had not advanced from the narrow point between the two rivers.

Part of him was beginning to hope that the Heronai and mercenaries had done more than bloody the nose of the Dacian allies – perhaps they had broken it and they were not coming. 'Good work, boys,' he said to the two centurions.

'I have to admit,' Settus said, 'that I thought working with women would be a waste of time, but they've put in a good shift. Especially those Spartan ones when they arrived. Stuck up cows, though,' he added.

It was the truth – Valerian had his doubts about the effectiveness of female soldiers, but thus far, Lysandra's warriors had done themselves credit. He had had his own men, the mercenaries and Lysandra's troops drilling relentlessly, falling back from the wall to the redoubt, for hours at a time. They had impressed him with their hard work, their tenacity and their discipline.

As had Lysandra herself; she was becoming something of a legend to both the IV Felix and her own troops. It seemed that she could tweak the nose of Hades and come back with Charon's coins in her purse. Maybe her faith in her goddess had some merit after all.

'I'm going to get pissed,' Settus announced. 'But I could do with a shag. It's torture,' he said to Valerian. 'I'm so close to a whole legion of willing gash that I can smell it. But I can't do anything about it.'

'Dream on, Ganymede,' Mucius snorted. 'Willing, my arse! The only gash you're likely to get is if its owner is unconscious. Or dead.'

'Best you tease one out, Settus,' said Valerian, climbing the steps that led to the top of the wall. 'I don't want to have to crucify you.'

'Thank you, sir,' Settus saluted. 'With your permission?'

'Just go and have your wine.' Valerian waved his centurions away and they strode off, lying to each other about which of Lysandra's women were giving them the come-on.

It was growing late and the air turned much colder, as it always did in this gods-cursed place. But Valerian was satisfied as he took the salutes of the guards and surveyed the work of his men and the Heronai. The wall now stretched from bank to bank; the strongest part of it was the town proper. Here, he had ordered the construction of a strong redoubt. *Hope for the best; plan for the worst.* It was a saying of Frontinus and the wily old bastard was a good man to learn from.

Valerian had to assume that they could not hold the entire wall indefinitely – the redoubt would give them a last refuge on a narrower front. Still – he looked at Lysandra's artillery pieces, set up behind the length of the wall – the war machines would cause great losses to a massed enemy on the move. Perhaps even enough to stop them.

It was the north bank that gave him most cause for concern. The ground along the entire front was poor, but it was worst there. Any fool would know it, and that would be where the bulk of the attack would come. Water was an issue, constantly flooding the ditch below the defences and then washing out again. It was not ideal, but it was the best he could do.

'Legate!'

He turned to see Lysandra approach, wrapped in a scarlet cloak. Her face had been badly cut – a deliberate stroke with a knife. He did not have to imagine the terror she must have felt being in the hands of the Sarmatians – he had experienced it already. 'Strategos,' he said with a smile. 'What can I do for you?'

'I have news. Please come with me.'

'What news?' he asked, but the Spartan had already turned away and was climbing down the steps. He rushed after her, but she was striding off at pace, forcing him to trot to catch up with her. 'What news?' he said again as he drew level.

'It would be better that you heard it for yourself.'

He opened his mouth and thought better of it: he was not close to Lysandra, but he knew her well enough to know that asking again would be pointless and would probably anger her, and the last thing he wanted was an irritated woman. There were, after all, thousands of them less than a bowshot away on the other side of the camp.

Lysandra took him to one of the intact buildings in Durostorum town – a longhouse – perhaps a meeting hall of some kind. Inside were a few of Lysandra's company – the priest, Telemachus, her bodyguards and her friend, the other Spartan, Kleandrias. Otherwise the room was filled with some of the captains of the merchant ships that had brought her here.

'Bedros!' Lysandra said. 'Tell the legate.'

A man came forward, short and with a simian look about him. He looked at Lysandra, but her gaze was cold and full of anger. He cleared his throat, shifting from foot to foot.

'What's amiss, Bedros?' Valerian asked, hoping the smile he gave was open and easy.

'We're leaving here, sir,' the merchant said. At his words, the captains rumbled in approval. 'It's too dangerous. We have families. We're not soldiers.'

Valerian glanced at Lysandra, understanding her anger. 'You've been paid,' he pointed out.

'And you've been supplied and we've delivered Lysandra. But the men want out. We're not soldiers,' he said again.

'If things go badly for us, you realise that your ships are the only way for us to leave.'

'We already went on one rescue mission,' Bedros said. 'We saved her people.' He gestured to the Spartan but could not bring himself to meet her gaze. 'We have families . . .'

'And you're not soldiers,' Valerian cut him off. 'Yes, I heard you the first time.'

'I did not expect this from you, Bedros,' Lysandra said. 'You owe me. If not for me, the *Galene* would be in the hands of pirates and you would be dead.'

'And I paid my debt,' the merchant replied, again not able to look at her. 'If not for me, your soldiers would be dead. And it is not my choice – we all voted.'

'You realise that when our soldiers see you sail away, it will damage their morale,' Valerian said. 'You carry our supplies.'

'You have enough supplies to last you weeks, legate. That's more than enough.'

More than enough, Valerian thought bitterly. Clearly, Bedros didn't rate their chances. He was probably right. 'Very well,' he said at length.

'What!' Lysandra stepped forward. 'We had an arrangement!'

'We can't make them stay. Unless we hold them here and have them murdered – which I am not prepared to do. Bedros . . . Captains . . . I ask that you keep your reasons for your departure a secret. Tell your men – and mine for that matter – that you are to sail for reinforcements. That at least will keep hope in the hearts of our troops.'

Bedros turned and looked at the men, all of whom were nodding in agreement – whether out of decency or the fact that they realised that Valerian had made no idle threat. He could have all of them killed before they got close to their ships.

'We will keep it secret, and lie if we are asked,' said Bedros.

'That is what you are good at,' Lysandra snapped. She turned on her heel, gesturing to her friends and left the building without another word. The remaining men shuffled about for a few moments, before they too began to file out. Bedros, however, remained.

'I . . . voted to stay,' he said to Valerian. 'I swear that I did.'

Valerian looked him in the eye, wanting to lash out, wanting to upbraid him, wanting to vent his anger – even if he could see that the man was telling the truth. But that would be beneath him; as Bedros had said more than once – he wasn't a soldier. Valerian offered him his arm, which the merchant took with some incredulity. 'I will tell her when she has calmed. She will not think badly of you.' He said. 'Good luck, Bedros.'

'And to you, sir.'

The merchant bowed his head, not knowing what else to do. He made his way out and closed the big wooden doors, leaving the legate alone. Valerian looked around the empty room, now heavy with silence. 'At least we have a wall,' he said to no one, his voice echoing slightly in the gloom.

Lysandra seethed at the betrayal. She had not expected it of Bedros, whose life and ship she had saved. She stormed though Durostorum town, leaving her friends in her wake. As she walked, she could hear the sailors lying to the legionaries about reinforcements and they made haste to their ships. She wanted to shout the truth of it to the heavens, but she knew she could not.

Lysandra made her way back to the wall, climbing to the top, acknowledging the challenge of a Roman guard with a wave of her hand; the man knew who she was. *All* of them knew who she was.

She put one foot up on the ramparts, leaned on her thigh and stared out onto the darkening plain before the town, imagining it blackened by hordes of warriors as they came on. And come they would, she thought to herself. She heard the guard challenge again and the very officious reply: 'Telemachus, Officer of Logistics – Heronai.' It made her smile, taking the sting out of her anger.

'You cannot blame them,' Telemachus said as he came to her.

'Why not? They are gutless cowards.'

'No. They are just normal men. This is not their cause, not their fight.'

'If we fail here, the gate to Hellas will be open! What is a more important cause than that, Telemachus?'

'Big wars don't concern small men. They care about their wives, their children and their livelihoods. And they can sail away if the axe falls on Hellas, Lysandra.'

She nodded. There was no arguing with that.

'Believe me, I was tempted to join them, Telemachus added, putting his hand on her shoulder.

She glanced at him and he winked; she knew well he was trying to make light of it for her. 'And you did not.'

'No. You need me. Priest . . . Officer of Logistics . . . and soon to be war hero.'

'And my dear friend,' she said, putting her hand to his bearded cheek. 'You are more than a friend. You are a brother to me, Telemachus.'

'Don't I know it,' he took her hand in his own. 'Sometimes, I wish I had never met Lucius Balbus. Life was simpler when I was an impoverished man working my devoted craft in Athene's shrine. Then I met you – and look where it has got me.'

Lysandra laughed; Telemachus had a way of lightening her soul. 'I made you rich. You enjoyed the hospitality of my Deiopolis . . .'

'Which I ran profitably for you . . .'

'And the hospitality of the Temple of Aphrodite. What skills did those girls bring to the Heronai?'

Telemachus flushed with embarrassment and coughed. 'Thebe had them working with the Asklepians – the healers.'

Darkness had fallen now, the black hand of the Dacian night smothering the plain like sack cloth. Around them, the Roman legionaries began to light braziers to keep warm and puncture the darkness. 'Thebe,' Lysandra said quietly, turning her eyes once again to the east. 'I wish . . .'

'And I. She was a good soul, Lysandra. You know as well as I that she now sits in Elysium, her cup filled with Ambrosia.'

'With Penelope,' Lysandra smiled at the memory of the lusty island girl. 'I made mistakes, Telemachus,' she said after a moment. 'I did not think that the ground would fail us. I assumed that I was right.'

'What strategos doesn't? You've read more books on this than I, but even I know that most battle plans go wrong the moment you meet the enemy – because they have plans of their own.'

'Yes, but I should have known better. Because of my mistakes, Thebe is dead. Hundreds are dead.'

'You did what you could with what you had. The Romans needed time to finish the wall. You gave them that time. They all believe the goddess is with you now, Lysandra. Not least that you bring a thousand Lysandra's with you. Your Sisterhood is something to behold. It is plain to see Athene's hand in this.'

'She is with us. She saved me, Telemachus. I should have died back there, but I did not.' As Lysandra spoke, she felt the truth of the words in her heart.

'You should have died when Illeana struck you down and you did not,' he replied, impersonating her accent for the last few words. 'Come on,' he said. 'Let us get down from here. You can bore – sorry . . . regale me with tales of your youth.'

'I am still young, Telemachus,' she replied and allowed him to lead her away.

Neither they nor the guards on the wall saw the dark shape crawling towards the ditch. One man alone – a brave man. A Sarmatian, strong, proud and loyal to his Clan Chief.

He had a good eye for detail and he reckoned he knew how wide and how deep was this wall of theirs. And that knowledge would serve Amagê well.

News of the returning cavalry patrol had spread fast and the wall was crowded with Heronai and Spartans on the southern side. The north and the town proper were held by the Romans with Euaristos's mercenaries linking the north and south wings.

The morning was hard and cold, clouding Lysandra's breath as she stood on the ramparts looking out to the east. Illeana was by her side and the bitter wind whipped through her hair. They watched as the *turma* trot towards Durostorum. The town's main gate opened and burly legionaries staggered out, carrying a thick gangplank in an upright position – to the 'encouragement' of their comrades. On reaching the lip of the ditch, the soldiers let go of the huge plank and it slammed down, affording the cavalrymen a quick entrance to the town proper.

The *turma* clattered across the makeshift bridge and the unfortunate soldiers were tasked with dragging it back inside – again to the hoots of derision both from their fellow legionaries and the mercenaries who had been derided by the men of the IV Felix for not being 'proper soldiers'.

'That was the last patrol,' Illeana observed.

'I know,' Lysandra replied, meeting her gaze. Illeana continued to look at her, clearly trying to implant her thoughts without speaking. Lysandra shook her head, a smile playing about her lips. 'You are keen for me to find out what is happening, then?'

Illeana tipped an ironic salute. 'Yes, strategoi,' she said.

'*Strategos*,' Lysandra corrected, she turned and shouldered her way through the women gathered on the ramparts and made her way to the town proper. She was pleased that when she reached the Roman section the men saluted her as she passed; it bolstered her confidence to have their recognition despite her failures.

She saw Valerian rushing to meet the decurion in command of the *turma*. Halkyone and Euaristos were striding towards him. Valerian glanced over to her and beckoned her on; around her, Roman legionaries were loitering, craning their necks, trying to listen in only to be harangued by their centurions and optios to get back to work.

'Report!' Valerian said to the decurion. 'You're the last men in. Are they on the move?'

The decurion nodded. 'Yes, sir. They saw us watching and didn't even bother to send a patrol to see us off. They broke camp – in some sort of order – and have commenced their march. Heading right for us. Good thing the merchantmen are bringing more bodies. There's an awful lot of the bastards heading this way.'

Valerian glanced at Lysandra – the lie had taken hold at least. 'How long?'

'Two days,' Lysandra said. 'It is a two-day march from the narrow point to here.'

Valerian nodded and turned back to the decurion. 'Thank you, decurion. You and your men get yourselves some food in your guts and some wine down your throats. Have your relief ride out to find Iulianus. Report this news and tell him that . . . that, whilst we expect to be reinforced, we cannot confirm when they will arrive. It may well be too late. Tell him . . . tell him that we will do our duty and we hope to welcome him and his men to Durostorum soon.'

'Sir!' The decurion saluted and made off, leaving the commanders standing in a loose semi-circle.

Valerian turned to the others. 'Euaristos . . .'

'Sir.'

'Your casualties . . .'

'Serious. But we can hold our ground, sir. Old soldiers endure.'

'Halkyone?'

'Look to your own soldiers, legate,' Halkyone replied. Lysandra admired her – tall and strong, her red cloak wrapped around her, dark hair streaked with grey, the crow's feet at her eyes; she looked every inch the Matriarch she was born to be. Lysandra promised herself that when this was over, she would rebuild the temple in Sparta in thanks to Halkyone and the Sisterhood. 'I have reinforced Lysandra's troops with my Spartans,' Halkyone said. 'We alone put fifty thousand barbarians to flight. We will do so again.'

'Spartan confidence,' Valerian chuckled.

'Spartan honesty,' Halkyone replied evenly.

'And Lysandra,' Valerian looked her in the eye.

'I will not fail,' she said, and in that moment she felt the goddess at her side and believed what she said. 'We will hold.'

'I was expecting you to add *or die*,' Valerian joked.

'She has spent too much time with you *xenoi*,' Halkyone said. 'We will hold. Or die. That is the Spartan way.' She said it with a straight face, but there was mockery in her eyes.

'All right then,' Valerian said. 'One day to prepare. One day to make sure that the preparations are good. And then we fight. You know the plan. Hold the wall. If you are hard pressed, throw in your reserves. If other units can stiffen you, they will be sent. If not, we'll order a fighting retreat back to the redoubt. All of us.'

'What if we're winning on the left and losing on the right?' Euaristos wanted to know.

'Doesn't matter,' Valerian said at once – with all the confidence of a man who had asked that question of himself a hundred thousand times. 'They have men to spare and we don't.' He lowered his voice. 'We can't win here. But we can save the Empire – and Greece – if we hold. And to hold, we have to do it together. Romans. Athenians. Spartans. Men and women. Infantry. Artillery. Archers. Cooks. Healers. All of us. We are one Army. We all depend on each other now.' He let that hang, seeming to gauge each of them and perhaps, Lysandra thought, he was gauging himself as well. Lysandra had often thought Valerian a weak man – he was too kind by far, his heart soft. But yet, she sensed he had grown into this role – he was no Caesar, no man of blood and thunder, fiery speeches and pounding of the chest. Instead, he appealed to the decency in the hearts of all of them. His words would bind them stronger than she suspected he realised.

'Legate,' Halkyone said. 'You spoke of preparations.'

'Yes,' he said. 'Drill will continue. And also, some gardening.'

'Gardening?' Halkyone arched an eyebrow.

'We're going to plant some daisies.'

★

The disruption caused by the Greek raid on their encampment had been far reaching. It had taken an inordinate amount of time to herd the horses. Not all had been recovered and many of those that had were now being used as beasts of burden.

This was no work for a horse, Sorina knew — they were noble creatures and she, like tens of thousands of the plainspeople had learned to ride as she had learned to walk. Scythian, Sarmatian, Magyar, Hun, Dacian — all of them shared the love of these animals. But, as she had said to Amagê, this was a war like no other. Decabalus aped the Romans and Amagê used horses to drag planking carved from the bones of Dacia.

It was an act of necessity. Their scout had reported the structure and strength of the Roman defences in detail: they would need to cross the ditch swiftly and with ease to avoid would be a repeat of the fiasco against Lysandra.

Sorina should have killed her on sight and she cursed her desire for a drawn-out revenge now. She had desperately wanted to debase the haughty Spartan, to see her ravaged, abused and tortured to pay for her crimes. Instead, Sorina had been cheated of her vengeance and now she prayed that Lysandra had made it back to Durostorum. This time there would be no hesitation, no taunting, no capture — if she had the chance, she would cut Lysandra down on sight. Then she would take her eyes, her ears and her tongue so that her shade would wander Greek Hades forever blind, deaf and dumb. An eternity of torment.

'It seems that your Decabalus has had his way after all,' Amagê said to her, bringing her back from her dark thoughts.

They had been riding for some time, each step bringing them closer to Durostorum. To Lysandra. Sorina forced herself to concentrate. 'I told you the truth,' she said. 'But you are right . . . we have delayed and the Romans will be dug in like tics now.'

'I was wrong before,' Amagê said, her voice soft. 'Many died because of my impetuousness. I underestimated your Lysandra. I will not make the same mistake again. I promise you that, my love.'

The epithet lightened Sorina's mood. 'You did what anyone who fights with honour would have done,' she replied. 'And, heed me when I say, what is done is done. Nothing can bring those we lost on the field back to us. But we can revenge ourselves on those who defy us. We can save our way of life and drive a sword into the heart of Rome and her Empire. What happens here in the east will resonate throughout the world. I pray, Amagê, that is the death knell for all those who would cut roads on the face of the Earth Mother, make their fortunes on the slavery of others and destroy the natural order of things.'

Amagê laughed. 'Big thoughts, Sorina. I just want to kill the Romans after what they did. And you're mad if you think this will change anything. There will always be kings, always be queens and always people that want more than others.'

Sorina knew her glance was sidelong. She loved Amagê and she knew now that the Clan Chief loved her back. But she knew also that Amagê loved power. And if the younger woman was forced to choose, Sorina feared that she would be second in the Sarmatian's heart. 'We can only hope, Amagê,' she said after a time.

'I am hoping for a quick victory,' Amagê replied. 'I will not make the same mistakes again.' She looked over at Sorina. 'You'll have your vengeance.'

'I just want it to be over,' Sorina replied. The words came from her soul, she knew. She hungered for revenge it was true, but the corpses by the river would be as nothing to the amount they would leave behind when this battle was finished. Decabalus would have his way: these tribes would be, to use a Roman term, *decimated*.

They rode on, the army moving at a fair pace, but not a taxing one. Amagê wanted her warriors fresh when they arrived at Durostorum, ready to fight and eager to kill. Midway through the second day of their march, they – as lead riders – saw it first.

397

The wall.

Fully complete and gleaming with iron, it plugged the gap between the rivers far more effectively than Lysandra's meagre staves. Even from a distance they could see the ditch and ramparts, the latter bristling with wooden spikes in standard Roman fashion. Higher still, the wall proper, manned with armoured soldiers. She did not doubt they would be backed with archers that would take a heavy toll on the plainspeople before they got to grips with the legionaries, gladiatrices and mercenaries that made up the defence. The southern bank was their strongest position – there lay Durostorum and any fool could guess that this was to be the Romans' last refuge. If the wall fell, they would stand there and die. They couldn't run – there was nowhere for them to go.

Everything now rested on Durostorum.

Lysandra looked out across the plain as the first riders appeared; dark smudges at first, they soon came into relief, spreading out across the grasslands as they came on. To her right, in the centre, she saw Euaristos's men leaning forwards on the wall, talking amongst themselves; they knew what was to come, as did her own forces holding the northern point of the line; holding the south and Durostorum town was the IV Felix. They were far from an elite legion, but they had been trained in the Roman way: that was usually enough to defeat barbarian armies of vastly superior numbers. She had to trust that Valerian and his command had prepared them well – as Thebe had done with the Heronai.

'I had thought that our presence here would have deterred them.'

Lysandra turned and found Deianara at her side, grinning. She had had little chance to spend time with her old friend in the past days in the frantic drilling and final preparations for the forthcoming assault. 'Perhaps they will learn again that Spartan invincibility is no myth,' she replied.

'The only thing around here that is invincible is your self-belief, Lysandra,' Deianara said and swatted her on the backside.

'I am supposed to be the strategos,' Lysandra gritted.

'Of course. Have me flogged when this is over.'

Lysandra shook her head. 'You are incorrigible.'

'So what now?'

'Now we fight. Until we win.'

'Or die?'

'Naturally.'

'I plan on winning.' Deianara laughed. 'This is what we trained for, all those years. Oh, Lysandra, sometimes I envied you.'

Lysandra turned. 'Why?'

'A statue of you in the square . . . fighting in the arenas of Rome . . . honouring the goddess . . . a Roman senator commissioning a frieze of your fight. It is the stuff we all dreamed of. Whereas I . . . I marched up and down a lot and trained.'

'That is the Spartan way.'

'I know. But the men at least would put it into practice. Now, we have our chance again – as it was when Pyrrhus came to Lakedaimonia.'

Lysandra was about to say something blithe, something that a friend would say to another. After all, what contact she had had with her old sisterhood had been full of banter and jocularity. But what she had said was true, and even if Deianara and the others took the rise out of her, she was still a leader and had to act as one. 'Listen, Deianara. I do not believe what Valerian said. I think we can win here. The wall is high, our spears are sharp and the ground groans with the weight of our artillery stones. We can break them – you and the Sisterhood have proven that already. They will break again.'

'She is right,' Kleandrias approached, Cappa and Murco in tow. 'We will forge a great victory here. And I will stand by you, Lysandra.'

'What are you trying to say?' Cappa bristled. 'We're her body-guards.'

'That you are,' Lysandra interrupted. She wanted no bickering while the enemy marched on them. 'And Kleandrias is my dear friend. It would help me to have him at my side. Titus is ready?' she asked Murco.

'He's trying to use up all the tallow for the want of something to do,' Murco informed her. 'Pacing up and down, shouting at a bunch of girls. He tried it with the archers . . . the Artemisians,' he added. 'But they told him to piss off, so he went back to haranguing the artillery.'

'A prickly bunch,' Kleandrias agreed.

'I must head back to my own prickly bunch, brother,' Deianara said to Kleandrias. 'You should not take shit from the *xenoi*,' she added, looking at Cappa and Murco.

'Fuck off.' Cappa made a little waving gesture as one would to a child.

Deianara shook her head and then donned her Corinthian helmet. At once, her pretty features were obscured in dark shadows and she seemed to become something more than she was, as if Athene imbued her with her strength. 'Fight hard, Lysandra. I will see you soon. Cappa. Murco,' the red crest on her helmet bobbed back and forth as she nodded at them.

'Good luck,' Murco said. 'For a Greekling, you speak pretty good Latin.'

'I am flattered you think so,' Deianara said and made off with an over dramatic swirl of her red cloak.

Lysandra turned her eyes once more to the plain. The advance had stopped and it was clear the barbarians were readying themselves for the assault.

★

Mucius sniffed wondering if he was developing a cold. His back hurt and he was scared – and he knew his mind was making all the excuses that every man made before a big fight in case he faltered. Every man, apart from Settus it seemed.

'Fuck *them*, Settus said. 'I've seen far worse in Britannia – the blueskins were hard cases – as well you know it. I mean, yeah, there's a lot of them, but at the end of the day, they're just cunts,' he went on. 'Lysandra, a bunch of girl gladiators and a few fucking Greeks had 'em the other day, for fuck's sake.'

'You're shitting yourself, aren't you,' Mucius said.

'As if.' Settus sneezed and rubbed his nose on the back of his hand. 'Think I'm getting a cold, though.'

Mucius grinned. 'Listen, Settus,' he said. 'I know we didn't see eye to eye before, but you're a good soldier. Your boys are tough. You did a good job.'

Settus regarded him, his hard brown eyes glittering. 'Don't talk like that, you twat,' he said after a moment. 'You'll regret it when I'm taking the piss out of you at the *caupona* once we've stuck these cunts full of iron. And speaking of cunts . . . when this *is* over, you reckon we'll be allowed to . . . you know . . . fraternise? Some of Lysandra's lot are well tasty.'

'I dunno,' Mucius said, a little miffed that his words had gone over Settus's head. 'Maybe, but don't keep saying 'cunt', would be my advice.'

'You're right,' Settus nodded solemnly. He saluted. 'I'd best get back to me men. Good luck, *Primus*.'

'Good luck, Settus.'

Settus turned about and made off, his *segmentata* clattering gently with his gait; then he stopped and turned around. 'Mucius.'

'Yeah?'

'Thanks. For what you said. You know what I mean. First round's on me, all right.'

401

Mucius nodded but did not reply. What needed to be said had been said.

Valerian was about to wrap his cloak around him as the chill wind kicked up, but he felt the eyes of the men on him and decided against it. He placed his palms on the wall, looking across the plain at the enemy. They were milling around, forming up, dismounting – a kind of organised chaos, but there was no mistaking their intent.

He looked down the line of battle: the Felix, Euaristos's auxiliaries in the centre and then, holding the north, Lysandra's Heronai with the red cloaked Spartans in the midst of them. A lot of bodies, he thought. But there were more on the other side of the wall. Many times more. His forces had the wall. The ditch. The artillery. The discipline.

But would all that be enough? As he had said to the commanders – they didn't have to win, they just had to hold. Hold and hope that Iulianus won out and came to their aid. But that, he knew, was in the hands of the gods – all he could do was his duty.

Duty.

It seemed to Valerian that events had swept him along, taking his feet off the ground and bringing him back here to this gods-cursed country. He tried not to think of the past and, the truth of it was, that he had so much to do in command he had little time to dwell on such things.

But this place was a plague on his fortunes. Defeated here. Dishonoured and abused here, it had taken everything from him. And then he had met Pyrrha and hoped to build a new life with her; but she had died – at Lysandra's hand – in the arena. He looked to the centre once again and he could see the Spartan, a scarlet splash in the grey of her troops; he could not bring himself to hate her. She had tried not to kill Pyrrha, begged her not to fight – it had been an accident.

That was the truth, but it didn't alter the fact. Pyrrha was dead and Valerian had allowed fate to drive him back to Dacia for revenge. To regain his lost *virtus*. Or, probably to end up dead serving the Empire that had treated him so poorly.

'You all right, mate – sir, I mean?'

Settus walked up to him, and he forced a smile. 'Settus. You should be with the Tenth.'

'Yeah, I know. Just wanted to ask if . . . you know . . . after this, the fraternisation ban will be lifted.'

Valerian regarded the former optio for a moment: it was clear that Settus had not come all the way from his century to ask that. He knew the little man and could read him well. The smile on his face reached his eyes. 'I don't know about that,' he said. 'I doubt they'd be interested. They're religious women.'

'I'll make believers out of them all right,' Settus made an obscene gesture. Then he spoke, lower. 'Listen. We got this far. We'll go all the way. You were made for this sort of shit, Valerian. The blokes all trust you. I trust you. Get us through it, all right.'

The words lifted him. 'All right.'

'All right, then.' Settus saluted. 'When it's over, I'll see you at the *caupona*. First round's on me. Good luck, mate.'

'And to you, Settus.'

'Don't need it. Those cunts won't kill me.' Settus didn't wait for a reply, simply turning on his heel and shoved his way through protesting legionaries back towards his own century.

'Sir!' A legionary shouted to him. 'They're on the move!'

And they were. The front line of the barbarian horde seemed to ripple and shift and then, slowly and deliberately, they began to walk towards the wall. No mad rush as he had heard happened at the narrow point. Behind the leading warriors came a number of horse soldiers and Valerian wondered what they were about. No cavalry could assault a wall – probably their chiefs, he reasoned.

They came on and, as they got closer, his men began to shout abuse, jeering the barbarians, daring them to attack them. One wag climbed onto the wall and bared his arse at the enemy before being dragged down by his optio and dressed down by his centurion.

Valerian looked to the rear and could feel Titus's eyes on him. But it was too soon, they were not yet in range. He looked back to the field and the barbarians walked on. Back to Titus and a slight shake of the head. Then he heard it – a high-pitched scream from the barbarian ranks. Then another. Then the shrill whinny of a horse as it went over. He waved at Titus.

Moments later the first flight of arrows flew overhead and into the struggling ranks of warriors.

They found the daises then, he said to himself.

LXIII

Sorina's horse screamed in pain and fell, toppling her to the ground. The animal kicked and thrashed about, forcing her to roll away as it whinnied in terror and uncomprehending agony. Around her, warriors and beasts were down, the men and women clutching their legs.

Sorina looked around and saw that the ground had been disturbed in many places; she scrabbled on a patch of dirt and withdrew a caltrop – a barbed metal spike embedded in a thick shank of wood. Once through flesh, the tip would lodge and be almost impossible to withdraw.

Then the arrows began to fall and the front line erupted into chaos. 'Back!' she shouted needlessly as people in their thousands were retreating away from the field. Some were leaping onto the wide, ditch-spanning gangplanks the horses were dragging, causing more disorder. 'Back!' She herself scrambled away. Amagê was reaching down and, with a leap, Sorina threw herself onto the back of the Clan Chief's mount.

It was a rout without them having engaged the enemy, thousands of warriors fleeing and screaming at those behind to halt. The cries were soon cut short as volleys of arrows fell from the grey skies, silencing man, woman and beast.

'Bastards!' Amagê said as Sorina dismounted.

On the walls, the distant figures rippled – infantry falling back, archers taking their places. But no further volleys were forthcoming. 'We're at far range,' Sorina said. 'They won't waste their arrows.'

'Not yet,' Amagê was grim. 'We'll have to clear the field. They think they will have easy targets.' She was looking at the horses dragging the gangplanks, now being cut away by concerned riders.

'Those things will be the saving of us,' Sorina said.

'Let us find some order here,' Amagê turned her mouth down. 'And clear the field.'

A warm glow of satisfaction spread through Valerian as the barbarian advance halted before it began. The first ranks were thrown into utter chaos, all plunging horses and falling warriors, pandemonium erupted within moments, compounded by a withering flight of arrows from Titus's Artemisian Priestesses.

At his signal, they came forward, exchanging places with Euaristos's mercenary auxiliaries at the front of the wall: no need to protect them now, they would shoot until they ran out of arrows or the barbarians got close enough to shoot back at them. As it was, the stall in the advance had bought more of what they needed most: time.

The men were celebrating the small victory, laughing and joking amongst themselves as the barbarians fell back in disarray. It was all to the good, he thought. The Felix had proved itself in the initial assault on Durostorum. The men that had survived now counted themselves rightly as veterans.

They watched their cowed enemies deciding what they were going to do next. Distant figures milled about for some time until, finally, there was forward movement on the front. Valerian squinted, trying to make out what was happening.

Columns of warriors were moving out in good order and it seemed to Valerian they were holding something aloft as they went. Titus had seen it too and, without a direct command, he ordered a volley, lofted in a high arc. The arrows, cheered by the men, rose and then fell. He could hear the distant sound of them impacting, but it was not the thud of iron into flesh, but rather a sharper sound, as though the barbs were hitting a target. And none of them pitched forward to roll in the dirt. Another volley followed with the same result.

'Cease shooting!' he barked. The barbarians had some sort of defence and, after a moment, he realised what they were about as the warriors put down their burdens and hoisted them forward. Makeshift wooden 'walls' sprouted up, held in place by the men behind it. They were not tall – but long enough, Valerian realised, to effectively bridge the ditch below.

The barbarians would use their gangplanks to protect themselves as they ridded the field of the daisies. For a moment, he toyed with the idea of sending men out to widen the ditch, but the risk was too great. The Felix, Heronai and mercenaries were safe where they were and getting large numbers of people in and out of the defences would be a time consuming task. And there were trees aplenty in Dacia – all the enemy needed to do would be to chop more wood if they saw his people at work. 'Deflowering' the field, however, would take time, and each moment that passed was precious to the defenders of Durostorum.

'Legate!' A female voice made him turn – one of the Artemisian Priestesses had been dispatched to him. She was tall and lithe, with a pretty nose and heavily oiled blonde hair tied in a queue at the top of her head. This was a fashion with these archers

– they were different to the rest and liked to show it. 'Centurion Titus requests orders. Are we to shoot or conserve?' she asked.

'Conserve,' Valerian said at once. 'We'll have no idea if we've hit anything.'

'With respect, sir, we can hit them. The goddess guides our shafts.'

'Of course . . .?'

'Breseis, sir.'

'Tell me, Breseis. Does Artemis also provide fresh arrows for those that we lose?' Breseis looked at him as though she was about to argue for a moment, but she held her tongue. 'Conserve, if you please.'

She saluted and made off, ignoring the appreciative looks of the men close by. A good thing, Valerian thought, that the fraternisation order had been taken seriously. Otherwise there would have been more chaos behind the walls than beyond them.

It was taking hours and Sorina could see that, with each passing moment, Amagê was becoming more frustrated with the progress, even if she did not voice it. The army had retreated to a safe distance as the warriors out front, protected by the gangplanks, dug out the caltrops that the Romans had planted. They also had to refill the holes they left – each one could turn an ankle or break it. Every injured warrior took two more to carry them from the field.

The Romans were truly the masters of war. For all their progress, their art – stolen from the Greeks as Lysandra would have it, their science, their buildings and their laws, conflict was their greatest field of endeavour. It seemed to her that they were a race obsessed with finding easier ways to live and quicker ways to kill.

At last, Amagê spoke. 'We will lose another day.'

'But tomorrow, we will clear the field and the advance can continue.'

'Tomorrow,' she shook her head. 'It is beginning to grate on me now, Sorina.'

Sorina touched her face. 'There will be time for fighting soon enough,' she said. 'We will be within a hundred yards of them come the night. Tomorrow, we will be over the walls, and this will be over . . .'

There was a monumental crash and the screams of men as she spoke. She and Amagê turned in horror to see great boulders lofting from over the Roman walls. The rocks had been coated with pitch and set afire, tails of flame streaking from behind them like god-hurled things from the sky. They smashed into the gangplanks, splintering wood and bone and those that missed hit the ground making clods of earth explode around them. Some bounced towards the mass of warriors causing a ripple of panic but it was soon obvious that they didn't have the range to cause harm to the main body.

Amagê was stunned and Sorina guessed that she had never seen this before – but even as the thought occurred to her, more burning rocks were flung skywards, plummeting towards the exposed men on the field. There must be many engines, she thought, many more than a legion would usually have. There was a shiver down her spine and she felt the laughter of the Morrighan, and knew in that moment that Lysandra's hand was in this. Amagê had still not spoken, her slate grey eyes alive with desperation and panic. She didn't know what to do.

'We have to attack!' Sorina said, shaking her.

'But the caltrops . . .'

'We'll never clear the field under this! Amagê – order the advance, we have to risk it!'

'Sorina! We cannot advance into the teeth of that! Thousands will die!'

'And we run now, we lose – everything. The Romans will send more men and more and more . . . you've seen what they can do. Amagê, I don't care about Decabalus and his war now . . . but we can't retreat. Even if Decabalus wins out there, he'll have to face this army. We have to dig them out!'

'But . . .'

Sorina was filled with purpose then. 'Come *with* me, Amagê.'
She ripped her sword from its sheath and screamed a war cry. Without
waiting to see if the Clan Chief followed, she ran towards the Roman
wall and whatever dark fate the Morrighan held in store for her.

LXIV

Alone barbarian broke from the milling throng and began
running towards their lines. Moments later another
followed, then another and soon the entire host was on
the move.

Lysandra looked to her left to see the Artemisians rushing away
from the walls – threading through the mass of auxiliaries that were
trying to take their place. Shoddy, she thought to herself, but nobody
could have foreseen that the barbarians would launch an attack so
late in the day: not when the risk of injury from the Roman caltrops
was so great and certainly not into a storm of artillery shot. But
they were brave warriors.

Titus kept up an unmerciful rain of fire and death from the
onagers at the rear; the sound of them, along with the ballistae and
scorpions were a constant comfort, the ratcheting sound of the
winches being pulled back, the bark of orders to loose and then the
whump-crack of the projectiles being released.

It was murder, pure and simple. The barbarians fell screaming as
their feet were pierced by the caltrops only to have the life smashed
from them as the shot rained down. The stone spheres wreaked
havoc, cutting bloody swathes through their ranks, blood and gore
erupting from shattered bodies as they ploughed through.

In the centre of the defence, the auxiliaries formed up and soon the Artemisians added to the woes of the attackers, launching flight after flight into the milling throng. Yet for all of that, they came in such *numbers*. Lysandra could see them clearly – the vantage point of the wall gave her a much better view than of her previous battle. It was as though a packed-out Flavian amphitheatre had emptied onto this bloody field.

Was Sorina out there, Lysandra wondered, or was she already dead? She pushed the thought aside, focusing on the job in hand. She should say something to encourage the Heronai but, before she could open her mouth, another voice rang out.

'Here they come, girls!' Illeana shouted. 'We've faced them before and back there we only stood behind sticks. But we held them off. *All* of them. Now look – they're dying in their hundreds and they're nowhere near us. When they get to the wall, they'll be tired and tired fighters make mistakes. I should know – I've sent enough of them to Hades in my time! Stand fast. Hold the wall. Kill them! Kill them all!'

The Heronai roared in response, weapons clattering on shields and some began to chant Illeana's name. Absurdly, it irked Lysandra: once again Illeana was the darling of the crowd and everyone's favourite. She surmised that that was the way it was always going to be. Some people – like Lysandra herself – the gods had blessed with intelligence, skill and of course Spartan blood. Illeana may not have the blood, but she had charisma to spare – the touch of Aphrodite must be on her, and Lysander reflected how even Athene, the Virgin and the Wise, held no power over the Cyprene.

The pounding from the artillery was relentless. Titus's spotters were organising the elevation, ensuring that the stones and bolts delivered maximum carnage. But the barbarians did not break – there were too many, Lysandra realised. This fight would end as she knew it must – hand to hand, eye to eye – as it was in the arena.

Burly warriors were heaving the heavy gangplanks towards the wall and behind them, hundreds carried makeshift ladders. Lysandra was forced to duck as arrows began to hiss back from the horde: they were not organised volleys but rather a constant erratic rain that, in some ways, felt more dangerous. 'Keep your shields ready!' she ordered, 'and your heads down.' She herself gripped the *secutrix scutum* in her hand tighter and raised it so that only her eyes peeked over the top, the rest of her head protected by her red-crested helmet. With that and her cloak, she knew she made herself a target. At her sides, Cappa and Murco stepped in with Kleandrias close by. 'I need room,' she snapped. 'Like Illeana, I have killed many – probably more than all three of you put together!'

'Just doing our job, strategoi,' Murco said.

'*Strategos*!' This from Lysandra, Kleandrias and Cappa.

It was the last thing Cappa ever said. An arrow from the horde below whizzed by Lysandra's face and went through his neck. Blood spurted from the wound on both sides as he gagged, eyes rolling in pain and terror; he reached out and clutched at Lysandra before his legs gave way and he fell onto the fighting platform, the dead weight too much for her to bear. He lay there, kicking his legs, his body trying to live as Hades pulled him close. The desperate, heaving rattle of this throat trying to draw breath and the wet, whistling sound of the air exiting the wound was obscene; Lysandra could hear it above the sound of the barbarians below, the shouts of the Heronai and the artillery shot.

'Cappa!' Murco threw himself to his knees, not knowing what to do. 'Get a healer! Get a healer here, now!' Asklepian Priestesses in white tunics came running up the steps to the platform but as they arrived, Cappa had stopped moving. 'Cappa!' Murco began sobbing. 'Oh no!'

Kleandrias dragged him to his feet. 'He is dead!' he shouted into the other man's face. 'We live. *They* killed him,' he gestured in the direction of the attackers. 'We can do nothing for Cappa's body, Murco. But we can make sure his shade has plenty of slaves in the

Dark Hall.' Murco was staring at him, the shock of Cappa's death still freezing him. 'Come *on*!'

Murco blinked and, white-faced, he nodded and stepped back to Lysandra's side. Kleandrias took up Cappa's position on her left. 'We will avenge him, Murco,' Lysandra said.

Below, the barbarians had reached the ditch.

'Stand ready!' the woman next to Illeana shouted at the top of her lungs. Helena was her name – or Tough Boots as she was called behind her back. She had been with Lysandra in her *ludus* and stayed with the Spartan when she had built her temple. She was a *lochagos* – a line commander and all the women respected her.

Huge men threw the great wooden planks across the gap as the Heronai hurled javelins and stones down at them. Not all the walk-ways stuck – some fell short and plunged into the ditch others dug in and then slid away. But a quick glance up and down the lines told Illeana that hundreds of them were succeeding.

Behind the Heronai the archers and artillery kept up a withering hail of shot and barb, the ordinance falling into the middle ranks of the barbarians.

'They're going to be annoyed,' Helena said to her out of the side of her mouth.

'True enough,' the *Gladiatrix Prima* responded. 'But I keep thinking of what they did to your girls back there,' she added, louder. 'Think on that when the first one of those bastards puts his head above this wall!'

They would not have long to wait. The barbarians were pounding across the walkways now and Illeana could hear their guttural language, the screams and shouts as they came close. The first prongs of a ladder clattered against the wall and Illeana shoved it away. Moments later, it was back again. She reached out.

'Wait,' Helena stopped her. Then: 'With me . . . now!'

They both pushed – the ladder was heavier because a man bearing

412

a sword was clambering up it, behind him, a woman clad in animal skins bearing an axe. Both of them fell back into the swarming mass below. An arrow careened off the wall close by Illeana and skittered away. She shook her head and looked at Helena who raised her eyebrows. There was no time to talk – another ladder hit the stone bulwark.

Another ladder thudded against the wall.

'Fuck me, you stupid bastards, push it off!' Mucius shouted. 'Look alive there!' All down the line, the barbarians were crossing their portable bridges and coming at the wall en masse. Behind the front-runners, there were tens of thousands of them in the field, helpless against the carnage that the artillery and archers were causing. But the enemy milling below the wall on their walkways added their own ordinance to the fray: spears, stones, arrows even axes were being pelted up at the Felix as they ducked and shoved, desperate to keep the barbarians from gaining purchase.

'Keep it up, keep it up!' Mucius's optio, Livius, was pacing up and down the fighting platform, ignoring the screams of wounded men as they were struck by Sarmatian missiles. He approached Mucius. 'I have a bad feeling about this,' he informed him – as he always did.

Mucius laughed, the fear in his guts dissipating. 'If you get killed, I'll make sure I'll toast your shade.'

'Look out!' Livius shoved him hard, sending him off the fighting platform and down to the ground. Mucius landed flat on his back, stunned; reserves crowded around him, hoisting him to his feet, many voices asking him if he was all right. He pushed them aside, looking up at the platform just as the corpse of a tattooed warrior crashed to the ground in front of him, pierced by a dozen wounds. He'd made the platform, then – and Mucius realised that Livius had saved his life: the bastard must have been behind him. Livius looked down and waved at him briefly before turning back to the fight.

Mucius pushed and shoved his way through the men of the Felix, wading towards the steps and ran up, back to the platform. Casualties mounted, the missiles from the attackers took their toll on the men – but they were holding. As the thought occurred to him, he saw one lad take a stone straight in the face; he fell back, spitting teeth and gobs of blood. A huge tribesman hoisted himself up where the legionary had been standing and began to clamber over. Another man went to stab him, but then another head appeared above the wall, forcing him to turn and cut the enemy down.

'Shit!' Mucius drew his *gladius* and charged the giant who was flailing about with a sword that the centurion reckoned was half as tall as a man. Behind the barbarian, another was up and over. The warrior cut down with his blade, splitting a legionary's head in two, helmet and all. Blood and brain matter spattered those close by as the Sarmatian – or whatever in Hades he was – roared, lost in battle fury. The men were backing off and as they did, more of the enemy were getting up onto the platform.

Mucius pushed one of the lads out of his way and ran right at the barbarian, but as he drew close, Livius grabbed his long hair and pulled his head back. The optio's blade sprouted from the giant's torso before he withdrew it and shoved him off the platform – to the curses and shouts of the men below.

The barbarians fought with an insane, desperate kind of courage, as though death held no fear for them. Mucius had seen this before: they could overwhelm you with their force and their raw courage, but it was a fragile thing and if you stood firm, you could overcome them.

But as more men – and their damned screeching Amazons – reached the wall, he began to fear that they had so many bodies to throw into the fight that they would just keep coming and coming and coming until it was the Felix and her allies that broke and ran.

Run to where? He looked down and across at the second wall: Valerian's redoubt. And then? Then it would be all over. They had to stop them here. Because while the redoubt might seem like a safe haven, in Mucius's experience, if it came down to retreating there, they'd be down to the *triarii*.

Fear.

Not the kind of desperate, frantic terror that you felt in the thick of the fight where everything happened so fast. This was different and Valerian had never felt it before – not even when he had been watching Pyrrha fight. This was a churning, gut wrenching sense of hopelessness; the die had been cast and there was nothing he could do but watch and hope. The commanders on the front were rotating their forces, keeping fresh troops at the wall so that they would not become exhausted; Titus and the Artemisians were raining a constant hail of missile shot over the walls and onto the attackers; all Valerian had in his hands was the decision of when and where to throw in his reserves.

For now, he could see everything from his vantage point, but it would be dark soon. The sky was turning and if they could just hold out, it would buy another day. Another day for Iulianus to win his fight and come to their aid. All down the line, the fight raged, thousands of voices lifted in fear, rage and pain, the endless cacophony of weapon on weapon, sword on shield.

Decabalus's allies were on the wall, first – worryingly – at the Felix's position; the men, though, were having none of it and those attackers who reached the fighting platform were being despatched. He saw with satisfaction – even from this distance – that the centre and the notionally weaker north end where Lysandra commanded were holding. The enemy was failing there. Lysandra's gladiatrices, *hypaspistai* and her Spartans were fighting like Olympians. Below them, the barbarians hesitated as bodies fell in increasing numbers, crashing back to their walkways or tumbling down into the ditch.

A female warrior gained the platform. She was bulky, her black hair shaved short at the sides of her head. With an axe, she cleaved her way to the centre, striking about her like a mad woman, hewing into Euaristos's men like a Fury. Behind her, huge warriors – one of whom threw himself in front of a sword stroke that should have killed her. A chieftain, he reckoned, or a chieftain's wife or daughter. Either way, she was backed by elite fighters, well kitted, huge in size and ferocity.

Valerian could see it happening before his eyes – the auxiliaries backing away, eyes on the new threat as yet more and more Sarmatians gained the wall. He reached for the whistle around his neck and blew three sharp blasts. It was picked up by his signallers and the *buccinas* responded in kind, calling in a reserve from the Felix. The legionaries took off at a trot and he could see Settus and his ill-tempered optio, Slainius, leading the run. The Eight and Tenth of the Tenth centuries were good men – not as good as Mucius's First of the First, but hardy enough – and no one in their right mind wanted a fight with Settus. Valerian hoped their arrival would bolster the faltering troops before it was too late. Two centuries was not a great number, however. He hesitated, unsure if he had thrown enough to support the centre. But if he put more in there, what if Lysandra's corps came under pressure – they were, after all, only women. And the barbarians had gained their first successes in his sector.

He just didn't have enough at his disposal to cover all the options: another blast at the whistle, and two more centuries from the Tenth began the run to the centre line.

Which, he realised, was beginning to crumble and break apart.

LXV

Sweat drenched her body, her lungs desperate for breath, but she had pushed on, eyes blinded by the salty, stinging rivulets that ran into her eyes.

But Sorina had made it unscathed, through the gauntlet of stone and arrow and across pitted ground. Behind her, she had heard the plainspeople following her, urging her on as she led them to battle. Soon, the younger, fleeter ones overtook her and, like a swarm, they descended on the wall, their gangplanks thudding down as the defenders pelted them with javelins.

She doubled over, hands on her thighs, heaving for breath, a dribble of vomit escaping her guts and spilling out down her chin. A heavy hand clapped her on her shoulder: Amagê, her broad face florid with exertion and spattered with sweat and mud. 'You're insane!' she shouted, pulling Sorina up. She looked her straight in the face then, saying nothing, but her eyes expressed her gratitude. Amagê had frozen and it was she, Sorina, who had taken charge.

Thousands rushed past them, hurling their bodies into the fray, every man and woman amongst them desperate to outdo each other in feats of courage. There would be legends carved out today.

For some.

Sorina looked back at the field; the arrows rained down and the onagers shot carved swathes through the crowds. The ground was littered with the injured, some screaming, transfixed by ballista bolts, others rolling in agony with the caltrops piercing their feet. Hundreds. No, she realised, thousands. It was a killing gallery for the Romans as they took lives that they could not even see.

Amagê's bodyguard arrived some moments later, angry and tired, weighed down by their armour and weapons and, Sorina reckoned, unaccustomed to joining battle on foot – as was she, she thought, ruefully.

They found themselves in the centre of the line, looking up at the auxiliaries who were hard pressed to stem the tide but – as yet – no one had gone over the top as the soldiers shoved ladders away from the wall and sent warriors tumbling away.

'What do you think?' Amagê asked her.

Sorina scanned the walls. On their right, the Romans – the best of the best – were taking the brunt of the assault. Sorina reckoned that most were veering to their left to avoid the arrows and shot: it was illogical, but then – she looked around – this was all madness. In the middle, they had gained no headway and on their left she could see the gladiatrices and, right in the middle of them, the red-cloaked priestesses from Lysandra's temple. They and the other *hoplomachai* were giving bloody hell to those trying to gain the wall, their huge round shields and long spears creating a second wall – but one that had iron teeth. Either side of them, *secutoriae*, fighting with small *scuta* and *gladius*, killing, killing and killing again. Of all the fighters, Sorina realised, Lysandra's were the most skilled and the most deadly. How would that be received in Rome, she wondered? The women outfighting the men.

Scuta. Gladius. Hoplomacha. Secutrix. She cursed herself – these were Roman words and they had become part of her.

'Well?' Amagê pressed.

'The centre,' Sorina decided. 'We'll break their body and cut off the arms. Look there,' she pointed with her sword to the right. 'The wall is thick with legionaries – the strongest point of the defence. They can't lose the town, Amagê, if they have nowhere to hole up if we take the wall. Over there, on the left, Lysandra's women are too well kitted for the fight. But here,' she jerked her chin at the wall, 'if we can take them here, we'll win this.'

'Then let's take this fucking wall!' Amagê hefted her axe and Sorina could tell she was about to charge straight into the fight.

She reached out and grabbed her arm. 'Wait here,' she said.

'Why!'

'Because they are fresh, and you are too important to throw your life away. Wait a while.'

Amagê gritted. 'I am Clan Chief, I must lead the charge – it shames me to hang back.'

'Better shame now and defeat later, Amagê. You fall and the Sarmatians will lose heart – and so will the others.'

'They will think me a coward if I do not fight!'

'And you will fight. But not yet. Trust me – we'll wet our swords in Roman blood – but when the time is right.' Amagê screamed in frustration and turned away, knowing Sorina was right and hating the fact that she was.

Sorina looked back to the battle, waiting. Above, the sky was turning dark; Sorina's eyes narrowed. If the night came too early, it would hand the Romans a victory and they would have preserved their wall for another day.

Unless . . .

Events on the right interrupted her train of thought as the first warriors were gaining the heights. They were few in number, but they had proven with their lives that it could be done. The Romans were not done yet, she knew. They would fight until they were dead – or someone with a red, ermine trimmed cloak told them to stop.

The fight raged on, Amagê pacing around in frustration as yet more of her kin ran past and up to the walls – and were thrown back. Behind them, the rain of death from the artillery kept up, though the rate of shots was slackening now. The Romans too knew the dark was coming and they were conserving their ammunition. If she were a soldier, fighting along that wall, she would be thinking the same thing. The night is coming – all I have to do is stay alive until the dark. And I will live another day.

There was a roar of triumph up ahead – the warriors had finally gained the top of the wall and were pouring over it, a river of iron and flesh. 'Now,' she said to Amagê. 'Now is the time!'

Amagê needed no second command, like a hound let off its leash, she bounded forward, her bodyguard in tow. Sorina gathered herself and rushed after her. Amagê was shoving her own people out of the way, her bodyguards forcing their own number off the walkway and into the ditch as they piled forward towards a ladder and it was into this breach that Sorina ran, her long legs eating up the space they left in their wake.

Amagê almost flew up the steps and disappeared over the top of the wall – and a head flew into the air no sooner had her feet hit their fighting platform. The bodyguards were close behind her and then Sorina found herself clambering up the rough wooden rungs and until her fingers touched the stone at the top. She took a deep breath and hurled herself over.

Amagê was causing carnage on the packed fighting platform, her axe rising and falling with deadly efficiency – a fearsome weapon – a terror weapon that the auxiliaries were not used to. But she had no shield and it was dangerous – a man leapt at her – a commander if the cross-crest on his helmet was anything to go by.

'Amagê!' Sorina screamed, but her voice was lost in the din as the officer thrust his blade at her lover. If Amagê had not heard, one of her bodyguard's had: there was no time for him to block, cut or parry – he simply leapt before her and took the sword blow in the chest.

The auxiliary commander stepped back, withdrawing his bloody iron. 'Look alive there you men,' he shouted. A Greek, she realised – Athenian, the same accent as Balbus's catamite back at the *ludus*. It was cultured and urbane – like the man himself, she reckoned. His cloak was fine, his armour expensive. An Athenian dandy. 'Hold them! Hold them!' That, Sorina decided, would be the last order the bastard gave. She moved in, attacking him from the side. He turned sharply and raised his blade to block move, the impact juddering down her arm and into her shoulder.

Fast, she realised. He punched out with his shield in the Roman way, his *gladius* held high and close to the left rim. Sorina stepped back, banging into someone fighting behind her and kicked out – the old gladiatorial trick. Her foot crashed into the boss of his shield and the Athenian shrieked in pain, his *scutum* falling from his grasp. She had broken his wrist – she could see the sick pallor of pain whiten his face, the sweat sheening as she cut down with her sword.

He had courage and his own blade came up to parry, the shorter blade allowing him to counter cut, the tip of the *gladius* missing her throat by a finger's breadth. He had missed his killing strike and, in doing so, had exposed his right side to her. She thrust hard with the longsword, the blade piercing his armour just under the pit of his arm. He cried out in pain, blood exploding from his mouth as the cold iron ruptured his internal organs. The Athenian fell and nearby, she heard his men groan.

'Euaristos!' one of them shouted. 'Euaristos is down!'

It was as though this Euaristos was the spine of them. At his death and with Amagê's relentless assault, men were falling to her blade like wheat to the sickle and the fight seemed to drain from the auxiliaries. They were falling back – about to break.

'Come on!' she screamed. 'Come on!' A man engaged her, but he was old and fat – a man that should have been with his grand-children by the looks of him. Once he may have been skilled, but Sorina was too quick for him, ducking under his thrust and sweeping her sword down, its edge biting into his thigh, shearing through muscle and flesh. He fell and she stuck him through the throat, leaving him to choke on his own blood.

She attacked another, but he backed off, falling over a corpse and crashing down. Sorina leapt at him and rammed her sword into his groin and revelled his piteous screams of agony. In that moment, she was young again. They were breaking – she could feel it.

More men were piling up the steps of the fighting platform, Romans this time, led by a centurion. In all the chaos it was a strange thing to see that he had tattoos on his arms. He screamed obscenities as he charge into the battle and, backed by his optio, began to seize back the ground the plainspeople had won.

Amagê faced him and her axe bit into his shield, ruining the bronze rim and splitting it. The centurion let it go, unfazed and stepped forward as Amagê swung her axe at his ribs. But the little man was too quick and was inside her guard. Sorina's heart was in her mouth but the centurion was too close in the press of bodies to use his *gladius*. His shieldless left arm looped over Amagê's right and he jerked her elbow upwards, causing her to cry out. The centurion's head jerked forward and he butted her in the face with his helmet – Amagê fell back and she could hear that tattooed Roman calling her a 'fucking cunt' before he was forced to deal with one of her bodyguards.

Sorina went in from the side, reckoning she could take him but, like Amagê, the centurion had guards of his own. His optio rushed her, a big man with chipped teeth and an evil expression. He tucked in behind his *scutum* keeping it close to his body and jabbed his sword at her. She parried, realising she had hardly seen the blow coming.

Because it was nearly dark.

The optio charged her and there was nothing she could do – the battle swirled around her, there was no room to manoeuvre – she could only leap back and hope that there was no one behind her. 'Kill her, Slainius!' she heard the centurion scream as he picked up a fallen shield and threw himself elsewhere into the fray.

She struck out at Slainius, but the man was canny, taking the blow on the *scutum* and stepping forward – as he must have drilled ten thousand times in the past and, again, the viper's tongue of his *gladius* spat out, forcing her to parry. And this, she realised, was what he had been waiting for. He punched out with the shield, the boss cracking her on the forehead and Sorina's world became white as she fell back. Her heels hit something solid and she crashed to the wooden fighting platform and, as Slainius rushed to kill her she realised that, in death, Euaristos had had his revenge on her – for it was his corpse that had tripped her. Fear welled in her as Slainius's arm went back, ready to strike.

Amagê's axe cut his head from his neck, sending blood fountaining skywards, drenching her with its hot stink. The Clan Chief's face was sheeted red, a livid wound above her hairline where the centurion had butted her, but she was still strong and dragged

Sorina to her feet. 'It's getting dark!' she shouted over the din.

'We can't stop!' Sorina said. 'They're expecting us to flee with the night — we can still break them. We can do this.' It was true — even though the centurion's counter-attack had done damage here, the plainspeople were spilling over the wall in numbers now. She could not see left or right and did not know if the Romans and Lysandra still held. But she did know if they broke the centre they could flank them both.

Victory was in their grasp — and they would seize it by night.

LXVI

Valerian bit his lip as the mercenaries began to give way. He'd seen it before — here, in Dacia — how quickly a cohesive fighting force could collapse and become a disorganised rout. The Tenth and Eighth of the Tenth had joined the fight, but were soon swallowed up, indistinguishable from the mercenaries in the half-darkness.

He was seized by indecision. Should he throw more men into the centre and hope they threw back the assault or cut and run, back to the redoubt? Night was falling fast and the enemy was showing no signs of aborting their attack. And for all the drilling, he had not thought to conduct the exercise of retreating to the redoubt in the dark.

And because of that — because of *him* — thousands could die. He could lose here; the Empire could fall because of it, because he had not thought of everything. Even now, as he hesitated, people were being killed. The wall had to hold, he decided, bringing the whistle to his lips. He blew again, longer blasts this time — sending the remaining centuries of the Tenth cohort into the centre and hoping that this would be enough. As they ran forward to the sound of the *buccinas*, he could barely see them.

Night had come to Durostorum. And as it did, the centre of the line collapsed. And Valerian knew that the reserves would arrive too late.

The Heronai were holding.

But night had come and Lysandra was finding it harder and harder to see what was going on down the line. It looked bad in the centre, but she trusted Euaristos was canny enough to throw back the enemy.

'At least they will not see how few we are if they get up here,' Kleandrias said to her.

'Let us hope they do not get up here, then,' Lysandra replied. She was coated in blood and gore, her right forearm slick with it, her shield battered and scored. Kleandrias himself looked like Ares, fresh from the Field of Troy. 'Murco,' she turned to him. He too had a ghastly aspect, his armour spattered crimson. 'Are you all right?' She did not mean physically: clearly, he was hale, but Cappa's death must have cut him deep.

'I'm alive,' he said shortly. 'Look out!' he added, causing Kleandrias to spring into action, cutting down as a head popped up. It was a wild-haired woman with stray coloured hair. She didn't even scream as he opened the top of her head with his blade, she simply dropped down and out of sight. He and Lysandra shoved the ladder away from the wall, but no sooner had they done so did another come a few yards down the line.

'This is bad,' Kleandrias observed. 'I can hardly see as it is.'

Lysandra nodded, her lips pressed into a thin line. 'The night favours them.' She was about to speak again when Murco stumbled into her. For a moment, she thought that he had been hit by missile shot, but it was clear he had just stumbled. The gladiatrix next to him was down, scrambling to get up when the next in line fell over her. A sick feeling of panic welled up inside Lysandra; she knew at once what was happening. And there was nothing she could do about it.

Illeana cut the man's throat and shoved him in the face, tipping him off his ladder. 'Helena!' she shouted, not needing to add anything as the *lochagos* heaved the ladder away from the wall.

'This is just like the arena!' Helena yelled. 'Fighting by torch-light!'

'Except there isn't any torchlight!'

'You Romans are always complaining!' Helena was about to speak again when the woman next to her stumbled and crashed into her. Illeana risked a look down the line and saw that it was becoming compressed and ragged. She could hear screams and shouts of surprise – and the sound of Spartan voices cursing their allies as they ordered them to turn about.

Something told Illeana to move: it saved her life as an axe whis-tled past her head. A warrior, huge and black in the darkness, was standing atop the wall and he leapt down – foolishly as she smashed him in the face with the edge of her sword, shattering teeth and bone. She struck again, this time in the neck, killing him outright. 'What's going on?' she shouted at Helena.

'I don't know!' the *lochagos* admitted. 'Just keep fighting till we get the order to withdraw!' But again she was knocked sideways by the girl next to her and careened into Illeana, knocking her down.

For a moment, a terrible fear welled up in her that she would be trampled, but she was hoisted to her feet from behind. There was no time to thank her benefactor as dark hands scrabbled at the wall and warriors hurled themselves over. Illeana hacked down, feeling her blade bite deep into a shoulder: she had been aiming for the skull, but in the dark it was impossible to strike accurately. She withdrew the *gladius* and stabbed forward, hitting something again

425

– head or torso, she couldn't tell which. Someone grabbed her and she felt a thud on the collarbone as a sword hit her – it was a man, big and strong, but unskilled. She head butted him and stamped on his foot, giving herself stabbing room and rammed her sword into his guts, feeling hot blood drench her wrist. He screamed in pain as she twisted the blade to disengage it from his entrails, hearing the wet, popping sound as it came free. With it came a torrent of gore and the stink of shit as he fell. Her collarbone hurt like Hades but she knew it was not broken and, thank the gods, the armour had done its job.

Thank the gods. Lysandra would be pleased if she knew that Illeana was finding some use for religion after all.

'I can't see *anything*!' A legionary shouted at the top of his lungs.

'I can see *you*, Marcus!' Mucius heard Livius scream back in his best parade ground vocal. 'And I can see you're not fucking fighting! So face the front and put iron to the enemy or I'll carve your balls off and use the sack for a fucking purse! A *small* fucking purse!'

Mucius couldn't believe that the fight was still going on: it was as black as pitch now and still the barbarians were throwing themselves up the wall. It was as dangerous for them as it was for the Felix and her allies, but he reasoned their leaders knew that they had the bodies to waste and his people didn't. He could hear thumping on the platform as boots from without landed within and the screams and curses of men in close quarters battle. This was the Roman way, though. The lads had been trained for this – punch – stab – punch – stab. A thumb's worth of iron would put a man out of the fight.

'Contact left!' he heard the panicked shouts ripple down the line. 'Contact left!'

Contact on the left could only mean one thing. He looked up to see if the legate was going to give any orders, but he heard no whistle and nor could he see Valerian in his vantage point, the darkness having swallowed him whole. 'Ignore that!' he shouted at his own men. 'Eyes front and fight front – let the lads on the left deal with the left. We have to hold this fucking wall!'

A gladiatrix fell before she'd even known what had hit her. Sorina exulted as she pushed forward. They had forced the mercenaries from their fighting platform and had gained the centre. Now, the plainspeople were spilling out, left and right, attacking the defenders in the flanks. It was like lighting papyrus – at once panic began to spread amongst them and she cut another down, hacking her longsword into the girl's un-armoured thigh and sending her crashing to the fighting platform. Amagê was by her side, the axe chopping down as the Clan Chief screamed and exulted in her power.

She was like the War Goddess, Sorina thought, a fearsome energy flowing around her as she hurled herself forwards, the axe raised. It came down like a lightning strike from the heavens, the broad blade severing a gladiatrix's head, sending it spinning off into the night.

Ten fell, then ten more as the plainspeople sliced through the flank of Lysandra's fighters as easily as an oar cut the water: it was the dark, too, she realised. The defenders knew they were outnumbered and knew that the wall was their only defence. Now it was breached and now they could not tell friend from foe – and fear was spreading amongst them like wildfire.

She heard the Roman trumpets sounding as she killed another faceless enemy in the blackness, feeling their life spray out all over her face and neck. And then, like Amagê, she lifted her voice in a fierce war cry, a fire flooding through her as she heard them shouting in Greek and then Latin. '*Recipio*!' She reached out and grabbed Amagê, pulling her back. Bodies rushed past them in the dark as she pulled the Clan Chief to face her. 'Amagê! They're running – that is the order to retreat.'

Amagê laughed, her teeth and eyes white in the darkness. 'Let's finish this,' she said and turned back to the fight, eager to kill and kill again.

Valerian wanted to weep but he could not. He had delayed and because of that, he had lost. He should have ordered the retreat as soon as the line began to buckle, but he had hoped against hope that the mercenaries would have reformed – but something had shattered their confidence and even the late arrival of the Tenth Cohort had not been enough – the barbarians had gained the platform and now . . . Now what? He could no longer see a thing.

He blew the whistle, its mournful sound cutting across the screaming and dying and it was answered by the *buccinas*. The ground behind the wall was still theirs, he lied to himself. They knew it well, they had been camped there long enough; he had to hope that they could find their way in the dark.

There was a sound then, a great hiss and a thump that seemed to come from the very earth itself. And all at once, the scene was bathed in a hellish glare of fire. Huge towers of flame erupted from the rear ranks, burning pillars that scraped the sky, burning at even intervals all the way down to the river in the north.

Titus had ordered the onagers to be fired. And by their light, Valerian prayed that they still had a chance.

Lysandra was grateful to hear the order to retreat and more grateful to Titus – the old centurion's quick thinking might yet be the saving of them. This, she told herself, was one war story of his that she would not interrupt.

It would be a fighting withdrawal, complicated by getting down the steps, but even now she saw many of the Heronai foregoing that and leaping off to the ground. There was little she could do to stop those that chose to – but a turned ankle could mean death for those that chanced it. Kleandrias and Murco pulled closer to her and began to shuffle away towards the steps, shoving Heronai aside as they did so. 'Make way,' Kleandrias shouted. 'Make way for Lysandra!'

They made it unscathed and ran for it, down the steps and into the chaos below. To their credit, the troops were forming up before trotting off in good order – not enough barbarians had yet got over the top to hinder the general retreat and pride swelled in Lysandra's breast as she saw her *hypaspistai* and the Spartans forming a phalanx, side by side, to protect the rest as they retired.

The Romans still held their portion of the wall and she could hear the *buccinas* sound as Valerian ordered his men into the fight to deal with the barbarians who had spilled off the centre platform and onto the ground beyond. As they turned to face this threat, the Heronai ploughed into them from behind, ramming them with shield and spitting them on the points of their swords.

But there was no time now to check a kill – the closer they got to the ladders that led to the redoubt, the faster they ran. It was human nature, she knew. They were close to safety and even she, Kleandrias and Murco went for it, running hard for the redoubt.

Here again, it became congested and many fell, trampled to death so close to succour. Behind, the fighting was intensifying as the barbarians came on in greater numbers. Lysandra could feel their rage, their frustration – they had nearly won their prize and it was being snatched from them.

'Go, Lysandra!' Kleandrias lifted her from the ground and almost threw her up the ladder. 'Go! We are right behind you!'

She clambered up and eager hands hauled her over – the Artemisians had made safety, grim faced and dour, they were doing the lifting of Heronai, legionary and what remained of Euaristos's mercenaries.

She remained with them, watching the fight as it crept closer to the walls, living each death as it happened, exulting as another barbarian fell. There were so many of them – and what had started in good order was descending into a rout as the enemy poured more and more bodies into the attack. Each passing moment saw ten or more armoured figures cut down and swallowed by the mob. They were losing more in the frantic scramble to the redoubt than they had the entire day.

'Archers make ready!' She heard Titus's baritone rasping in the night. 'Ready . . . Loose!'

Now the Artemisians rained shot down on the advancing barbarians and Valerian's whistle sounded. The legionaries that were engaging them backstepped and backstepped again. Then, to a man, they dropped their shields and ran for it. Their backs to their foes, hundreds were cut down as they fled, hindering each other in the desperate flight to live.

Men hurled themselves at the ladders and the Artemisians ran back, forming up again and loosing what munitions they had left to cover the retreat. Lysandra herself stayed at the walls, hauling the desperate men into the temporary safety of the redoubt.

It was like a scene from Tartarus as the Romans were slaughtered by the barbarians as they fought to gain the wall, screaming at their fellows to climb faster, begging for their lives as they were cut down.

A man – one of the last – gripped her wrist and she pulled, overbalancing as she dragged him over. They fell, thudding down hard on the fighting platform.

'I thought they had me there!' Settus exclaimed. 'Oh! It's you! Glad you're alive, love.' He gave her a crack-toothed grin before scrambling to his feet and began screaming orders at his men.

Hundreds of warriors died as the close range volley smashed into them, hurling them from their feet as the cursed archers shot at them from their redoubt. Sorina felt the mood change as the exultation turned to anger and fear as the black-barbed death flew from the narrow – and packed – redoubt.

The plainspeople – so close to victory – began to back away.

'Tomorrow,' Amagê said to her, glaring death at the Romans. 'Tomorrow, they will all sing to Zalmoxis. Those fires,' she gestured to the burning onagers, 'will be as nothing.' Her face glowed like gold in the firelight and her eyes burned with fury – and for a moment, Sorina feared her and knew that she would make good her vow.

LXVII

Lysandra had seen this before on a smaller scale, under the great arena of Halicarnassus and also after Domitian's spectacle. But there was a part of her mind that had erased the worst of it.

She moved through the buildings of Durostorum where the wounded and dying had been housed to be saved or breathe their last. Her Asklepian Priestesses worked alongside the Roman Army surgeons, doing what they could for those that would live and ending the suffering of those they could not. At least Bedros had left enough medical supplies for them before his betrayal.

The stink and noise inside the biggest building, the same one in which they had met the merchant and his captains, was overpowering. Pain made children of them all in the end and the suffering of others did nothing but heighten the fear in everyone else. There was sawdust on the floor – it was there to soak up the blood, but there was too much and the ground was a dark crimson mulch that stuck to the soles of her boots.

Telemachus was there, looking gaunt, thin and faintly ridiculous in the armour he wore. He was comforting those he could and she wished she had sent him away with Bedros. He looked over at her

431

and his smile almost broke her heart: even now, he did not judge her.

There were so many in here, she thought as she looked around. So many wounded and so many dead on the other side of the wall. The exultation of surviving the barbarian counter-attack had been short lived when she realised how few of them remained – Euaristos's men having been all but wiped out. Even the Athenian himself had not survived and the knowledge cut her deeply. He was a good man at heart and a loyal friend. But he was dead now. Along with Thebe, Cappa and thousands of others.

'Lysandra,' Kleandrias came to her side. 'Valerian is looking for you.' She nodded briefly and turned away, hating herself for being glad of the excuse to leave.

Lysandra breathed deeply of the cold night air outside and looked up at the sky. Above, the stars twinkled far off, beautiful and uncaring. There were campfires everywhere for those who had not found bedding inside the buildings that remained, people huddled in small groups, talking in low tones. As she walked with Kleandrias, she heard many snatches of conversation. Some felt that Iulianus would be here soon, others that Bedros would return with reinforcements and still others that she feared spoke the truth. That, come first light, the barbarians would get over the redoubt and it would be all over.

'We will hold them,' Kleandrias said as though reading her thoughts.

She looked across at him and smiled, feeling the wound on her face pulling as she did so. 'Of course we will,' she replied.

He saw through it. 'It is not like you to be fatalistic, Lysandra. The goddess is still with you.'

'I know she is,' Lysandra replied. 'But she promised me a life full of hardship and pain in her service – and that I would lift my shield in defence of my homeland. I am doing so here. I wonder . . .' she trailed off. 'I wonder if the Morae had already marked me to die by Illeana's hand – if the life I have led since then is one of borrowed time.'

'If that were so, then you would have fallen back there at the river,' he was full of earnestness. 'You are special, Lysandra. I cannot believe that Athene would save you only to forsake you again.'

'Perhaps.'

There was no more time to speak as they approached the *praetorium* and went inside. Lysandra was shocked at Valerian's appearance – he seemed to have aged ten years since she had last seen him, his skin was grey and he had dark smudges under his eyes. With him was his *Primus*, Halkyone, Titus and Illeana, the three of them coated in blood as she and Kleandrias were. She went to Titus and, to his surprise, she embraced him and kissed his bearded cheek. 'You saved us all,' she said.

Titus flushed red. 'I was just doing as I ought,' he coughed, trying to extricate himself.

'Good initiative,' Halkyone looked at the former trainer with something like respect. 'You saved many lives, old man.'

'I'm not that old,' Titus muttered, breaking the embrace.

'I am glad you are alive,' Valerian said to Lysandra.

'As am I,' she forced a sternness into her tone that she did not feel. It was as though the day's battle and retreat had taken something from her that she could not replenish. 'I am surprised to see you here, Illeana. Is Helena . . .?'

'No, she's alive.' The Roman still somehow managed to look like a dramatic heroine rather than a bedraggled, bloody mess. Looking at her now, Lysandra wished that their paths had been different. That they could have perhaps shared something of what she and Eirianwen had shared – they were, as they both had acknowledged, similar creatures. 'She took one in the thigh when we made a run for it. She's getting stitched up, but she'll be all right.'

'Are *you* all right?' Lysandra asked her.

'Tired, sore shoulders, but otherwise unharmed,' Illeana smiled.

But Lysandra saw that it did not reach her eyes. 'So,' she looked at Valerian. 'How do we get out of this?'

Valerian leaned back in his chair. 'I don't know,' he admitted. 'I don't think we can. I . . . I have failed us all.'

'Don't talk like that, sir,' the *Primus* spoke at once. 'We have men yet. We'll hold them.'

'That we will,' Kleandrias put in.

'Despair is for weaklings,' Halkyone said. 'You shame yourself by such a display.'

'That's helpful,' Illeana interjected.

'I am speaking the truth . . .'

'He is not a Spartan, Halkyone,' Lysandra's interruption was weary.

Valerian sought her eyes. He did not speak but she could see the gratitude there. 'I did not think they would press an attack by night. I should have thought of it – made proper preparations. As it is, my error of judgement has cost us all dearly. I am sorry.'

'All commanders err,' Lysandra said. 'Even me. My errors cost lives. Yours have. That is war, and you should not need a woman to tell you that, legate. And Halkyone is right . . . we cannot give in to despair.' It was a lie – they all had succumbed to it. The losses of the retreat had been catastrophic and everybody knew it. Except perhaps Halkyone. Halkyone who was as Lysandra would have been had she stayed in the Temple of Athene. Halkyone who still spoke with all the arrogance Lysandra herself had once possessed, staunch in her belief that her blood made her superior to all others. 'There are no war tricks we can call on,' Lysandra continued. 'We must fight until we win,' her eyes flicked over to Halkyone who, thankfully, saw fit not to joke, 'or until we are overcome. Think on this,' she added. 'We have lost many, yes. But we have killed thousands of the enemy. *Thousands*. And wounded more.'

She felt the touch of Athene, forcing her to speak bold words to lift them and she pressed on. 'I make no secret of it – my being

434

here is of divine intention. Believe it or not, it matters little to me. I thought once that my Mission would be to raise my shield in defence of my homeland – but the goddess also promised me a life of pain and hardship. Perhaps my Mission ends here – in defence of my homeland and something greater. How long, Valerian, do you think the enemy can continue to take such losses? And even if they win here and kill every one of us, what have they won? A small town? And lost an army doing it?'

'Pity we never went for the cripple,' Illeana said, causing all to turn to her. 'Something Pyrrha – Varia – once said to me. Go for the cripple before the slow kill . . .'

' . . . Because a slow kill might have enough left in her and kill you before she dies,' Lysandra finished for her. Titus, her old trainer, smiled and Illeana had the look of someone for whom mystery had been solved. 'We must assume they will, at some stage, gain the wall. Then we will fight them in the town – house by house, street by street. This will favour us, not them. The Spartans are heavily armoured, each one of the Heronai is a veteran of the arena, well used to fighting up close. Your men,' she jerked her head at the *Primus*, 'are armed and trained for close quarters battle. Big shields, one thumb of iron is your credo, is it not?'

'It is, Lady,' the Roman responded.

'We will litter this place with their dead,' Lysandra said. 'The memory of it will haunt them for generations . . . a story to frighten their children. A memory that will shame those of them that survive. For what in fact did this great army of theirs face? A wall of wood, a wall of hastily thrown up stone, a ditch and an army made up of slaves, boys, geriatrics and women gladiators. You question your command, Valerian? Look what you have accomplished here. Because of you, Rome will live. If we do our jobs tomorrow, we will have dealt them such a blow that we will render them impotent.'

'If Iulianus has won,' Valerian reminded her.

'If he has not, history will remember his failure and your valour.

Rome gave him everything they had, Valerian, and she gave you nothing. In return, you have given them everything. *Virtus* is yours and no Roman has more right to it than you. If we fall tomorrow, you will fall with your sword in your hand . . . and in your heart you will know that you did your duty.'

'You have led us to our Thermopylae, Lysandra,' Halkyone said, her eyes glittering in the light of the brazier. 'Our temple is dust and here we stand at the arse end of the world, spears in our hands, fighting for Athene herself. By the gods, what an end, eh, brother?' she said to Kleandrias. 'No regrets,' she added. 'Athene – Minerva – has decreed. Here we stand. Let us break their spines in the morning.'

'You all sound like you're going to die,' Illeana said. 'I'm going to live through this.'

'How do you presume that?' Halkyone asked.

'Venus has my back.' She winked at Lysandra. 'I'm too beautiful to die in a shithole like this.'

Murco was waiting for them outside, his face still wrapped in grief. Lysandra was about to speak when she saw Telemachus approaching, weighed down by his mail shirt.

Halkyone clapped her on the shoulder. 'If you cannot sleep, Lysandra, come to us. And if I do not see you on the morrow, have a good death.'

'And you, Halkyone,' Lysandra said. It would have been unseemly to embrace her, so she simply nodded and watched as the Matriarch of a temple that was no more made off into the night. Illeana did likewise, walking with Titus towards where the majority of the Heronai had made their beds.

'I am glad you survived,' Telemachus said to her.

'Many did not,' she replied, suddenly weary. 'Murco,' she turned to the bodyguard. 'I wish to release you from my service.'

'Why?' he exclaimed. 'I have served you well . . .'

'Yes, you have. Better than I deserve. But I need you now, more than ever. I need you to stand back from the fight tomorrow. And if it goes badly for us, I need you to help Telemachus. He is not a fighting man. My last order to you, my friend. Get him out of here if you can.'

'I would stay with you, Lysandra,' Telemachus said. 'I will not abandon you here.'

'Kleandrias will keep me safe. But I cannot fight if I am worried about you, my friend. Please. Do this for me. Besides . . . who will write all of this down if I fall? My tale will surely need some Athenian embellishment.'

'Do not speak of such things.' Telemachus pulled her close. His body shook and she knew he was sobbing.

'Get out of here,' she whispered in his ear. 'Get out of here and live if you can.' She pushed him away gently and jerked her chin at Murco who nodded.

'I'll look out for him,' the Roman said. 'Come on, Priest,' he added. 'Let's get you out of that armour and find something that doesn't make you stick out so much.'

Lysandra watched as the two walked away before she too made off, Kleandrias at her side. He walked with her in silence towards her quarters and, without being asked, came in with her.

'Spartan,' she observed as she looked around. It was lit and heated by a single brazier. A low bunk was in one corner and a table with a jug of wine on it in another. She picked it up and sniffed; it was still good. 'Wine?' she asked him. He nodded and she poured for them both. 'We should get out of this armour,' she said. 'I am weary of it.' They both struggled out of their kit, weapons and armour clattering to the floor.

They stood in the half-light, close to each other and poured a libation before sipping the wine. He looked at her as though she was the only thing in the world and she saw again what Illeana had seen. Kleandrias loved her. He had stood by her, fought for her, bled for her and had wept like a child when he thought her dead. She wished in that moment that she loved him, but there was nothing for him in her heart but warm affection. But she knew they would be dead tomorrow, so tonight she could lie to him. Tonight, she could do something for somebody other than herself.

She placed her cup down on the table. 'Hold me, Kleandrias,' she said. He pulled her close, patting her on the back, thinking to comfort her. 'No,' she pulled away, holding his bearded face in her hands. 'Not like that.' She saw disbelief in his eyes and she could not hold his gaze so she kissed him softly on the mouth, her tongue seeking his. 'Love me.' He responded, surprising her with his gentleness, caressing her face with his bloodstained hands as he kissed her. She lifted his tunic away and ran her hands down his hard chest, puckered and ridged with scars. He kissed her again, more urgent but still as though she was something fragile, something he could break. Her own tunic came away and he looked at her, marvelling as though he had never seen her thus before.

'You are the most beautiful woman the gods ever put on this earth, Lysandra,' he said, his voice thick with emotion.

Lysandra went to the bunk and lay down, reaching out her hand and he joined her, his great male form arching over her. For a moment she was afraid: Nastasen and his men and the attack in Halicarnassus, sickening fear remembered. Kleandrias kissed her face, stroking her hair as his thighs parted her own. She could feel him pressing against her, his body yearning to join with hers, seeking the font of her sex.

He pushed and she gasped as he entered her, shocked at the feeling of another body joining her own, not by force. Kleandrias moaned in joy and kissed her again, beginning to move, slowly, gently so as not to hurt her.

Lysandra closed her eyes as she gave her body to him. She wept as he made love to her, thinking of Eirianwen, of Varia, of Thebe and all those she had lost. She wept for her sins, her selfishness and her failures. But most of all, she wept for Kleandrias, who was a fool because he now believed that she loved him too.

He moved faster, losing control and she moaned in response so that he would not know that her mind was elsewhere and then he cried out as he came into her, filling her with his seed, the sweat of his body mingling with hers.

'I love you,' he whispered.

She kissed his neck but offered no reply.

The grey sky was smudged with the smoke from the burnt onagers, the acrid stench of scorched wood floating to the defenders of Durostorum. Red-eyed and weary, they looked out at the killing field that separated them from the enemy host. It was littered with corpses, a glut of Roman and Hellene bodies where the fighting had been thickest. Out of bowshot, the barbarians were working feverishly, retooling their ramps – with these they would clamber up to the redoubt and this time, there was no artillery to pound them, no 'daisies' to slow them down. Little did they know that the fearsome Artemisians were now so low on arrows, they could make no difference. At least not with their bows. Dacia's allies would come on unimpeded; there was nothing to stop them but swords and shields and those who stood behind them.

Valerian walked the line of the redoubt, offering a word here and there, trying to will courage into his men, being careful not to burn himself on the bubbling cauldrons that they had prepared as a welcoming gift for the barbarians.

He crossed from the Felix to the Heronai lines, seeing Lysandra and her ever-present protector, Kleandrias by her side. The big man looked relaxed and almost happy. This, Valerian supposed, was this 'Spartan way' they kept mentioning. They were a fatalistic bunch, but all seemed content that there would be a bloody battle and the prospect of a painful death at the end of it.

Lysandra herself looked untroubled and indeed resplendent in her red war cloak and bloody armour. She nodded as he approached. 'Legate.'

'Strategos,' he replied. 'Last night . . .'

'I spoke the truth,' she cut him off. 'You are a good man, Valerian. Let today bring what it may.' He was about to respond but her eyes told him not to – Lysandra was not one for small talk and platitudes. She looked away, turning her strange, ice-coloured eyes towards the field. 'You should go,' she told him. 'They are coming.'

He saw the great mass of bodies undulating forward, big men at the front heaving the walkways with them. The barbarians were yelling battle cries, taunting the defenders, the sound of their voices rolling towards the redoubt like an ocean swell.

Valerian took a step up onto the wall, facing the enemy. He wanted to turn, to make a dramatic speech, something that would inspire the defenders to greater courage, to make them fight harder. But he had nothing. So he drew his sword and pointed it to the sky in defiance of those that came to kill them. Some god chose the moment to kick up the wind that caught his cloak, making it flutter to one side and, at the sight of him, the defenders cheered. He heard a woman's voice – Illeana's – begin to chant his name and soon it was taken up by the rest: *Valerian . . . Valerian*. His heart swelled with pride and gratitude because he knew in that moment that their faith in him had not faltered – even if he had failed them.

There was nothing he could do about the past or the future. Lysandra's words stirred in his memory – *virtus*. He had recovered it here. A shame, he thought, that he would probably die here before he got to tell anyone about it. Valerian lowered the sword and kissed it, swearing that he would fall upon it rather than be taken again.

'Orders, sir?' one of Lysandra's Heronai called out.

Valerian turned and raised his voice. 'Fight!' he glanced at Halkyone and her Spartans. 'Until we win. Or die.' He jumped down from the wall and made his way back to his own section, taking up a position by Mucius.

'Not much of a speech, if you don't mind me saying so, legate,' he said, handing Valerian a spare shield.

'Didn't have a lot more to say, *Primus*. Unless you've got any ideas?'

Mucius laughed then. 'No, but there is something that has been bothering me. Something that Settus said.'

'What's that?'

'*Is* shitcunt one word or two?'

Sorina gripped the spear tight in both hands as she trotted towards the wall, leaping over bodies both friend and enemy. They had looted the corpses all night, and now many of her people had armour and shields. Those that had lacked swords now carried them – they would turn the weapons of the Romans and Greeks against them. The spear in her hands had once belonged to one of Lysandra's 'invincible' Spartans. For all her vaunted training and supposed superiority, the bitch had died like any other.

With Amagê at her side, she felt a sense of freedom; she had been wearying of war, but now she knew that she had been lying to herself. This was truly living. And the future would bring what it would. She ran on, realising that they were not yet under attack. 'They have no arrows!' she shouted to Amagê. 'They have nothing left!'

She carried on and could make out Lysandra, red cloaked amongst the grey of her gladiatrices and, further down the line, the crimson and bronze wall of the Spartans. Then the Romans – there would be more on the other side of the wall, she knew. And she knew that, come the noonday sun, they would all be dead. She prayed to the Earth Mother that she would meet Lysandra in battle and bring her low.

In front, the walkways had reached the pitiful Roman redoubt and the men were raising the platforms. Rocks, spears and even crockery rained down and then Sorina heard screaming as the defenders poured boiling pitch down on top of them. She vowed vengeance for this too: they had wronged the plainspeople and the Dacians and soon they would pay.

There was little else the Romans could do as the walkways came up, their legs catching the top of the wall and fitting into place. No sooner were they down than the soldiers were pushing them off – a dance went on for a time as the archers among the tribes peppered the wall with arrows, forcing them to lift their shields or duck out of the way.

The advance stalled as the men at the front struggled to get the walkways to sit, but soon, the defenders were out of munitions save for rocks and these could not halt them for long. The bottom of the redoubt was strewn with bodies but worse were the wounded, men horribly burned and blinded, screeching with pain, begging for succour that would never come.

Then the first walkway bit and their warriors began to stream up it, right into the teeth of the Roman legion. Sorina screamed encouragement, angling her run towards the gladiatrices. She wanted Lysandra. This time, the Spartan would not escape.

'How's the leg?' Illeana asked Helena – not for the first time.

'It's still fine,' the *lochagos* replied.

'They'll be up this side soon,' Illeana observed as the barbarians charged up their makeshift bridge to meet the Felix. At once, the shouting began as battle was joined. She saw Valerian in the thick of it, his red cloak flying as he fought with his legionaries.

'I was hoping they'd have given up by now,' Helena said. She jumped in shock as a walkway crashed into the wall right by her. 'Quick!' She ducked down and put her shoulders under it and Illeana did the same. They heaved but the weight was too much.

'They're coming!' someone shouted.

The women exchanged a look and extricated themselves. 'I was hoping that too,' Illeana said. She jerked her head to one side as a spear flew past her. 'But you have to say – they have guts.'

'Let's spill some, then,' Helena said as the first of the enemy charged up to meet them.

The kid's lifeblood flowed out and it dropped to the floor, dead.

'Save them, Athene,' Telemachus prayed. 'Save them because they fight for you.'

Outside the small hut, Murco paced up and down, a sword held loosely in his hand. Telemachus could feel the man's eyes on him as he prayed, but some things could not be rushed. He spoke no more but raised his palms and silently begged the goddess for deliverance; his heart was open and she would know that it was also for himself that he prayed. He was her servant and she had put Lysandra in his life and to this gods-cursed country he had come.

Telemachus was not a warrior and he was desperately afraid. He was ashamed that he felt relief when Lysandra had commanded the tough bodyguard to protect him and shame that he felt it.

Lysandra.

He loved her like a younger sister, for all her faults. Life had been harsh with her and she had endured more in her few years than many would in a hundred lifetimes. And she deserved to survive this, he told the goddess. She was not perfect, but her faith in Athene was unshakeable – it was the cornerstone of her life, her devotion – and that devotion had brought her here.

'Ever has she done your bidding,' he said aloud. 'She deserves to live.' He lowered his hands and turned, hearing the first of the screams.

'It's started, Priest,' Murco said to him. 'We'll have to wait till the killing on this side starts and see if we can slip away in the chaos. Stay close to me, alright? I'll protect you.'

'Thank you, Murco. Should I find a sword?'

The man's mournful face lifted for a moment. 'Best you don't.'

Telemachus looked toward the walls. All around them, the fighting raged and even he could tell that it was hopeless. His guts churned with fear and he wondered how men – and now women – could do this to each other. Heads flew from bodies, torsos were spitted on sword and lance, limbs were cut away – and the noise; the song of Ares was loud, screams of terror and pain, the clash of weapons. It was madness.

He watched as the fight raged and saw the defenders giving way as the unstoppable tide flooded over the walls, forcing them away and to the ground. It was chaos then, men and women falling or climbing or leaping to the streets of Durostorum. He saw Lysandra's red cloak billow behind her as she threw herself to the stones. Kleandrias landed by her side and dragged her to her feet.

Halkyone and her Spartans were forming up alongside the *hypaspistai* – making a shield wall to protect both legionary and Heronai as they rushed to regain their formations.

'Won't be long now,' Murco told him.

Valerian did as he had been trained to do, punching out with the shield and thrusting with the *gladius*. He ducked low behind the big *scutum*, exposing only his eyes and shins as he fought. The press in front was immense as more of the attackers piled in and Valerian found himself being forced backwards, crashing into the man behind him as the barbarians hurled themselves at the shield wall.

'Don't fall!' the man behind shouted, pushing the boss of his shield into Valerian's back, righting him. He used the momentum to stab a woman that rushed at him, her sword raised. As he caught her in the throat, he realised she held a *gladius*. It tumbled from her

444

dead fingers and her place was taken by a warrior who cut down with an axe. The blade cut through the rim of the *scutum* sending wood chips flying. Valerian yelled in fright and dropped it, ramming his blade into the Sarmatian's side; the iron went in deep and he had to twist to free it. The warrior's hands were clawing at his face, his filthy nails gouging the flesh. Valerian put his hand under the man's chin, forcing him away as he struggled desperately to free his weapon.

The man next to Valerian fell, crashing into him and a barbarian stepped into the gap, killing the next ranker. 'Close the ranks!' Valerian's voice sounded shrill in his own ears as he finally dragged his *gladius* free. He heard the blast of Mucius's whistle and gratefully spun away as the man behind him – the man who had saved his life – stepped up and took the brunt of the next attack.

Breathing heavily, Valerian staggered to the rear of the line, taking the pats of encouragement from the men as he did so. He looked around, craning his neck to see the state of the battle and it made for a grim sight.

A seemingly endless tide of enemy warriors still poured over the walls; those that had reached the streets were forcing the defenders back on all sides. The Felix were fighting hard, but Lysandra's Heronai were being pushed back on the leftmost flank. Their centre and right were held by the Spartans and *hypaspistai* – their weapons and armour were ideal for this fight, the long spears and big shields keeping the enemy at bay, cutting them down in large numbers.

They were godlike. But they were *not* gods – and they, like their sisters of the main Heronai corps, were being killed. But they were holding.

Valerian found himself moving forward, a few steps each time the whistle sounded. He had no shield now, so he asked for one from the man who was rushing past to take his place in the rear. 'Look after it for me,' the fellow said, glad to be rid of its weight.

Moments later, Valerian spun forward and hurled himself back into the fight. He gritted his teeth and punched forward, felling a warrior with the boss and followed up with a downwards thrust.

Then there was sharp, searing pain. Valerian heard himself cry out and he looked to see an Amazon withdrawing her spear from his side. Blood spewed from his armour in a fountain and his legs went. The woman's triumphant scream was cut short as a soldier plunged his *gladius* into her neck and rough hands grabbed Valerian, saving him from a terrible death at the feet of his own men.

The sound of the battle began to fade and he heard panicked men shouting 'Get him to the *medicus*!' He was being carried, the world tilting crazily, the combat playing out like some dim and distant dream. He saw the Heronai breaking, as even their valour could not hold back the tide against them. Some of the attacking warriors stopped mid-fight to ravish the fallen women in the heat of battle. 'Thin the line!' he croaked. 'Bridge the gap or we're done for!'

But no one heard him. And even if they did, there was nothing they could do about it now.

Illeana was tired, her hair plastered to her head, drenched in sweat. Her helmet was gone; she'd taken a hit on the top of the head and it had dented inwards, opening a cut. It was intolerable to wear it, so she'd cast it aside. She was no student of war, but anyone could see that they were losing the battle.

Helena still lived, but the Heronai had been pushed back. As it was, she was at the rear of the 'line', but in truth it was more a mob fight now. Only the Spartans and *hypaspistai* retained any sort of order, but they, like the rest, were being forced back, their ranks thinning as exhaustion began to overcome even the elite warriors.

'We've had it!' Helena shouted. 'I'm not going to let those bastards take me alive,' she added. 'Look!'

The enemy were raping the wounded. The sight set fury aflame inside of her, a helpless rage because she knew that there was nothing she could do to save them. She thought of the crowds at the Flavian, cheering her on as she killed for sport. For fun. Romans in love with death. But most of them had never seen it up close. *She* had never seen it up close. Not like this. 'I'm not going to let them take me, either,' she said. As she spoke, there was a groan and a roar of triumph as ever thinning line of Spartans and *hypaspistai* finally broke apart. Without the group cohesion they reduced to fighting alone or in small knots.

A heavy-set young woman with dark hair – short at the sides and spiked on top – roared in triumph as she cut down one of the Spartan Priestesses, the blade biting deep into the woman's chest. A splash of blood flew as the woman fell and the Corinthian helm fell from her head. Illeana recognised her as Deianara – Lysandra's blonde friend from childhood. She recognised the barbarian too: it was the one who had taken Thebe's head.

'I'm going to kill her,' Illeana said to Helena, 'and then think about what to do next,' she said. Without waiting for a response, she walked forward, a strange sense of calm settling on her.

The battle had broken down now – a thousand fights and individual duels raging on the streets of Durostorum. The dark haired Sarmatian seemed to sense her coming and she looked up. Illeana pointed her bloody sword in the woman's direction and she nodded, bounding towards her, axe held confidently in both hands.

'You're pretty,' the woman said to her in Latin as she drew close.

'And you're fat,' Illeana replied.

Big men came to aid the warrior – her bodyguards, Illeana realised. She must be facing a chieftain. 'She's mine!' the woman barked.

Illeana came forward with her *gladius* – 'going for the red', as Pyrrha would have had it. The Sarmatian was fast, though, and she skipped back, swinging the axe out as she did so. The tip of its blade caught Illeana in the temple and opened it up, stunning her. Too tired, she realised as she hit the ground, rolling away on instinct and coming up again. She knew she would have been dead if there had been any force behind the blow, but it had been delivered when the chieftain had been off balance. As it was, she felt hot blood sluicing down her face and the smile on the barbarian's face told her that the cut was bad.

Warriors from both sides rushed past them and Illeana saw from the corner of her eye that several Heronai were engaging the body-guards – seizing her chance, she came into the attack again, ducking under a swing from the big woman and executing a cut across her ample belly. The chieftain gasped and stepped back, her hand flying to the wound.

The pain seemed to galvanise her and she roared in fury and flew at Illeana, the blade of the axe spinning in a terrifyingly intricate pattern; she could not block, nor could she attack for fear of breaking her sword.

'Coward!' the chieftain snarled, snagging back her blade and stamping forward. 'I'll send you to your gods!' She swung the axe in a vicious uppercut and Illeana saw her chance, stepping to the side and smacking the haft of the weapon away. She rotated her wrist and skipped past her enemy, the iron biting deep into her fleshy bicep. Bright blood flew and the woman shrieked in pain. She spun around, flailing with the axe, but Illeana had found her speed and silently thanked Venus-Aphrodite for it, stepping back as the blade hissed past her.

Illeana lunged forward, going for the red – the woman's side, exposed by the swing of the axe. The *gladius* went in deep and blood geysered both from the wound and from the chieftain's mouth as the cold iron ruptured her internal organs. The axe fell from her hands and Illeana pressed harder with the sword, forcing it in further. 'I've only just found religion,' she said. 'Too early for me to meet my gods just yet.' She twisted the blade savagely, making the woman cry out in agony and then dragged it free.

The chieftain fell to her knees and Illeana finished her with a thrust to the throat, watching with satisfaction as she fell in a heap, choking on her own blood.

She looked up and saw men pouring over the western wall. They looked like legionaries from the Felix, but she realised that their tunics were red and their shields had a different blazon.

Roman soldiers.

Around her, the barbarians that should have been hacking her to pieces were backing away and, at first in ones and twos and then in greater numbers, they began to run.

Illeana fell to her knees and began to sob and laugh at the same time.

Because Iulianus had come at last.

LXIX

Sorina screamed in anguish as she saw Amagê fall at the hands of the beautiful warrior. Beyond, she saw the first shields of the Roman legions and knew that she had lost. They were few at first, but she knew that they would come in their thousands and slaughter or put to flight the brave warriors who had given so much for the freedom of her lands.

Her heart rent in two, she staggered through the fight that still raged, viewing the carnage as though it were a bloody Roman mosaic. The streets were scattered with thousands of dead and dying: Roman, Greek, Spartan and people of the Tribes. She heard someone screaming and realised that it was her own voice that rent the sky with its anguish. Tears clouded her vision as she stumbled on, lashing out with her spear at any enemy that came close.

Then she saw her through a veil of tears. Tall, red cloaked, the arrogance exuding from her as she exulted at the arrival of the Romans.

Lysandra.

Laughing for joy, she hugged a man close to her, a big man with a beard. Sorina snarled and called out loud to the Earth Mother for vengeance and cast her spear with all her strength. It flew as though the Mother had hurled it herself, fast as an arrow and with all her hatred and anger behind it.

Above the bloody streets, crows circled and as the warhead slammed into the big man's side, Sorina was sure that she heard the laughter of Morrighan Dark Fate.

Lysandra fell to her knees at the man's side, holding his hand, her glee turned to grief as he writhed in pain, his life pouring out on the ground. She held his hand as he died, leaning close to him, comforting him. He reached out to her and she bowed her head and kissed him.

And then his hand fell and Sorina knew she had killed someone Lysandra had loved.

Again, the voice of the Morrighan whispered to her. *For did you not kill Eirianwen too?*

Lysandra looked up and Sorina saw the shock and grief writ clear on her pale face, a face now scarred with the tip of her own blade. Lysandra rose slowly and unfastened the scarlet cloak at her neck. It fell to the ground, red cloth on scarlet stones. She drew her *gladius* and walked forwards, her strange eyes burning with fury. She stooped and picked another sword from the ground. Sorina looked around and grasped the blades of the fallen around her. They too were *gladii*. She gripped them tight.

Sorina was drenched in blood, her hair thick with it. 'Your lover?' she asked as Lysandra approached her. 'I am glad I killed him. I will kill you now as I should have done before.'

Lysandra could not speak for fear she would weep. It was over – it should have been over. The fight still raged, but the Romans had come and it was *over*. The barbarians should have run. Kleandrias should have lived. Perhaps, she thought, she could have learned to love him. Or at least pretended long enough to make him think that she did. But, because of Sorina, he now lay dead, one amongst thousands of others.

Hardship and pain.

The goddess always spoke the truth.

Lysandra stretched her neck from side to side, breathed out sharply through her nose and spun her swords twice before dropping back into her fighting stance. 'Come, Sorina,' she said. 'Let us be done with this.'

Sorina stepped back and put her weight on her rear leg, left sword facing towards Lysandra, the right held at an angle above her head. Lysandra too led with her left, her right carried lower, behind it. They stood thus for long moments, measuring each other. Images flashed in Lysandra's mind's eye, images of Sorina at the *ludus*, her battles in the arena, her killing of Eirianwen. It was all so long ago yet the memories burned bright and vivid. She imagined it was the same for Sorina and both of them had known – had always known – that it would come to this.

There would be no *missio* here. Not this time. This was war – and one of them would die.

Sorina cried out and attacked from the rear, her right blade scything down in a diagonal cut that Lysandra took high on her left sword, cutting for Sorina's ribs with her left – only to find it parried with Sorina's own weapon. Lysandra kicked out, her foot thudding into Sorina's midriff and sending her staggering back. Lysandra came at her hard, a left cut to the head followed with a sweeping right cut that scored the armour on Sorina's shoulder, splitting the mail.

The Dacian came back at her, left blade spearing straight at her face; Lysandra stepped off, but felt the impact of Sorina's right sword on her ribs, the tip of the blade parting the links of her armour and sinking into her flesh. She gasped as the pain from the wound flared within her. It was not deep enough for a cripple or a slow kill, but still it seared her. She lashed out with her own right, but Sorina was way too canny and ducked the clumsy swing and struck again, this time to Lysandra's sternum. Her armour held, but the blow staggered her and she was forced to back step as Sorina pressed her advantage; her attack, swift, brutal and unrelenting. Her blades moved fast and it was all Lysandra could do to parry and fend her off. But she saw the sweat beading on Sorina's brow, glistening at the grey of her temples and she let her come on.

Lysandra circle-stepped backwards, opening the gap between them, taking the risk of evading rather than parrying, swaying this way and that, twisting and dodging. Sorina tried a downward cut; instead of blocking with a classical cross block, Lysandra stepped off to one side, and swung both blades at Sorina's exposed ribs. The Dacian cried out in pain as the iron thudded into her and Lysandra heard the crunch as her ribs broke with the impact.

Sorina backed away and coughed. Blood dribbled down her chin as she did so, her teeth pink with it. She snarled and came at Lysandra again, ignoring the pain she must have felt; she seemed fired with strength because of it. Her left blade lanced through Lysandra's guard and crunched into her shoulder, again piercing her armour and this time she knew the wound was deep as she felt hot blood coursing down her body. She raised her right sword just in time to block a cut that would have taken her neck; she twisted on the balls of her feet and smashed the pommel of the sword into Sorina's face, smashing her front teeth.

The Dacian staggered, knees bent and Lysandra spun her left blade and, holding it like a dagger, rammed it through Sorina's thigh with all her strength. It went all the way through, shearing muscle and flesh. The Dacian went down and Lysandra went in for the kill.

Sorina raised her sword – still so fast – hoping to kill Lysandra as she rushed in, but the goddess was with her and she cut downwards, severing Sorina's hand at the wrist. Sorina screamed in agony as the wound gouted blood; she pressed it under her arm, pinkish, splintered bone protruding from it as, unable to stand, she knelt before Lysandra.

Lysandra looked at her. There was no feeling of exultation, no heady rush of victory. The truth of it was that Sorina was old. She was old and she had still nearly beaten her. Around them, the Romans were putting the tribespeople to flight, cutting them down as they fled. 'Look, Sorina!' she said. 'It is the ending of your world.' The Dacian stared at her in mute agony, tears falling down her weathered cheeks. 'I told you. No barbarian army can stand against disciplined troops.' She turned her back on her enemy and began to walk away.

'Lysandra!' Sorina croaked. 'Finish it.'

Lysandra stopped and turned back. 'Why should I?' she asked, walking back towards her. 'You were going to burn me alive, Sorina. Torture me. You killed Kleandrias. You killed Penelope. You killed Eirianwen. I would have my vengeance on you. No clean death for you, Sorina of Dacia. You will be paraded through the streets of Rome, mocked and derided by their mob. And they will say, "there is Sorina of Dacia, the barbarian fool who thought she could defy Rome".' She was about to say more, but the words would not come.

She looked at Sorina and saw not the mighty warrior or the *Gladiatrix Prima*. She was what life had made her. And she had lost everything. Lysandra remembered once again that there could have been a healing between them and that it was she, Lysandra of Sparta, who, in her youth, had thrown it back in Sorina's face.

And whatever else she may have become, Sorina had been a gladiatrix. And she had once loved Eirianwen.

Lysandra screamed and spun about full circle, her blade cutting into the flesh of Sorina's neck, severing her head from her body. It rolled away, bouncing on the stones of Durostorum to lay amongst the detritus of battle.

Sorina's body toppled backwards, blood oozing from the ragged stump of her neck to pool on the ground behind her like a crimson pillow.

In her mind she heard the voice of the goddess and in her heart she knew it was for the last time.

'You have served me well. We are all but done, you and I.'

Iulianus's men were both appalled and impressed by the carnage. They wandered the main square where the majority of the fighting had taken place taking note of where the fighting had been thickest, where the barbarians had been stopped and where they had broken through.

Lysandra sat on the ground, staring at them as they gathered the bodies for the funeral pyres, her hair hanging about her face. She was too numb even to feel the pain of her wounds, her mind shot, her emotions drained. She saw Halkyone and Melantha walking among the red-cloaked Spartan dead. Both had backs as straight as javelins, but she could see Melantha was in shock, her hands shaking, her face as white as a tomb. Halkyone was ashen and to Lysandra she seemed to have aged a decade in a single morning.

She, like Sorina, had now lost everything; the temple itself was gone, taken by the gods and the Sisterhood was smashed, hundreds dead on the stones of Durostorum. A Roman funeral party approached and began to lift the Spartan corpse from the ground and Lysandra saw the flowing blonde hair of Deianara hanging as a man hoisted her from the ground.

I am going to kill you one of these days.

The words she had spoken to her friend so long ago had come to pass.

Halkyone said something to the Roman who bore Deianara and he stopped, nodding and listening before gently lowering to the ground once again. The funeral party moved off and the message was obvious: the Spartans would tend to their own dead.

Lysandra's eyes flicked to Kleandrias's still form. Kleandrias who had loved her and died for her. She felt sick with guilt. She had brought them here; not just her friends but the thousands of others who had followed her – the women of the Deiopolis, Euaristos and his mercenaries – all of them who had trusted her word and now lay dead.

But they had won. They had paid the ultimate price and their sacrifice had bought lives beyond counting. People in Hellas and other lands who would never know the names of the people that laid down their lives for them – and even if they did, would have looked down upon them. Slaves, women – Greeks and arena fighters at that, old men, boys and mercenaries – the lowest of the low.

Illeana was walking towards her, her green eyes for once dull and listless, her hair clumped in bloody hanks, her hands black with filth and dried gore. She looked dead on her feet. Wordlessly, she sat at Lysandra's side and rested her head on her shoulder, her hand seeking Lysandra's own. 'I wanted to see this,' she whispered after a time. 'It wasn't what I thought it would be.'

She looked up to see some men of the IV Felix that were not injured acting as guides to their brother legionaries from Iulianus's relief force, mocking them for 'not being in a real fight'. They joked and laughed, demanding wine and, when mocked in turn for fighting with 'a bunch of girls', they lied about the favours the Heronai bestowed on them to 'keep their morale up'.

'How can they be so . . . nonchalant?' Illeana said.

'They are not women,' Lysandra offered. 'There is a reason that men fight and women nurture. You. Me. The Heronai, my Sisterhood

– every woman that picks up the sword is an anomaly. Men love war, I suppose. I pray that I never see this again.'

'I feel sick,' Illeana said. 'Sick and guilty, even though I have done nothing wrong. I killed them because they were trying to kill me – no different to the arena. But I feel like something has been taken from me and I don't know what it is. I feel . . .'

Lysandra looked around at the bodies and turned her eyes to Illeana. 'Like you have left a piece of your soul here. That it has sunk into this ground like the blood that has been spilled. Dacia has taken something from us that we can never recover.'

Illeana nodded, her peerless green eyes wet with tears. 'I knew you would understand. We are similar creatures, you and I.'

Lysandra forced a smile to her lips and nodded. She turned away and saw Titus; he was hale and beckoning to her. 'Come,' she said to Illeana, forcing herself to her feet though all she wanted to do was sit there forever.

'Titus,' Lysandra greeted him. 'You are alive, thank the gods.'

'I've seen a few battles in my time, Lysandra. If you had ever let me finish a tale, you would have known how I managed it.' He smiled briefly and then sobered. 'Valerian is asking for you.'

'I am weary, Titus,' Lysandra said. 'A report can wait.'

Titus shook his head. 'He doesn't have long.'

Valerian lay on a cot in his *praetorium*. His usually tanned skin was pale and sheened with sweat; bandages were wrapped around his torso, sodden with blood and there was a small mountain of them on the floor, mute testament to the severity of his injury.

He was asleep, tended by a surgeon and two of Lysandra's Asklepian Priestesses. They looked up as she walked in with Illeana and Titus. One of them caught Lysandra's eye and shook her head slightly.

There were others in the room – Settus, the tattooed centurion who was known to Illeana and Lysandra both, and a tall patrician Roman of middle years with a stern expression and aquiline nose.

Another, somewhat younger man – a tribune, Lysandra guessed.

'Lysandra of Sparta.' the taller man stated.

'Yes,' she replied. 'Sir.'

He accepted that with a grunt. 'Tettius Iulianus,' he introduced himself, 'and my tribune, Quinctilius Spurius Nolus.'

'This is Titus . . .' Lysandra trailed off. After all these years, she had never known his *trinomen*. She realised that she had never even thought to ask.

Titus saluted. 'Titus Atronius Cassianus, sir.'

'And . . .'

'The *Aesalon Nocturna*,' Iulianus smiled. 'I have seen you several times at the Flavian,' he added. He glanced at Lysandra and left it unsaid that he had seen Illeana defeat her.

'Lysandra . . .' Valerian's voice as he woke was a low whisper, cracked and parched.

She went to his bedside and crouched down. 'Legate,' she said, forcing a smile to her lips. 'My priestesses tell me that you will recover.'

He returned the smile and ignored the lie. 'I wanted Tettius Iulianus to know that it was you who carried the battle to the enemy. Without you and your Heronai, the enemy would have come fast upon us. Without you, our wall would not have held them at all, and they could have come upon the legate before he was prepared. And . . . I wanted to . . . thank you.'

Lysandra was confused. Varia had died at *her* hand; she loved the girl as her own daughter, but Valerian, she knew, wanted to marry her. 'You have nothing to thank me for, Valerian,' she said.

'I would have not come to this place if Py . . . Varia . . . had not died. Because of you, I am here. Because of you, I found what once was lost to me and I thought it unrecoverable. *Virtus.*' He stiffened in pain and Lysandra could see the life ebbing out of him, soaking through the already sodden bandages. 'I lost it here. And found it again. I have no sons . . .'

457

'But you have a father,' Nolus spoke up, ignoring the glare from Iulianus. 'I have lived in a house that was once yours,' he said. 'I make this oath, before my legate and these witnesses, that I, Quinctilius Spurius Nolus, adopt you as my son. Your image will adorn the walls of our *atrium*. I will see to it that your name is revered.'

'You do me great honour, Nolus.'

'Honour you have earned.'

'*Virtus*,' Valerian murmured.

'Fuck all this!' Settus moved forward with an apologetic glace at Iulianus. 'Why is everyone acting like he's copped it?' the little man crouched down by the bed as Lysandra moved away. 'You soppy cunt,' he said quietly. 'Can you stop fuckarsing around. You're going to be all right, mate. We'll fuck this lark off and go back to Rome as rich men. Think of the whores . . . It'll be fucking great! We'll own that *subura* . . . Me and Mucius been cooking up a few business plans . . .'

Valerian stiffened in pain, arching his back. He coughed and blood oozed from his mouth. Settus grabbed his hand, squeezing tight. 'Hang on, mate, hang on . . . it'll be all right . . . just don't give in. You can hack it . . .'

Valerian's hand went limp, and he gave a low, bubbling sigh, his eyes closing for the last time.

'Valerian!' Settus's hard dark eyes were moist, his voice cracked, but Lysandra could see that he held back his tears by force of will. 'Valerian! Come on, mate . . . you can't die . . . you can't. You're . . .' He looked around helplessly at the surgeon and the Asklepian's who wore the expression all in the room had seen many times before, be it in a surgeon's tent or in the caverns under an arena. 'You're my friend . . .' Settus looked up at Lysandra. 'He was my friend.'

Lysandra nodded and met Iulianus's eye. 'He was a friend to Rome.'

Iulianus regarded her. 'I will mention this in my despatches to Frontinus,' he said.

She did not say it, but Lysandra knew this to be a lie. History would not remember Gaius Minervinus Valerian. Iulianus would ensure that this victory was his and his alone.

Lysandra placed the coins on Kleandrias's eyes and kissed his forehead. She knew he was in Elysium now and prayed to an unanswering Athene that he was happy and had the honour a Spartan warrior deserved.

She climbed down from the pyre to see a river now glutted with the Roman transport ships to carry them home and walked over to join those of her friends that had survived. The fields outside the walls of Durostorum were a forest of deadwood, hundreds upon hundreds of funeral pyres rising from the earth, temporary monuments to a forgotten legion that had saved an empire.

Iulianus's men had marched out in pursuit of the barbarians who had fled the field, determined to fulfil their mission of *summa exstinctio*. So it was The IV Felix, bolstered by those few mercenaries who had not been killed, that was on parade. At their side, as it had been in the battle, were the Heronai, but it was the Spartans – those who survived – who began the funerary wailing. At this signal, men tasked with lighting the fires thrust their brands into the wood and the pyres burned bright, their smoke hecatombs to Athene, for whom they had all – knowingly or otherwise – served and died.

They mourned for hours, and all sung the paen to the goddess till their throats were raw, the sound a final battle cry that honoured the Virgin and the Wise, and until the pyres began to collapse in on themselves.

Lysandra wrapped her cloak around herself, somehow cold despite the heat of the flames and saw Halkyone and Melantha walking towards her. This then, was the sum of her life. Those from her childhood, Titus and Murco who had trained her, Telemachus who was her brother, and Illeana whom she had fought and had come to love.

Halkyone looked at the Spartans' pyre as it blazed brightly. '*O xein', angellein Lakedaimoniois hoti teide keimetha tois keinon rhemasi peithomenoi,*' she said.

'*E tan e epi tan,*' Lysandra offered. Then: 'What will you do now, sisters?'

'Return to Sparta,' Melantha said. 'Where else would we go?'

'To rebuild?'

'Yes,' Halkyone replied. 'And no. I had a dream last night, Lysandra. I know the goddess speaks to you and I know my dream was true. She told me that our order had served its purpose. She told me that the time had come to put down our spears. That, because of our actions here, Rome – and with it Hellas – would endure for many lifetimes. And that all our names – save your name that is not your name – would be as dust.'

Lysandra stepped forward and embraced them both, first Halkyone and then Melantha.

'Find us if you return.' Melantha gave her a final squeeze and broke away. 'It was good to see you fulfil your potential, worm.'

'And though the cost was great, it was good to fulfil ours,' Halkyone said. 'The Mission is complete.' She nodded at the others and turned away. Neither she nor Melantha looked back as they joined the thin line of the Sisterhood and made their way towards the waiting ships.

'We're for Asia Minor,' Titus announced. 'Me, Murco, Mucius and Settus. With the money from all this, we're going to set something up.'

'What kind of something?' Illeana asked.

'Wine,' Murco said. 'We're going to become wine merchants.'

Lysandra allowed herself a smile. Murco had always been a lover of the grape and considered himself an expert on the subject.

'I'm for Rome,' Illeana said. Rested and scrubbed, she was as beautiful as a May morning, her eyes green and bright. 'I have had my fill of all this. I just want to go home. And then . . . And then I will see. You should come with me, Lysandra.'

There was something in her eyes that lifted the gloom of the funeral from Lysandra's heart. A promise, perhaps?

'She will come to Athens with me,' Telemachus put his arm around Lysandra's shoulder, the protective older brother. 'All of us need time to heal our wounds from this, Illeana. Those without and those within.' And Lysandra knew he was right; Telemachus had ever been a balm for her soul and she for his.

Illeana nodded, clearly understanding this. She stepped forward and kissed Lysandra's lips as a lover would and held her close. 'That time on Bedros's ship,' she murmured. 'I think now that I was not only teasing you. We are similar creatures, you and I. I *will* see you again.'

And with that she turned away, Titus and Murco in tow, leaving Telemachus and Lysandra – her heart beating fast in her breast – staring after her. Illeana was truly touched by Aphrodite. They had not gone far when the beautiful Roman turned back. 'What did Halkyone say to you at the pyre?'

Lysandra smiled.

> *'Go, tell the Spartans, stranger passing by,*
> *That here, obedient to their laws, we lie.'*

EPILOGUE

It had been years since she had looked down the valley.

The last time had been over her shoulder when Halkyone had come for her and taken her away to the temple, yet she was surprised to find that every rise of ground was the same. The stream still trickled past, the slaves still worked in the fields beyond. The old house with its red tiled roof had not changed, the walls still as white as she remembered.

Lysandra nudged her horse, Hades, onwards, the tiny bundle in her arms nestled close to her breast. The daughter of Kleandrias stirred in her sleep as their journey ended, but she did not wake.

Lysandra slid from the saddle and tethered the horse at the gate. The knife marks were still there: the *lambda* for Lysandra and the word *Stahya* – tall. Her fingers traced the faded notches from an all but forgotten childhood.

Steeling herself, she walked towards the door and knocked. There was a shuffling from inside. After what seemed like an eternity, it opened.

He was still a tall man, taller than herself. The beard that had been iron black was now shot with grey but his shoulders were still mighty. His right arm was scored and scarred by a multitude of sword cuts, his chest wide and strong. As he recognised her, she read the stark shock in his eyes. The ice blue eyes that she had inherited.

'Hello, father,' she said. 'This is Kassandra.'

He regarded her for a moment and then jerked his chin at the

462

babe. 'Give me the child,' he said. Wordlessly, she passed her daughter to him, watching as he shook her free of the swaddling cloths. Slowly, he turned her this way and that, examining her. 'She is well formed and strong. The father?'

'Kleandrias of Sparta. He died in battle with wounds in front. I bring my daughter here, father, because this is my home, and – '

'Your home?' he interrupted her, cold scorn flashing in his ice-coloured eyes. 'You have no home, Lysandra. Many times you could have come *home*. I heard tell you were in Sparta not two years ago, entreating the Matriarch of your temple for spears. Did you think to come *home* then?'

'I was ashamed. Afraid.'

Her father grunted, dismissive. 'Your mother died in the earth-quake that followed your departure. All she had of you had been the monument to you in the town square. Never seeing you as a grown woman save for on the Holy Days when you paraded in your war gear. Too far away for her to hold. Too in love with your goddess to notice us. I was a fool when I thought it an honour that they took you.'

The news cut Lysandra like a knife and she felt sick with shame and remorse. 'I am sorry, Father.'

He looked her in the eye, ice meeting ice. 'I care not what your reasons were and I care not for your sorrow and regret now. For you cared nothing of mine or ours.' He drew the child close to his chest. 'You owe me a life. Let us hope that she is a better daughter to me than you ever were. Goodbye, Lysandra.' Slowly but with finality, he closed the door firmly in her face.

She stood there for long moments, the mother in her warring with the sinner, the guilt fighting with the warrior that urged her to go inside and take back what was hers.

But her father was right. She did owe him – and what was he now but an old man, wracked with the grief of losing his wife? Her mother, whose face she could no longer bring to mind.

Hardship and pain.

She knew then, that this was the final fulfilment of Athene's prophesy. Her final sacrifice for the life she had been given back.

Lysandra walked back to her horse and mounted up, kicking his flanks gently and steering him back up the valley from whence she had come and then reined him in.

She sat for long moments, recalling Melantha's offer to her to join them in their new temple that was now just like any other in Hellas, no longer ringing with the sound of sword on sword. But she was no longer a priestess. She had served her goddess and the price had been high.

So very high.

She looked to the north. There lay Athens and Telemachus. As always, he had cared for her, nursing her while she carried the child she had called Kassandra for her mother. She was about to ride, but hesitated. As she had served Athene, so Telemachus had served her. She could not lean on him forever.

Lysandra turned Hades to the west. To the road that, like all roads, led to Rome.

AUTHOR'S NOTE AND ACKNOWLEDGEMENTS

Like *Gladiatrix* and *Roma Victrix*, *Imperatrix* is of course a work of fiction. Where this third chapter in the story of Lysandra differs from the first two is that in those novels I worked very hard to ensure that the tales were as historically accurate as they could be. With *Imperatrix* this is not the case: whilst it is probable that women fought with the tribes of the steppes, it is highly unlikely that the 'more civilised' nations would have countenanced such a thing. As such, the events portrayed in this book are born of my imagination.

Certainly, Tettius Iulianus led a punative expedition against Decabalus, which ended in a credible draw for both sides. Decabalus would ultimately be crushed by Trajanus, and the events of that campaign would be brought vividly into relief on the famous monument, 'Trajan's Column', that still stands in Rome.

Why *Imperatrix* drifts away from historical accuracy is something that I feel I ought to explain.

When writing *Roma Victrix* I felt that the only realistic way to go with the story in a third book would be to have Lysandra back in the arena – perhaps older, perhaps facing up to the fact that she was no longer as strong as she had once been. This would have become an inversion of the roles of the first book – with Lysandra in the Sorina role, facing up against a younger, hungrier opponent

– and I realised that this was not the way I wanted the story to go at that time, hence the setup at the end of *Roma Victrix* with Lysandra 'raising her shield in defence of her homeland.'

In *Imperatrix*, I wanted to reflect some of what is happening in our own time: in Britain, we are contemplating adding women to our front line regiments, something many other nations, the USA included, do already. I think this is right: women should not be excluded from any vocation once they prove they are capable of doing it.

As with the first two books, I was trying to illustrate that women are equally capable as men in their capacity to fight and compete, that they have the will to win and that not every heroine needs a man to complete her. To tell that story with characters and situations set in the ancient world, I had to break some of the rules and take a further step into the realms of historical fantasy (the first of which was with Lysandra's fever dream of Athene at the end of *Roma Victrix*).

I apologise to the history buffs out there if this is not what you wanted from this (almost certainly final) chapter of Lysandra's tale. If you can put my liberties with the facts aside, I hope I have managed to craft an entertaining story, which is what I set out to do in 2008 when I started writing *Gladiatrix*.

There are so many people who have supported me in this endeavour since back in the day. My agent, Robin Wade, fellow (and far better) writers Tony Riches, Ben Kane, Harry Sidebottom, Giles Kristian, Robert Fabbri, Doug Jackson, Scott Oden, Simon Scarrow and of course, the genius Donna Gillespie who inspired me to start writing 'for real' in the first place. Maybe a fourth book would see Auriane and Lysandra face off at last?

Something that the internet age has made possible is real contact with the people that read the stuff that you write. It's great to have made friends with those people who have enjoyed what I've written (and the fact that I kill one or two of them off in every book). Steve "Settus" Setters, Dave "Slainius" Slaney, Andy "Cantius" Canty,

Isabel "Ankhsy" Picornell, Daina Price, Alistair Leslie, Robin Carter, Peter Harborn, Edna Russell, Mick Cunningham, Leila Annani, Phillippa Taylor, Gerda Du Plessis-Snyman, Tina Drysdale, Siobhán E. McKendrick, Nikki Hewitson, Elizabeth Ball, Katie 'can I have a signed copy' Oliver, the legend that is Jason Frost and so many others. Thank you all so very much.

Special thanks to writer Maria Janecek: Maria contacted me a while back and gave me some great feedback on the books and was working on a story featuring the *Aesalon Noctunna* herself. From that, she began developing a stand-alone novel that takes place around the same time as *Imperatrix*. I really look forward to reading this and I expect Lysandra and or Illeana to be seen at least in the background! Good luck, Maria, and thanks so much for all the kind words and inspiration.

Also to Nikki Green – my dear friend and accomplice; thanks, Niks, for reading and being a real support.

A special mention here. Every year or so, Ben Kane gets myself and Tony Riches horribly drunk and coerces us into doing a charity walk weighed down in Roman armour. Through Ben's efforts, we've managed to raise a huge amount of money for Combat Stress and Medicins Sans Frontiers, but whenever I think of these walks, I think of Colin Brame and his lovely partner Lynette Hartman. During our Hadrian's Wall walk, I was dead on my feet – I really didn't have anything left halfway through the third day. Or at least I thought I didn't. Colin, an expert in long distance walking, picked me up by the chinstraps and explained where I was going wrong. He and Lynette got me through that day and I'll always be grateful for that. Thanks so much, guys. You rule.

On the Italian walk, it was Riches who had to put up with my constant complaining and without him, I'd never have made it from Capua to Rome whilst the instigator of the campaign, Ben, had to sit out a few days with serious injury. This was tragic for Ben who had trained so hard and more tragic for Tony as he had to put up with me. As did our wonderful guide Emiliano Tuffano, Phil, Lewis, Stuart and Tom from Urban Apache who filmed the whole thing and managed to make me look less of a twonk than I actually was with skilful editing. Beers on me, boys.

My thanks as usual to my publisher, Ed Handyside, to Steph Roundsmith for proof reading and to artwork designer Lisa Brewster at Blacksheep, who always manages to make sure Lysandra is well turned out.

I have to thank my beautiful and long-suffering wife, Sally, for supporting me in this endeavour, and indeed in everything I do. Everything that I have, everything I've achieved, every good thing that I've ever done is because of you. I love you very much.

To my daughter Samantha: Sambo, you're too young to read these books right now, but when you are old enough to read these words, please know that (even though I tell you every day) I am so very proud of you. You *are* a warrior and you make my world complete.

Et Lysandra. Ave atque vale, gladiatrix.

Also by Russell Whitfield:

GLADIATRIX

'A great debut that shines an entirely new light on the glory and the bloodshed of the Roman arena. Whitfield paints a vivid picture of the fights and the passions of women combatants. It's exciting stuff, with well-rounded characters, nail-biting duels to the death and vividly depicted settings. *Gladiatrix* makes *Gladiator* look very tame indeed!'

Simon Scarrow, author of
Under the Eagle* and *Centurion

'What a brilliant novel! Whitfield has taken one of history's curiosities — the role of the female gladiator — and woven from it a savage and splendid tale of the Roman arena . . . a tale that, once sampled, cannot be easily forgotten.'

Scott Oden, author of *Men of Bronze* and *Memnon*

'. . . brutal, fast-paced . . . a great first novel.'

Gareth Wilson, *Falcata Times*

PAPERBACK: [ISBN 978-1-905802-09-8]

£7.99

Also by Russell Whitfield:

ROMA VICTRIX

'. . . a compelling and gritty in-your-face account of life for women gladiators ... I couldn't put it down! Lysandra the Spartan has returned, and she's more lethal and more arrogant than ever . . . full of thrilling gladiator fights, real blood and guts, and sex – what more could a reader ask for?

**Ben Kane, author of *Hannibal*
and *The Forgotten Legion Chronicles***

'Roma Victrix is brutal, bloody and loaded with authenticity. Just the way I like my historical fiction.'

**Anthony Riches,
author of the *Empire* series**

PAPERBACK: [ISBN 978-1-905802-41-8]

£7.99

If you enjoyed the Gladiatrix novels, you may like to sample the action-packed apocalyptic trilogy by award-winning thriller writer, Jon Grahame:

REAPER

Jim Reaper started to plan a murder as thousands began to die in a natural disaster that almost killed the world . . .

Lonely and embittered ex-cop, Jim Reaper has nothing much to live for... until the man who raped and killed his daughter is released from prison after serving only three years.

Obsessed with plans for vengeance, Reaper is largely indifferent to media reports of what the world has labelled 'SuperSARS': a virulent pandemic sweeping westwards from China.

It is the apocalypse that everybody predicted but nobody believed would ever happen. It wipes out 98% of the world's population as well as every vestige of government, law enforcement and civilised society. Still traumatised by the loss of loved ones, many simply struggle to survive while hoping to rebuild decent lives for themselves in a world of fear and uncertainty; where every town and city is a hell of shadows, smoke and distant screams; where feral gangs simply take what they want and savagery is rife.

All Jim Reaper had ever wanted to do was take his revenge and then die. But the fates that have taken the lives of so many others have different plans for Reaper: his destiny is to become an instrument of both salvation and retribution in a torn and desperate land.

PAPERBACK: [ISBN 978-1-905802-52-4]

£7.99

ANGEL

I'm 18, going on Death . . . and this is the Age of Terror . . .

After its bloody confrontation with the murderous paramilitaries of 'Muldane's Army', the North Yorkshire community of Haven licks its wounds. Both Jim Reaper and Sandra Hinchliffe harbour the pain of having lost loved ones in the conflict. More people are flocking to the sanctuary. They bring new skills and the hopes of finding peace and security and a return to civilisation.

But Reaper knows that just as decent people are coming together in ever-greater numbers and with more sophisticated technology, so too, inevitably, are the predators and the depraved. And so Reaper and Sandra venture further afield, seeking early intelligence of the threats that lie over the horizon while dealing with evil wherever they find it – and in the only way they know how.

But Sandra is no longer an apprentice: the loss of her husband has turned her hard, efficient and ruthless. Across the isolated settlements of England a modern legend spreads. And it speaks of the Angel of Death.

PAPERBACK: [ISBN 978-1-905802-84-5]

£7.99

REDEMPTION

After the apocalypse comes Armageddon . . .

Jim Reaper and his small band of 'enforcers' have successfully defended the North Yorkshire settlement of Haven and it has become the hub of trade and cooperation between the dozens of peaceful settlements that comprise most of what's left of northern England.

But further north, Newcastle and its environs have become infested by a feral horde that must sooner or later turn its rapacious gaze towards Haven and the peaceful communities under its protection.

And to the south is a regime called Redemption, rumoured to be the new seat of British government – with Prince Harry as its patron – and luring hundreds of survivors with the promise of a return to civilised order and normality, backed by a full battalion of regular soldiers.

Reaper and his ruthless young protégée, Sandra, set off to learn about Redemption for themselves and are soon embroiled in a bloody power struggle that imperils the whole country.

And then, with Reaper and Sandra far from Haven, the feral horde takes to the road.

PAPERBACK: [ISBN 978-1-905802-86-9]

£7.99

Coming soon – Craig Smith's epic story of one man's struggle for survival in Ancient Rome's civil wars:

THE HORSE CHANGER

Messala Corvinus said it best of the opportunist Quintus Dellius: "he was the horse changer of our civil war". In the course of a year, Dellius served first Dolabella, then Cassius, and finally Mark Antony . . .
Seneca the Elder

ROME 46 BC

Dreaming of service to the great Gaius Julius Caesar, the young Tuscan knight, Quintus Dellius, secures the patronage of the youngest of his generals, the dissolute Cornelius Dolabella. Dellius distinguishes himself in Caesar's Spanish war against Pompey, becomes a tribune of cavalry in Caesar's army and looks forward to an assured and glittering career.

But when his hero is assassinated, the Roman republic is plunged into chaos as both his heirs and enemies jostle for power. In the civil wars that follow, Dellius is soon caught up in a maelstrom of shifting allegiances and the young soldier will need to discover reserves of both tenacity and ruthlessness if he is to survive.

As he journeys from the orgiastic salons of Rome's Palatine Hill to the Palaces of Alexandria, the rocky fortresses of Judaea and the bloody field of Philippi, he manages to incur the enmity both of Egypt's queen and Rome's future emperor, but also to snare the affections of a beautiful and cunning young senator's wife, Livia Drusilla.

PAPERBACK: [ISBN 978-1-910183-13-7]

£8.99